THE NOBLE PATH

Also by Peter May

PETER MAY

THE NOBLE PATH

riverrun

First published in Great Britain in 1992 by Piatkus
This revised paperback edition published in 2019 by

riverrun

an imprint of

Quercus Editions Ltd
Carmelite House
50 Victoria Embankment
London EC4Y 0DZ

An Hachette UK company

A CIP catalogue record for this book is available
from the British Library.

PB ISBN 978 1 78747 795 7
EBOOK ISBN 978 1 78747 796 4

10 9 8 7 6 5 4 3 2 1

Typeset by CC Book Production
Printed and bound in Great Britain by Clays Ltd, Elcograf S.p.A.

For Jancie

'I did not die, and did not remain alive; now think for thyself, if thou hast any grain of ingenuity, what I became, deprived of both life and death.'

– Dante's Inferno

FOREWORD

I first had the idea for *The Noble Path* in the mid nineteen-eighties. I had wanted to explore the idea that in certain circumstances innocence can be a more corrupting influence than evil – simply because it knows not what it does.

The story itself was a departure from my usual crime/thriller genre, though I suppose it might loosely be described as a thriller. But I see it more as a very human adventure set against the brutal canvas of south-east Asia in the 1970s.

It takes place in the aftermath of the war in Vietnam, when the murderous and anarchic regime established by the Khmer Rouge in neighbouring Cambodia systematically annihilated three million people. This was not so much ethnic cleansing, as the eradication of thinking and educated people. The Khmer Rouge saw intelligence, and the expression of ideas, as the biggest threat to their existence.

Rereading the book nearly thirty years later, I note with some sadness that one of its primary themes – a refugee crisis caused by the mass migration of people trying to escape war and poverty – is with us every bit as much now as it was then.

Replace the 'boat people' of Vietnam with the sub-Saharan Africans dying in their thousands today, as they try to escape war and poverty by crossing the Mediterranean Sea in dangerously flimsy boats.

To facilitate the writing of my story I made a trip to Thailand, but was unable to journey into Cambodia, which was still an unstable and dangerous place. And so most of the research that followed was achieved by tracking down and reading copious numbers of books dealing with the recent history of the region. No internet then, or easy access to video footage.

I was at the time working as a script editor on the Scottish TV soap opera *Take The High Road*. To write the book I took a two-month sabbatical from the show, bought an old manual typewriter, and drove down to south-west France in my Suzuki Jeep, where I rented a *gîte*. Every morning I drove into the town of Saint-Céré and established myself in a corner of the Café des Voyageurs, where I wrote around 1,600 words a day using the Pitman's shorthand I had learned as a journalist. At night I sat alone in my *gîte* typing up my shorthand, and fighting off the large numbers of brown bugs that somehow managed to crawl in under the door.

At weekends I generally found myself invited to dinner parties hosted by expat Brits and Americans. It was at one of these that I had the great good fortune to meet a lady called Maud Taillard, then in her sixties. Seated next to her at the dinner table, I soon discovered that she had spent several years living in Phnom Penh, the capital of Cambodia. There her late husband had been physician to the King, and she told me of their many adventures, including nightly visits to an opium den in the city.

I went on to call on her at her impressive home in the thirteenth-century medieval village of Carennac, where she showed me mementos and photographs of her time in Cambodia.

The daughter of a French father and English mother, Maude became the model for one of the book's characters, La Mère Grace, the madam of a Bangkok brothel. I was concerned when she read the book that she might take offence. I needn't have worried, as she proudly told anyone who would listen, 'That's me, darling!'

I didn't finish the book during that time in France, and it wasn't until I had quit *Take The High Road* a little over a year later that I had the time to do so.

I have edited the original manuscript very lightly. The biggest change involved cutting much of the sex that I was told at the time was a prerequisite for a bestseller. Reading it all these years later, I revisited the embarrassment I had felt writing those graphic scenes. Times and tastes change, and I think the book is much the better without them.

I am proud and happy to republish it now, nearly thirty years on.

Peter May
FRANCE 2018

PART ONE

PROLOGUE

Cambodia: April 1975

There is a seventeenth-century proverb which says, 'When war begins hell opens.' In this once lovely country in the heart of Indochina, hell opened when the war ended.

This, then, was liberation. Sullen youths in black pyjamas and red-chequered scarves cradling AK-47s with all the warmth they could not feel for their fellow human beings. It wasn't hate in their eyes. It was hell.

A breeze brushed the faces. The thousands of faces all along Monivong Boulevard. It carried the smell of smoke, a city burning in places.

It carried the smell of fear. They said the Americans were coming to bomb the city; it would be safer in the countryside. No one believed it.

It carried the smell of death. They had emptied the hospitals. Broken bodies wheeled out on hospital beds, the tubes and wires of a discarded technology trailing behind, plasma and blood in their wake. Those who could walk leaned on crutches. Those who could not, died. The debris of this once elegant colonial city littered the street; a child screaming, an old man coughing blood on the pavement, the weary shuffling of a million pairs of feet on a dusty road to oblivion.

There is another proverb: 'Hell is a city.' On 17 April 1975, that city was Phnom Penh.

CHAPTER ONE

Ang Serey was a handsome woman, though you would scarcely have guessed it. Her face was blackened by smoke, and you could not tell if it was sweat or tears that made tracks through the filth. Her eyes were red-rimmed and bloodshot, and afraid to stray to one side or the other lest they betray an emotion. Her feet shuffled in open sandals among all the others. Ahead of her she pushed a cart bearing a few meagre belongings. On either side were the children she dared not look at. 'Hold on to me so that I can feel you are there,' she had whispered to them. 'If anyone speaks to you, say nothing. Let me speak.'

For days she had worked her hands until they blistered and bled. Digging in the soft earth among the suburban bougain-villea, rubbing the dirt into the sores and blisters till her hands were red raw. She had made her children do it, too. The boy had cried at first, waving his stinging hands in the air. Why did his own mother make him do this? She had struck him when he refused to go on. And when his tears dried they were replaced by a sullen stare of hatred. The girl was older, yet it seemed she understood even less.

5

Ang Serey was an intelligent woman. She knew she must use that intelligence to hide itself; the black, peasant pyjamas, the hands of one who worked the land. Somehow she had to make the children understand. For if she couldn't, their betrayal of the truth meant certain death.

There had been so little time. Just five days since Yuon had flown out on one of the last helicopters with the American evacuation. Ten days since he had told her, tears streaming down his cheeks, that he had been unable to get a place for her and the children. He had cried most of that night. Her eyes had been dry. She wondered if he expected her sympathy. It would break his heart to leave them, he had said. But still he left. Perhaps they could mend broken hearts in the West.

She lifted her head slightly towards the clear blue sky and felt the heat of the sun on her skin. They had passed by the smoking cathedral and the railway station, all those shuffling feet.

CHAPTER TWO

South Armagh, Northern Ireland, October 1978

McAlliskey sat on a bench in a darkened corner of the pub, nursing the last of the Guinness in his pint glass, pulling distractedly on a hand-rolled cigarette held loosely between nicotine-stained fingers. The pub was quiet. A small, old-fashioned country pub, its wooden bar worn smooth by years of use. A group of farmers stood in a knot sinking pints and shorts, talking in low voices that rose occasionally in muted laughter. Big men, grimy caps pulled down over leathery faces.

'Jaisus! If the beasts's going to die anyway, youse are as well pumping the stuff into it yourself and saving the vet's bill!'

An old woman behind the bar polished glasses, listening idly to the conversation. From time to time she glanced across at the stranger in the corner. She didn't know him. She didn't want to know him. This was bandit country and it was dangerous to know too much, dangerous to ask questions. Curiosity killed.

McAlliskey had crossed the border from the Republic three days earlier and spent two nights in different safe-houses. He stirred uneasily and flicked a look at the clock behind the bar. O'Neil was late, and he was aware of the woman's attempts to avoid taking an interest in him. Which meant she would remember him. Where in God's name had O'Neil got to? If something had gone wrong McAlliskey would be vulnerable here. He had the taste of fear in his mouth – a taste he knew well, had lived with these ten years past. But he could sink a dozen pints and not achieve the high he got from the adrenalin that was pumping through his veins right now.

A tiny stab of fear pricked his heart as the door opened and a man stepped into the pub, bringing the damp night air with him. O'Neil. Dark eyes set deep in a pale thin face. There was mud on his boots, rain on his collar, death in his eyes. He paused only momentarily, his gaze flickering past McAlliskey to the men at the bar. They seemed not to notice him.

He nodded to the woman. 'Twenty Players plain.'

She reached for a packet from the shelf behind her and put it on the bar. 'A wee whiskey, sir, to warm you on a cold night?'

He shook his head and dropped a note and some coins on the counter and glanced again at the little group of farmers. Still they showed no interest. He slipped the cigarettes in his pocket, nodded to the old woman and went out.

McAlliskey sat on for several minutes before draining his glass and taking a final draw on the remains of his cigarette. He rose from the bench, turning up his collar, and left, aware of the old woman watching him go. Outside, the cold caressed him like the icy fingers of a deceitful lover. A fine drizzle drifted down the main street, making haloes around the feeble yellow of the street lamps. The car was parked fifty yards away. He walked briskly to it, hands in pockets, and slipped into the back seat.

'What the hell kept you!'

O'Neil looked at him in the driving mirror. 'Another dud bloody detonator. Where in Christ's name do you get the stuff?'

'Come the day you need to know, I'll tell you.' McAlliskey took a battered tobacco tin from his pocket and started to roll another cigarette. 'It's set?' O'Neil nodded. 'Let's go, then.'

They parked the car at a road end where a dirt track led up through a gate towards the woods above. Below them, the road ran steeply downwards between high hedgerows. To their left, a narrow lane led away around the side of the hill, hugging its contours before dropping down again to feed into the network of roads that fanned out through rolling farmland, south towards the Republic. O'Neil switched off the engine and killed the lights. He took a map from the glove compartment and shone a flashlight for McAlliskey to see. There were three routes traced in red, each an alternative escape to the south. They had been lettered A, B and C with a red marker. 'To keep our options open,' he said. 'If anything goes wrong.'

McAlliskey nodded. He didn't much like O'Neil, but he was thorough. And good with explosives.

They left the car and O'Neil led the way down the hill about two hundred metres. Then he stopped and whistled softly. A faint whistle answered his, somewhere away to their left, and the two men followed the sound, finding a deep-rutted tractor track that led them down to a drystone dyke at the corner of the field. A figure was crouched there, with a holdall tucked in under the wall to keep it dry. He flashed a light briefly in their faces.

'Turn that fucking thing off!' McAlliskey spoke softly, but his voice carried the authority of rank. The third man doused his light without a word.

'Flaherty,' O'Neil said.

McAlliskey crouched down beside him and saw that he was no more than a boy of sixteen or seventeen with fear in his eyes. 'You should know better, son.'

'I'm sorry, Mr McAlliskey.' And there was awe in the boy's voice. McAlliskey was almost a legend in the organization. The boy wasn't sure what scared him more – McAlliskey or the bloody business they were about on this dark Irish night.

'How long?' McAlliskey asked.

''Bout fifteen minutes, sir.'

O'Neil opened the holdall and took out a small, hand-held radio transmitter. He extended the aerial and flicked a switch. A red light came on. He glanced at McAlliskey. 'You sure they'll be?'

'They'll be.'

And they settled back against the wall in silence, listening for the first distinctive sound of the army APC rolling up the lane towards them. From here, they had a perfect line of sight, and would see its lights early – the same lights that would illuminate the white marker O'Neil had planted at the roadside, in line with the twenty pounds of plastic explosive skilfully secreted just below the tarmac. O'Neil wondered how McAlliskey got his information. But he knew better than to ask.

McAlliskey took out his tobacco tin, leaning forward to keep it safe from the rain, and rolled another cigarette. He struck a match to light it, hands cupped around the box.

A hundred and fifty metres above them, a man lay still against a slight rise in the ground, below the shelter of the treeline. He had a livid white scar running back across one cheek where a bullet had grazed the flesh and taken off the lobe of his left ear. His dark hair was cropped short, greying at the temples. His eyes were blue and cold as steel. He saw the brief flare of the match light up the smoker's face.

He had already picked out McAlliskey as he and O'Neil made their way across the field. Amateurs, he thought. He tucked the butt of his US M21 rifle into his shoulder. The weapon had been modified to his own specifications. He put his eye to the lens of the long, telescopic, infrared sight mounted above the butt end of the barrel, centring it on McAlliskey's head, and he too prepared to wait.

They saw the lights of the APC before they heard the distant whine of its engine. Headlights raked the sodden green of the fallow winter fields, swinging one way then the other as the vehicle wound up the road towards them.

McAlliskey and the others crept further along the wall to a

11

clearer vantage where a white gate opened into the lane. The man in the woods kept them in his sights and adjusted his position.

The engine of the armoured personnel carrier had become a roar now as it approached the marker on the road below. The muscles tightened across O'Neil's chest and his finger hovered over the button on his handset. McAlliskey watched, impassive. Twenty metres, fifteen, ten. The APC lumbered inexorably towards the marker. A fine, cold sweat beaded across O'Neil's forehead, his hands clammy. The boy glanced at him anxiously, his heart in his throat, almost choking him. The marksman in the woods focused on McAlliskey's right temple. Gently he squeezed the trigger. The rifle sounded, like the crack of a dry branch underfoot. McAlliskey slumped forward, a neat round hole in his temple, blood gouting from the back where the bullet had passed through, taking half his head with it. O'Neil pressed the button involuntarily, and the explosion below ripped up the road, the APC still five metres short. But O'Neil barely heard it as he stared in horror at McAlliskey. He had hardly a chance to turn before the second bullet struck him full in the face, and his head cracked back against the wall.

Flaherty froze in a moment of panic, two men dead beside him, the shouts of the soldiers below as they fanned out from the APC, a searchlight sweeping the hillside. He looked up instinctively towards the woods and saw, for a second, a face caught in the searchlight glare. Then he took off, running hard in the direction he knew O'Neil had left the car.

The young captain shone his flashlight on the faces of the two bodies. The first was unrecognizable, but he held the beam on the second. His sergeant arrived breathless at his side.

'Jesus! McAlliskey!'

'Somebody just saved our lives, Sergeant.'

The sergeant spat. 'A lot of lives. And a lot of bloody trouble.'

Elliot walked briskly up the ramp towards the Shuttle desk and presented his ticket. He had already passed through the stringent security at this airport on the hill, above the besieged city of Belfast. No problems. He wore a neatly pressed grey suit, white shirt and dark tie. With his slim black attaché case, a raincoat over his arm, he looked like any businessman on a return flight to London. He was thirty-nine but appeared older, his face unusually tanned for the time of year. The girl who handed him his boarding card assumed he was recently returned from a winter sunshine holiday. But Africa had been no holiday. Her eyes were drawn to the scar on his cheek, which stood out white against his tan, and she noticed that his left ear lobe was missing. He returned her stare, and her eyes flickered away self-consciously. He took a seat in the departure lounge.

He would collect the second half of his fee in London. This had been a departure for him. A one-off. Although, he considered, it wasn't really so different from what he had been doing for the last twenty years. Just better paid. And he needed the money. He hadn't been told who his paymasters were, but had a shrewd idea. The English establishment embraced hypocrisy with a greater ease than it did democracy.

He had not been told to take out O'Neil. Only McAlliskey. But he had judged it dangerous not to take O'Neil at the same time. He had no idea why he had left the boy, nor would he ever know just how great a mistake that had been.

He had not seen the two men standing idly by a newsstand in the terminal building. One of them, little more than a boy, pale and drawn and still shaking from the horror of the night before, had nodded in his direction.

'That's him.'

The other had glanced at the boy appraisingly. 'You sure, kid?'

'Sure, I'm sure.' The boy had watched Elliot with hate in his heart. It was a face he would never forget.

CHAPTER THREE

I

London, December 1978

It was raining. Cold. The clutch of black umbrellas around the grave shone wet, dripping on the feet of the mourners. One of them – death was his business – held an umbrella over the vicar as he read from his prayer book. Dust to dust, ashes to ashes . . . meaningless words reeled off for countless dead. The vicar hurried through it. He was cold, and the umbrella was dripping on the back of his neck. He hadn't known the woman. Another faceless soul dispatched for judgement. He wondered, wearily, what had happened to the faith he had known in his youth. Perhaps, like listening to the same piece of music over and over, faith, like the melody, palled. He glanced at the daughter and felt a stab of guilt as she stooped to throw a handful of wet soil over the coffin. The young man beside her offered his handkerchief. She waved it away.

She too felt guilty, and was glad of the black veil that hid her face. No one could see that there were no tears. Her eyes were so dry they burned. She looked around the sad little gathering: a woman who'd worked with her mother, a couple of neighbours, the vicar, the professional mourner – and David. And David was only there because of her. These were all the friends her mother had to show for thirty-seven years. A strange, shy, introverted woman, her mother had not made friends easily. Lisa reconsidered. No, her mother had not made friends at all. Perhaps if Lisa's father had lived . . . But her mother had never even spoken of him. A young soldier killed in Aden in the Sixties. Lisa had only been fifteen months old. She had no memory of him at all. Not even second-hand. Her mother had locked away all the photographs. 'No point in living in the past,' she'd said. And Lisa had never thought to question it.

Thirty-seven! To Lisa's eighteen years it seemed old. But she supposed it was quite young really. Too young to die. Cancer of the breast. Her mother had been aware of the lump for over a year and been too frightened to see a doctor. It was Lisa, finally, who had made her go. But too late. I didn't love her, Lisa thought. I can't even cry. She knew she was depressed only for herself, for her future – alone.

David took her arm to lead her away from the graveside. David. Yes, she had forgotten about him. He wanted to marry her, he said. But she was too young and he was too keen. And, anyway, there had to be more to life, hadn't there? Yet still she felt safe with him, like now, as he put a comforting arm around her shoulder. She glanced back as the gravediggers moved in to shovel earth carelessly over the coffin, burying her mother, her past.

'Come on, love.' David urged her gently away. She turned back towards the future with a heart like lead, and saw a man standing under the trees at the far side of the churchyard. A tall man in a dark coat, hands pushed deep into his pockets. He had no umbrella, no hat, and his short-cropped hair glistened in the rain. Lisa paused and David followed her eyes. 'Who's that?' he said.

Lisa drew back her veil to see more clearly. 'I don't know.'

'Well, I don't like the way he's looking at you.' And David hurried her away. But the vision of the man remained with her. Something about his eyes.

'That was an ugly scar on his cheek,' she said.

II

At first she just wandered around the house touching things. *Her* things. The chair by the window where she sat nights reading her cheap romances, as though she might discover in them what she had failed to find in life. In the bedroom a brush lay on the dresser, her hair still tangled among the bristles. Lisa teased some out and ran it between her fingers. Soft, shiny. In the wardrobe her coats and dresses hung in neat rows. Lisa ran a hand along them. She picked out a jacket, held it against her face. Smelled it. Her mother's smell. It is hard to believe, she thought, that someone is dead, when you can run their hair between your fingers, breathe in the smell of them from their clothes.

This was still her mother's house. Always would be. A neat little semi in a neat little south London suburb. A place for everything and everything in its place. She had been ordered, fastidious to the point of obsession, Lisa just one more possession with a place in the order of things. Cared for, but without love, without warmth. Lisa had always known it, but never rebelled. Been unhappy but safe. Now anger welled inside her and she grabbed an armful of clothes from the wardrobe, throwing them across the room. She swept her arm across the dresser, sending make-up, perfume, brushes, ornaments clattering on to the floor. She stood for a moment, breathing hard, exulting in the violence of her rebellion. A rebellion that had come too late, full of sound and fury, signifying nothing – a remembered scrap of schooldays Shakespeare came back to mock her. Self-pity fuelled her anger as she ripped the sheets from her mother's bed, lifting a pillow and slamming it repeatedly against the wall until it burst and filled the air with feathers, like snowflakes on a still winter's day. And something inside her broke, releasing all the tears that had refused to come earlier. She fell on the bed sobbing wretchedly. Her mother had no right to die! How could she have done this to her?

It was almost dark when she rolled over and realized that she had slept. The bed was still damp where she had spilled her tears. She looked around at the chaos and felt numb. Why had she been so insistent that David did not come back after the funeral? They had almost fallen out over it. But he had conceded, finally, hiding his hurt, and said he would call tomorrow. She wished he was there now. Someone to hold her, to keep her safe and warm. She shivered, realizing how cold she was, and went downstairs to turn on the fire and make herself a mug of coffee.

She tried to think dispassionately about David. He was twenty-four, good-looking with his green eyes and mane of fine red hair. A night-shift reporter on one of the London papers. She had met him a few months earlier when he had guest-lectured as an ex-student on the journalist course she was taking at college. He still lived with his parents. Steady, middle-class people. Very pleasant, very dull. Her mother had liked David, the first boyfriend she had allowed her. He was safe and sensible. 'That boy's got his head screwed on,' she used to say. But Lisa kept seeing him thirty years on, a clone of his father. Safe, sensible, dull.

She cupped her hands round the mug. There had to be something else. Nice! It was the word her mother used to describe everyone and everything that offered no risk. What she meant was safe. Lisa reflected that there must be a lot of her mother in her. It was what drew her, too, like a moth to a light. Safety. Only, she knew it was an illusion.

She wandered through to the living room. On the mantelpiece stood a framed photograph of herself aged twelve. A child with a pleated pony tail and a neatly pressed school uniform. Where was that little girl now? Time. It all seemed to slip away, like a shadow at the end of the day. She felt more like eighty than eighteen. As though her life was already over.

She gazed for some time at the photograph before she remembered the trunk in the attic. Years ago, as a child, she had found and opened it. She could have been no more than five or six. But she remembered the photographs, dozens of them in albums and a shoebox, faded black and white prints. There had been all manner of papers and documents in it, and an old jewellery box. Her mother had found her there with the trunk open and screamed at her and slapped her face. Never was she to go near that trunk again. She was confined to her room for the rest of the day. Some weeks later, while her mother was in the garden, she had crept back to the attic to discover that the trunk had been made secure with a heavy padlock.

The trunk was still there, behind a pile of cardboard boxes, thick with dust, untouched for years – perhaps since the time her mother had first padlocked it. The bulb in the attic had blown, and Lisa had to manoeuvre carefully by torchlight. She tugged at the padlock ineffectually and wondered where her mother might have kept the key.

She turned the house upside down but could find nothing that resembled the key she was looking for. The phone started to ring, loud and insistent in the empty house. It stopped Lisa in her tracks, her heart thumping. It could only be David. She stood uncertainly for a moment, then decided to let it ring out. Finally, she took a hammer and chisel from the toolbox under the sink and carried them up to the attic. Balancing the torch on a nearby box, she directed the beam on to the padlock and set about trying to break the lock. She quickly realized that wasn't going to work, and turned to the clasp on the trunk itself, gouging with the chisel at the wood behind it. It took ten minutes of hacking and splintering before finally it broke free. Then she paused, breathless, almost afraid now to open it. With trembling hands she took the torch and lifted the lid on the past she thought had been buried with her mother.

A couple of layers of dry brown paper covered the contents. She tore them away, revealing again those things she had seen as a child. The pile of old photo albums, the jewellery box, an old rusted deed box, a shoebox filled with loose photographs – her mother as a child on holiday with her parents somewhere. A beach, an old-fashioned guest house, faces Lisa had never seen. Faces of people long dead. A fox terrier being cuddled lovingly by a small girl with hair tied back in ribbons. She put the box down, and lifted out a bundle of old, faded newspapers, which she laid aside without a second glance.

Then she took out the first of the albums, her mouth dry as she opened it. A confusion of more strange faces looked back at her. People standing in awkward groups grinning at the camera. Men in ill-fitting morning suits hired for the day. Her mother in white, smiling, almost beautiful. Lisa hardly dared look at the face of the man standing proudly beside her. A young, shy face, smiling nervously. A tall man with short dark hair, leaning slightly to one side, awkwardly holding the hand of his bride. Lisa's father.

She suffered a feeling of anticlimax. And, yet, what had she expected? He was in army dress uniform, a very ordinary-looking man. She noticed several more uniforms among the guests as she flicked through the pages. Bride and groom cutting the cake. Then a full-sized close-up of the happy couple, arms linked, each with a glass of champagne. She examined her father more closely. He looked no more than twenty or twenty-one. There was something, she thought now, familiar about the face. Something about the eyes. Piercing, looking straight into hers. Then, quite suddenly, she felt every hair on the back of her neck stand up, her scalp tightening, the shock of it bringing the sting of tears to her eyes. Staring back at her, in the yellow light of the torch, was the face of the man she'd seen standing under the trees in the churchyard. A tear splashed on to the page. Her whisper filled the dark. 'He's alive!'

Four hundred miles away in a small, darkened room on the top floor of a building off the Falls Road in Belfast, Elliot's face was drawn from a large beige envelope. The face was older than in the wedding photographs, and had by now acquired its distinctive scar. The photograph was placed in the centre of a bare wooden table. There were three men seated around it. The man who had taken the print from the envelope turned it through ninety degrees in order that the others could see it clearly.

'John Alexander Elliot.' He spoke with a thick Belfast brogue. 'Ex-British army. Now freelancing. He killed McAlliskey. And O'Neil.' He paused. 'We want him dead.'

CHAPTER FOUR

Elliot pulled up his collar against the cold London night and turned into Dean Street. He found the Korean restaurant halfway up on the right. A pretty oriental girl in a long black skirt approached as he entered. 'A table for one?'

'I'm meeting someone. Mr Ang Yuon. He booked the table.'

'Thank you very much. He is waiting for you.' She took his coat. 'You follow me, please.' She led him through the bamboo and ricepaper partitions to a black, lacquered table in a discreet corner at the rear of the restaurant.

Ang Yuon rose to greet him. He was a small dapper man, black hair streaked with grey. His face was pale, cheeks peppered by ugly pockmarks, but remarkably unlined. Elliot thought him about forty, though he looked younger. Fine slender hands. Manicured nails. He smiled, but only with his mouth. The eyes remained dark and impenetrable. Elliot thought he detected in them a deep sadness. 'Mistah Elliot. I am happy you could come.' The trace of an American accent. His handshake was clammy.

Elliot nodded. 'Mr Yuon.'

'No.' He smiled again. 'Mistah Ang. In Cambodia first name is last, last name is first. Please sit.' Elliot felt uncomfortable about this encounter. The call had come from his usual contact, but the circumstances of the meeting were unusual.

'You know Korean food?' Elliot shook his head. 'Shall I order?'

'Sure.'

Ang waved the waitress over and ordered something called *boolkogi* with steamed rice, and *yachi bokum*. Then he smiled again at Elliot. 'You are very ruthless man, Mistah Elliot.'

Elliot remained impassive. 'Is that so?'

'Oh, I know all about you. Shall I tell you?'

'I'll take your word for it.'

Ang shrugged. 'You know nothing of me.'

Elliot clasped his hands under his chin. 'You're a wealthy Cambodian, Mr Ang – politician or businessman. Probably corrupt. You're about forty, and you've never done a day's physical labour in your life.'

Ang raised an eyebrow. 'And how would you know that?'

'That you've never worked the paddy fields? Your hands, Mr Ang. Hands tell you a lot about a man.'

Ang glanced at his hands then looked at him thoughtfully for a moment. 'Corrupt?'

'Nobody ever got wealthy in Cambodia without being corrupt. And I'd say you probably did well out of the Americans.'

Ang's expression hardened. 'There are worse things than corruption – or Americans.'

Elliot said evenly, 'The Khmer Rouge would never have taken power if the Americans had not brought down the Prince.'

Ang was irritated now. 'I did not ask you here to argue politics, Mistah Elliot.' He paused to collect himself. 'And wealthy?'

Elliot inclined his head in a slight ironic gesture. 'The manicure, the cut of your suit, the quality of your English. And if you didn't have money you couldn't afford me.'

A waitress brought small round dishes of soy sauce and spring onion, a large dish filled with strips of raw marinated beef, and a hotplate which she placed on one side before lighting a gas ring beneath it.

'Chopsticks?' Ang asked Elliot.

'Sure.'

The girl smiled and brought them each a pair of finely engraved ivory chopsticks. She returned with a bowl of shredded Korean vegetables, soaked in a bitter dressing, then started arranging the meat on the hotplate with a pair of wooden chopsticks. The beef sizzled and spat as she moved it around, and the air was filled with a delicious aroma of exotic spices. Two bowls of steamed rice were brought before she served them the cooked meat, bowed and took her leave. Elliot tried it. Ang watched.

'Good?'

Elliot nodded. It was. 'Excellent.'

They helped themselves to rice and vegetables and Ang arranged more meat on the hotplate. Two small jugs of warm sake arrived. Ang poured them each a cup and raised his. 'To a profitable relationship,' he said.

Elliot sipped his sake. 'I'll wait till I hear what the deal is.'

Ang drained his cup in a single draught. 'What do you know about Cambodia, Mistah Elliot? Or should I say, Democratic Kampuchea?' He could not hide the bitterness in his voice.

Elliot shrugged. 'Since the Khmer Rouge took over, not much. Except that they seem to be killing a lot of people.'

'Not a lot, Mistah Elliot. Millions.'

'An exaggeration, I think, Mr Ang.'

'No. The stories have been confirmed by the refugees coming across the northern border into Thailand. And they have come in their thousands. I know. I have spent a lot of time in the refugee camps there, Mistah Elliot, off and on for more than three years.'

'You don't look much like a refugee to me.'

'Perhaps not. But I am, nonetheless.'

'A rich refugee.'

If Ang detected Elliot's sarcasm he gave no sign of it. 'As you supposed, I was not without influence with the Americans. I succeeded in getting most of my money out of the country in the months before Phnom Penh fell to the Khmer Rouge.'

'And yourself with the American evacuation, no doubt.'

'Yes.'

Elliot detected a moment of pain in the Cambodian's eyes.

'Unfortunately my influence did not extend to the evacuation of my family.' Ang glanced at Elliot and saw the contempt flicker across his face. A look he had seen on many faces since 1975. He examined his hands. 'My wife, Serey. My daughter,

Ny. She will be seventeen now. And Hau, my son. He will be twelve.'

'If they are still alive.'

'Oh, they are still alive.' The light of hope burned brightly for a moment in Ang's eyes.

'How can you know that?'

'I did not spend all that time in the refugee camps because I had to, Mistah Elliot. I have American citizenship now.'

'Amazing what money can buy – and what it can't.'

Ang faltered only momentarily. 'I was there through choice. I talked to hundreds, maybe thousands, of refugees. They all told the same stories of what was happening in Cambodia – of the atrocities these murderers are perpetrating in my country.'

Elliot recalled the infamous Nixon pronouncement after the US bombing of Cambodia in 1970 – *Cambodia is the Nixon doctrine in its purest form.* No involvement. As if bombs were somehow neutral.

Ang was still talking. 'There were always those in the camps seeking news of relatives or friends. Some were lucky, most were not.'

'And you?' Elliot found himself interested, in spite of an instinctive dislike of Ang.

'I had almost given up.' He remembered the hopelessness of it all. The skeletal figures with their pathetic bundles of ragged possessions who came out of the jungle day after day. Some had lost wives or husbands, fathers and mothers, sons and daughters. They thought they had escaped to freedom, when all that awaited them were the camps, and the indifference of the West. Barbed wire, rows of long insanitary huts. A Thai regime that didn't want them was determined to keep them there, without home or country.

'Until six weeks ago,' he said. 'I had a reported sighting at a commune north of Siem Reap. A woman who had known my wife in Phnom Penh. It was promising, but uncertain.' He had recalled the woman vaguely. Her children had gone to school with his. She had told him it could have been his wife she saw. But one face looked much like another in the communes, she said. Blank. People did not speak. Recognition was dangerous. The past could kill. 'I still needed confirmation. I got it ten days ago. No doubts. My wife is alive. And my daughter.' He paused. 'My son I do not know about.' He sat silent for a long time, then he looked up. 'Mistah Elliot, I will pay you half a million US dollars – everything I have left – if you will go into Cambodia and get them out.'

CHAPTER FIVE

The sun had been merciless, beating down in waves like physical blows, her only protection the conical hat and ragged black pyjamas she wore. Hands like leather worked the wooden shaft of the hoe to a rhythm that was as much a part of her now as breathing.

Serey had lost track of the passage of time since her death. For that was how she saw her life under the Khmer Rouge. A living death. An existence, nothing more. The endless hours in the fields, the indoctrination sessions when the sun went down. Young fanatics haranguing the new breed of Cambodians. Automatons serving the needs of Angkar – the Organization. Mercifully, these had become less frequent since moving to this commune. At first the speakers had been seductive, appealing to those with an education, those with technical, medical, administrative skills, to come forward and serve Angkar on a higher plane. Angkar needs you, they said. Angkar will reward you. And at first there had been those who succumbed. But they all knew now that a call to Angkar meant torture and mutilation in the woods. A bayonet in the stomach or, if you were lucky, a bullet in the head. The weak, the sick, all those who could not work went to Angkar.

There was no conversation, no friendly chatter in the fields, no eye contact, lest it be seen by the guards who watched them from the shade of the trees. The only sound was the scraping of countless hoes in the dry earth, and the idle talk of the guards as they smoked or ate from hampers of fruit and meat and rice. Serey could not remember the last time she had eaten fresh meat. She had eaten grubs, worms, all manner of insects, anything she knew would provide her with at least some protein. And there had been the berries she picked in the jungle, the tubers she dug from the earth. The three meagre portions of rice they were provided with each day would never have sustained her. But still she had the sores on her arms and legs and face that came from vitamin and protein deficiencies.

Ten metres away an old man buckled at the knees and fell face first into the earth. The nearest of the guards shouted at him to get up. He did not stir. The guard approached and kicked him in the ribs and struck him several times across the back with a bamboo staff. The faintest groan escaped the old man's lips. At a signal from the first, a second guard came across and they dragged him away. Another sacrifice to Angkar. There was not the faintest flicker of acknowledgement among those left hoeing. Not a head turned. The rhythm of the hoes continued unbroken. In the early days Serey had heard stories of guards dragging people into the woods, using bayonets to cut open their stomachs. It was said they removed the livers of their still-living victims and ate them raw. She had found it hard to believe. Now she believed anything, and nothing.

Her back ached, her whole being ached, but she no longer felt the pain. Many times she had wished they would come and take her to Angkar. It would, perhaps, have been easier. But she'd had to stay strong for Ny, even though she could no longer acknowledge her as her daughter. Nor Ny her as her mother. Families divided loyalties. They owed loyalty only to Angkar.

It was a miracle that she and Ny were still together after the frequent moves from commune to commune. Somehow they had always contrived to be aboard the same truck. Here they even shared the same hut – with a dozen others. But their only contact was the occasional exchange of glances, a brushing of hands as they passed. Hau, she knew, was in a commune across the river. She had seen him once, sitting in the back of a truckful of guards as it rumbled through their village. He had an automatic rifle slung across his shoulder, and wore a *kramar* – the red, chequered headscarf of the Khmer Rouge. Twelve years old and they had made him one of them. He had seen her, too, she was sure. But he had turned his face away. She wondered if he, like some of the other children, had been made to pick out those whose faces he did not like, and watch as plastic bags were pulled over their heads to suffocate them.

It was almost dark as the siren sounded and they shuffled from the field back to the village and their respective huts. The women in Serey's hut ate their rice in silence, slowly, without passion. Serey glanced at Ny and felt her eyes fill with tears. She had more flesh on her bones than the others, fewer sores, a lustre to her hair and a burning hatred in her eyes. Seventeen and beautiful – or should have been. So many things she should have been. So much that life should have offered.

Ny was aware of her mother looking at her, but kept her eyes down, ashamed to meet her mother's gaze. She was consumed by shame, and hatred for the young cadre who would come for her before very much longer.

Most of the women were asleep, curled up on the hard wooden floor, when she heard the creak of his step on the ladder. Then he appeared in the open doorway and nodded curtly. Silently, she arose and followed him down the steps. He smiled at her. 'How are you tonight?'

'Well,' she said.

He took her arm and led her quickly between the stilts of the huts, beyond the perimeter of the village and into the woods to the place he always took her.

'Undress,' he said. She did so, without a word, as he slipped out of his black pyjamas. She lay down without being told. She knew the routine well. First he kissed her, his lips wet, his tongue probing her mouth. She had to fight to keep down the bile. His hands slipped easily over her breasts, pinching, squeezing. She felt the pressure of his erection against her stomach and clenched her teeth as he entered her, digging her nails into his back in what he always mistook for passion. He was quickly spent, grunting as he came inside her, then sighing, breathless, allowing his full weight to press down on her. He lay for a short while until he softened and then withdrew, kissing her lightly on the lips and brushing her long hair back from her eyes. 'You're a good girl,' he said.

He got up and dressed quickly. She shivered, though the night was warm, wishing she could wash it all away. From her body and her mind. When she had dressed he handed her a small cloth sack of food, some dried meat and fruit, an extra portion of rice. Ny was never quite sure whether it was a payment or a penance, for afterwards, passion spent, he always seemed embarrassed. She took the sack without a word and hurried back to the hut.

Serey heard her coming in, felt the warmth of her closeness as she leant beside her and filled her bowl with half the contents of the sack. Serey feigned sleep, as she always did. Nothing was ever acknowledged between them. The shame would have been unbearable.

CHAPTER SIX

I

David tutted irritably. 'Well, why didn't you answer?'

'I was in the attic,' she lied.

'But I let it ring for ages.'

'Oh David, never mind! I want you to look at these.' She had the contents of the trunk spread across the table in the dining room. She opened the wedding album.

'Wedding photographs,' he said, without enthusiasm. He was tired. He had only come off the night shift at seven that morning, and she had phoned him at home at eight. He should have been asleep by now. But there had been an urgent quality in her voice. So he had driven over and found her in a state he could only describe as near-euphoria. Sometimes death affected people that way. Down one minute, on a high the next. He had been prepared to play the role of comforter, but had not been prepared for this. She stabbed at a picture of the bride and groom.

'Look,' she said.

He recognized her mother. Very young, quite pretty, not at all like the haggard, pinched woman he had known. He shrugged. 'What do you want me to say? It's your mother.'

'Not my mother! The groom!' She could hardly contain her impatience.

He looked at the groom without interest. 'So, it's your father, I suppose.'

'Don't you recognize him?'

David almost laughed. 'How could I recognize him? He's been dead for years. Look, Lisa, you didn't get me all the way down here just to look at old wedding photographs, did you?'

But she was insistent. 'Look again, David, please!' He sighed and looked at the face more closely. And, oddly, there did seem something familiar about him, now that he gave the photo more attention. Lisa saw his frown. 'See, you have seen him before, haven't you?'

He was reluctant to admit his doubt. 'It's not possible.'

'At the churchyard yesterday. The man under the trees. The one with the scar.' She was desperate for confirmation, needed to know she wasn't imagining it. He frowned uneasily as he recalled the face of the man he had seen standing in the rain. And his sense of unease deepened as he remembered the way the man had looked at Lisa.

'This guy doesn't have a scar,' he said.

'Oh for goodness sake, David! That photograph must be twenty years old.' She paused. 'It's him, isn't it?'

'Are you trying to tell me we saw a ghost?'

'Did he look like a ghost to you?' His silence spoke for him. 'He's alive,' she said.

'But it doesn't make sense, Lisa. Why would your mother have told you he was dead? And if it was him, why didn't he come over and speak to you?'

Lisa shook her head in frustration. 'I don't know.' They were questions that had been rattling around her head all night, a night without sleep, a night of so many questions and so few answers. She slumped wearily into a chair. 'I phoned my mother's lawyer first thing. I've made an appointment to see him at twelve. Will you come with me?'

David saw a day without sleep, and a long, tiring night ahead of him in the newsroom. But he nodded. It was as well to get all this out of the way as soon as possible. 'Well, I suppose if anyone can tell you the truth he can.'

Lisa closed her eyes, a wave of relief and fatigue sweeping over her. At least with David there she wouldn't feel quite so alone, quite so vulnerable.

'Lisa . . .' Something in David's voice made her open her eyes sharply. He had been leafing idly through the bundle of old newspapers. He held one up. 'Have you seen this?' It had never crossed her mind to look at them. There was a group photograph of four men in army uniform. A headline: VERDICT IN ADEN MASSACRE. She felt the blood rise on her cheeks as she recognized one of the men as her father.

II

Wiseman was in his sixties, with more than half an eye on retirement. His life had been one long succession of conveyancing, divorces and wills. Long gone were the heady ambitions of the student lawyer; the Bar, the Old Bailey, the triumphs and intrigues of criminal law. Instead, life had brought him to this small, seedy office in an insignificant south London legal partnership. He was the senior partner now, but it was little consolation. Nothing was more difficult in life than coming to terms with your own limitations.

This, however, was something rather different. He examined the young lady seated at the other side of his desk, a desk piled with conveyances, divorces and wills. Her thick blonde hair was cut short, swept back from a strong-featured face. Full, sensuous lips, a fine straight nose and clear blue eyes. She wore no make-up and there were deep shadows under her eyes. He supposed he wasn't seeing her at her best, having just buried her mother. But he could see she was a good-looking girl, slim, her blouse tucked loosely into her jeans. She wore a long dark jacket which hung open, a leather satchel slung from her shoulder. Her hands were clasped between her thighs as she sat slightly forward listening earnestly. She was not at all like her mother – a bitter, brittle woman whom he had never liked.

Her young man sat back in his chair, arms folded across his chest, listening with a sort of grim detachment. Wiseman had taken an instant dislike to him, but the girl had insisted that he sit in on their meeting.

'Of course, you realize it was your mother's wish that you never know,' he was saying.

'I think she'd already gathered that,' the young man said impatiently.

'David,' Lisa admonished him.

Wiseman flicked him a glance of disapproval. 'However,' he went on, 'since you have found out for yourself, I don't see any harm in telling you as much as I know.' He scratched his chin thoughtfully. 'It also releases me from the obligation of trying to conceal from you the source of the money your mother has left you.'

'What money?' David asked, suddenly interested.

'I think, Miss Robinson, this is a matter we really should discuss in confidence.'

'I've nothing to hide from David,' Lisa said.

'The world,' Wiseman said evenly, 'is full of fortune hunters.'

David contained his annoyance. 'I am not a fortune hunter, Mr Wiseman.'

There was just the hint of amusement in Wiseman's eyes. 'Then you won't be disappointed to discover that the young lady has not inherited a fortune.' He turned back to Lisa. 'But it is a sizeable sum.'

Lisa shook her head. 'I don't understand. My mother didn't have any money.'

Wiseman clasped his hands on the desk in front of him.

'When your mother divorced your father there was a settle-
ment. A small monthly sum. She opened an account into which
she had the money paid direct. The payments have been made,
unbroken, for almost sixteen years. But for the last nine or ten
years there have been additional, if infrequent, payments of
considerable amounts. Your mother always refused to touch
the money in that account. She told me that one day it was to
go to you, but you were never to know its source.' He paused,
picking his words carefully. 'She seemed to feel that the money
was somehow . . . dirty. And that by denying it to herself she
was in some way cleansing it for you.'

Lisa's thoughts were confused and uncertain, as though all
this was, or should have been, happening to someone else.
She had grown up in a cocoon of ignorance, and now that she
was breaking free of its protective shell, discovering that she
wasn't who she thought she was.

'She did make one exception,' Wiseman went on. 'About
four years ago. She lifted enough from the account to pay off
the mortgage on the house. Naturally, she has left that to you.'

'So what's the balance?' David asked.

Wiseman sighed, reluctant to impart the information in
this young man's presence. 'I do not have an exact figure, but
it is somewhere in the region of one hundred and eighty-five
thousand pounds. With the house, and various other bits and
pieces, the young lady should be worth over four hundred
thousand.'

David whistled softly. Lisa sat motionless, filled with a

39

great sadness. It wasn't right, or fair. She had done nothing to deserve this. She didn't want the money or any part of it. She wanted her mother back, along with the lost belief that her father was dead. She wanted to climb back into her shell and hide. But it was broken now and there was no way back. Wiseman cleared his throat discreetly. 'Miss Robinson . . . ?'

She looked at him. 'I'm sorry?'

'I know all this must have come as a bit of a shock to you . . .'

She cut in. 'What about my father?'

'I'm afraid I know very little about him. You've read the newspaper reports. You know he spent five years in a military prison after the court martial. You know as much as I do.'

'But how did he make the payments during the years he was in prison?'

Wiseman spread his hands in a gesture that told her he could not help.

'I want to find him,' she said.

David looked at her, shocked. 'Why?'

'Because he's my father.'

'It might be difficult after all this time,' Wiseman said.

Lisa looked at him defiantly. 'You're a lawyer. You find him. I can afford it.'

Wiseman sighed. 'I can try, I suppose.'

David shook his head. 'Lisa, this is ridiculous.'

Wiseman headed off a row. 'There is one more thing you should know.' Lisa looked at him, wondering what more there could possibly be. 'After the divorce your mother reverted to the use of her maiden name. She was ashamed and humiliated by what your father had done, and wished to protect you. But you are still, strictly speaking, Lisa Elliot. It's the name on your birth certificate. It was never legally changed.'

Outside, a watery winter sun cast pale shadows in the street. 'You're mad,' David said, trying to keep up with her. But he had seen that determined set of her jaw before and knew she would not be argued with. For a young woman of eighteen years she could be frustratingly immature, almost childlike, with a child's blindness to reason. The result, he knew, of an obsessively shielded upbringing. Her mother had been a strange woman locked away in a world of her own, a world of protective darkness in which she had forced her daughter to live too. He had wondered why she should unlock the door to him. Perhaps she had known she could not hold on to Lisa for ever. Perhaps she had seen him as her successor. Lisa kept walking, hardly aware of him. She just wanted to walk and walk, run if she could. He said, 'I mean, along with the rest of them he killed a whole bunch of innocent civilians in cold blood.'

'We don't know that.'

'He was found guilty, wasn't he? They put him in prison. What more do you need to know?'

'I want to know why.'

'Does there have to be a why?'

'Of course there does.'

'What, just because he's your father?'

She stopped suddenly, turning to face him, tears of frustration welling in her eyes. 'Yes,' she said defiantly. 'Just because he's my father!' And she turned and ran off through the shoppers as the tears began to spill.

CHAPTER SEVEN

A rare blink of winter sunshine sparkled on the slow-moving waters of the Thames. The slightest breeze rattled among the leafless branches of the willows that wept along the embankment. London seemed a long way away here, in the quiet affluence of this Upper Thames village. In the summer, lovers would pass idly by in punts, drifting gently among the backwaters, somnolent and languid in the afternoon sun. Picnics on the embankment, the murmur of bees. But now it was cold, deserted, save for one old man swaddled in coat and scarf walking an equally old dog along the riverside.

Elliot watched them absently from the warmth of the sun lounge, large windows that in hot weather would open on to the garden, now providing a winter panorama across the river. 'You still take lemonade in your whisky?' Blair turned from the drinks cabinet.

'Nothing changes,' Elliot said.

Blair grinned. 'Heathen!' He turned back to pour lemonade with reluctance into a generous measure of amber liquid. He was a tough, wiry, old Scot approaching his middle fifties, a

43

fine head of grey hair over a lean, tanned face. He wore a faded army-green pullover, leather patches at the elbow, and a pair of baggy trousers that concertinaed over dirty white tennis shoes. 'How'd it go in Africa?'

'Bloody disastrous.' Elliot ran a finger gently along the line of his scar. Even after all this time it still occasionally hurt, like toothache. 'Lost nearly half my men before we crossed the border.' He snorted his disgust. 'Freedom fighters! A rabble. No training, no discipline, no balls. Last time I'll take on a job like that. Barely got out alive myself. Didn't get bloody paid, either!'

Blair chuckled. 'Times are tough, eh?' He handed Elliot his whisky and Elliot noticed he hadn't poured one for himself.

'You not joining me?'

'Too early.' Blair eased himself into a deep leather armchair. He paused, his smile fading. 'I saw the death notice in the paper.' Elliot nodded. 'I'm sorry.'

'Don't be. It was all too long ago to mean anything now.'

Blair eyed the younger man with affection. 'What about the girl?'

'She's well provided for.' Elliot sipped his drink. 'I need weapons and kit.'

Blair smiled ruefully. No matter how hard you tried you never got beneath the skin. 'Where this time?'

'Thailand.'

Blair whistled his surprise. 'Jesus Christ! What are you doing in Thailand?'

'Thailand's just base. I'm taking a team into Cambodia.'

The older man laughed. 'Taking on the Khmer Rouge single-handed, are we?'

Elliot smiled. 'It's a small private job. Man's paying me a lot of money to go in and get his family out.'

'How far in?'

'About a week there, a week back. It'll be a small team. Just three of us. I'll want automatics, pistols, grenades, knives, kit, radio, rations and medical supplies. And maps. Can you do it?'

'Thailand's tricky. Can't get anything in. Have to procure locally.'

'I don't want to know how difficult it is, I want to know if you can do it.'

''Course I can do it. Have you ever know your old sergeant to let you down?' He rose. 'I think I *will* have that drink.' He crossed to the cabinet to pour himself a stiff measure. 'Can't guarantee what I get you, though. Be either Russian or American. Probably Russian.'

'I'd prefer American.'

'Might cost more.'

'So, it'll cost more.'

Blair sipped his whisky and rolled it around his mouth. 'Who are you taking?'

'Slattery.'

'That bloody Aussie! Man, he's aff his heid!'

'He's good. I phoned Sydney this morning. I'm meeting him in Bangkok.'

Blair shook his head. 'The two of you loose in Bangkok. That would be worth seeing.' Pause. 'Who else?'

'A pal of Slattery's. A Yank called McCue. Vietnam vet. Ex-Big Red One. Tunnel Rat. Stayed on in Bangkok after the war.'

'When you going?'

'Flying out later this week. I want to be ready to move in a fortnight.'

Blair emptied his glass. 'You're aff your heid, man!' Another pause. 'Don't suppose you'd like to take a fourth?'

Elliot grinned. 'You're too bloody old, Sam.'

'I'm as fit as you are.'

'No chance. The only place you're going to die now is in your bed.'

CHAPTER EIGHT

Lisa had not gone back to college. The Christmas holidays were coming up and, anyway, she couldn't have faced it. The sympathy of her friends, the questions she wouldn't want to answer. And she was no longer sure she was the person she had been just a week ago. College, and a future in journalism, seemed unimportant, trivial.

She had wandered around the house for days, unable to settle, picking up a book, reading a few pages then laying it aside. She had phoned Wiseman several times, but he had no news. David had called every day and she had put him off each time. Somehow he belonged to the person she had been before, to Lisa Robinson, the shy orphaned eighteen-year-old who had stood so helplessly at her mother's graveside only a few days earlier. Lisa Elliot was someone else. Who that person was, she could not yet tell. Just that she was different. She had money, independence, and a father who'd killed women and children in cold blood.

Then, on the fourth day, came the call she had been waiting for. Wiseman's voice at the other end of the line. 'We can't guarantee,' he said, 'that he'll still be there. But it's the last address that we can find.'

Lisa's mouth was dry and her hands trembled as she stepped out of the taxi into the King's Road. She had not wanted to take the cab right to the door. She needed time to walk, collect her thoughts, summon the courage to make her way to the mews address Wiseman had given her, to knock on the door and face the man she had always thought was dead. Her father.

She realised very quickly that had been a mistake. All she'd done was make time for her courage to fail. What would she say to him? What if he didn't want to know, and shut the door in her face? What would she do then? She walked slowly, dreamlike, through the late evening Christmas shoppers, tinsel flashing in shop windows, Christmas lights tinting the faces of passers-by. She caught a glimpse of her reflection in a window. A pale, frightened face staring back from the glass. She focused beyond the reflection. An ice-cream parlour. And she shivered. A little girl holding her Daddy's hand as he bought her a two-flavour cone, her face alight with pleasure, her father's smile of fond indulgence. Ice cream at Christmas. Moments Lisa had never known. She caught her reflection again and looked quickly away.

Now or never.

The cobbled mews lane was deserted, feeble pools of yellow light falling from old-fashioned coach lamps mounted on each cottage wall. One or two lights shone in upper windows. A red Porsche stood parked on her left as she entered through an archway. You needed money to own a mews house here.

Number twenty-three had a lacquered, oak-panelled door. There was no name plate, no light in the upper windows. She pressed the buzzer and heard it sound faintly within. She waited, but already she knew the house was empty. She tried again, an automatic response, and stepped back to look up. The darkness in the windows mirrored her despair. She turned away.

A net curtain flickered at an upper window as her footsteps receded down the mews.

'She's gone. Probably some woman he's been two-timing.' The man turned away from the window as his companion again turned on the flashlight and quickly completed the wiring Lisa's arrival had interrupted. He lifted the top casing of the telephone answering machine and slipped it carefully back in place, dexterously tightening the screws at all four corners.

'That's it,' he said, and placed each of the specialist tools of his trade into the pockets of a folding canvas carrier which he rolled up and dropped into a soft leather holdall. He switched off the flashlight. 'Let's get out of here.'

The other man lifted the holdall and patted the answering machine gently with his gloved hand. He grinned. 'Merry Christmas, Mr Elliot.'

CHAPTER NINE

Elliot looked down as his plane circled before coming in to land at Bangkok's Don Muang international airport. Below, the paddy fields caught and reflected the light of the moon, hundreds of silver-paper shapes arranged in random geometric patterns. The airport was crowded and hot. A sticky heat you could almost touch. It came as a shock after the hours of incarceration in the air-conditioned fuselage of the aircraft that had left London shivering at minus ten. Elliot felt his clothes go limp. He had a long, irritating wait to clear customs and immigration, Thai officers inspecting him with inscrutable dark eyes. Slattery was waiting for him at the international arrivals gate in a short-sleeved, sweat-stained shirt.

'Hey, chief!' His big hand grasped Elliot's. Elliot had a great affection for this voluble Aussie, and a great respect too. As a soldier of fortune in the early days of the war in Nam he had adapted quickly and easily to the guerrilla tactics of the VC, realizing long before the Americans that this would be no conventional war for conventional soldiers.

Elliot grinned. 'How are you, you ugly bastard?'

'Getting uglier.' Slattery pulled playfully at Elliot's scarred cheek. 'And you get prettier every time I see you.'

He was a man of indeterminate years, though probably in his early forties. His coarse blonde hair had been crew-cut to little more than a stubble. He was short, about five-nine, but broad-built, stocky, with enormous strength and stamina. He had a striking face, squat and ugly, made almost remarkable by the pale grey of his eyes. His deep tan was ruddy rather than brown, his eyebrows bleached nearly white by the unrelenting Australian sun. But Elliot's first impression was that he had lost weight.

Slattery drove the battered Peugeot hire car with a deceptive carelessness, smoking constantly, one hand on the wheel, dodging in and out of the traffic, cursing other drivers. He talked incessantly. 'There I was, all set to spend the summer on the beach, a couple of girls lined up. You know, the kind who know how to amuse themselves when I'm not in the mood. House rented right on the surf, king-sized bed for three, the works. And then I get your call. Jesus! There goes my summer. And there go the girls. So then I think, okay, a bit of R and R in Bangkok. Can't be bad. How long we got before we hit the shit?'

'A week to ten days.' Elliot had listened to all this in brooding silence.

'Jeez! Time enough to catch the clap and take a cure.' Slattery laughed too loudly. 'What's the agenda?'

'I want to see your man, McCue.'

51

'Sure. Tomorrow do?'

'Now.'

'Aw, hey, chief. The night's young, and so are the women. I thought we'd break a bit of sweat our first night.'

'I want to see him tonight.' Elliot spoke quietly. Slattery glanced at him.

'Something bugging you, chief?'

Elliot said, 'I don't rate our chances on this trip at better than fifty-fifty. I want you and the Yank to be under no illusions. If either of you are going to pull out I want it to be tonight. I'll need time to recruit another team. And I want to see this guy for myself before I give him the green light.'

Slattery nodded and felt a tightening across his chest. He had calculated the odds differently, had known from the first that this outing would be his last. A quick death in action, adrenalin pumping. It was preferable to the lingering death sentence passed on him by the young doctor. 'A wee touch of cancer,' Slattery had joked. But the doctor had not smiled. He had been as cold and clinical as the tiles in his surgery.

'You have six months to a year, Mr Slattery, if you respond to treatment.'

'Fuck the treatment,' Slattery had told him.

Elliot's call had come like a beacon in the darkness. The prospect of a summer on the beach had loomed like a shroud waiting slowly to descend. There had been no girls, no king-sized bed, just long hot months of lonely boredom stretching ahead, leading inexorably towards the inevitable.

'Well, I reckon you can count me in, chief,' he said brightly. 'You know me. Try anything once. Suck it and see, eh?'

Elliot smiled. Slattery had a habit of picking up odd clichés, using one till he had burned it out, and then picking up another. On their last outing it had been bite on the bullet, the time before, the nature of the beast. Everything had been the goddamned nature of the beast! Now he was sucking it and seeing. But Elliot had also detected a false bravura in the Australian, a chill behind his grey eyes that the grin could not hide. It worried him a little, but he said nothing.

They drove the rest of the way in a silence punctuated by Slattery's curses, down Rajadamri Road, past the Royal Sports Club on the right and Lumpini Park a little further down on the left. The traffic was still heavy, buses, trucks, private cars, taxis and *tuk-tuks* – small three-wheeler samlors, extended motor-scooters with two seats at the back for passengers. Great multi-storey blocks rose up now on either side of them, cheek by jowl with the mean little rows of Chinese and Muslim shops, multicoloured, multilingual signs hanging out over shambolic broken pavements from which rose the stench of the sewers below.

They crossed Rama IV Road at a busy junction and turned into Silom Road, where the nightlife was gathering momentum in the sticky heat. Past Patpong Road with its noisy clubs and bars, sexual floorshows and hundreds of bar girls who were little more than children. Slattery pulled in outside the Narai Hotel. It towered above them, rising into the inky black of the south-east Asian night. Elliot got out and Slattery pushed his case at him. 'You check in, chief. I'll park the car then come and find you.'

The chill of the air conditioning beyond the sliding glass doors was delicious after the humidity outside. Tourists sat drinking coffee in a pizzeria coffee shop while young girls, white robes glowing in the ultraviolet of the Don Juan bar, smiled alluringly as he passed. An incongruous Christmas tree sat in the lobby, erected no doubt to make Western tourists feel at home. It seemed peculiarly out of place in this deeply Buddhist country. Elliot filled out the paperwork at the reception desk, feeling tired for the first time. It was almost ten o'clock, though it was not yet three back in London, and he had been in the air for more than thirteen hours. He never slept on aeroplanes.

It was a relief to get to his room. He sank back on the bed and closed his eyes, the drone of aircraft engines still in his ears. A scraping noise at his door made him sit up abruptly. A small card had been slipped beneath it from the corridor. Elliot picked it up and smiled wearily. A massage parlour somewhere in Chinatown. They didn't waste any time. A sharp knock at the door startled him. Slattery stood there grinning. 'Saw some greaseball slip a card under your door.' He took the card from Elliot and examined it. 'We could go see McCue tomorrow.'

Elliot shook his head. 'Don't you ever give up?'

The grin again. 'Only kidding. Got a *tuk-tuk* waiting downstairs. Ready when you are, chief.'

The *tuk-tuk* spluttered and bumped its way perilously through the traffic in Silom Road, taking a right into Charoen Krung Road and then sharp left down to the Oriental Hotel landing stage. The jetty was ablaze with light, crowded with all manner of people – children with mothers in black pyjamas, men in smart evening wear, monks in saffron robes – all coming and going on a variety of craft, large and small, that bobbed gently on the slow-moving waters of the Chao Phraya river. A hubbub of voices competed with the noise of the traffic on this east bank, haggling over the price of a cross-river trip on a water-borne taxi.

'Back in a sec, chief.' Slattery slipped off through the crowds to do his own haggling. Elliot was content to leave him to it. Slattery was an old Bangkok hand, knew his way about. Elliot let the city night wash over him. He had forgotten how many people in this sprawling river port lived on or over water, along the hundreds of *klong*s that ran like veins off the main artery of the river. He had read somewhere that Bangkok was sinking at the rate of half an inch a year. The incredible sinking city. In the rainy season you had to wade hip-deep through some of the streets. Perhaps, he thought, most of its people would one day be living on or over water – and some of them under it.

Slattery re-emerged from the crowd, wearing his habitual grin. 'Alright, chief. Got us a ride and saved us a few *baht*.'

The ride Slattery had got them turned out to be in a sleek yellow *hang yao* canoe. The propeller that powered it was fixed at the end of a long driveshaft which the toothless Thai driver

used as a rudder. The driver showed his gums in what was
clearly meant as a friendly grin. His eyes were glazed, and
he babbled something incoherent as Elliot climbed in. Elliot
turned to Slattery. 'He's pissed!'

''Course he is. These guys don't function without at least a
half-bottle of Thai whisky inside them.'

Still showing his gums, the driver gunned his engine and
they powered away from the landing stage, knifing through
the wash from the overladen rice barges that trafficked up
and down the river. They headed south, the hot breeze and
cool spray in their faces, exhilarating. Under the Krungthep
Bridge, then turning in a wide arc into the Dao Khanong Canal,
their progress shattered city lights reflected on dark waters.
Tall lamp-posts rose from the water on either side, wooden
poles linked by a confusion of arcing cables carrying electricity
and telephone lines. They slowed suddenly, turning again, this
time into the maze of *klong*s, a shambles of teak houses raised
on stilts overhanging the banks, linked here and there by ramshackle wooden bridges that spanned the waters.

Lights shone in most of the houses, many of the stilt-raised
shops still trading. A confusion of sounds filled the night air
– a babble of voices giving way to the tinny blare of Thai pop
music and the Americanized jingles of a million television sets.
They passed men and children bathing in the water at the foot
of wooden steps leading to their homes, women perched precariously on narrow wooden terraces, peeling potatoes. Myriad
small boats gave way to the *hang yao*, resentful faces briefly

glimpsed, raised voices calling after them in the dark. 'Tell him to slow down,' Elliot shouted. 'We're going to hit someone!'

Slattery called something to the driver, who shrugged and pulled back on the throttle, slowing them down to a walking pace, and reducing the roar of the engine to little more than a throaty idle. They cruised slowly through the maze for another ten minutes or more, turning into increasingly narrow canals, thick vegetation and leaning palms crowding in on either side, choking the gaps between the houses. Slattery leaned forward and spoke to the driver, who pulled over at the foot of a short flight of wooden steps leading up to a narrow drooping teak house that stood in darkness atop its spindly legs. He cut the engine and a silence encroached with the night, broken only by the constant gentle slapping of water against stilts. A rank smell hung in the air. Rotting vegetation, human waste, woodsmoke. Something heavy thudded against the side of the canoe. Slattery leaned over to take a look, shining a small pocket torchlight into the water.

'Dead dog,' he said, and grinned. The decaying creature, bloated by putrid gases, drifted away. 'We're here.' He jumped out on to a tiny landing stage and Elliot followed.

'He lives here?' Elliot asked incredulously.

'Sure. Married a Thai girl, a bar girl. I bet she thought she was escaping from all this.' He laughed softly, ironically. 'And all the time it was old Billy doing the escaping. Don't worry about the driver. He'll wait.'

As they climbed the steps, Elliot glanced back and saw the

driver taking a long pull from a murky-looking bottle. A veranda with a rickety rail ran the length of the house at the front. It creaked under their weight, and an old rocking chair tipped slowly back and forth. Mosquito nets hung loosely in open windows. Slattery rapped gently on the door. 'Hoi, McCue!' His voice sounded inordinately loud in the whispering silence. 'Get out yer scratcher. Got a man here wants to see you.'

A light came on somewhere within, then after a moment the door opened and McCue appeared in a dirty white singlet and shorts, barefoot and blinking in the light. 'Shit! What time of night's this to come calling?' He was a small man, no more than five-five. Sinuous, wiry arms and legs, lean-faced with a nose like a blade and a chin with a cutting edge. His eyes were dark and hostile, and his skin tanned a deep, even brown. His black hair was tousled, and had it not been for the Midwest drawl, at a glance you could have taken him for a Thai. He was younger than either of his visitors. Early thirties, Elliot guessed.

'Hey, Billy boy, that's no way to greet an old buddy. The chief wanted to meet you.'

McCue eyed Elliot darkly. 'You'd better come in.'

Inside, the main room was neat and spotless, stone jars lined up against one wall, a wooden dresser with a water bowl and jug. There were no chairs, no table. McCue squatted cross-legged on the floor and indicated that they should do the same. As he sat, Elliot saw, through an open doorway, a half-naked woman slipping into a *panung*, a large sarong-like garment drawn up between the legs like an Indian *dhoti*. Beyond her, a mosquito net hung from the ceiling over a big square mattress on the floor. Inside, a baby stirred restlessly. 'You hungry?' McCue asked.

'Starving,' said Slattery.

McCue called into the back room and the woman appeared in the doorway. She pressed her palms together and bowed solemnly to the strangers. You could see she had once been very beautiful. Thai girls are considered by many to be the most beautiful in the world. But it is a beauty that fades quickly with a life that is hard, features coarsening, skin withering, so that by forty they can often look like old women. This woman – Lotus, McCue had called her – was perhaps thirty. Already well down that road. McCue spoke to her curtly in stuttering, guttural Thai. She nodded, and without a word moved off into another part of the house.

'This is Jack Elliot,' Slattery said.

McCue reached out a hand for a cursory handshake. 'Elliot.'

'How much has Mike told you?'

'Enough to know it's fucking madness.'

'So why do you want to go?'

'Because there's a big fat pay cheque at the other end.'

Elliot glanced around him. 'Thinking of moving upmarket?'

McCue inclined his head towards the back room. 'This ain't no place to bring up a kid. I'm taking him home with me.' He spoke softly with a voice like Thai silk, his face expressionless, his eyes impenetrable.

'Shit, Billy, you could have gone home anytime.'

'I never wanted to before. But then, I never had a kid before.'

Elliot looked at him thoughtfully, taking in the scars on his thighs and calves. 'What's your track record?'

'Three tours in Nam, sixty-nine to seventy-one.'

'Nobody did three tours.'

'I volunteered for the other two.'

'With the Big Red One?'

'First Engineer Battalion, First Cavalry Division. Sergeant, Tunnel Rats.'

The Tunnel Rats had been an eight-man elite team operating in the Iron Triangle north of Saigon, flushing VC out of the hundreds of kilometres of tunnel networks where the communist guerrillas lived and fought – a dark, subterranean existence where they had contrived sleeping chambers, food and ammunition dumps, and even makeshift hospitals. It was an extraordinary complex of tunnels, dug by hand out of the hard, laterite soil over twenty years, built on several levels to protect against flooding and gas. They were riddled with booby traps.

The VC would pop out of hidden trapdoors on the ground, catching American GIs unawares, and then vanish again into the tunnels. The soldiers sent down after them were almost invariably killed, either by booby traps, or by VC waiting with grenades or AK-47s. The twisting dark tunnels were only big enough to allow a small man to crawl on his belly. Operating here took special skills. Techniques for engaging the enemy, and a very special kind of soldier, quickly evolved. The Rats were formed in 1967.

'You knew Batman, then?' Elliot asked.

Sergeant Robert Batten Batman had been the most famous of the rats, and the most feared by the Viet Cong. So much so that he had made it on to their ten-most-wanted list. All the VC in the tunnels knew his name. McCue shook his head. 'Before my time. But I heard the stories.'

'Why were you picked?'

'I wasn't. I volunteered.' A slight ironic smile hovered on his lips. 'I loved it in the tunnels,' he said. 'When they told me they had a VC down there I came unglued.' The most dangerous moment for the Rat, when he was most exposed, was when he was lowered into the hole. Often a VC would be waiting for him at the bottom with a poisoned bamboo *punji* stake, or a grenade, or he would just cut the Rat in two with a burst of automatic fire. It was one of those moments that had finally got to McCue, a split second when he lost his nerve and just couldn't do it any more. Just six weeks earlier he had almost been killed in a tunnel. He remembered the cold horror of the moment. They knew there was a VC somewhere up ahead in the dark. McCue had inched his way forward, his flashlight held out to one side in his left hand, his gun in the other. A second Rat followed about five metres back – the distance at which a grenade would not be lethal.

As they came to a bend, McCue had reached round and fired three shots into the blackness. Nothing. So he had moved on.

The tunnel straightened out and came to a dead end. A slight earth-fall betrayed the presence of an overhead trapdoor. As he reached it, sweat running in clear rivulets down his blackened face, the trapdoor slid into place. The VC was right above him. His mouth dry, he had raised his pistol, ready to fire, and pushed the trapdoor up. Something fell, almost into his lap. 'Grenade!' he screamed, and started scrambling back along the tunnel. The explosion ruptured one of his ear drums, and his legs were peppered with grenade fragments. The second Rat had dragged the bleeding and half-conscious McCue back along the tunnel. It had taken nearly an hour to get him to the surface.

The smell of cooking came to them from the back of the house. Outside, the cicadas kept up an incessant chorus and the murky waters of the *klong* lapped constantly at the stilts. Slattery passed round cigarettes and the three men sat smoking in silence for some minutes. At length McCue looked at Elliot and broke the silence. 'You were responsible for the Aden massacre.'

Slattery glanced at Elliot anxiously, but the Englishman was impassive. 'It's what they said at the court martial.' He stared back at McCue, unblinking.

'Apart from that, I don't know anything about you,' McCue said.

'No one does, Billy boy, no one does,' Slattery said cheerfully. 'But he's the chief. And take my word for it, a handy man in a scrap.'

McCue's eyes never left Elliot. 'What's your experience in south-east Asia?'

'Nam.' McCue raised an eyebrow, and Elliot answered the unasked question. 'Freelance.'

A flicker of distaste crossed McCue's face. 'A headhunter.'

'I only counted them.' It wasn't a defence. Just a statement of fact. In the early days in Nam, some of the mercenaries had been paid by the head. Literally. Elliot had not been squeamish about it. Just practical. Heads were bloody and cumbersome. He knew McCue was weighing him up, and he liked that. Soldiers who thought before they acted stood a better chance of survival. He had already decided that McCue was in.

McCue said, 'When do we go?'

And Elliot knew that he, too, had passed muster. 'Ten days. My fixer in the UK has set us up a contact here in Bangkok. He'll provide arms, kit and supplies. We'll make contact tomorrow. He'll also provide passes to get us into selected camps along the border. I want to do a recce, talk to some of the refugees. And we'll need a guide. Someone to get us across the border. Then we'll be on our own. Initial planning meeting in a week.'

Lotus brought in half a dozen bowls of steaming food on a tray and laid it on the floor beside them. With a careful, elegant precision, she knelt down and placed each of the bowls on the floor in the centre of the small circle of men. McCue described each dish. '*Kaeng jeud*, soup with vegetables and pork. *Khao phat muu*, fried rice with shrimp. *Phat siyu*, noodles and soy sauce. *Plaa priaw waan*, sweet and sour fish. *Phat phak lai yang*, stir-fried vegetables. *Yam neua*, hot and sour grilled beef salad.'

'Jesus, that's some spread, Billy. Tell the little lady it's much appreciated.'

She nodded, unsmiling. 'Thank you.' She passed them each a bowl and chopsticks.

'Tuck in, chief. Thailand's finest. All cooked in lovely *klong* water, that right, Billy?' McCue inclined his head in acknowledgement. 'Wash, shit and cook in the stuff.' Slattery glanced at Elliot. 'But don't worry, chief, suck it and see. You've had your cholera booster, ain't ya?'

On the way back Elliot was silent. The hot air battered against his face as their driver, now glazed and unreachable, drove their *hang yao* through the myriad waterways with a reckless disregard for the safety of anyone. Slattery hung on to the side of the boat grinning maniacally, eyes on fire. 'Fantastic, chief! Absolutely fantastic!' They had consumed enough *Mekong*, a distilled rice concoction, to leave them with as much disregard for their safety as their driver.

Elliot was miles away. McCue's total commitment to his child had touched a raw nerve. However little he cared for himself, or even his wife, he was prepared to die to provide the chance of a better future for his son. Elliot had a picture in his head that wouldn't go away. Of a young woman in a churchyard, all in black, lifting her veil and looking at him without recognition. Somehow that had been more painful

PETER MAY

than the years of denial. He had known her at once, felt he would have known her anywhere. And he had provided for her, hadn't he? After a fashion? He shook his head. It was the *Mekong* talking, not his conscience. He had no conscience, or if he had it had never offered him guidance, only pain, somewhere deep inside, buried away from public gaze.

'I could do with a real drink,' Slattery shouted above the roar of the engine.

Elliot looked at him. 'What age do you reckon McCue is?'

Slattery frowned. 'I dunno. About thirty? Why?'

Elliot shrugged. 'Doesn't matter.'

'So what about that drink?'

'Why not.' Elliot felt like getting drunk.

CHAPTER TEN

Lisa opened a small, white-painted wooden gate and started down the path through the trees towards the house. It was a mock Tudor building, white with black-painted cross-beams and latticed windows. The garden was extensive and well kept, a path leading round the side to a large lawn at the back which sloped down towards the river's edge. The weather had changed overnight. It had been bitterly cold, threatening snow for Christmas. But today it was unseasonably mild, an almost springlike warmth in the sun that slipped out periodically from behind the scudding white clouds that raced across the winter sky.

She was apprehensive, but the passing days had blunted hope and she expected nothing. She had returned several times to the mews house, but always there had been no one there. If this proved another dead end, she had resolved to put it all behind her, return to college after the holidays and try to build a new life for herself. She would tell herself that, after all, her father really was dead as her mother had always told her. In time she might even grow to believe it. She would probably marry David, raise children and lead a normal life. Normal! Whatever that was.

She knocked on the door and waited, praying that at least someone would answer, even if only to tell her she had the wrong address. Not knowing was the worst. The sun slipped behind a cloud and a shadow fell over her like fading hope. She knocked again and was about to turn away when the door opened abruptly. A grey-haired man in a green pullover, baggy trousers and tennis shoes peered out at her. She hesitated, not quite sure now what to say. 'Yes?' the man asked.

'Sergeant Samuel Blair?' she stammered, aware of the colour rising on her cheeks. He frowned, eyeing her suspiciously.

'Who wants to know?'

'I'm Lisa Elliot,' she said.

Blair was at a loss for words. He had figured her for some young reporter trying to dig up an old story. It happened from time to time. But he saw now that she was too young, her face flushed with uncertainty.

'You'd better come in,' he said at length.

He led her through to the sun lounge and indicated the chair where her father had sat only a few days before. 'Tea? Coffee?' She shook her head. He sat on the edge of his leather armchair opposite her, leaning forward, hands clasped between his legs. He stared at them for a moment. Big rough hands, speckles of age like large freckles spattering the back of them. 'So how can I help you?'

'I'm looking for my father.' She was hesitant. Not sure how much she should tell him. But there was something warm in his eyes that drew her on. 'I have an address in a

Chelsea mews. I know he did live there, but it seems to be empty now.'

Blair nodded, reluctant to commit himself to anything yet. He examined her face. Pretty. And he thought he saw something of her father in her. Was it the blue of her eyes? Maybe something in the set of the mouth, or the line of the jaw? 'How did you find me?'

'Luck really,' she said. 'And a journalist's training.' He allowed himself an ironic smile. He hadn't been so wrong, after all. She added, 'I went through all the names of those convicted at the court martial and looked in the telephone book. Yours was the only one listed. But, even then, I couldn't be sure it was the same Samuel Blair.'

Blair made a mental note to change his number and go ex-directory. 'I understood you'd been told Jack was dead.'

'Jack? Is that what you call him?' It was odd hearing him referred to by name by someone who knew him. It made him more real. 'I thought it was John.'

Blair shrugged. 'He's always been Jack to me. And you haven't answered my question.'

'I didn't know you'd asked me one.' She caught his look. 'I'm sorry,' she said, 'I *was* told he was dead. Then this man turned up at the funeral . . .'

Blair was taken aback. 'He was at the funeral!'

Lisa nodded. 'I didn't know who he was, of course. But then I found all the newspaper cuttings in the attic, and some old photographs. My mother had shut them away.'

He saw a large tear gather itself on the brim of her eye before it rolled down her cheek.

'All those years he was alive, sending money. And I grew up without a father. And then I find out he was a – a murderer!' She looked at him, daring him to contradict her, her eyes blurred and wet. 'And you were, too.'

Blair was embarrassed by her tears, hurt by her words, sharing the pain of them. 'You mustn't be too hard on him, Lisa.'

And immediately she punished the inadequacy of the only words he had been able to find in response. 'Why not?' Her eyes blazed at him. 'Do you think it wasn't hard on me? All the other kids had dads. Dads who took them skating, picked them up from dancing, read them stories.'

'And all those dads had little girls to pick up from dancing, to read stories to. It goes both ways, Lisa.'

'Maybe. But whose fault was that? Mine?' All the resentment that had been growing inside spilled out in bitter words. Now she knew why she wanted to find her father so badly. She wanted someone to blame. Blair reached across and took her hand. Such a small hand in his. There was compassion in his eyes. Understanding. And Lisa wondered how it was possible that this man, too, was responsible for killing all those women and children.

'I think you could do with some air,' he said. A wry smile. 'I think I could, too.'

*

Lisa said, 'Not having a father, not knowing anything about him, I invented him for myself, made up stories about him.' She felt better for the fresh air, strangely comfortable with this man, able to talk to him as she had never talked to anyone before. They followed a path through the trees by the water's edge, scuffing through the dead leaves that still lay thick and rotting on the ground.

'He was very handsome and kind, and brave, and he died in some heroic gesture trying to save the lives of his men. It had broken my mother's heart and it still hurt her deeply even to talk about him, so she never did. It's what I told my friends. There was a time, I think, I actually believed it myself. But somewhere, deep down, I suppose I always knew it wasn't true. And as I got older I started to hate him, blame him for dying and leaving us. Just as I blame my mother now for leaving me to face everything on my own. Not very rational. How can you blame someone for dying?'

'It's quite common when someone close to you dies,' Blair said. 'You feel let down, betrayed.'

Lisa glanced at him, sensing that he wasn't generalizing, that he was speaking from personal experience. But she didn't ask. 'I was never close to my mother, though,' she said. 'I didn't love her, and I'm sure she didn't love me. Sometimes I even felt that she resented me. Maybe she did. Maybe all I was to her was a constant reminder of my father.' She shook her head. 'But if that was true, why did she go to such lengths to protect me from the truth? From ever knowing anything about him?'

'Perhaps,' said Blair, 'she wasn't so much protecting you as punishing him.'

Lisa looked at him, startled. But he refused to meet her gaze. Of course! It would fit with her mother's twisted logic. The thought had a profoundly depressing effect on her.

'But that's probably oversimplifying it,' Blair added lamely and too late.

They came to a bench overlooking the river and sat down, watching the slow movement of the water in silence for some time. Finally she asked the question that had been consuming her for days. 'What's he like, my father?'

Blair shrugged. 'That's like asking how long is a piece of string.'

'But you know him – or did.'

The Scot shook his head. 'Jack's not a man you ever know. Not really. Though I suppose I'm the closest thing he's got to a friend. But even then, I don't know him. He's a complex character. If you're asking if I like him the answer is yes. Very much. I admire him and respect him, but I also like him.'

'How can you like someone you don't know?' And immediately she recognized the paradox of her question. She didn't know the man she had asked it of, but she knew she liked him.

'Jack never confided in me,' Blair said. 'At least, not anything personal, never what was really in his heart. But there was always a rapport between us. Sometimes it's the things left unsaid that say the most. He never spoke of your mother, or of you, but I knew he was hurting. And he still carries the scars of that hurt, though you can't see them like you can the scar on his face.

'When they sent him to prison he asked me if I would make sure that you were both provided for – until he could pay me back.'

'It was you that paid the money into my mother's account?'

He nodded. 'And, of course, he did pay me back. It wasn't easy for him at first, when he got out. He went to Vietnam for a spell and fought for the Diem regime. And then in the Seventies to Africa. Rhodesia, Angola.'

'A mercenary?' Lisa could not hide her distaste for the word.

Blair smiled wryly. 'A soldier of fortune,' he said. 'After all, it was all he knew, soldiering. It was what he was trained for, and he was very good at it. If it hadn't been for Aden . . .'

'Why did you do it?' Lisa broke in, accusation again in her voice. 'How could you shoot all those people in cold blood like that?'

Blair got up and walked a few paces towards the river's edge, hands in his pockets, remembering how it had been. The heat. That scorching, dusty, white heat. The casualties, on both sides, the dead and the dying, men with horrific injuries. Betrayal and counter-betrayal. Never knowing who to trust. And the flies. Always those damned flies, crawling into every gaping wound, getting in your mouth, your eyes. He breathed deeply, drawing the chill clean English air into his lungs. 'Whatever it was, it wasn't in cold blood,' he said. 'We were all of us tired and scared. We'd been drawn into an ambush at a town on the edge of the southern desert. False information. They'd sucked us in and were cutting us to pieces. We all thought we were going to die.

'We'd been coming under heavy fire from a large building in the middle of town. Jack reckoned if we could take and hold that building we could secure our position, at least for a while. We lobbed a couple of grenades through the ground-floor windows and moved in under covering fire. That's when the white flag appeared. Not a flag, really. A piece of dirty white cloth in one of the windows. But, Jesus, if we'd stopped then we'd have been sitting ducks. How were we to know that they'd already withdrawn, that all that was left was a bunch of women and children?

'Jack ordered us to keep going, ignore the flag, and he was right. I'd have done the same. We all would. But he was the officer, he gave the order, he took the fall.' He paused, fists clenched in his pockets, eyes tight shut trying to black out the horror of it. Then he opened them wide and saw it as clearly as he had every night in the dreams that had haunted him all the years since.

'We went in, guns blazing, just like in the movies. Only when the dust and the smoke cleared we were looking at the bodies of women and kids, dead, dying, bleeding.' He turned to face her, but found that he couldn't meet her gaze and his eyes flickered away.

'It didn't read like that in the newspaper reports of the court martial,' she said.

'No – but, then, courts only deal with facts. The truth – well, the truth is something else.'

'Truth is subjective.'

He looked at her, surprised by the insight in one so young. But her eyes carried no condemnation, only pity. And, perhaps, he thought, that was worse. 'It was all a long time ago,' he said. 'I suppose I really don't know what the truth is any more. All I know is the truth I can live with. And, God knows, that's hard enough, lass.'

They walked back to the house in silence. 'Would you like to stay for tea?' he asked when they got in.

'No, I must go.' She turned at the door. 'Where is he, Mr Blair?'

Blair hesitated. There was a good chance Elliot would never come out of Cambodia alive. Then, 'Thailand,' he said.

He sat for a long time in the dying day after she'd gone, full of doubts. The room was sunk in a deep gloom when he finally reached for the phone. He listened to Elliot's voice on the other end, thin and unreal on the tape of his answering machine. After the tone Blair said, 'If she hasn't found you before you get this message, Jack, your daughter knows you're alive and she's looking for you.'

And the machine was primed.

CHAPTER ELEVEN

Tuk Than had a villa on Sukhumvit Road. It was an impressive house built in the French colonial style, anonymous and cool behind shuttered windows. The brief chill of early morning had given way to the fierce south-east Asian sun which was rising high now above the Bangkok skyline, smeared by a haze of heat and humidity. Slattery's face was red and beaded with sweat. He tugged uncomfortably at his collar and loosened his tie. 'Jeez, chief, did we have to get all togged up for this?'

'It's expected,' was all Elliot said, and Slattery wondered how he managed to look so cool in his dark suit.

A demure young Thai girl in yellow tunic and long silk skirt bowed and led them through the delicious cool of the house, where ceiling fans turned lazily in darkened rooms. Out through French windows into the heat once more. Elliot and Slattery screwed their eyes against the glare. The large walled garden was lush and green, still dripping after its early morning sprinkling. A white table and four chairs were set in the shade of a tall, broad-leafed tree at one end of a lawn like billiard baize. Tuk was taking breakfast at the table, short black hair brushed stiffly back from his brown face. He wore an immaculately pressed white shirt and pale slacks. Everything about him – hair, hands, clothes, his smile and his English – was as neatly manicured as his lawn.

'Good morning, gentlemen.' He made no attempt to rise, but waved expansively towards the empty chairs. 'Won't you join me? I'm having a little late breakfast.'

'Thank you, we've already eaten,' Elliot said. He and Slattery sat down.

'Mr Elliot, I take it,' Tuk said.

'That's right.'

'And . . .' Tuk's eyes flickered towards the sweating Slattery.

'Slattery,' Elliot said. Slattery nodded, uncomfortable and untidy in his crumpled, ill-fitting white suit.

'So . . .' Tuk clasped his hands and beamed at them. 'Our friend in London has told me of your requirements, and of course I can supply – at a price.'

'Naturally.' Elliot was already wary of him. He was too squeaky clean, too ostentatiously wealthy – calculating and obsequious. His aftershave, liberally applied to his freshly shaved cheeks, was too expensive and carried the reek of corruption. His hands, Elliot noticed, were like a woman's. He was small and slim, possibly in his early forties. Wariness was turning to distrust.

'I have arranged passes allowing you access to the Mak Moun refugee camp north of Aranyaprathet on the Cambodian border. I can take you down tomorrow. There I can also put you in touch with a man who will take you safely across the border.' He smiled. 'We can discuss terms later, but first . . .' He raised an arm and snapped his fingers. The girl who had brought them in appeared at the French windows and he uttered some clipped instruction. 'I insist that you join me in a drink.'

'I won't say no to that,' Slattery grinned.

The girl brought three amber-coloured drinks in tall glasses, ice ringing coolly against the glass. 'A *Mekong*-based cocktail, mixed with various fruit juices,' Tuk said. Slattery eyed the girl as she retreated towards the house. Tuk followed his eyes and smiled. He inclined his head and raised his glass. 'Here's to your success.' They sipped the bitter-sweet cocktail and Tuk dabbed his brow with a small white handkerchief. 'You realize, of course, that the Thai authorities would not approve of your little venture into Democratic Kampuchea.'

'I didn't think your people were on the best of terms with Pol Pot and his pals,' Slattery said.

'They are not, Mr Slattery, but they wish to avoid a war at all costs. There is a large army presence along the border. It is well patrolled. Naturally, if the police or the army were to discover your intentions you would most certainly be arrested. They would not like to provoke an incident with the Khmer Rouge. The risk, therefore, to myself in supplying you is increased.'

'Like the price, no doubt.'

Tuk smiled at the irony in Elliot's voice. 'It goes without saying. The greater the risk, the greater the recompense. I imagine you would not be undertaking this – adventure – if the rewards were not very great.'

'A calculated risk,' Elliot conceded.

'And your calculations will doubtless include the knowledge that the area east of the north-west sector is thick with Khmer Rouge units.'

'It's our only possible crossing point,' Elliot said. 'I've looked at all the other possibilities. There's the Dangrek mountains to the north, and the Phnom Malai mountain range, thickly wooded as I understand it, to the south.'

'Which is precisely why there is such a heavy concentration of troops in the north-west. It is from there that any Cambodian invasion of Thailand will come. Conversely, it is this area that the Khmers see the need to defend against any imagined threat from the west. And, of course, it is through this area that most of the refugees have come. The forests are mined and booby-trapped, and well patrolled by the Khmer Rouge.'

Elliot had done his homework. He already knew much of what Tuk was telling them. 'I'm banking on a decreased presence because of the continuing border confrontations with the Vietnamese in the south,' he said.

'Then you are banking on a fantasy,' Tuk replied. 'You must realize, Mr Elliot, that the regime of Pol Pot is neither rational nor sane. I myself heard the famous broadcast from Radio Phnom Penh last year, which claimed that one Kampuchean soldier was capable of killing thirty Vietnamese, and that, therefore, only two million Kampuchean troops would be required to wipe out the entire population of Vietnam.' There was contempt in his smile. 'They are sacrificing thousands of *yothea*s – child soldiers – in the border war with Vietnam. Children of ten and twelve years, Mr Elliot. And if they refuse to fight they are shot in the back by their own people. As I understand it, Phnom Penh has committed only thirty to forty thousand troops in the south, while the Vietnamese have massed around a hundred and twenty thousand along the border.'

Slattery glanced at Elliot. 'Tougher than you thought, then, chief?'

Elliot seemed unfazed. 'I need more first-hand intelligence on the ground we'll be covering. It makes it all the more important for us to talk to refugees who have recently come through the north-west sector.'

There was hardly a breath of air in the sheltered silence of Tuk's garden. The late morning heat was intense, the humidity rising. Slattery finished his drink with regret and felt the now familiar tightening across his chest, a dull pain growing acidly from somewhere deep inside his solar plexus. His concentration wandered as Tuk sat back languidly in his chair, dabbing his forehead, clearly in a mood to talk. 'What do you know of Democratic Kampuchea, Mr Elliot?' he said.

'Only what I've read in the newspapers,' Elliot said. 'There isn't much information coming out of the country.'

'Enough to know that there has been genocide on a massive

scale.' Tuk sipped at his drink. 'Stone-Age communism, the Vietnamese call it. Even the Chinese, who have backed Pol Pot from the start, are embarrassed by what has been happening since he took power. The Khmer Rouge are giving communism a bad name. They have been trying to build what they see as a classless society, based on an agrarian economy. They have emptied the cities, wiped out their intelligentsia. Anyone who could read or write, or speak another language. If you wore glasses you were shot as an intellectual – even if you had been no more than a simple fisherman. They are fanatical, almost beyond belief. Even Stalin would have been shocked.'

He leaned back reflectively, enjoying what he knew, savouring it from the security of his villa in Sukhumvit Road, passing it on to lesser mortals with a careless generosity.

'The strange thing is that it is a peculiarly Cambodian phenomenon. These are Cambodians destroying fellow Cambodians. Incestuous genocide. You must speak to a Cambodian friend of mind about it.' He glanced at his gold wristwatch. 'If you care to have another drink while you wait, she will be here very shortly.'

'Wouldn't do no harm, chief,' Slattery said eagerly.

Elliot shrugged. 'We've nothing better to do.'

The drinks came and Tuk spoke for some time of Thailand, of the Prime Minister, General Kriangsak Chamanan, a moderate military figure, he said, who had cut back Thai support for the Khmer Serei – the Free Khmer – guerrillas who were based along the border and dedicated to the downfall of the

Khmer Rouge. Elliot seemed to Slattery to be listening with interest, but Slattery himself had no interest in any of it. He looked around the garden, reflecting on how good life could have been. Not that he had been disappointed by his forty-odd years. He had enjoyed most of them, living often close to death, something that always somehow heightened the pleasure of life itself. How could you really know life, he thought, until you had faced death? But he had never had money. Not real money. How differently he might have felt about life, and death, if he had. But, then, he thought wryly, even money can't save you from the Big C.

It was Slattery, lost in his thoughts, who saw her first. Radiant, all in white, stepping through the French windows. He blinked in case he was dreaming. She was, he thought, the most beautiful woman he had ever seen. She wore a calf-length, white, cotton dress, cross-cut in a deep V over her small breasts and tied loosely at the waist by a red cord. Silken black hair cascaded over her shoulders, so black it was almost blue as it caught the glare of the sun. Her skin was the colour of teak, her eyes a deep, almost luminescent brown. There was just a touch of rouge on her fine high cheekbones, a hint of blue on the lids of her eyes, the merest trace of red on her full, wide lips. She moved with a slow assured elegance across the lawn and he realized that she was tall, perhaps five-six, and not of pure Asian blood. Tuk rose as she approached, and Elliot turned his head to see her for the first time. And he knew from that first moment that she was something very special.

'My dear,' Tuk said. He stood and made a little bow. She kissed him on each cheek in the French manner and took his hands in hers.

'Than. You are well, I hope?' she said with an accent that owed more to French than Cambodian.

Tuk smiled with genuine affection. 'Of course,' he said. 'But I have no need to ask it of you. You are radiant, as always.'

She inclined her head in acknowledgement with the assurance of one accustomed to admiration. Slattery saw now that she was older than she appeared. Tiny lines around the eyes and the mouth, a slight loosening of the skin at her neck. She looked thirty, although she could easily have been forty, or even more. But age enhanced rather than diminished her beauty. She was flawed only by her lack of innocence. A look, knowing and calculated, in her eyes. She turned, ignoring Slattery, and looked directly at Elliot with an unwavering gaze of naked interest. 'Are you not going to introduce us, Than?'

'But, of course. La Mère Grace, Mr Elliot. A business associate from England.'

'Oh? And what kind of business are you in, Mr Elliot?'

'I make war,' Elliot said.

She offered him a cool hand, small and perfect, which caressed his for the briefest of moments. Then she looked at Slattery. Tuk said, 'And Mr Slattery.'

'And do you make war also, Mr Slattery?' she asked.

'Only when I get paid.' Slattery grinned and added, 'But I prefer making love.'

She raised an elegant eyebrow. 'Then we have much in common. I, too, prefer to make love. But only when paid.' Her eyes flickered back to Elliot.

Tuk watched with amusement. 'Grace runs the best brothel in Bangkok,' he said. 'Please, do sit.' They all sat and Tuk called for another drink.

'Brothel is not a word I care to use,' La Mère Grace said. 'It has . . . connotations. My girls entertain only the most discerning of clients. I have other establishments to cater for the more basic clientele.' She looked again at Slattery. 'We can cater for almost every taste.' Slattery shifted uncomfortably under her gaze, feeling like a book that had just been read and discarded.

Tuk offered her a cigarette and lit it, then lit one for himself. He did not extend the offer to Elliot or Slattery. She took tiny puffs, exhaling the smoke through pursed lips.

'La Mère Grace ran the most celebrated house in Phnom Penh until the early Seventies.' Tuk leaned back and ran a hand through his hair. 'She only just escaped the country before the Khmer Rouge took over. Unfortunately she was unable to bring her girls with her.'

'I very much fear they were killed by the communists,' she said with no apparent trace of regret. 'I have had to find and train new girls. Thai girls.'

'I was telling Mr Elliot,' Tuk said, 'that he must speak to you of Cambodia. He and Mr Slattery intend visiting it in the not too distant future.'

A look of surprise flickered momentarily in her eyes, but she knew better than to ask. 'Of course,' she said. 'If I can be of any assistance.'

Tuk stood up. 'And now, gentlemen, I have other business to attend to. At which hotel are you staying?'

Elliot rose. 'The Narai.'

'Then I shall pick you up this evening at seven and take you to my warehouse to examine the merchandise. And we can also make arrangements for our trip tomorrow.'

His dismissal was brief and pointed. Slattery raised himself to his feet and grinned at La Mère Grace. 'Pleased to have met you, ma'am.'

She smiled perfunctorily and held out a card to Elliot. 'Call on me tomorrow night. Both of you. I'll expect you at nine.'

She watched them walk across the lawn towards the house. 'He doesn't say much,' she said. 'The dark one.'

Tuk rubbed his chin thoughtfully. 'It is often the quiet ones who are the most dangerous. We would, each of us, do well not to underestimate him.'

CHAPTER TWELVE

David poured the last of the wine into their glasses. Lisa had drunk most of the bottle, since he was driving. Before the meal she had gone through three gins and tonic. He wasn't sure now whether she meant to be vague or whether it was the drink. It was she who had called and suggested they go out for a meal – the first time she'd called him in days. But she had been strangely formal and uncommunicative, and done nothing to assuage his growing exasperation with her. He was beginning to lose patience.

She was toying absently with her glass, staring vacantly at some spot on the table. It was as though he wasn't there. He felt an anger welling in him. He did appreciate that she was going through an emotional crisis – the death of her mother, the discovery that her father was alive. But she was refusing to share it with him, to let him in, to let him help. Now he was feeling used. Why had she asked him to take her out for a meal, and then sat through it silent and morose, refusing to give a direct answer to any of his questions? He restrained an impulse to snap at her, and asked with a patience that he did not feel, 'Why won't he see you?'

She lifted her head and seemed surprised. 'Oh, it's not that he won't see me. He can't.'

'Why not?'

'Because he – he's out of the country. He doesn't even know I know he's alive.'

'So how do you know he's out of the country?'

She sighed. She hadn't wanted to go into it all. She could have told him over the phone what she was going to do, but felt she at least owed him an explanation in person. But faced with him like this, she wasn't finding it easy. 'It's a long story,' she said.

'I've got time.'

She hesitated, then reached a decision, drained her glass and said, 'Alright, I'll tell you. But take me home first.' She didn't want a row in the restaurant.

He bit back a retort and signalled the waiter that he wanted the bill.

They drove back to the house in silence. He glanced at her once or twice, but she was still miles away. The house was cold and dark when they got in, and she lit the gas fire in the living room, drawing the curtains and turning on a small table lamp. 'You want a drink?' she asked.

'I'm driving.'

She nodded and poured herself a large gin and tonic.

He said, 'Don't you think you've had enough already?'

'No,' she replied simply. 'If I want to get pissed I'll get pissed.' She took her glass, almost defiantly, and squatted on the rug in front of the fire. He sat in her mother's armchair and thought how childish she was being. What had he ever seen in her? She was a good-looking girl, intelligent, brimming with potential. But if he had once believed it was a potential he could shape, he was already beginning to entertain doubts. It wasn't as though they even had any kind of sexual relationship. She'd always been strange about that, as if sex frightened her. And, like most things about her, he didn't begin to understand because she would never tell him. Anything. She was like a book with an exotic title that excited the interest. But she had never allowed him to open it.

'So,' he said. 'You were going to tell me.'

She looked at him and wondered why she had felt she owed him anything. She didn't love him. Oh, she had thought so at first. He was so good-looking. Thick red hair swept back from a fine face. A voice that came from his boots. He looked as though he should have led a Bohemian existence in the Paris of the nineteen-twenties. And he had seemed so caring and sincere at first, with all his deeply held views on social justice. Social justice! she thought with irony. The only social justice he was interested in was his own. He was so possessive about everything: his job, his future, his life. And she was just another of his possessions. The only reason, it occurred to her, that he hadn't already given up on her was because he would have counted it a failure. His failure. And David couldn't bear to fail at anything. And, yet, in spite of it all, there was something about him she still liked. She shied away from the idea that it was the sense of safety she felt with him. She wanted to believe it was more than that.

'Well, are you going to tell me or aren't you?' he asked. She sipped her gin then took a deep breath and told him. Everything. The mews house in Chelsea where there was never any reply, the searches through the phone book, the visit to the Sergeant's house, everything that he had told her, everything she had told him. David listened gravely, just letting her talk. It occurred to him that it would make a good feature for one of the Sunday papers, then he was shocked that he had even thought of it and realized how little he really cared. It worried him, sometimes, how little he felt for other people, how little their problems touched him. Life was all a performance, the way you were expected to behave. And hurt was only what you felt, never what the other person felt. He decided to be sympathetic.

He sat down on the floor beside her, slipping an arm around her waist, squeezing her gently, letting her rest her head on his shoulder. He ran his hand back through her hair, then traced the line of her nose, lips and chin lightly with his fingers. The smell of her perfume, the warmth of her closeness, began a stirring in his loins and quickened his heart. What was it about her that made him want her so much? 'Poor Lisa,' he said. 'I'm sorry. You must have thought me very unsympathetic.' For the first time he felt he was making progress. That she was on the point of opening up the book to him at last. And he relaxed as he felt her respond to his touch.

Lisa closed her eyes and felt the drink spinning her head. She should have known David would understand. But she'd been frightened to give him the chance. He'd been so antagonistic when she had gone to see the lawyer.

Now, just having told him felt good. Someone else to share the weight of it all. She felt his lips on her neck, gently brushing her skin. His breath sent a shiver down her back. He bit her softly and she felt the first stirrings of arousal. She turned her head towards him and his lips found hers, barely touching. He kissed her – a light, loving kiss. Then again. This time more fiercely. She felt herself responding, felt his hand slip under her top and push up her bra, felt it warm on her breast. A thrill ran through her, leaving her weak. She pushed herself against him and they slipped over gently on to the floor, the softness of the rug beneath them, the warmth of the fire on their skin. His mouth was everywhere. Her lips, her neck. Her bra had come away, her top pushed up. She heard herself moan, a distant voice that belonged to someone else. She felt him hard against her leg. She opened her eyes and saw him looking down at her, the strangest look on his face, eyes burning with a passion so violent that suddenly it frightened her. She went cold.

'No,' she said. It wasn't right. He didn't own her, she didn't love him. 'No,' she said again. 'No, David.' And she tried to push him away. He resisted, pressing down on her hard.

'It's alright, Lisa. It'll be alright.'

But she knew it wouldn't. 'No!' And with a great effort she pulled herself away from under him, sitting up fastening her bra and pulling down her top. He looked at her, mouth tight, eyes filled with anger.

'What the fuck's wrong with you!' he shouted.

'There's nothing wrong with me,' she said, with all the control she could muster. But her voice was trembling. 'I think you'd better go.'

'I think I had.' He got to his feet and looked at her with patent hostility, running his hands back through his hair as if trying to smooth his ruffled pride. 'Don't expect me to call.'

'I won't,' she said to his back as he turned towards the door. 'And even if you did I wouldn't be here.'

He stopped, frowning. 'What do you mean?'

'I've already applied for my passport,' she said. 'I'm leaving early next week.'

'For where?' He glared at her in consternation.

'Bangkok,' she said. 'To find my father.'

CHAPTER THIRTEEN

The long dusty drive south-west to Aranyaprathet was tedious. The unbroken flatness of the paddy fields stretching away on either side of a long straight road that sat up on an embankment rising a metre above the surrounding countryside. The air conditioning in Tuk's car made it difficult to believe it was hot out there – crucifyingly hot under the December sun.

'In the rainy season,' Tuk said brightly, 'this road is impassable, under almost a metre of water.'

Elliot, Slattery and McCue sat in the back, silenced by the monotony of the drive, while Tuk sat in the front beside his driver, chatting animatedly.

Mak Moun camp, he told them, was effectively controlled by a man called Van Saren, a captain in the army of Lon Nol before the Khmer Rouge victory. Tuk turned in his seat and smiled. 'Well, so he says. He might have been a lieutenant, but even that's doubtful. He calls himself *Marshal* and claims to be the most honourable of the Khmer Serei. It is he who will arrange your border crossing.' He laughed. 'Actually, he smuggles teak and artefacts out of Cambodia for me. He's a nice man. You'll like him.' He laughed again, and Elliot felt there was something unpleasant in the laugh.

The previous night Tuk had taken the three of them to Bangkok's dockland, to a lock-up among a jumble of deserted warehouses. There, under the watchful eyes of armed guards, they had selected weapons and equipment from what was virtually an arsenal. The Colt Commando variation of the M16 automatic rifle, M26 anti-personnel hand grenades, Colt .45 automatic pistols. McCue had picked out a long, lethal hunting knife that hung from a belted sheath that strapped high up round the shoulder. He handled it with a kind of reverence and had to be persuaded to take an automatic rifle. 'Never carried one in the tunnels,' he said. 'Too goddam clumsy!'

They were to travel light, but Elliot insisted that Slattery pack a shortwave radio-receiver. Tuk had promised to have everything delivered to a pick-up point near the border once it had been decided exactly where they were to make their crossing. And now that he had been paid, he was full of false bonhomie. Not one of the men in the back of the car trusted him.

Aranyaprathet had been transformed from a sleepy, forgotten little border town into a thriving and expanding mini-metropolis by the influx of refugees, and by the medical and relief agencies that had moved in to meet their needs. The town was thick with foreigners and commerce and traffic of all kinds. Bars and shops and clubs had sprung up everywhere, as they had in the North American goldrush boom towns. Only here the gold was flesh, and the currency human misery. There was a large Thai army presence and a growing administration complex, the fruits of a burgeoning bureaucracy, to control the comings and goings of all manner of people – refugees, journalists, troops, traders, prostitutes, and large numbers of workers from the international relief agencies. Trucks lumbered in from Bangkok throughout the day, bringing the decadent goods of an alien Western culture to feed the black-market economy.

'The trucks only travel by day,' Tuk said. 'The road is controlled by bandits after dusk. Cars and trucks are attacked and robbed, and the drivers often killed. The army surrenders control after the sun goes down.'

They spent a hot sticky hour below a broken ceiling fan in a room filled with the human flotsam of war, while Tuk spoke long and heatedly with recalcitrant Thai officials. Finally Tuk and the officials disappeared into another room. When they came out again, ten minutes later, Tuk was smiling broadly. 'All fixed,' he said. 'We can go now.' Vacant eyes watched them leave.

Outside the heat of the sun seared the skin and the senses, and it was a merciful relief to slip back into the air-conditioned comfort of Tuk's car.

Mak Moun came as a shock, even after the poverty and corruption of Bangkok and Aranyaprathet. This largest of the Cambodian encampments on the border was little better than a rural slum. The place was black with flies, a huge depressing sprawl of small huts crammed together, refuse piled in stinking heaps, broken bottles and empty cans, decaying scraps of food scraped from meagre plates, a flyblown chicken carcass. Men and women and children squatting to defecate in a nearly dried-up stream running through the camp were almost obscured by the flies. The stench of human excrement was choking. Young Thai soldiers carrying rifles or automatic weapons wandered arrogantly between the rows of huts, occasionally shouting at the children. Any who dared to argue with them were rewarded with a blow from a rifle butt.

As they drove through the camp they watched a soldier strike an old woman several times about the head with a long cane, until blood appeared oozing from her hair. Elliot felt his scalp tighten with anger. Tuk grinned back at them and shrugged philosophically. 'Life in the camps,' he said. 'But what can one do?'

'We could kick the shit out of that bastard for a start!' Slattery growled.

'That would not be very wise, Mr Slattery. Van Saren's people would only shoot you. The Thai army presence here is for show only. They are happy to let Van Saren police the camp. People are often shot trying to leave. Van Saren could not have his position undermined by allowing a foreigner to attack a soldier. Oh yes, and remember,' he added, 'to call him Marshal. Marshal Van. He is a little eccentric, but his control is very effective.'

'Effective in what way?' Elliot asked.

'He controls distribution of the food that the ICRC and

UNICEF truck in every day. And on the border, Mr Elliot, food is power.'

The car drew up outside a hut near the camp's administration centre and they all got out. Tuk waved at the hut. 'Van's kingdom,' he said. Not ten metres away a squalid, half-starved group of women were trying to wash themselves in the same dried-up slick that doubled as an open sewer.

'And I thought I'd seen everything,' Slattery said, brushing the flies from his face. 'Jeez, if the world needed an enema this is where they'd stick the fucking tube.'

Elliot glanced at McCue, who had remained silent throughout their journey. He was impassive, his face betraying no trace of emotion. But his eyes missed nothing, and Elliot sensed a tension in him. He was beginning to regret having come here at all.

They climbed the steps and entered the empty hut. It was a shambles: two-tier bunk beds down one wall, crates of beer stacked against another and under the beds, empties strewn everywhere. Slattery kicked one across the floor and it rolled into a corner. There was a large desk and a swivel chair by the window. An electric fan whirred and clattered on the desk making erratic sweeps and stirring the papers strewn across the desktop. Several sheets had fallen to the floor. Crumpled cigarette packs lay on the desk, ashtrays brimming with half-smoked cigarettes. A window blind had slipped down to hang at an angle. The floorboards were crusted with dried spittle and the room stank of human sweat and stale cigarette smoke.

'Cosy little place,' Slattery said, and spat out a fly that had crept in at the corner of his mouth.

Tuk turned in the doorway. 'Ah, here comes the Marshal now.'

Van Saren strode across the compound towards the hut, a small figure, ridiculous in US army trousers tied above the ankles, open sandals, a khaki shirt open to the waist and a pork pie hat set squarely on his head. A large crucifix hung round his neck, glinting in the sunlight. He had a cocky swagger emulated by the three thugs who accompanied him, all in khaki, bandoliers slung across shoulders, AK-47s tucked under arms. Each had a dirty scarf tied around his head.

Van grinned as he saw Tuk, revealing several gaps in a mouthful of yellowed teeth. He greeted him in Thai. The thugs ignored the newcomers, pushing past and propping their automatic rifles against the far wall. One climbed on to one of the top bunks and flopped across the sweat-stained sheet. Another dropped into the swivel chair and cast an indifferent glance over the strangers. The third sat on the edge of the desk and lit a cigarette.

Tuk made the introductions. He seemed out of place and ill-at-ease in these surroundings, dabbing again at his forehead with a now grubby handkerchief. 'Saren, this is Mr Elliot and his colleagues.'

Elliot nodded and Van looked at them appraisingly before smiling broadly, as though proud of his bad teeth. 'Welcome to Mak Moun,' he said. 'Here you under my protection. Protection of Khmer Serei.' He paused. 'You want go Cambodia, Than tell me. No problem. You enjoy stay my country.' And he laughed uproariously, pleased with his joke. 'I take you. No problem. When you want go?'

'A week or so,' Elliot said. 'But I want to talk to some of your refugees first.'

Van waved a hand dismissively. 'They talk you. No problem. I tell them. You want drink?'

'Sure.'

Van giggled. 'Hah! "Sure." I like "Sure."' And he snapped an instruction at the thug sitting on the desk. Wordlessly the man rose and opened half a dozen bottles of beer to hand them round.

'Not for me, Saren,' Tuk said.

Van chuckled. 'Sure you drink with us, Than. No problem.' He turned to Elliot. 'Than like glass with beer from refrigerator. He think we very uncivilized here.'

Tuk took a bottle reluctantly from the thug, who showed his first emotion in an evil grin. Van said something in Cambodian and all the thugs laughed. Then he raised his bottle. 'Death Khmer Rouge bastard!' he shouted.

Elliot took a swig from his bottle. The beer was hot.

The sound of raised voices made them turn. Through the open door, across the compound, outside the administration hut, they saw two white men engaged in an argument. One was big, unshaven, wearing jeans and a T-shirt, a Colt .45 stuck in his paunch. The other man was smaller, fair-haired,

97

in pressed trousers and white shirt. The argument was heated and in English, although from the hut there was no telling what they were saying.

Suddenly the big man stepped forward and pushed the other back, his voice rising to a pitch of fury. The smaller man stood his ground, trying to calm aggression with reason. Then the big man swung a fist like a football and hit him full in the face, so that he staggered back and fell in the dust, blood pouring from his nose. As the big man advanced he scrambled backwards, getting hurriedly to his feet. He stood off, holding a handkerchief to his face, shouting angry words before turning and striding quickly to a jeep parked at the edge of the compound. He got in and drove off fast, tyres spinning in the dirt.

As the big man started towards their hut, Van turned grinning to the others. 'That Garee,' he said. 'He clearing today food distribution with Red Cross. No problem.'

Tuk moved next to Elliot and said quietly, 'I would advise caution with this man. He can be – unpredictable.' He turned to McCue. 'A fellow countryman of yours, Mr McCue.' And Elliot saw McCue's jaw set.

'Cool it, Billy boy,' Slattery said softly. McCue said nothing.

The big American climbed the steps and stopped in the doorway, taking in the new faces. 'Who the hell are these guys!' He didn't look happy to see them.

'Friends of Mr Tuk, Garee,' Van said. 'They want we take them cross border.'

The American grunted.

Tuk said, 'Mr Ferguson is Saren's Minister of Defence for the National Liberation Movement of Cambodia.' Elliot picked up the irony, but it seemed to elude Van and Ferguson.

'Marshal Van is the father and saviour of all Cambodia,' Ferguson said, in a way that defied anyone to contradict him. He pushed his way past McCue and Slattery and flicked his head at the thug in the swivel chair. It was vacated at once. Ferguson slumped into the chair. 'Fucking Red Cross think they own the place!' His feet thudded on to the desk.

'You tell them different, Garee,' Van said.

'Fucking right I do.' He looked at Elliot. 'And I'm not taking any shit off you guys either. Got that?'

'Sure,' Elliot said evenly.

'Hah,' giggled Van. '"Sure." I like "Sure."'

But Ferguson was glaring with ugly hostility at Elliot. 'I don't like your tone, pal. You show some respect for my father.'

Elliot looked at him steadily. 'I'm surprised you have one.'

Ferguson frowned. He simmered for a moment, then seemed to explode from the inside out. 'Marshal Van is my father! You trying to say something different?' He was on his feet, hands on his hips, swivel chair clattering backwards.

Elliot said, 'I said I didn't think bastards had fathers.'

Slattery wondered at Elliot's coolness and he began to feel good, adrenalin pumping. He glanced quickly round the room. The three thugs were taut and alert. Tuk was pale with fear and had stepped back towards the door. Van just watched, apparently quite relaxed. Outside somewhere a baby was crying.

Ferguson was puce with rage. He drew his pistol from his belt and levelled it at Elliot's head.

'You apologize to my father!' he shouted. 'Or you're a dead man!'

Slattery caught the slightest movement out of the corner of his eye, and a long blade glinted at Ferguson's throat, the point drawing blood. McCue. He'd forgotten about McCue. Slattery swivelled round, snatched an AK-47 from the wall and turned it on the three thugs, almost before they could move. 'Don't even think about it, boys.'

Ferguson had gone rigid and he glanced quickly sideways to see McCue's face very close to his own. He felt the heat of his breath, smelled the beer on it. McCue's eyes chilled him. 'Move that trigger a hair's breadth and I'll cut your fucking head off – pal.' McCue's voice was barely a whisper.

Elliot reached out and took the Colt from Ferguson's hand and tucked it back in the belt below his paunch. 'Didn't anyone ever tell you it's dangerous to point guns at people?' he said.

The tension was broken by Van's laugh, high-pitched, almost a giggle. 'Good. Very, very good. Nice thing they on our side, huh Garee?'

Elliot nodded to McCue and Slattery. Slattery lowered the automatic and McCue slowly withdrew the knife, his eyes never leaving Ferguson for a moment. Ferguson slapped at his neck and looked at the blood smeared on his fingers. 'Hey, you guys,' he said. 'Just a goddam joke.'

''Course it was.' Elliot smiled and turned to Van. 'How about letting me talk to some of those refugees now?'

'Sure, sure. No problem. Garee, he take you.'

They walked through the camp, Elliot, Ferguson and one of the thugs, who kept a wary eye on Elliot. Ferguson seemed preoccupied, animosity apparently forgotten. 'Hey, Elliot,' he said. 'Who is that guy?'

'McCue?'

'The runt with the knife.'

'Vietnam vet.'

'Shit, ain't we all?'

'Tunnel rat,' Elliot said. 'Did three tours.'

Ferguson whistled, an expression of awe. 'Hey, I heard about them guys.'

Elliot smiled. 'Be glad he didn't fillet you.'

Ferguson lapsed again into contemplative silence, leading them abstractedly between rows of mean little huts. A group of children stopped and stared at them. Big brown eyes in shrunken faces, looking out through a film of indifference. There were no games played here, no cries of joy or petty squabbles, just the lacklustre eyes, brittle sticks of arms and legs poking out from torn T-shirts and dirty shorts. There was no curiosity in their stares, not even fear. Flies crawled over their faces, in mouths and nostrils, children too inured to them to bother.

Elliot was uneasy, disconcerted by their gaze. He had felt eyes like these on him before. But it was only now, for the first time in his life, that he realized what it was in these eyes that so troubled him. It was an emptiness. Where there's no hope, what else could there be? It was a look he and the others had seen for more than sixteen years in the eyes that looked back at them from their shaving mirrors each morning. Strange, he had never thought of soldiers as victims before. Soldiers fought, lived or died, won or lost. These, these children, they were the real victims of war. Yet he knew that he, too, somewhere, at some time, had become a victim. He looked away, seeing only himself reflected in the dull stares. Ferguson shouted at the kids and waved an arm. But they continued to stand watching, unmoved.

It was dark in the huts after the glare of the sun. The air was fetid. Rows of makeshift beds, groups of ragged refugees, sometimes whole families camped in the gloom, eating, sleeping, dying there. The food dished out by Van Saren's thugs was never quite enough, the medical services provided by the overstrained relief agencies at best inadequate. Prompted by the threats of Ferguson, often translated by his indifferent rifletoting deputy, they told their stories. Elliot had wanted to ask questions – numbers of Khmer Rouge, the lie of the land, roads, rivers. But all he could do was listen, silenced by the simplicity of the narratives, the unemotional, undramatized pictures of hell painted in single bold brushstrokes.

One man sat on his own, squatting on the filthy blanket that covered his bed. His hair was matted, his face blank, his eyes dead. Ferguson's deputy barked at him in Cambodian. The man ignored him and looked at Elliot. 'I speak English,' he said. 'Are you another newspaper man?'

Elliot shook his head. 'Just interested.'

'No one is interested without a reason.'

Elliot felt rebuked, though there was no hint of it in the man's voice. He acknowledged the truth. 'I have a reason.'

The man shrugged. He didn't want to know what it was. He had no cause to be interested. Ferguson sat on the bed opposite, picking his teeth with a bamboo splinter. 'Get on with it!'

Elliot caught a movement out of the corner of his eye and saw McCue standing there. Ferguson glanced at him with unconcealed hostility. He didn't like anyone to get the better of him, especially another Yank. 'Where's Slattery?' Elliot asked.

'Drinking.' McCue pulled up a broken stool and sat down. 'Thought I'd listen in.'

'I ain't got all day,' Ferguson snapped. He prodded the refugee with his cane. 'I told you to get on with it.'

The man shrugged. He told them his name was Chan Cheong and that he was twenty-eight. Elliot was shocked. He would have taken him for forty. 'I was a truck driver in Lon Nol's army,' he said. 'I lived with my wife, Key, and my two sons, in Phnom Penh. My oldest boy was eight, my youngest not yet two. When the Khmer Rouge came I threw away my uniform and when they emptied the city we took what we could carry and went north.

'The road was choked with people just like us. Thousands and thousands of them, young and old, sick and dying. When the old and the sick fell in the road the soldiers made their families go on, and if the ones left behind were not dead already, they were shot and pushed to the side of the road or dumped in the fields to rot. That first day there were so many people on the road we covered no more than two or three miles. By the end of the day we had thrown away most of what we had, because it was too heavy to carry. And always the soldiers pushed us with their guns to make us hurry, or fired shots in the air.

'Every so often there were checkpoints where they asked questions. Endless questions. And those they thought had been soldiers they took away, and made the rest go on. But we knew that the soldiers were shot. For myself, I said I had been a taxi driver and they believed me. They made us walk for days, and we did not dare to stop to rest or sleep. We had to walk through the night and carry our children. Children cannot walk for ever without sleep.

'After about a week, we reached a town called Kompong Thom. There, a woman I had known in Phnom Penh identified me as a military driver. I said she was lying, but they took me away and made me join a work party of what they called liberated soldiers. We worked until we dropped, every day from first light until well after dark, building a dam. If anyone stopped for a rest he was shot. So for as long as we could stand we worked without stopping.

'Sometimes they gave us a day off and told us we were invited to a merit festival. But those turned out to be long hours of indoctrination. We had to sit and listen to endless communist slogans blasted out from loudspeakers. The only good thing about the merit festivals was that I had the chance to be with my family again, if only for a few hours.

'Then one day we were told there was to be a big freedom celebration for all the newly liberated who had arrived from Phnom Penh. We were to wear our best clothes for the occasion, and were taken in buses to a Buddhist temple on the mountain. There were about two hundred of us gathered there. Former soldiers, officers, doctors, nurses, teachers. Everyone was very frightened when they locked us in. But the guards would not answer our questions, telling us only that everything would become clear to us at the meeting that night.

'It was raining and dark when they started to call us out, one family at a time. I think I knew then that we were to be killed. Everyone did, but no one said it. It was nearly three hours before they called my name, and Key and myself went out carrying our boys. A soldier told us to follow him and took us down a path through the woods. Another group of soldiers was waiting at a clearing. They were sheltering from the rain under the trees and smoking. When we came they got up and tied our hands. But I held my arms taut so that the knot was not tight and I could loosen it. They asked me again what my work was. A taxi driver, I told them. You're lying, they said. You drove for the military. Then they asked my wife, what did your husband do? She was in tears and could lie no longer. He drove for the military, she said. And I knew that we had no hope.

'They took the baby from her arms and she pleaded to let them die together. She screamed when they blindfolded her and then bayoneted the child. Then they bayoneted my oldest boy. They had not blindfolded me. I was to watch as they stripped my wife and stuck their bayonets into her. I turned and ran into the woods, trying to free my hands as I went. They fired after me, dozens of rounds, but I was more frightened of the bayonets than the bullets. Then I fell down a steep slope and into a dry stream bed, and rolled under some ferns that hid me. A grenade went off and I was showered with damp earth. But in the dark they could not find me and finally they gave up. I think, maybe, I was the only person in the temple that night to escape with his life.

'Early next morning I started to walk, heading north until daylight. Always I walked at night and slept in the day. It did not take me long to reach Siem Reap. But there were many soldiers there, so I circled the town and went by Angkor Wat. I had never before seen the temples and I wept at the sight of them.'

He paused for a few moments and brushed a fly carelessly from his lips. 'There is not much more to tell. I kept myself alive foraging for food in the forest, walking, walking, always north and then west. I saw many patrols, and once or twice I was nearly caught. But I was lucky. Eventually I reached the border with Thailand.' He dropped his head a little then looked directly at Elliot. 'I cannot say I am free. I cannot say I am alive. I wish I had died by the bayonet with my wife, so that our blood should have run together in the soil of my country.' There was no emotion in his voice, or his eyes, and Elliot understood what he had meant when he said he was not alive.

'You finished?' Ferguson asked. The man nodded.

Elliot turned to McCue. 'Let's get out of here.'

Outside they blinked in the sunlight, flies in their hair, on their clothes, in their faces. Ferguson went off shouting at a group of children. 'I never had a reason for killing before,' McCue said quietly.

Elliot looked at him. 'The only reason you need is the money that's going to buy your boy a better life.' There was an edge to his voice that made McCue turn his head. Elliot stared back with cold, hard, blue eyes. McCue held the look for some moments then shrugged and walked away towards the hut where Slattery was still drinking beer with Van Saren.

CHAPTER FOURTEEN

I

Lotus sat repairing a shirt by the light of an oil lamp. It saved electricity. Old habits died hard. Billy had gone out the night before without telling her where. He had returned late and left early again in the morning. He had said nothing of the men who came two nights ago and talked with him for several hours. She had not needed to ask who they were. She knew. She knew by their eyes, for she'd seen that look in Billy's eyes, too. In the early days, when he had first come from Vietnam.

In the back room the baby gave a little cry. She turned her head and listened. The child shifted restlessly for some moments and then was silent. Asleep still. Dreaming. She wondered what he dreamed. His dreams would not be like hers. She dreamt very little now. Her waking dreams had long since faded. Dreams of America, of an escape from poverty and squalor, from endless nights in darkened bars where every groping GI made promises of freedom, promises that were never fulfilled. Sex had been mechanical, a living earned with a false smile and a soft caress, rewarded by money and brutality, void of emotion, empty of hope.

Billy had been different, quiet and gentle. At first he bought her things, took her places during the day. They never spoke much, just sat in cafés, walked by the river. But, bit by bit, she had told him everything about herself: her family in the north, the paddy fields and the poverty. The brothers and sisters her father could not feed. She had been only fifteen when they sent her to the city to sit behind a mirrored screen, a number pinned to her blouse, alongside eighty or a hundred other girls all with the same story to tell. The doctor came to examine them once a week, like a butcher checking the freshness of the meat.

Billy had told her nothing about himself. Then one day he had said that he no longer wanted her to work the bars. She had protested. How was she to live? She needed to work. For a while he had said no more about it. He had been morose and cold. Then nothing. He just disappeared. Two weeks, maybe three, and she had thought she would never see him again. It happened. A man took a fancy to you, lavished you with money and gifts, told you he loved you and wanted to take you away from it all. Then he would be sent back home and know that he could not take you with him. A brief illusion. A candle that burned too bright to be real. Then Billy turned up at the club one night, took her by the hand and pulled her out into the street.

'You're quitting. Now,' he said. She had pulled herself free and told him he was mad, and he'd said quite simply, 'I want to marry you.'

He had looked her straight in the eye, and she knew that he meant it. He had never told her he loved her, or promised her anything, but it was all there in his dark tragic eyes. She had wondered what America would be like. Reality, she knew, could never be like the dream. But she was never to know. He had bought them a house on the *klongs*. He was never going home, he said.

But it had been an escape of a sorts. She had not loved him, not then, had not known what love was. But they had found peace together, a kind of happiness she had not experienced since childhood. He had never told her where the money came from, though sometimes he had been away for weeks on end. But they had never wanted for anything and so she never asked.

She had found herself returning to the ways of her mother, and her mother before her. All the values she had rejected, the heritage she had wished to trade for the dream that had been America. She was Thai, and she was happy in the knowledge of who she was.

But Billy had changed since their child was born. The inner peace they had found together was gone, like the still surface of a pond broken by the monsoon rains. And the trouble in his heart was reflected in his eyes, like mirrors of his soul.

She finished with the shirt, and was padding through to check the mosquito net around the baby's sleeping mat when she heard the bump of a small boat against the landing stage and Billy's step on the stairs. Something had happened, she knew. It was in those eyes that spoke to her more eloquently than the words he used so seldom and so sparingly.

'When will you be going?' she asked.

He shrugged, avoiding her eyes. 'A week.'

'And when will you be back?' She felt the tension in him.

'Listen,' he said, 'when I get back we're going home.'

'This is my home. I thought it was your home too.'

He glanced through to the room where the baby slept. 'There's more chance for him in America.' She squatted on the floor and examined the shirt she had mended. He lit a cigarette. He had been smoking more these past two days. 'If – if I don't come back . . .' She looked up. 'If I don't come back, I want you to take him anyway. There'll be plenty of money and my folks'll look after you.'

She shook her head. 'I don't want money, or America. I want a husband, and a father for my child.'

He stood for a moment, then turned and went out on to the terrace. She heard the creak of his old rocking chair. After some minutes she rose slowly from the floor and went out beside him. The sky was thick with stars, like the eyes of Heaven gazing down upon the affairs of men. She didn't even look at him. 'Don't go, Billy,' she said. 'I love you.'

He looked up and felt the sting of tears in his eyes. She had never told him that before. No one had.

II

'There's a gentleman been waiting to see you,' the receptionist told Elliot when he got back to the hotel. She nodded towards a man sitting on one of the large sofas dotted around the reception lounge. Elliot and Slattery turned to look.

'It's Ang,' Elliot said. 'I'll catch you later.'

Slattery disappeared towards the lifts. Ang rose and held out his hand as Elliot approached. Elliot sat down without taking it. Ang's smile of greeting faded and he resumed his seat. 'Do you have the stuff I asked for?' Elliot said.

'Yes.' Ang lifted a large buff envelope from the seat beside him. 'The daily routine and layout of the commune near Siem Reap. It was not easy to come by, Mistah Elliot.'

'Is it accurate?'

'As accurate as the recollection of half-starved refugees can be.' Ang paused. 'The money has been lodged and credited to the account number you gave me.'

'I know,' Elliot said. 'I checked.'

'The second payment will be released just as soon as my wife and family are delivered safely to me here in Thailand.'

Elliot looked at Ang with ill-concealed contempt. He remembered the story Chan Cheong had told him in that stinking hut in Mak Moun. He remembered the dead look in the eyes of the refugee. Eyes that had watched his wife and children bayoneted to death. *I cannot say I am free. I cannot say I am alive*, he had said. And here was a man who had left his wife and family to their fate. Here was a man who *was* free, who *was* alive, who had the money to buy off his conscience and the memory of his betrayal.

'Will there be penalties?' Elliot said. 'If I don't come back with a full complement.'

'I don't think I understand, Mistah Elliot.'

'I mean, are you paying by the head? A third each for your wife, your daughter and your son? After all, we're not even sure where your son is.'

Ang faced out Elliot's contempt impassively. 'They paid you by the head in Vietnam, did they not?'

Elliot was momentarily taken aback. Ang had done his homework. The little Cambodian pressed home his advantage. 'I'm paying you to try, Mistah Elliot.' And a moment of pain flitted across his face. 'If you succeeded in bringing only one . . .' But he shied away from the thought.

Elliot said, 'I wouldn't raise your hopes, Mr Ang. It'll be a miracle if you see any of them alive again.'

III

Slattery lay back in the darkness of his room and felt the pain spreading from below his ribs. He imagined the cancer inside like a giant crab gnawing away at him, growing fat as he grew thin. He had taken some painkillers and knew it would pass. But he knew, too, that it would return, again and again, with ever-increasing frequency, stealing the life away from him. The worst part was that he didn't want to die. He looked back with a bitter irony over all the years he'd thought he hadn't cared, the risks he'd taken, the life he had laid on the line time and again. But then, death had never been a certainty as it was now. Death was what happened to the other guy.

He screwed his eyes tight shut and knew he was only feeling sorry for himself. And he despised self-pity. It could turn a man, change him, make him afraid. He'd never been afraid of anything or anyone in his life. And he didn't want to start now. Didn't want to become a man he would not recognize. It was too late to start trying to come to terms with a new self. He'd had enough trouble with the old one. His only regret was that he'd never had children. Then, perhaps, some part of him might have lived on. After all, that's what it was all about, wasn't it? Procreation. Go forth and multiply, said the Lord.

He smiled wryly to himself. Well, it hadn't been for want of trying. And he felt better knowing that in the midst of all his self-pity he could still smile. The old Mike Slattery was still there somewhere. Shit! He wasn't going to let this bastard cancer beat him without a fight.

A soft knock at his door startled him. 'Yeah?'

'It's Elliot.'

'Come on in, chief.' Slattery sat up on the bed self-consciously, as though Elliot might have been listening in on his thoughts, like a conversation overheard in the dark. He turned on the bedside light as Elliot entered. 'What's the score?'

Elliot looked at him curiously, and Slattery felt uncomfortable. 'You mind if we talk?'

Slattery knew he wasn't being asked. 'Grab yourself a chair.'

Elliot pulled a seat out from the dresser and sat down. 'Got a cigarette?'

'Sure.' Slattery tossed him one and lit another for himself. He knew Elliot only smoked when he felt stressed.

Elliot lit his cigarette and watched the smoke rise gently in the stillness. 'It's hot in here. Air conditioning broken down?'

Slattery shook his head. 'Naw. Can't sleep with it on, chief. Dries me out.' He paused. 'Something on your mind?' Why did he feel that Elliot knew exactly what was going on in his?

'Been worrying about you, Mike,' Elliot said at length.

Slattery smiled unconvincingly. 'No need to worry about me, chief. You know that.'

'Do I?'

'Well, I mean, why would you?'

'You've lost weight. You've been behaving – oddly.' Slattery said nothing. 'I made a couple of phone calls last night, Mike. Mutual acquaintances Down Under.'

The skin tightened across Slattery's scalp. 'You know, then.'

Elliot nodded. 'Why didn't you tell me?'

'Would you have taken me with you if I had?'

'No.'

'That's why I didn't tell you.'

'I don't like being lied to, Mike. Especially by a friend.'

'I never lied to you, chief.'

115

'By omission. It comes to the same thing.'

Slattery looked away. 'I couldn't face dying in a beach house somewhere. Just wasting away. Not me, chief. Not after what I been through.'

They were both silent for a long time. Then Elliot said, 'I didn't take you on so you could go and get yourself killed. I need you, Mike.'

'I won't let you down, chief. Honest I won't. I'd just rather take the chance of dying like I've lived, you know? Rather than the other way.' He looked directly at Elliot. 'You're still taking me with you, chief, aren't you?'

Elliot seemed to look right through him. He drew slowly on his cigarette, then said, 'Sure I am, Mike.' He paused. 'But I'm bringing you back, too.'

Slattery nodded. 'You want a beer?'

Elliot smiled and drew a half-bottle of whisky from his back pocket. 'The real MacKay,' he said. 'I thought we might get pissed.'

Slattery grinned.

CHAPTER FIFTEEN

Ny lay awake on the hard wooden floor with dread and hate in her heart, listening for the footfall of the young cadre on the steps of the hut. Perhaps tonight he would not come. The pain and discomfort of her period had been a merciful release from his nightly visits, and she had told him it was still on her for several days after it had passed. He would know it must be over by now, so she expected he would come. All the other women, her mother as well, were asleep. Escape for a few brief hours from this living death. At the far end of the hut one of the women moaned in her shallow slumber. Perhaps she was dreaming of how life used to be. Or perhaps her dreams were of soldiers in black pyjamas and red-chequered scarves, and Angkar, and fear and death. Perhaps, for some, even sleep was no escape.

She heard a creak on the wooden steps and tensed. He had come for her, and from somewhere she must summon the strength and courage to face again the shame of his sexual gratification. But she wondered how much longer it would be possible. She had known others to take their own lives, but she did not think she had the courage for that.

The silhouette of the cadre appeared in the open doorway as she sat up. He seemed smaller, was wearing a scarf round his head. 'Ny,' he whispered. He had never called her by her name before, yet the whisper of it was familiar. She rose and moved quietly to the doorway and found herself looking into the dark face of a young boy. A face she knew from somewhere in her past. But still it took her a moment to recognize it.

'Hau!' Her brother's name slipped involuntarily from her lips, and though whispered, seemed loud in the quiet of the night.

'Shhhh!' He put a finger to his lips and signalled for her to follow. She slipped quickly down the steps behind him, and in the shadow of the hut they embraced. She held him tightly, never wanting to let go, emotion choking her. How often she had known the heat of his body when he had slipped into her bed on cold nights and snuggled up to her for warmth. But how was it possible? She held him at arm's length to look at him and brush the hair from his eyes.

'Hau, what are you doing here?'

He still had the face of a boy, but his eyes were much, much older and he spoke quickly and with quiet authority. 'Ny, they are sending me away.'

'Away? Away where?'

'To Phnom Penh. They say the Vietnamese might attack, and they want more soldiers to defend the city in case of invasion.'

Ny was stunned. It was the first she had heard of it. A Vietnamese invasion! Perhaps, then, there was still hope. For surely the Khmer Rouge could not withstand the might of the Vietnamese army. But her heart froze with the same thought. They were sending her brother to fight. And the fanatics of the Khmer Rouge would urge their troops to fight to the last, and shoot those who refused. 'Oh, Hau,' she whispered. 'You must not go.'

'I have no choice,' he said. 'But I will not fight. I will run away.'

'They will kill you.'

'I will take the chance,' he said simply.

'I will get Mother.' She turned towards the steps, but he stopped her.

'No. I cannot face my mother.' And there was a look of shame in his eyes. 'I have done things,' he said. 'They made me do things . . .' And he could not even face his sister.

Ny took him again in her arms. 'Oh, Hau.' When she looked once more into his face she saw that he was crying. He brushed away the tears, ashamed of them too.

'Tell her,' he said, 'that I will go and hide at our house in the city. If our country is freed then she must look for me there.'

Ny looked at him with pain in her heart. She knew it was impossible. They heard footsteps and drew back further into the shadows. Ny saw the young cadre approach the hut and climb the steps. 'You must go,' she whispered urgently to Hau. She kissed him. 'We will look for you.' And she hurried out to the foot of the steps as the cadre climbed back down. He looked at her suspiciously.

'What are you doing here?'

'I was waiting for you.'

He seemed surprised, then smiled. 'Come,' he said. 'I have not much time tonight.' And he led her quickly away through the stilts. She glanced back and saw the shadow of Hau darting away between the huts, and she wondered if she would ever see her brother again.

CHAPTER SIXTEEN

A crystal chandelier hung overhead, tinkling gently in the breeze of the air conditioning. The air was cool rising from the cold marble floor. Elliot and Slattery stood uncomfortably in the opulence of their surroundings. A beautiful Thai girl in a long pink silk skirt and white blouse had let them in, asking them to wait. She had then tiptoed away into the depths of the house. Somewhere, they had heard a bell ring twice, followed by a deep silence. Slattery scuffed his heels impatiently, hard leather on marble echoing around this grand entrance hall. Erotic Greek statues stood on plinths, a chaise longue against one wall beneath a painting of a Renaissance nude, white and plump with blue-veined breasts. Velvet curtains were drawn on tall windows.

'I thought you might like to see some of my acquisitions before we go back to the house.' La Mère Grace's voice echoed off marble. They looked up to see her descending the broad staircase, elegant and beautiful, bearing herself with a poise that comes only with age. Her white dress buttoned up to a high collar at the neck, and clung to her contours in an elegant sweep to her ankles. It was split up one side, almost to the top of her thigh, allowing her to move freely and reveal glimpses of a long, shapely leg with each step. Her black hair was piled high to show off her fine-boned features and small, perfect ears. Her smile was radiant, betraying a hint of ironic amusement. 'My car is waiting,' she said.

The car was large, black and American, with smoked windows. It was driven by a girl in a chauffeur's uniform and peaked cap who drove them smoothly, and with assurance, through the night traffic of Bangkok to a nightclub for members only. A small waiter in a perfectly fitting dinner suit bowed, led them to a reserved table and brought them drinks. The hostesses – they were not bar girls here – were discreet and extremely beautiful, all in white like their mentor, but without her poise. A band played soft seductive American jazz, and, through an archway, wealthy men dined with elegant women. Subdued lighting was concealed above red velvet drapes and the drinks, served from a long polished mahogany bar, were expensive. But they paid for nothing.

'Here we cater for Bangkok's elite,' Grace said. 'Government ministers, high-ranking civil servants and army generals, the captains of Thai industry. The Prime Minister himself dines here on occasion. But it is, I think, not quite your style. As I told you, we cater for all tastes.' She pushed her glass languidly away. 'Drink up, gentlemen, and we shall take a little trip downmarket.'

Downmarket, it transpired, was one of the better massage

parlours on Patpong Road. A girl rose from a desk, pressed her palms together, and bowed as Grace led them in. 'Madame,' she said deferentially.

'These gentlemen would like to see the facilities we offer here,' Grace said.

'Of course.' The girl led them through to a red-carpeted lounge dotted with deep, soft sofas and armchairs. A crimson flock wallpaper covered three walls and the ceiling. The fourth wall was a large window looking on to a chamber where something like a hundred girls sat in tiers, chatting idly. Each had a number pinned to her dress. Some were plain, some pretty, others indifferent. Most looked bored, and all were very young. None, Elliot thought, over twenty.

'Here, discretion is assured,' Grace said. 'Our customers need not feel embarrassed, for the girls cannot see them.' She ran a cool hand lightly across the glass. 'A two-way mirror. All they can see is a reflection of themselves.' But Elliot noticed that none of the girls looked in their direction. Perhaps they were ashamed of their own reflections. 'A man may choose a girl by her number, and he will be taken to a small room where the girl of his choice will shower him and then give him a body massage. Soap or oil is applied for maximum lubrication. Any further activity is a matter for private negotiation between the girl and the customer. Naturally we take ninety per cent. And, of course, our girls are very clean. They are checked regularly by our doctor.'

'I've heard,' Elliot said, 'that many of these girls are sold to establishments like this by their families. Peasant girls straight from the paddies. Bought and sold like slaves.'

Grace looked at him with feigned surprise. 'Do I detect a hint of disapproval, Mr Elliot?' She shook her head. 'Do you really think they would be better off in the paddies, working from dawn till dusk, thigh-deep in water, legs scarred by leeches, skin burned by the sun? Such women are old by the time they are thirty, dead by fifty – if they are lucky. Here they make more money than they could ever have dreamed, are well fed, receive the best medical care.'

'And end up in squalid little *klong* houses, working sleazy bars up dark alleys when they are no longer young enough or attractive enough for your customers.'

Grace smiled and turned to Slattery. 'Are there any of my girls who catch your eye, Mr Slattery?'

'Two of 'em, actually, ma'am.'

She called over the girl who had shown them in. 'See to it that Mr Slattery has everything he wants, with my compliments.'

The girl bowed and Slattery grinned. 'See you back at the hotel, then, chief.'

In the car Grace said to Elliot, 'I thought we would never get rid of him.'

Her room was on the first floor of her rambling mansion house, known throughout Bangkok as Chez La Mère Grace. 'It was what they called my house in Phnom Penh,' she said. 'The house there was my mother's really, and I took on the name

PETER MAY

when she died and left me the business. She called herself Grace. She wanted an English name. She thought it very chic.'

'She was a Cambodian, your mother?'

'Oh, yes. Her real name was Lim Any. I was the result of a liaison with a high-ranking French diplomat. But they never married.' She finished pouring their drinks at a glass cabinet, kicked off her shoes, and padded across the thick-piled carpet to kneel opposite him on one of the huge soft cushions scattered around a foot-high circular table. The room was sumptuous. Velvet drapes, antique cabinets, exotic trunks with gold clasps. There were mirrors everywhere you looked, even on the ceiling above an enormous circular bed spread with red silk sheets and white cushions. Two or three discreetly placed lamps cast light on key areas, and left others in pools of mysterious darkness.

'You would have loved Cambodia,' she said. 'The Cambodia I knew.'

'Tell me about it.' He settled back with his drink.

Her smile seemed distant as she drifted back to a world gone for ever, a world she had loved like life itself, and for which there could never be a satisfactory replacement. 'Were you ever in Phnom Penh?' He shook his head. 'It was a beautiful city, Mr Elliot. It had all the grace and style of the French, the brashness of the Chinese, and yet at its heart was still very Cambodian, full of history. You have seen photographs of Angkor Wat?'

'Sure.'

'Then perhaps you will understand a little of Cambodia. But you must see it to feel it. The temples symbolize everything that was great about a race that once ruled the whole of Indochina. Then, lost for hundreds of years, they were rediscovered in the last century by a French explorer, a mirror on a long-forgotten past.'

'I think we could skip the history lesson,' Elliot said.

She smiled with something like condescension. 'Perhaps you have to be Cambodian to understand.' She sipped her drink thoughtfully. 'The Fifties and Sixties were a golden era in our more recent history, under the rule of that fat little man, Prince Sihanouk.'

'I heard he was a bit of an eccentric.'

'Oh, yes, he was eccentric, Mr Elliot. But you mustn't mistake eccentricity for stupidity. The Prince was successful in keeping Cambodia out of the war in Vietnam for nearly twenty years before the Americans bombed our country in 1970. Oh, some people thought him mad. He had a penchant for making his own movies, in which he nearly always starred himself as some awful gangster. Of course, I was invited to the palace on the banks of the Mekong many times with my mother. I saw several of his films. They were truly dreadful. He played the saxophone, too. Not badly. And wrote music for performances by the Royal Dancers. He preserved many of the traditions of Cambodia. The people turned out in their thousands every year for the *Fêtes des Eaux*, a sort of Oxford and Cambridge boat race on the Mekong, held during the rainy season when the waters

PETER MAY

of the river and the Tonle Sap reverse their currents and flow
back on themselves. It is one of the wonders of the world.'

Elliot yawned and she chided him with mock severity. 'I
don't think you are taking me very seriously, Mr Elliot.'

'Tell me about Chez La Mère Grace.'

Her smile was resigned. 'At Chez La Mère Grace,' she said,
'time was unimportant. There were no clocks, as you will see
there are none here. Sex cannot be measured by the minute
or the hour, or even by the day. Nor is it something to be done
in the dark, furtive and secret.' She paused. 'Another drink?'

'Sure.'

She rose and crossed to the cabinet to refill their glasses. 'Of
course, not everyone came to Chez La Mère Grace for sexual
gratification. A night out in Phnom Penh was not complete
without a visit to my house for a few pipes of opium. I had one
of the best boy pipes' – she pronounced it *peeps* – 'in the city. A
couple would dine at a club along the river then come to the
Rue Ohier, in the fashionable centre of Phnom Penh, to smoke
in one of my upstairs rooms.' She came back with their drinks
and curled up on a cushion, revealing the curve of one of her
legs all the way up to the top of her thigh, brown and smooth
and tempting. 'A good boy pipe is a very rare commodity. He
must be able to cook the opium over the flame of a candle so
that it does not burn but remains soft and malleable in order
that the pipe may be primed to perfection. Only one or two
pulls at each pipe are necessary to achieve that pitch of exquis-
ite harmony and peace that the smoker seeks.'

Elliot took a pull at his second drink. 'How did the war affect you?'

'At first not at all. We were all very sad when the Prince was driven into exile after Lon Nol's coup. The General was little more than an American puppet, and that gave the Khmer Rouge a popular support which they had never previously enjoyed. If it had not been for the interference of the Americans, the Khmer Rouge could never have taken power. They would have remained a small, ineffectual group of guerrillas buried away somewhere in the jungle.

'We sometimes heard the sound of distant guns from the swimming pool where we would spend our afternoons in the sun, cooling ourselves in the water and sipping chilled Chablis. I could never understand why the Cambodian people felt it necessary to fight, to make war.'

'Understanding is seldom found in swimming pools and glasses of chilled wine.'

The contempt in his voice stung her to reply. 'Nor is it to be found in England or America, where you know nothing of Cambodia or its people. Cambodians are a lazy, happy people, Mr Elliot. They live in a rich, fertile and beautiful land. They have never had reason to do other than smile and give thanks to Buddha.'

Elliot remembered the face of the refugee at Mak Moun. He had had no reason to do either.

'In the last months it became clear that the Khmer Rouge were going to win,' she said. 'Lon Nol's army was corrupt, had no will to fight. The officers sold the food for the troops, the money for the war effort lined their pockets. Dollars for Cambodia. When the Khmer Rouge were only a few kilometres from the city they would still prefer to spend their nights drinking or smoking opium or buying favours from my girls. Eventually I barred army officers from my house. And a few weeks later I was forced to close up, take what I could, and flee the country. I would certainly have been killed had I stayed.' She got up and moved to a trunk by the bed. 'All I have left now of Cambodia are my memories and my jewellery.'

With a small key hanging on a fine gold chain round her neck, she unlocked the trunk and threw back the lid. She lifted out tray after tray of necklaces and earrings and gold and silver bracelets, rings and brooches. 'These' – she held out a necklace and bracelet set of hand-engraved silver – 'were my mother's. Made for her by the Prince's own silversmith, Minh Mol. There are others, too. Earrings, cufflinks, brooches, crafted by men now dead whose skills have been lost for ever. Only in Cambodia could you find such men.'

Elliot examined the fine detail of the engraving. Miniatures of many of the scenes hewn out of the stone of the temples of Angkor Wat. 'And this' – Grace passed him a small, round, pink tin box, scraped and dented – 'is my most prized possession. Given me by one of my regular customers.' Painted in faded gold on the lid of the box was the name of the shop where it had been bought: BIJOUTERIE HUE-THANH, 121 RUE OHIER, PHNOM PENH. 'It is such an unprepossessing little box,' she said, 'I could not imagine what manner of cheap jewellery it might contain.'

Elliot lifted the lid to reveal a gold bracelet on a bed of tissue. It was a good inch wide, comprising thousands of tiny links, each hand-crafted in the form of a miniature star. He lifted it carefully out. It was heavy, flexible, every link moving freely. He turned it over and marvelled at the way a human hand had ever been able to work such tiny pieces of metal with such fine precision. 'It's beautiful,' he said.

She smiled. 'I took it to a jeweller in Paris one time, and he could not believe it had been made by hand. He said there was not a jeweller in France who could make such a thing.'

Elliot put it back in the box. 'Did you go to Paris often?'

'I was educated there, and in my teens was trained as a ballet dancer. I still do the exercises to keep me supple and fit. The body is like a musical instrument, Mr Elliot. It requires care and fine tuning for it to perform at its best.' She ran her hands down over her breasts and the flatness of her stomach as if to illustrate her point. 'I am very proud of my body. I am forty-five years old, but I have the body of a woman half that age. And I have the benefit of age and experience to make me a better lover than any twenty-year-old.'

She took the pink tin box and shut it away in the trunk with the rest of her jewellery. 'I cannot keep calling you Mr Elliot. You have a name, I suppose?'

'Jack.'

'Ah, Jacques. It was the name of my mother's lover. My

father.' She pulled a bell cord by the bed. And almost immediately the double doors of the room were opened by the girl who had admitted them earlier. She bowed and Grace spoke to her briskly in Thai. Then she turned to Elliot. 'If you will follow my girl she will take you to your room.' He raised an eyebrow. 'Do not worry, Jacques. This is not goodbye. Only *au revoir*.'

Elliot followed the girl down a long hallway, through an arch, and she opened the door to a large bedroom all in white – white carpet, white walls, white furniture, white silk sheets on the bed. Another door led off to a shower room. She left him, and he wandered around the room touching things, wondering about Grace. This was not what he had expected. He turned as the door to the bedroom opened. Two young women in long white robes padded in. One was slightly taller than the other, with long dark hair. The smaller girl had her hair cut short. They were both pretty. They bowed, and the shorter one giggled. 'We undress you,' she said. Elliot shrugged. He wasn't about to protest.

They undressed him slowly and with care, hands drifting caressingly over his chest and stomach, his buttocks and thighs. He allowed them to lead him into the shower room, where they both disrobed to reveal their nakedness. The shorter one turned on the shower, testing the water until the temperature was just right. They all stepped in together, and the girls began to lather him with scented soap from coloured bottles. Their hands slid over him with an effortless professionalism, leaving no part of him untouched.

Then somewhere in the depths of the house he heard a bell ring, and the girls drew away leaving him breathless and aching for fulfilment. 'La Mère Grace want you now,' said the smaller one. They slipped him into a towelling robe before taking a hand each and leading him from the shower. 'You come with us.'

He was stung by a sense of shock as they swung the doors open. Grace lay naked, stretched out on the red sheets, a girl rising from between her legs to stand by the side of the bed. Grace's eyes were closed. 'Come to me, Jacques. Come to me now, quickly,' she called.

As he approached the bed, the girl moved aside and melted away. Slowly he stepped from his robe and lowered himself between Grace's thighs, her dancer's body lean and perfect.

Afterwards they lay for a long time, bodies tangled, sweating and breathless. She kissed him gently all over his face, his nose, his eyes, his mouth, before taking his hand and rising from the bed to lead him to the shower.

When they had washed and dressed a girl brought in a tray from which she served them sweet-scented tea in tiny bone china cups. 'Tea is always so refreshing,' Grace said. 'Don't you think?' She had a glow about her now and, if anything, looked even more beautiful. Elliot shrugged. He would have preferred whisky.

She emptied her cup and rose to take a wooden box, inlaid with ivory, from a cabinet at the far end of the room. She brought it back to the table and opened it. Inside were several rings and a pendant necklace, each set with the same large, translucent purple stones. She handed him one of the rings. 'Alexandrite,' she said. 'Hold it up to the light and turn it slowly.' Elliot did as she asked. The stone changed from purple to red, to green and then blue, as its cut surface refracted the changing light source. One colour bleeding subtly into the next. 'I had them cut for me in Phnom Penh. They are not very expensive, but they are very beautiful.' She paused. 'Do you like the ring?'

Elliot turned it again in the light. 'I don't think I've ever seen anything quite like it.'

'Keep it,' she said. He looked at her, surprised. 'To remember me by.'

'But I will see you again.'

She shook her head solemnly. 'No.'

'Why not?'

'Because, Mr Elliot, it would never be the same a second time.'

It was some hours later that Elliot closed the door of his hotel room and switched on the bedside lamp. He lay back on the bed and felt strangely empty as he fingered the cold cut surface of the alexandrite ring in his jacket pocket. As though she had stolen something from him, something from deep inside. The memory of her face still filled his eyes, the warmth of her skin against his still burned. Of course, he knew, she was right. It could never be the same again. The telephone rang and he reached out absently and picked up the receiver.

'Where the hell you been, chief? I been trying to get you for hours.'

Something in Slattery's voice rang an alarm bell. Elliot sat up, suddenly alert. 'What's wrong?'

'You mean you ain't heard?'

'For Christ's sake, Mike . . .!'

'Bloody Vietnamese have just invaded Cambodia.'

PART TWO

CHAPTER SEVENTEEN

I

The road was pitch black as the tyres of their jeep bumped and rattled over its uneven surface. Tuk sat uncomfortably in the back with Elliot, Slattery and McCue. He glanced at them uneasily, all three dressed in jungle camouflage jackets, shirts, and army trousers tucked into US army boots and wrapped around with strips of cloth to make puttees. Elliot and Slattery both wore green berets, and McCue had a black cotton scarf tied around his head, the ends trailing loose down his back. Their hands and faces were smeared with dirt rubbed into an evil-smelling insect repellent. They were silent and tense. Tuk moved one of their backpacks to make room for his legs and tried to stretch them. A pothole rocked the jeep and jarred his spine. He had not anticipated this. The Vietnamese invasion had taken him too by surprise, although it had always been a possibility at this time of year. The phone call from Elliot had woken him up.

'We're going now,' Elliot had said.

In two hours Tuk had arranged everything, but he was far from happy. He would have liked more time to set things up, although he had already had two detailed sessions with Van and Ferguson. He was nervous now, and felt that the eyes upon him were filled with suspicion.

But Elliot was paying little attention to Tuk. His mind was occupied, sorting mentally through kit and provisions. Maps, compasses, ropes, radio. Biltong, protein biscuits, salt tablets, water purifiers in case they had no chance to boil their water, malaria tablets, first-aid kit. Water bottles, sleeping sacks, folding canvas mats. They were to pick up their weapons and webbing at a house near the border. Tuk had assured him that everything was ready and waiting. Though there was something odd in Tuk's manner that had put Elliot on his guard. He glanced at him now and saw a nervous tic fluttering above his left eye. Tuk shifted uncomfortably.

'Thought you said this road was controlled by bandits at night,' Slattery shouted across the roar of the engine.

Tuk smiled feebly. 'It is,' he shouted back.

Jesus, Slattery thought, the guy's got a finger in every pie. 'Where are we going?'

Tuk said, 'Van Saren has quite a comfortable bungalow a few kilometres back from the border.' He smiled at Slattery's surprise. 'You did not think he lived in the camp, did you?'

Up ahead, there was an unexpected flash of light on the road and the driver braked sharply. Another vehicle pulled in behind them, headlamps shining in the back. 'What's going on?' Elliot snapped.

Tuk leaned forward and exchanged a few words with the driver. He turned back to the others. 'Just a road check,' he said.

'Army?' Slattery asked.

'My people,' Tuk said. McCue drew out an old US army-issue Colt and slipped off the safety catch. Tuk blenched. 'There is no need for that, Mr McCue. It will only cause alarm.'

McCue lowered the pistol between his thighs, leaning forward on his elbows so that it was concealed, the barrel pointing straight at Tuk. 'Anything goes wrong,' he said quietly, 'I'll blow your balls off.' Tuk paled visibly.

The jeep drew to a halt and there were voices in the road. Then a man with a dark, ugly face whipped aside the canvas cover at the back and looked inside. He wore jeans and a T-shirt and carried an automatic rifle. The lights of the vehicle behind filled the inside of the jeep and the four men blinked, temporarily blinded by their sudden brightness. The man spoke and Tuk replied sharply. The name of Van Saren figured in the response. The man shrugged and let the canvas cover fall back. The rear vehicle revved its engine and pulled away, overtaking them and driving off at speed into the night. More voices in the dark, then all the lights went out again and the jeep jerked into motion, picking up pace and lurching violently on the uneven surface. Tuk was still tense. He looked at McCue. 'I think you could put that away now, Mr McCue. It is a bumpy road and I am sure we would both regret it if your gun happened to go off by accident.'

The faintest flicker of a smile crossed McCue's face as he slipped on the safety catch and tucked the Colt into the belt below his jacket.

'Where the hell did you get that, Billy boy?'

McCue glanced at Slattery. 'It's the one I used to take down the tunnels with me. Guess I must have forgot to hand it in. Just wish I'd some ammo to go with it.'

Slattery grinned and looked at Tuk, whose silent annoyance showed in the line of his mouth. He turned to Elliot. 'Being threatened by one of your men was not part of the deal.'

Elliot shrugged. 'Like the man said, it wasn't loaded. Your balls were quite safe, Mr Tuk.'

Another fifteen minutes, and they could see the lights of Aranyaprathet in the distance. They turned off the main road, left on to what was little more than a dirt track. They criss-crossed paddy fields that reflected the light of the rising moon and seemed to bear east for some time before swinging south again, the paddies left behind, jungle closing in on either side. The track was scarred by deep ruts in the mud made by the wheels of vehicles during the rainy season. Then the trees thinned and they drew into a clearing fringed with small patches of cultivated land reclaimed from the jungle.

A bungalow with a long wooden terrace was raised a few feet from the ground on short stilts. Lights in all the windows threw long slabs of yellow light out across the clearing. Several battered vehicles were parked outside, and an armed guard sat idly on the rail of the veranda smoking a cigarette. He swung his automatic rifle lazily in their direction as the jeep pulled in at the foot of the steps. Tuk jumped down, clearly relieved to have arrived.

'Follow me, gentlemen.'

They climbed the steps past the guard and went into the bungalow. Inside, Van lounged on a settee in front of a television set, beer in one hand, a half-smoked cigar in the other, watching *Dallas*, the decade's most popular American soap opera badly dubbed into Thai. He was wearing combat shirt, trousers and boots and, like McCue, had a cotton scarf tied around his head. He turned and beamed as they came in.

'One minute, please. I want see what happens Bobbee here.' And he turned back to the television.

'Saren, Mr Elliot is keen to get started,' Tuk said impatiently.

'Garee see to them,' he said, without taking his eyes from the screen. Somehow the show's camp villain, J.R., did not carry the same authority in Thai.

A door opened from a back room and Ferguson swaggered in. He was kitted out in his old GI uniform, but looked incongruous, and faintly ridiculous, in a sweat-stained cowboy hat. He glared at them, surly and unsmiling, taking in their gear and the backpacks stacked by the door.

'You guys ain't travelling light, that's for sure. You'll get your weapons in back.' He jerked his thumb towards the back room and opened the fridge to get a can of beer. Slattery and

McCue followed Elliot through and opened the crates. They took out and checked their weapons – automatics, pistols, knives, grenades – and armed up, strapping on webbing and slipping long, lethal machetes into leather sheaths.

'He's right, chief,' Slattery said. 'With those backpacks we're going to be carrying some kit.'

'We're going to be a long time away from base,' Elliot said. 'You think there's anything we don't need, speak up.'

Slattery shrugged. 'I guess not.'

Elliot looked at McCue, who only shook his head.

'Okay.' Elliot moved across the room and closed the door. The atmosphere was tense in this small, darkened room only a few kilometres from the Cambodian border. He lowered his voice. 'I don't trust any of these bastards. Watch them. McCue, I want you to bring up the rear at all times. Slattery, you flank right, I'll take the left. Anything goes wrong, hit dirt. Whistle once for alright, twice for trouble. If we get split take a compass reading south-south-west from our last joint position. Take as straight a line as you can for about two kilometres and we'll try to rendezvous at first light. Don't use firepower unless absolutely necessary. If we fail to meet up, in an emergency fire a single shot and take cover.' The Australian and the American nodded. 'Alright, let's go.' He opened the door as the *Dallas* theme tune played over the closing credits.

II

Van Saren, Ferguson and two others sat with them in the back of the jeep as it clattered its way along the jungle track. Elliot eyed them warily and wondered why it took four of them to lead the way across the border. Tuk had seemed nervous as he shook their hands and wished them luck, and Elliot had not missed the look that passed between him and Van as they left.

Van kept up a cheerful front, babbling nonsense, grinning and showing the gaps in his teeth. Elliot could smell his breath across the jeep. Ferguson, by contrast, sat silent, staring sullenly at McCue. There was murder in his eyes.

After half an hour, the jeep drew in and Van said, 'Is as far we go in jeep. Very near border now. Ground open there, but no problem.'

Elliot, Slattery and McCue followed the leading group through the scattered trees in single file. With a bright three-quarters moon rising above them, their eyes adjusted quickly to night sight. The ground rose steeply and then fell away to a dry stream bed, rising again on the other side over a jumble of rocks to more trees. They moved quickly across the stream that would only carry water in the rainy season, and up the embankment into the subtropical forest, moonlight filtering through the canopy only in patches. The undergrowth was dense but not impenetrable, and they stuck to a network of criss-crossing animal tracks. Van led the way with McCue at the rear, just behind Ferguson. Because of the thickness of the undergrowth it was impossible for Elliot and Slattery to flank the group. Van was sure-footed and silent, moving with the assurance of familiarity. He had followed this route many times before.

Visibility was less than ten metres. The ground seemed to rise again before falling away to a valley that cut a swathe through the forest like a scar. Van found a track that led up the other side, smooth and well-worn, running at an angle to the right, then turning back on itself, though still rising, to take them over the ridge. More trees and dense undergrowth that caught and snagged on clothes with needles and thorns. Van stopped on the edge of a small clearing. 'You in Cambodia,' he said. 'You go on your own now. No problem. I go back TV.'

Elliot thought he heard something move at the far side of the clearing, saw a glint of moonlight on metal. Van signalled his men to move aside and let them past. 'Good luck,' he said. Elliot glanced at Slattery, who gave an almost imperceptible shake of his head.

'I think,' Elliot told Van, 'you should go a little way more with us.'

Van smiled. 'No need. You okay now. That right, Garee?'

'Sure is, father.'

Elliot swung his M16 up and levelled it at Van's chest. 'I insist,' he said. Slattery and McCue had the others covered before they could move, a clatter of gun metal against webbing.

'What the fuck are you guys playing at?' Ferguson hissed.

Elliot ignored him, his eyes fixed on Van. 'After you.'

There was fear now in Van's eyes. He knew that to step out into the clearing meant certain death. 'I send one my men,' he said, and turned to wave the nearest of his soldiers on. The man took a half-step back, shook his head and uttered something in Cambodian. Van barked at him, but the young soldier was terrified, before suddenly he turned to run back the way they had come, straight into a bullet from McCue. A burst of automatic fire rang out from across the clearing. The six remaining men dived for cover. Elliot rolled over behind a tree, snatched a grenade from his webbing, pulled the pin and lobbed it across the clearing. It exploded with a dull thud and somebody screamed. He saw two dark shadows running through the trees at the far side, not ten metres away. Two short bursts with his M16 and one of the shadows fell and lay still. The other kept going and disappeared into the forest. There was another burst of automatic fire somewhere to his left. He rolled over quickly, eyes raking the darkness, and bumped into a prone figure lying in the ferns. It was Van. Elliot turned him over with his free hand and saw the whites of frightened eyes staring up at him. 'You bastard!' he hissed. He looked up quickly then whistled once. A single whistle came back in response, and the crouched figure of Slattery crossed the path and moved up beside him.

'Alright chief?'

'Where's McCue?'

'Christ knows.'

'The rest of Van's men?'

'Two dead. Don't know about Ferguson.'

A rustle in the undergrowth made them turn. Ferguson stood there, pale and grim in the moonlight. Then he lurched suddenly forward, almost landing on top of Van, to reveal McCue standing behind him, M16 crooked in his arm, muzzle pointing skywards. Elliot jerked his head at him. 'Check out the far side of the clearing.' McCue nodded and melted away into the trees.

Elliot gripped the loose flesh at Van's throat. 'You sold us out, you fucker! Why?'

'Tuk's idea,' Van babbled. 'He trade you for big shipment gold artefact. He ask me fix it.'

'I knew there was something treacherous about that little creep,' Slattery growled. His gut was aching again.

McCue slipped quietly back through the trees and crouched beside Elliot. 'Three Khmer Rouge dead. Two hit by the grenade. You got the other with the M16.'

'And at least one got away,' Elliot said grimly. 'We're going to have to move out of here fast.'

'What about these two?' Slattery asked.

'Kill them.' There was no emotion in McCue's voice.

Elliot shook his head. 'Mike, take their weapons.' Slattery disarmed them, and Elliot pushed his knee hard into Van's chest, making him grunt. He leaned over, bringing his face very close to Van's. 'You tell Tuk I'll see him when I get back.' He nodded to the others and they rose and faded off into the forest. Van rolled over and vomited.

Ferguson crouched over him. 'Hey, you alright, father?'

Van was shaking. 'I scared, Garee. We lucky be alive.'

Ferguson spat. 'Yeah, well that could be the biggest mistake these bastards ever made.'

For the first hour McCue took point. Their need to move fast was tempered by the requirement for caution. They kept to the animal tracks, always running the risk of hitting landmines or booby traps. McCue's face was strained with concentration and tension, listening, scanning the ground, constantly checking ahead. It would be too easy to confuse the rustle of some night creature in the undergrowth for that of a man. But the opposite was also true.

Then from somewhere up ahead came what sounded like voices. He stopped, stood motionless, and listened, his hand raised to halt the others. There it was again. Definitely voices. He turned and hurried back along the track. 'Someone coming,' he whispered. Elliot nodded curtly and waved them into the undergrowth at the side of the path where they each lay flat, pressing into the soft damp earth beneath the cover of the ferns. Now they all heard the voices. Then the sound of feet on hard earth. A patrol of six Khmer Rouge soldiers, walking in single file, passed within inches of where they lay. The soldiers carried their AK-47s carelessly over their shoulders. They talked and laughed without caution. Clearly they were not expecting to encounter anyone here. Elliot waited for several minutes before he signalled the others back out on to the path.

'I'll go point,' he whispered. 'McCue, you ride shotgun.' He took a compass check. They were still heading south-east towards the small town of Sisophon, though they would not reach it for a day or more.

The next two hours passed without incident, and they were caught almost unawares by the sudden light of dawn. Elliot had forgotten how quickly night both lifted and fell near the equator. They had reached the edge of the forest now, and stood looking out across a flat valley of neglected paddy fields, an occasional line of trees breaking the regular monotony of the broken-down irrigation ditches. Early morning mist rose like smoke across the fields. Beyond, shimmering in a blue haze, the ground rose again, covered by a thick blanket of trees.

It took them fifteen minutes to find a secure place to set up camp and try to grab some sleep during the hours of daylight. The site was flanked on one side by a tall bamboo thicket, and on another by an almost impenetrable jungle undergrowth. It was nearly dark here, still under the thick canopy of the trees. While Slattery collected tinder and kindling to set a fire, Elliot cut lengths of bamboo to feed through the loops on either side of their canvas sleeping mats. He hammered two pairs of sharpened bamboo stakes into the ground, six feet apart, lashing them together to form two A shapes over which he placed the poles to stretch the mats and make comfortable bunks raised twelve inches above the ground. They only needed two, as there would always be one of them on watch.

Slattery's fire crackled fiercely, fuelled by the dry standing dead wood he had collected. It burned almost without smoke. What little there was filtered through the canopy overhead, where it was lost in the rising mist. McCue returned, having set two spring spear traps two hundred metres apart on the game track they had been following earlier. He had cut two strong saplings to use as springs, then sharpened short sections of bamboo and lashed them to the springs to act as spears. Short lengths of twine provided a tripwire. They would be lethal to the wild hogs that ranged through the woods, and could disable or even kill a man.

Over the burning embers of the fire Slattery brewed up coffee to wash down a handful of protein biscuits while Elliot took the first watch. McCue bunked down and was asleep almost immediately. Slattery took Elliot some coffee. The mist was dispersing now as the heat and humidity rose with the sun. The clamour of jungle life had grown around them with the coming of the dawn; the screeching of tropical birds, the howling of monkeys high up in the canopy, the hum of a million insects, and other sounds of unidentified life, large and small. Both men were sweating.

'What do you think, chief?'

'I think we were lucky last night. And we've still got a long way to go.' Elliot sipped his coffee thoughtfully. 'We've probably come through the most densely patrolled area of the border, but we're going to make slow progress if it's like this all the way. And getting back could be harder.'

Slattery nodded. 'Yeah, with a woman and a couple of kids.' He threw away the dregs of his coffee. 'Think I'll stretch my legs before I crash.'

He followed the path towards the edge of the trees, carefully skirting McCue's trap, and moved out on to a rock promontory overlooking the fields below.

Elliot tried to make himself comfortable in the undergrowth, from where he could cover both approaches along the path from a position of concealment. A silent approach to the camp was impossible through the bamboo thicket or the undergrowth, yet both provided instant cover should they have to abandon camp in a hurry. Elliot guarded the only other possible approach. He was tired, plagued by insects and heat, and he knew it was going to be a long and difficult two hours. The problem would be staying awake after the rigours of the night.

He still had the taste of Grace on his tongue, the smell of her in his nostrils. He was aware that he disliked her, while at the same time finding her irresistible. No one had ever aroused such passion in him. The alexandrite ring she had given him was tied on a thong around his neck, tangling with the chain of his tarnished St Christopher. Almost, he thought wryly, like the Lady's favour the Knight would carry into battle.

Suddenly he was alert. The sound of footsteps hurrying along the track. A soft whistle told him it was Slattery, and he relaxed just a little. 'Chief!' Slattery slipped through the undergrowth and crouched down beside him. 'You'd better come have a look.'

'What is it?'

'Soldiers. Down in the paddies.'

The two men darted back along the path, crouching low as they left the cover of the trees, and then dropping flat to inch their way forward to the edge of the promontory. Away below them, a group of twelve Khmer Rouge soldiers was escorting two ox-drawn carts across the fields. They seemed to be in no particular hurry. 'What's that they've got in the carts?' Elliot asked.

'Can't see.'

Elliot reached back and took out his binoculars. He checked the position of the sun before raising them to his eyes and levelling them towards the little procession. 'Jesus!' The oath escaped his lips in a breath.

'What is it, chief?'

Elliot lowered the glasses grimly. 'Bodies.' He handed the glasses to Slattery.

'Shit! Must be twenty or thirty of them.'

As they watched, the carts drew to a halt, oxen shuffling as the soldiers began pulling the bodies from the carts and dumping them into the liquid mud of the paddies, like so many sacks. No need to bury them when, in very little time, the mud would claim them.

When it had completed its grisly business, the procession of soldiers continued across the fields at the same unhurried pace. There was a sinister ease in the casual ceremony, as if death had grown routine. Bodies cast carelessly into disused paddies: the human refuse of an inhuman tyranny, incongruous in the morning sunshine.

Elliot felt a chill like the cold blade of a knife run through his heart. He recalled again the story of the refugee at Mak Moun. Bayonets flashing in the rain, the death of a mother and her children. And he remembered the flies and the heat of Aden. The smell of cordite, the clearing smoke – and all those bodies. Women and children. A white flag of truce ignored. Fear corrupting reason.

'You'd better catch some sleep,' he said to Slattery.

CHAPTER EIGHTEEN

They drove to Heathrow in silence. David glanced at Lisa sitting pale and impassive in the passenger seat. He suppressed lingering feelings of anger at her unreasonable behaviour. They had fought furiously over her trip. She had faced down his angry protestations with a childlike obstinacy. Of course she knew the dangers that faced a girl of her age alone in Bangkok! He knew she did not. And it was not just ignorance. She wore her innocence like a badge. Not even the death of her mother had brought her into the real world. She lived still in that strange, protected never-never land in which she had grown up.

Grown up! He almost laughed at the irony. She had never grown up. Never had to. She had the arrogance of the adolescent, the unswerving belief of the child in the triumph of good over evil, the certainty that if something bad was going to happen, it would never happen to her. In an odd way, it was this very naivety that had first attracted him.

And now he blamed himself for failing to protect her from her own innocence. His damned temper. He should have known better.

He had asked her how she thought she was going to find her father in a city of eight million people. Eyes blazing defiance, she had turned on him. 'I'm training as a reporter, aren't I?'

He hadn't been able to help himself. 'Reporter! You really have no idea, do you? Newspapers are for grown-ups, Lisa. You'll be lucky if you end up writing knitting patterns for the woman's page of the *Torquay Gazette*!' Instantly he had wanted to bite his tongue, but it was too late. She had turned away, her face red with anger and embarrassment, refusing to discuss it further, determined to prove him wrong. He was still cursing his stupidity.

There had been a reconciliation since then – of sorts. He had made all the running, apologized, said he was angry and frustrated and hadn't meant what he'd said. He asked her to reconsider. She refused, and was relieved when he seemed to accept it. In truth he had realized, at last, that there was no point in fighting her. She was obsessed with finding her father. So, let her find him. He could never live up to the myth she was creating in her own mind, or accord with the excuses she had been making for him. He probably wouldn't even want to know her – why else would he have stayed away all these years? But, whichever way it went, she would have to get it out of her system, and David had decided it was easier to swim with the current than against it. When the river of her obsession ran dry, as it was bound to, Lisa would be his again.

He still did not fully understand why it was he wanted her so much. Perhaps because she was one of the few things in his life that had not come easy. Winning had always come easy to David. Lisa was a challenge. One he was determined to beat.

For her part she was glad they had made up, was in need of his moral support. There was no one else, after all. She glanced at him as he drove. She wanted to say, I'm scared, but was frightened to admit it. All those brave words – I'm going to find my father. The reality was very different. And she was frightened, too, of the unknown. Of the stranger she was going to find. She would have liked to turn to David and say, I've changed my mind. But it was too late now. She was trapped by her own pride.

'Listen, I want you to telephone me when you get to your hotel,' David said. 'So I know you're alright.'

'I will.'

He allowed himself an inner sigh of relief. As long as she kept in touch by phone he would retain some measure of control over what she did.

They checked her in at the British Airways desk and took her luggage, and she and David sat in the departure lounge waiting for her flight to be called. She had gone very quiet, subdued by nerves. He took her hand and squeezed it.

'It's a long flight,' he said.

She nodded.

'I'm looking forward to meeting him.' She looked at him, surprised, and he forced himself to laugh. 'After all, he's the one I'm going to have to ask for your hand in marriage.'

She tensed and drew her hand away. 'Don't, David.' It was as though he was making fun of her.

'Oh, come on, I'm sorry. It was a joke, that's all. I know you don't want to hurry things. And I don't want to push you.' He took her hand again and decided to steer the conversation in a different direction. 'You know what hotel he's staying at?'

'The Narai.'

'And if he's not there?'

She hesitated. 'I went back to see the Sergeant.'

He turned his head sharply. 'You never told me.'

'I was going to. But I thought – well, I thought that you might be angry.'

'Why would I be angry?'

'Because you've behaved very strangely over everything to do with my father.' The defiance in her voice again.

I've behaved strangely! he thought. But all he said was, 'What did he say, the Sergeant?'

'He said he thought my father would still be in Bangkok. If he wasn't at the hotel he gave me another address to try. A man who might be able to help me. A man called Tuk Than.'

CHAPTER NINETEEN

McCue had been watching the pig for some time from a concealed position a metre back from the path. It was somnolent and off-guard in the late afternoon heat, snuffling about in the undergrowth, foraging idly for something to eat. Elliot and Slattery were sleeping, and McCue was nearly at the end of his two-hour stint on watch. He was refreshed and alert after five hours' sleep. The pig moved nearer the trap, infuriatingly slowly. But the tunnels had taught McCue patience. The beast was quite large and thickly haired with a long snout and two sharp tusks. McCue knew the dangers of provoking a wild pig into attack. It could knock a man over, and its tusks could inflict serious injury, often dangerously close to the femoral artery on the upper leg. He had seen a man bleed to death from such an injury.

Something close to McCue seemed suddenly to draw its attention, and it began lumbering down the path towards him, still contentedly unaware of his presence. As its forelegs broke the tripwire, the sapling sprang and the two sharpened bamboo stakes plunged deep into its chest. It let out a blood-curdling squeal and rolled over on its side, still twitching. It was not dead, but quickly failing. McCue approached with caution. It could still be dangerous. He raised the butt of his automatic and moved in to finish the job, clubbing the beast several times over the head. The twitching subsided and it lay quite still. A rustling in the undergrowth behind him made him swing round, drawing his knife to meet his assailant. It was Elliot.

'What the hell's happened!'

McCue smiled a rare smile. 'We got pork for dinner,' he said.

Slattery still slept while Elliot put water on the fire to boil and then made his way to the small clearing McCue had hacked out with his machete to prepare the dead animal. Four stakes were hammered into the soft earth and lashed together into A shapes, a bamboo pole laid across the top. The pig was hung upside down from the pole, tied by the hocks. McCue had made two neat incisions in the carotid artery behind the ears, allowing the blood to drain into a pot beneath the head. 'We should save the blood,' he said.

Elliot shook his head. 'We can't carry any more than we've got. We'll have to eat what we can and leave the carcase.'

McCue shrugged. 'Pity. This little mother could have fed us for days.'

Elliot watched, fascinated, as McCue wielded his hunting knife with dexterous ease to gut the pig. He pinched the abdomen as high as he could, raising a pouch of flesh and cutting a slit big enough for him to slip in two fingers. Using the fingers as a guide for the knife he cut upwards towards the anus, taking care not to damage the internal organs. Then he cut downwards the same way as far as the breastbone, holding back the gut with his left hand as it began to spill outwards. When he had completed the cut, he let the gut hang down so that he could inspect it for signs of disease. 'Looks okay,' he said. He removed both kidneys and the liver, then cut through the membrane covering the chest cavity and took out the heart and lungs and windpipe. 'Better bury this stuff.'

Elliot started digging a hole to take the animal's innards. 'You not going to skin it?'

McCue shook his head. 'You never skin a pig. We'll have to remove the hair over the fire. Did you boil that water?'

Elliot nodded. 'Where'd you learn to use a knife like that?'

McCue sat silent for a while, his lean cadaverous face taut and thoughtful. 'My Pa was a small-time farmer in the Midwest,' he said. 'He was a real hard bastard, but I guess I loved him. Ma died when I was just a kid and Pa had to raise me and my three brothers on his own. I was the baby of the family. When we was having bad times, like when the crop would fail or the animals got diseased, he would pack me off to his sister's. I spent half my life there when I was a kid, but I guess they didn't like me too much. I was none too happy staying there neither. I used to run off sometimes, and then I would get sent home and my Pa would beat the crap out of me. I didn't mind that, though. I just wanted to be home.

'He didn't have much patience, my Pa, and his temper worked on a short fuse, so I got the buckle end of his belt more times than I can remember.' He paused, lost in some childhood past. But there was reverence in his voice, more than rancour, when he spoke of the beatings. 'He taught me to use my fists. Stand up for myself. I was a bit of a runt, even then, and he said I had to be big in other ways.

'I was about nine or ten when he took me out in the yard one day and gave me a knife and told me it was my turn to kill a pig. 'You seen how it's done,' he said. 'So do it right. Kill it with the first stroke. You get it wrong I'm gonna beat the shit outa you.' So I got it with the first stroke. He taught me everything I needed to know about using a knife. Never needed nothing else since.'

'Is he still alive?'

There was a moment of pain in McCue's eyes and his voice took on an edge as sharp as his knife. 'Two of my brothers was killed in Nam. The other got a bullet in the spine. He's in some hospital somewheres for the rest of his days.

'While I was out there the bank foreclosed on my Pa's loan, tried to put him off the farm. Some shit, huh? He's worked that land all his days, two of his boys is killed fighting for their country, they give a third wheels for legs and stick me down a hole chasing gooks. They took all his boys, he wasn't about to let them take his land. It was his life, you know? So he blew his brains out in the back room.' He examined the blood on his hands. 'God bless America.' He got up to cut down the pig. 'Better get this old hog on the fire.'

Slattery awoke to the smell of meat cooking. 'Jeez,' he said.

'I had this dream. I was at this big medieval banquet. They was just about the serve up the pig when I woke up. Christ, I can still smell it!' He looked at Elliot and McCue crouched around the embers of the fire. 'Hey, what you guys doing? Shit, am I still dreaming?'

'It's no dream, Mike,' Elliot said. 'It may not be a banquet, but the pork's just about ready.'

It was dark when they set off again to cross the paddy fields in the valley below. The moon was not yet up, and it was fully twenty minutes before their eyes adjusted to the pale light cast over the land by the stars. Picking their way along the narrow paths that ran between the lines of irrigation ditches on either side of the paddies, it took them another half-hour before they reached the spot where the soldiers had dumped the bodies earlier in the day. The corpses, some still semi-clothed in torn black rags, others naked, were already being claimed by the mud. Men and women, some young, some old. Most had been stabbed, probably with bayonets. One or two had been shot in the head. Single bullets. The need to conserve ammunition Slattery crossed himself. An instinct from a long-forgotten past. But neither he nor the others spoke, and they moved on in silence.

They were almost two-thirds of the way across when Slattery slipped, the soft earth of the path falling away under his feet, and tumbled into the mud below the film of brackish water. He cursed under his breath and spat out a mouthful of sludge.

Elliot and McCue reached out hands to pull him out. But something had snagged on his backpack. He turned to shake himself free and saw a half-decayed hand clutching his shoulder. He let out an involuntary yell and thrashed about to try and get away, bumping into arms and legs and bloated heads, decaying skulls grinning in the mud.

'Get me outa here for Chrissake!'

The others grabbed him and pulled him free. He scrambled to his feet on the path, shaking, eyes wide, jaw chattering almost uncontrollably. It was not cold that made him shiver. It was naked fear.

'Jesus,' he panted. 'Jesus, did you see that!'

Elliot's voice was calm. 'We'd better move.'

But Slattery couldn't bring himself to put one foot in front of the other. 'Jesus Christ, this whole fucking place is one mass grave! There must be hundreds of them in there. All around us. Jesus, I wanna wash!'

McCue's face moved close to his, hot breath on his skin. 'If you don't move, Slattery, I'll cut your throat and chuck you in there with them.'

Slattery stared at him, the words slowly filtering through the film of fear that fogged his mind. Then he blinked several times and glanced at Elliot. Fear gave way to shame. He said, 'Sure, sure. Let's get the hell out of here.' And they moved on quickly, but careful not to risk another fall.

A sense of horror had gripped them all, turning the hot night cold, fear closing like icy fingers around their hearts.

Fear of what? Elliot wondered. The dead? The dead couldn't hurt you. But they filled your mind, touching your soul, a reminder that you too were only flesh and blood and would one day return to the earth. Dust to dust.

It was with relief that they reached the dark safety of the trees and followed the ground upwards again over a ridge. For nearly two hours they hacked their way through tangled undergrowth, compelled by the urge to put as much distance as possible between them and the paddy fields.

Sweating and breathless, Elliot finally called a halt and they dumped their backpacks and slumped to the ground, leaning back against the trees. They sat, recovering breath, each with his own thoughts, not a word passing between them for fifteen minutes or more. The mud on Slattery's face and outer clothing had dried and caked. He checked and cleaned his pistol and automatic and looked grimly at the others, giving voice for the first time to their unspoken thoughts. They had not come across a living soul or sign of life in more than three hours.

'Jeez,' he said. 'Is there anyone left alive in this goddam country?'

CHAPTER TWENTY

The truck bumped and rattled through the night over the shell-pitted road from the airport to the city. No one had bothered to repair the road after the fierce fighting for the airport and the capital four years earlier.

Hau sat in the back of the truck with a dozen other boy soldiers and their commanding officer, Ksor Koh, a small, ugly man of about thirty who enforced a sadistic discipline. Though it remained unspoken, the boys both feared and hated him. He worked them long hard hours and saw to it that they received only minimum rations. Tears, or the least display of childhood vulnerability, were mercilessly ridiculed.

There was one exception. Yos Oan, a burly, sullen boy, older than the others. Ksor's lieutenant, he saw to it that they followed their commanding officer's instructions to the letter. He carried a short, stinging cane with which he beat the others without pity if they so much as looked at him the wrong way. They had all suffered at his hand, and often watched with hate in their eyes and dark thoughts in their hearts as he wolfed down almost double their rations. Though he too had been

164

brutally beaten by Ksor on many occasions, he had accepted his fate with the philosophical forbearance of one who knows that there is always a price to be paid.

Since being trucked into the airfield at Pochentong, they had been worked from first light until well after dark, digging and repairing defences around the perimeter. Bone-weary, hungry and aching for sleep, they had been told by Yos that they were being taken south. And within an hour they had been herded into a truck and were heading for Phnom Penh. The rumour had spread quickly, in whispers among the boys, that from there they were to be sent south to Takeo to join in the fighting to repel the Vietnamese invader. There was fear in all their hearts, for they had heard rumours that the Kampuchean armed forces were suffering heavy defeats and that the Vietnamese army was making steady progress north. Why else would they have been building defences around the airfield?

Hau had been waiting and watching for a chance to escape. But not a single opportunity had presented itself. They were watched at all times. And now, as they approached the city of his birth, he knew that time was running out for him. He had told no one of his plan to run away, keeping his silence and his secret safe in a heart still with fear. He saw that Yos was staring at him – a long penetrating stare – and for a moment he wondered if it was possible that his heart had spoken aloud and that Yos had been listening. Or perhaps it could be read in his face. A surge of hatred welled up inside him, even greater than the fear that gripped him, and he turned away to look out the back of the truck where a canvas flap was whipping in the slipstream.

Not a light shone anywhere as they rumbled through the deserted, broken-down suburbs in the ghostly moonlight. Past the wrecks of armoured vehicles, a legacy of Lon Nol's defeated army, rusting cars lying abandoned at the roadside, refuse tumbling across the road in their wake. Not a sign of anything living, of any human existence, just the wreckage of another life, another time.

None of the boys possessed guns, except for Yos, who rested his AK-47 across his knees, a symbol of his privilege, carried with a careless arrogance. Ksor's automatic was slung over his shoulder, a pistol holstered on his belt. He sat with his eyes closed, swaying with the motion of the truck. Hau knew he would have to get the rifle from Yos, that he would probably have to kill to be free. But they had made him kill before. He owed them nothing but death. And yet he was still only a child, twelve years old. Old enough to take life, but not old enough to live with it. The nightmares were almost unbearable. He thought of his sister and his mother, the years of separation, the nights of secret, silent tears, the longing for the warmth of his mother's breast, his sister's lips, the fear of sleep.

He shook himself free of such thoughts. They would only make him weak, and he had to be strong.

The city centre, too, was deserted, apart from the occasional army truck or jeep that would rattle past. There was an eerie, haunted quality about the empty streets, the years of neglect, the absence of people or life where once they had thrived. Hau's fear was beginning to yield to despair. He knew that once aboard the truck south his chances of escape would rapidly diminish. And where would he go? He was not equipped to survive on his own in the jungle. The city was his natural habitat. It had to be here. Panic was planting irrational thoughts in his head. Of snatching the weapon from Yos and leaping out the back. But the road ran fast beneath them. He would surely be killed or badly hurt. He glanced desperately around the other faces. They were without expression, each boy silent, guarding his own thoughts. How many of them could he trust? Trust! It was a word he barely remembered – an act of free will that was little more than a distant memory.

Suddenly the truck lurched violently to one side, tyres screeching, a smell of burning rubber as it mounted the pavement and smashed into a derelict shop front. The shock flung them all from their seats, and in the confusion Hau heard Ksor shouting, demanding to know what had happened. He caught a glimpse in the moonlight of the driver's face as he turned, blood streaming from a gash in his forehead.

'A puncture!'

Ksor cursed and kicked his way through the confusion of bodies to the back of the truck and jumped down into the road. Hau saw Yos's AK-47 on the floor where it had fallen. He looked up and Yos's black eyes met his. Yos was on his knees, clutching his arm where he had hurt it in the fall. From the pain he knew it was broken. The two boys grabbed together for the gun, but Hau was faster. He swung it up and pushed the barrel into Yos's chest. Yos went rigid, his face taut.

'You wouldn't dare!' he hissed.

The other boys, too, had frozen, chilled to the bone by the drama unfolding in front of them. Outside they heard the voices of Ksor and the driver. Yos relaxed with Hau's hesitation, knowing that he *would* not dare. A slow smile spread across his face as Hau squeezed the trigger and a burst of fire flashed in the dark, sending the older boy thudding backwards, his smile replaced for an instant by disbelief, and then, for eternity, by death. Hau was wet, and wondered for a crazy moment if it was raining. Then he realized it was blood. Yos's blood. It was everywhere. Spattered across the clothes and faces of all the boys.

A shout, and feet running on the pavement, pulled him back from the horror, and he spun round to see Ksor's dark outline rising up at the back of the truck. He fired again and Ksor fell backwards without a sound. The bloodied face of the driver appeared briefly at the opening before he turned and sprinted away into the darkness.

The silence that followed was deafening. Small boys all with their eyes on Hau. He looked round the frightened faces.

'I'm not going to fight the Vietnamese,' he said. But no one spoke. He pushed through to the back of the truck and jumped down on to the road. Ksor lay on his back, eyes staring, dark blood pooling on the tarmac. Hau scanned the street. There was not a sound to be heard or a light to be seen. He knelt down and gingerly removed Ksor's pistol and picked up his automatic. He tucked the pistol in his belt, slung a rifle over each shoulder and started running, back they way they had come, long loping strides. When he reached the end of the street, he looked back and saw the dark shapes of small boys spilling out from the back of the truck and running off into the night.

CHAPTER TWENTY-ONE

Lisa was not prepared for the sticky heat of the Bangkok night, with its noise and babble of Thai voices and lazily swinging ceiling fans. She was still dressed for the English winter she had left behind. Jeans and boots, a cotton blouse under a thick woollen jumper and quilted anorak. She had known it would be hot during the day, but thought the nights might be cool.

She queued uncomfortably, anorak over her arm, at immigration, and was disconcerted by the unsmiling scrutiny of the immigration officer. He slapped her passport on the desk and waved her through. Baggage reclaim and customs was another trial, encumbered as she was by a large suitcase, her shoulder bag, her anorak and the jumper the heat had compelled her to remove. Flushed and perspiring, exhausted by the journey and the heat, she faced a bewildering confusion of signs and people in the terminal building. Seedy and crowded like some oriental bazaar, it was not at all as she had imagined it. Quite unlike the clinical, ordered efficiency of Heathrow.

'Excuse me,' she inquired of anyone in the crowd who would listen. 'Can someone tell me where I can get a taxi?' But no one paid any attention, bumping and pushing past, Thai faces flashing occasional curious glances. She was fair-skinned, fair-haired and alone. A curiosity here.

She felt eyes upon her as she struggled through the crowd, but they were eyes that wanted only to help themselves. She felt a panic rising in her breast. She was stumbling at the first hurdle and felt vulnerable and very much alone. Then, to her great relief, she saw a TAXI sign and hurried towards it. Through a doorway to find herself outside. Here, if anything, the night was even hotter and more airless. There was a line of taxis parked at the kerbside. A tout approached and tried to take her case.

'You want taxi, Miss. I get you taxi.'

She clung grimly to the case and pushed on towards the first in the line of cars. 'No thank you, I'll get one myself.'

A wizened old face leered at her from the driver's side. 'Bangkok?'

'The Narai Hotel,' she said with relief.

The driver pulled a lever inside the car, the boot swung open and she realized she was expected to put the luggage in herself. Trickles of sweat ran into her eyes as she lugged her case round to the back of the car and heaved it into the boot, slamming it shut as a small gesture of annoyance. No tip for you, she thought.

'You sit in front,' the driver said, patting the front seat beside him.

'I'll sit in the back, thank you.' She slipped in, sinking into the soft, worn leather of the back seat, leaning back and closing her eyes. God, she thought, on my way at last.

The taxi took off with a jerk and she clung tightly to the door handle. With her free hand she took out a handkerchief to dry her face, careful not to smear her eye make-up, and breathed deeply in a vain attempt to find more oxygen. She watched the city grow up darkly around her as they drove from the airport. Modern blocks of squalid flats, temples, shops and offices, curious ramshackle vehicles among the traffic that belched its black fumes out into the night. Sights and sounds unfamiliar and strange and slightly frightening.

They had been driving almost fifteen minutes when she noticed that there was no reading on the meter. She tapped the driver on the shoulder.

'You forgot to set the meter.'

His grin revealed a set of crooked brown teeth. 'Not working. I give you good price.'

She sighed and sat back in the seat. She didn't suppose there was any point in arguing about it. She would just have to pay whatever he asked. She closed her eyes again and felt a wave of fatigue sweep over her. For a moment she was back home on the rug in front of the fire, warm and slightly drunk, David there, hot hands on her breasts, his soft whisper at her neck, It'll be alright, Lisa. It'll be alright. And then she was jerked back to the present as the taxi drew in abruptly at the doors of the Narai, the driver grinning at her from the front.

'Four hundred baht.' She did not bother to work out the

exchange equivalent, but handed him the notes in the certain knowledge that she was being fleeced. Definitely no tip, she thought. He pulled the lever to release the boot as she got out.

She heaved her case out along with the rest of her bits and pieces and was damned if she was going to close the lid. She turned on the steps as the taxi pulled sharply away, and the lid swung down and snapped shut on its own.

Air conditioning, she decided, when she had passed through the sliding glass doors, was the best thing ever invented. She put down her case and stood for a moment, drinking in the cool sweet air, almost chill after the heat outside. It's strange, she thought, how when you are hot you cannot believe you could ever be cold again. As when you are cold, being warm is hard to imagine. She smiled to herself, feeling better. She'd got here, hadn't she? And she picked up her case and walked past the curious, faintly hostile stares of the girls in the Don Juan bar, to the reception desk.

'Lisa Elliot. I have a reservation.' The girl pushed her a form to fill out and asked to see her passport. 'Can you tell me what room Mr Jack or John Elliot is staying in?'

The girl checked through her files and shook her head. 'I am sorry, Mr Elliot checked out two nights ago.'

Lisa lay back in her room numb with disappointment. To have come halfway across the world and miss him by only forty-eight hours! The sergeant had not told her exactly what her father was doing here, though she suspected that she might not want to know. But she had expected him to be here for some time. She took a piece of paper from her shoulder bag and unfolded it. Tuk Than. Sukhumvit Road, Bangkok. She would call in the morning.

She washed and undressed ready for bed, and out of idle curiosity switched on the television set. The previous occupant of the room had left it on the video channel and the late movie was a soft porn one. God, she thought. Sex! The world was obsessed with it. She pressed the top button on the set and caught an old episode of *Rawhide* dubbed into Thai. The dialogue bore no relation to the lip movements, and it seemed incongruous to see a young Clint Eastwood squawking in a guttural alien tongue. She lay down on the bed, head propped against a pillow, and watched with amusement, eyes growing heavy as she drifted in a state that was neither sleep nor wakefulness. From somewhere deep in the memory of the Lisa she had been, she seemed to recall having seen a rerun of this episode as a child. She tried to remember how it went, but it was as elusive as her father, not quite tangible and always just out of reach.

She woke at eight to the hiss of the television, the screen a shifting mass of white dots. She dragged herself wearily out of bed and wondered if she had slept at all. She still felt just as tired as the night before. A coffee and croissant in the pizzeria downstairs helped to revive her, though she became uncomfortably aware of the many eyes that watched her here in the hotel lobby. Men and women seemed equally curious, though

PETER MAY

there was an intent in the dark eyes of some men that frightened her. She supposed it was unusual for a young Western
girl to be on her own in a place like this.

Back in her room, she asked the hotel exchange to get her
a number for Tuk Than. She rang several times over the next
hour, but there was no reply. Her spirits, which had lifted a
little with the morning, sank once again, and she began to
think this whole trip was nothing more than a wild goose
chase. She lay back on the bed and wondered what to do. She
could always phone later, or even call round to the house. In
the afternoon, perhaps. But what would she do till then? The
city scared her. A place like Bangkok, a girl on her own.

Oh, to hell, she thought. I've come all this way, I'm damned
if I'm going to spend the entire time sitting in a hotel room.
And, anyway, if I'm ever to be a reporter . . . She remembered
reading in a magazine on the plane an article about the Grand
Palace. So she showered, and changed, put on her make-up, then
went boldly down to the lobby and left her key at reception.

The city beckoned through the glass doors, a bustling street
thick with traffic and people. She summoned all her courage
and went out, and the heat wrapped around her like a hot,
wet blanket. The heat. She had forgotten about the heat, and
her courage wilted in it.

'Taxi?' One of several men loitering in a group outside
approached her, touts trying to scrape a living from the tourists. He leered at her suggestively.

She hesitated, for a moment about to turn back to the safety of the hotel, then looked him straight in the eye and said with a confidence she did not feel, 'Yes, please.'

He seemed surprised. 'You wait.' And he went down on to the pavement and waved an arm at the passing stream of cars. Almost immediately a white car with a taxi sign on the roof pulled in at the kerbside and a good-looking young man, with short, dark hair and a disarming smile, leaned across from the driver's side and rolled down the window. The two men had a brief exchange, then the driver nodded and got out the car. 'This man will take you,' the tout said.

Lisa felt quite pleased with herself. Perhaps she would manage better than she had hoped. She passed the tout a few coins and he grinned and nodded his thanks. The young driver opened the rear passenger door for her. And now she was surprised. Things were looking up after the unpleasant experience of the night before. She smiled and got in, grateful for the cool of the air-conditioned interior. 'Thank you.'

The driver spoke a polite, stilted English and, she thought, he really was very good-looking. 'Where would you like to go?'

'I have some time to kill. I thought I'd see the Grand Palace.'

'You are tourist, then?'

'Sort of.' And she supposed that's what she was, although it was not what she had come for.

'If you want, I take you on tour of Bangkok.'

She hesitated. That might come quite expensive. But she had money, hadn't she? She could afford it. 'Why not? Starting at the Grand Palace.'

'Okay.' He smiled at her and leaned on the back of the seat, waiting, as though expecting her to say something more. Then, 'How much?' he asked.

She frowned. 'Well – just set the meter.'

His smile widened and he shook his head at her naivety. 'In Bangkok,' he said, 'all taxis have meters. But they never work. You must agree price before or else driver will rip you off.'

'Oh.' She was not at all used to this. 'Well – how much do you want?'

He raised an eyebrow. 'You want me rip you off?'

She laughed at his directness. 'I'd rather you didn't. But I've really no idea how much.'

He began to laugh. 'You are too innocent, lady.' He thought for a moment. 'Two hundred baht, and I take you anywhere you want for the day.'

She made a quick mental calculation and was pleasantly surprised. 'Alright. But you decide where we go. I really wouldn't have a clue. Do you want the money now?'

'No, you pay after.' He put the car in gear, slipped out into the traffic and glanced at her in the mirror. 'You know anything about Bangkok?'

'Well, no, not really,' Lisa admitted. 'Except it's the capital of Thailand and Thailand used to be called Siam.'

He shrugged. 'Is a start.' He talked as he drove. 'You know that Bangkok is only what foreigners call our city?' She shook her head. 'In Thai it means place of olives , but it is only small part of the city. You want to know real name?'

'Well, yes, I suppose I should.'

Grinning, he took a deep breath . . .

'*Krungthepmahanakhornbowornrattanakosinmahintarayuthaya-mahadilokpopnparatratchathaniburiromudomratchaniwetmahasa-than.*'

She giggled. 'You're kidding!'

'No,' he said solemnly. 'That is official name. But many Thai people smoke cigarettes and have no breath left to say this name, so we call it Krung Thep for short – the city of angels.' Lisa was not at all sure that he wasn't pulling her leg. There was such mischief in those smiling eyes in the mirror. 'My name is Sivara,' he said. 'If you tell me your name I don't keep calling you lady.'

'I'm Lisa.'

'Lisa. This is good name.'

Sivara parked the car off Maharaj Road and walked her through the Grand Palace. Wide, elegant squares flanked by grand buildings and temples – built in the Ratanakosin style, he told her – inlaid with glittering mosaics of glass and ceramic and gold and precious stones. Giant statues of colourful Thai warriors guarded every flight of steps, every entrance. A long and elaborate fresco mural lined the inside walls of the compound in the shade of arched colonnades – the Thai version of the Indian epic Ramayana. He took her to the adjoining Wat Phra Keo. 'The Temple of the Emerald Buddha,' he said.

An armed guard stood in the doorway. A sign warned that visitors must not take photographs of the Buddha, and rolls of film ripped from the cameras of tourists who had ignored the warning hung from a wooden rack just inside. 'Can we go in?' Lisa asked.

'Of course. But you must take off shoes first and never point feet directly at Buddha. It is great insult.' They left their shoes at the door, walked into the cool of the wat and knelt on the cold stone tiles. The Buddha sat high up in a glass case draped with a fine shawl. 'To keep Buddha warm,' Sivara said.

Lisa stifled a laugh. 'Warm! In this heat?'

'It is our cool season,' he said gravely. 'The King himself changes the robe on the Buddha at start of each season.'

'God, if this is cool, I'd hate to be here when it's hot.' She looked up at the pale green carved Buddha and wondered if offering it a prayer might help her find her father. 'Is it really solid emerald?'

Sivara smiled knowingly. 'It says so in the guidebooks.' He paused then added, 'Actually, is made of jasper, like jade. Come, I take you to Wat Traimit, the temple of the Golden Buddha.'

He parked opposite the temple in Charoen Krung Road, in front of a row of dark shops that disappeared into the crumbling interiors of dilapidated buildings. Incurious Asian faces peered out from the gloom. The temple itself was an undistinguished building set in a small, scrubby garden. Inside, it was dark and smelled of burning incense, and against one wall sat the Golden Buddha. It stood a massive three metres high and shone brightly as though burning. Lisa looked at it in awe. 'It's never solid gold!'

She did not notice how Sivara ran appraising eyes over her body as she stared at the Buddha. 'Five and half tons,' he said. 'Solid gold. It was discovered only thirty years ago. It had skin of plaster and when it was being moved it fell and broke and they found gold underneath.'

'It must be worth a fortune.'

'Buddha does not measure life by wealth,' Sivara said. 'Is not important.'

She watched Thai worshippers buying small flakes of gold leaf which they stuck to images of the Buddha, and she turned to Sivara. 'If he places so little value on wealth, why is it all his images are made of gold or precious stone, or stuck with gold leaf?'

His smile faded. 'You have seen enough now? I take you back.' He turned away, out of the temple and across the road towards the car. She chased after him.

'Sivara, Sivara, I'm sorry – I didn't mean to give offence.'

'If I come to your country I do not say such things of your God,' he said.

Lisa said, 'I'm not sure I have a God.'

In the taxi she said, 'It must be about lunchtime. Can you take me somewhere to eat? You must know the best places.'

'Of course.' But he did not smile, and the mischief had gone from his eyes.

He pulled in on Siam Square, near the station, and pointed out a large noodle shop called Co-Co at the corner of one of the many alleyways leading off the square. 'Very good Chinese food,' he said.

'That sounds great.' She started to get out of the car, but he made no move. 'What about you?'

'I wait in car.'

'Oh, don't be silly, you must come and eat with me.'

'Is too expensive for me.'

'Not when I'm paying, it's not. Oh, come on.' She gave him a playful push on the shoulder. 'I don't want to eat on my own, and I wouldn't know what to order anyway.'

For a moment she thought he was going to refuse, then he turned and smiled, the mischief back in his eyes. 'How can I refuse beautiful lady like you?'

Sivara ordered, and endless bowls of rice and noodles and chicken and beef and fish in various sauces arrived at their table. They drank sake and laughed a lot at the way she was frightened to try things, and all the questions she asked before she would even take a taste. 'It's not like the Chinese restaurants at home,' she said.

She felt herself getting quite light-headed with the sake. She was relaxed and felt good for the first time in weeks. He told her about himself and his family, eyes sparkling at her the whole time. Fine, dark, laughing eyes. She laughed when he told her about his young brother who would arrange himself on the pavement, outside one of the big tourists hotels, early in the morning, so that he appeared to have no legs. He easily filled the bowl he placed in front of him, appealing to the fragile conscience of affluent Westerners. And at the end of the day he would get up and walk away with his takings on stiff legs. Sivara got up and did a stiff-legged walk around their table to impersonate his brother.

When he sat down again and her laughter had subsided, he looked at her very seriously and said, 'You really are very beautiful, Lisa.' And he slipped a hand over hers. She withdrew her hand slowly, not unflattered by his interest. And it occurred to her, through a warm haze of alcohol, that she had been picked up and was paying for the privilege.

Sivara ordered more sake and Lisa drank and felt giddy. But she didn't care. She was having a good time and Sivara was lovely. She suddenly remembered that she had not phoned David as he had asked. To hell with David, she thought. Sivara talked and talked. How he would like to visit England and America. He had seen so much of these countries on television and would really like to go. But he was only a taxi driver. He could not afford such a trip. Travel was for the wealthy. And Lisa told him how this was the first time she had ever been out of England. When the bill came she paid and asked, 'What shall we do now?'

'We could go to floating market at Thonburi,' he said. 'You like that?'

'Oh, yes, let's. Is it far?'

'We go by boat, on the *klong*s. But you must pay.'

'Oh.' She looked at the dwindling number of notes in her purse. 'I need to change some more money.'

'Is not problem. I will take you to money changer.'

In a small, airless room at the back of a shop in a nearby sidestreet, an obsequious little man with no hair and one tooth changed a traveller's cheque for her. Sivara sat waiting impassively in a chair at the back of the room, looking cool in his neatly pressed white shirt. 'Is this the proper rate of exchange?' she asked him.

He nodded gravely. 'It is very good rate, Lisa. This man is friend of mine.'

Lisa didn't much like the look of Sivara's friend, but he passed her a bundle of notes in exchange for her cheque and didn't even ask to see her passport. It was certainly simpler than going to the bank and, she thought, he had a funny face. When he closed his mouth his single yellow peg of a tooth protruded over his lower lip. But she was glad to get back to the taxi, sitting in the front now beside Sivara, as they drove down to the landing stage at the Oriental Hotel.

Sivara got them a *hang yao* and told her she would have to pay the driver, but that he had got her a very good price. She paid and sat behind Sivara, holding on to his shoulders as the long sleek boat powered its way down the Chao Phraya river and into the Klong Dao Kanong. Children, standing waist-deep in the *klong* water, waved as they passed. A boatload of saffron-robed monks smiled serenely. Lisa was exhilarated by the wind in her face, the spray from the water, the sights and sounds of an alien culture; teak houses on stilts, rickety bridges, and the dozens of boats, sampans, water-buses and rice barges that trafficked up and down the *klongs*. Old ladies, wearing reed-woven sunhats like upturned lampshades, sold hot meals from floating kitchens.

The floating market at Thonburi was thick with tourists and boats selling all manner of goods, from vegetables and live chickens to opium pipes and herbal remedies. Dozens of boats bobbed gently together on the water, owners engaged in lively conversations with competitors, or bargaining with potential buyers.

Sivara got their driver to cruise slowly among the boats so that Lisa could look at everything. She bought them some fruit, a straw hat for herself and, despite his protests, a couple of shirts for Sivara. 'That's for being so good to a stranger in Bangkok,' she said and kissed him lightly on the cheek. She did not see the look in his eyes, only the smile.

They bought drinks from one boat. A concoction of various fruit juices and Thai whisky. Lisa was a little dubious. But Sivara encouraged her. 'Is very good. Very refreshing,' he said. 'You like it.' And she did. It was cold and sweet, and she felt a glow across her cheeks. 'Another?'

'No,' she laughed. 'I think I've had quite enough. I feel as though I'm getting very drunk.' But more than the drink, she was intoxicated by the seductive allure of the Orient, by her new undreamed-of freedom, by the good-looking young Asian man who so clearly found her attractive.

On the way back she put her arms around his waist and rested her head on his back. 'I'm so tired,' she whispered. 'So tired.' He turned his head to look back and smile at her, and he squeezed one of her hands. She barely noticed.

It was almost dark when they got back to the Oriental landing stage, and Lisa put her arm through his as they walked to the taxi. 'I have to go back to the hotel,' she said, suddenly remembering. 'I have to make a phone call.' She turned to him as he opened the car door for her. 'Thank you, Sivara. I've had a really lovely day.'

He smiled, his hand brushing her arm. 'I enjoy it, too, Lisa.'

She got in beside him and they drove through the dark streets in silence. She felt pleased with herself. For a novice in these matters she had managed very well on her first day in the mysterious East. She was even beginning to get used to the heat.

They seemed to be driving for a long time through dark, narrow streets, away from the main thoroughfares. The buildings on either side were very old and shrouded in night. 'Are we nearly there?' she asked.

'I must collect parcel from friend first,' Sivara said. 'Will not be long.' And for the first time she had a dark sense of foreboding.

'Couldn't you drop me off first?'

'Quicker this way.'

'Please, Sivara. I must make that phone call.'

'Shut up!' His voice was sharp and ugly and hit her like a slap in the face. Her heart was thumping.

'Sivara, stop the car, I want to get out.' She grabbed the

wheel, and he turned and struck her viciously across the mouth with the back of his hand. The blow knocked her sideways and she struck her head hard against the side window. She felt dizzy and sick and her mind was fogged with fear and confusion. Why was he doing this? He had been so lovely, so kind.

The car turned into a blind alley and jerked to a halt. She heard the driver's door open, and then he was round at the passenger side, opening the door and dragging her out. She tried to pull away, but felt weak and sick and he was much too strong, hands holding her wrists with a grip like a vice.

'Sivara, please . . .' He threw her back against the wall and she struck her head hard and slid to the ground. She was aware of him grabbing her bag and taking out her passport and purse. He dropped the passport and pushed the purse into a back pocket and threw the bag away. Then he was standing over her, undoing the buckle of his belt. The mischief in his eyes had been replaced by lust and malice.

'English slut!' he hissed.

She tried to get to her feet, but he grabbed the neck of her T-shirt, ripping it away and exposing her breasts. Then he punched her in the face and her world went black.

The doctor looked cool in his white suit. He had cropped, silver hair and a wrinkled, brown face. He was carrying a small black bag in his right hand. Tuk was waiting for him in the hall at the foot of the stairs. He led him through to the study and poured them both a drink. He could smell the spice of the doctor's aftershave. 'Well?' he asked, and handed him his drink.

The doctor took a sip. 'She is concussed, of course. Has several nasty contusions about her face and wrists. But nothing serious, nothing broken. She is also in a state of shock. She should rest for several days.'

Tuk nodded thoughtfully. 'And?' he asked.

'There was no intercourse,' the doctor said.

'How can you be sure?'

The doctor smiled. 'Because she is still intact.'

Tuk was surprised. A virgin! 'What age would you say she is?'

The doctor shrugged. 'Late teens – eighteen, nineteen.'

'You will make your report to the police, of course.'

'Of course.'

Lisa opened her eyes and saw nothing but white, a brightness that almost blinded her. She felt as though her head were stuffed with cotton wool, and through it there was a distant sensation of pain. She closed her eyes and opened them again more slowly. This time, form gradually took shape in the light. Something dark passing in long, slow sweeps over her face. She tried to focus. It was a ceiling fan turning lazily in the heat. Now she felt the draught of it. As she tried to lift her head the pain drew closer, but she saw that she was in a large, square room with white walls and slatted wardrobes. Full-length white curtains were drawn on tall windows and a curious scent of spice hung in the air. A big soft bed enfolded her, her head sunk deep in a voluminous pillow. And then she realized that under the sheets she was naked, and she had a momentary, flickering image of Sivara standing over her, a face distorted by lust.

But full recollection was slow in returning. It came in fragments, pieces of a jigsaw that made no sense. Then, suddenly, the whole picture was clear to her, the full horror returning, and she tried to sit up, panic rising in her like bile. But her body would not respond.

She heard a door open, but could not raise her head far enough to see who was there. Then a man's face leaned over her, smiling, kindly, with fine black hair brushed back from his forehead. 'And how are you now, my dear?'

'Where am I?' The fear was clear in her voice.

'Now, you mustn't be afraid.' He sat lightly on the edge of the bed and carefully brushed the hair from her eyes. 'You are quite safe. My name is Tuk Than. You were coming to see me, I think. The police found my name and address in your handbag. When they contacted me, of course I insisted they bring you here. Unfortunately your passport and money were gone with your assailant.'

She looked at him, trembling. 'Did he – am I . . .?'

'The doctor says you were not violated, my dear. Perhaps he was only after your money. Perhaps he was interrupted. We will only know when they catch him. Now you must rest. The doctor has given you a sedative and we shall see how you are in the morning.' He rose from the bed. 'Perhaps, though, you might tell me what a pretty young English lady was doing carrying my name and address around in her handbag.'

'I'm looking for my father.'

He frowned. 'Your father?'

'Yes. Jack Elliot. I was told you might know where he is.'

And a shadow fell across Tuk's face.

CHAPTER TWENTY-TWO

*An estimated one hundred and twenty thousand Vietnamese troops
are making sweeping advances in the face of crumbling resistance from
the Revolutionary Army of Kampuchea. Outnumbered in the region of
three to one, almost half the nineteen divisions of Kampuchean troops
committed to the border by the Khmer Rouge have been encircled in
two massive flanking movements by the Vietnamese – at the Parrot's
Beak in Svay Rieng and the Fishhook in Kampong Cham. Independent
sources say that Kampuchean tanks and artillery are being destroyed
by superior Vietnamese firepower, and there have been reports that
Khmer Rouge cadres are being murdered by their own troops rebelling
against what is said to be intolerable repression within the armed
forces. A brief silence. This news comes to you in the World Service
of the BBC.*

Slattery switched off the shortwave radio and stowed it away
in his backpack. He looked grimly at Elliot. 'Looks like we
could be running out of time, chief.'

They had slipped from one year into the next almost without
noticing. But 1979 had not brought them much nearer to their
target. From their vantage point high up among the trees

they looked down on the main road east from the northern town of Sisophon. Their progress had been much slower than Elliot had allowed for. Tangled subtropical jungle had reduced their advance south to only a few kilometres a night. Almost impenetrable in places, it had forced them to take several detours to find a way through. The previous night they had reached Sisophon and made a wide sweep round the eastern flank to avoid risking a possible encounter with Khmer Rouge patrols. Having reached a point several kilometres south-east of the town, they laid up during the hours of daylight, catching a few hours' sleep and watching the activity on the road below. Armoured vehicles and trucks full of troops had been heading south-east to Siem Reap all day. The war with Vietnam was not going well, and the Khmer Rouge were having to commit more and more troops to the conflict.

It was dark now, and Elliot was examining several maps by the light of a pencil torch. McCue was on watch. Elliot acknowledged Slattery's observation with a solemn nod. 'We're going to have to make Siem Reap by tomorrow night at the latest. If they're moving troops in large numbers they may start to move civilians. I don't want to get there and find Ang's people gone.'

'Shit, chief, that must be a good seventy kilometres or more. How are we going to do that?'

They turned sharply as McCue slipped through the under-growth to join them from where he had been watching the road. 'There's a truck pulled up almost immediately below us.

Supply truck with a driver and two armed guards. Looks like they got a puncture.'

The truck driver glanced at the two guards smoking idly at the roadside and cursed under his breath. They would not condescend to lend him a hand to change the wheel. And he knew that while he had to drive through the night, they would be curled up in the back of the truck sleeping. He manoeuvred the large unwieldy wheel into position, lined up the holes with the bolts, and slipped it into place. Quickly, he screwed each nut as tight as it would go by hand, and then used the brace to finish the job. He lowered the jack and chucked the tools in the back.

'That's it. We'd better move,' he told the guards, and climbed up into the cab. The guards threw away their cigarettes.

From his position, lying flat in the bushes not five metres away, Slattery saw one of them hand the other his automatic and start walking towards him. *Jeez*, he thought, *he can't have seen me!* The other guard swung himself up into the back of the truck where Elliot's hand closed like a vice across his mouth, and a long blade glinted in the dark before it slipped between his ribs and into his heart.

Slattery watched the silhouette of the approaching guard until it was less than a foot away. The guard had stopped almost above him and was loosening the cord on his trousers. For a moment Slattery wondered what he was doing, and then truth dawned and he pushed his face down into the earth with sickening anticipation. A warm jet of urine splashed over his head and trickled down his neck. Slattery swore inwardly. Where the fuck was McCue! The jet lessened, became a trickle and stopped. The guard buckled at the knees and fell forward into the bushes, landing beside Slattery, eyes wide and lifeless and staring into his. Slattery looked up and saw McCue grinning down at him.

'Enjoy your shower, buddy?'

'Bastard!' Slattery hissed. 'You waited on purpose.' He shook his head, like a dog shaking off water, and moved quickly out of the bushes. Crouching, the two men ran to the back of the truck and climbed in. Elliot was bent over the prone figure of the other guard, stripping him of his black pyjamas and *kramar*. He chucked them at McCue.

'Put these on. You could almost pass for one of them in the dark.'

The driver revved the engine several times and shouted something from the cab. The three men froze and looked at one another. None of them had any Cambodian. Elliot leaned across and banged twice with his fist on the side of the truck. They waited for a tense moment, then the driver gunned the engine and the truck jolted into motion.

Slattery grabbed the chequered scarf from McCue and rubbed his stubbly wet head and neck with it vigorously. He threw it back. 'Bastard!' he said again. Elliot looked blankly from one to the other.

McCue shrugged and slipped on the black pyjama top. 'He finally got that wash he was after.'

The truck bumped and rattled over the broken surface of the road, trying to make up for lost time. Elliot prised open two of the crates stacked in the back. He whistled softly.

'Mortars!' He lifted out one of the lightweight 60mm mortar launchers and examined it. 'Chinese-made by the look.' He handed it to McCue. 'You can carry it.' And he turned to Slattery. 'You and I'll carry a couple of rounds each. We might need the firepower.'

McCue took out the dead guard's cigarettes and passed them around, and they all had their first smoke for days. After about an hour, the truck slowed and they went through a small neglected-looking town. Broken-down shops with corrugated-iron roofs. Decaying houses and empty gaps. There were no lights, no signs of life except for a dog that bayed at them as they passed. McCue sat up at the back beside the open canvas flap, in black pyjama top, chequered scarf wrapped loosely around his neck, AK-47 resting across his knees. Elliot and Slattery lay flat on the floor beside the stiffening corpse.

'Alright,' McCue said, and they sat up again as the town receded into the night.

'What place was that, chief?'

'Must have been Kralanh.' Elliot squinted at his map in the torchlight. 'That would put us about halfway to Siem Reap.' He checked his watch. 'It's early yet. We could be there by midnight.'

*

The driver turned his truck towards the lights in the centre of town, a refuelling stop for the convoy south.

Siem Reap was his home town, and a deep sadness ran through him at the ghost it had become. He remembered, as a boy, bathing in the palm-shaded river that ran through the town. People had loved to bathe in it then, dipping themselves in the milk chocolate-coloured water to cool themselves in the noontide heat. The rickety waterwheels that had once turned and creaked all day, feeding water into a crazy, wasteful network of bamboo conduits to water the little pocket handkerchief-sized gardens, stood idle now, broken and abandoned. The houses too stood empty, fallen into disrepair, perched on sinking stilts above long-decayed piles of garbage. Once, in a workshop here, Cambodian craftsmen had etched out scenes from the Ramayana on leather murals, squatting on the ground, dressing and marking out the hide with chalk and then punching out the patterns. They had enjoyed the patronage of the King.

The driver supposed he was lucky to be alive, but all that life held for him now was a handful of memories, like fading snapshots in a family album. A past that could never be recaptured, a future he was afraid to think about. He pulled the truck into the line of vehicles awaiting refuelling, and supposed he ought to try to find a replacement for his spare tyre, or at least attempt to have it repaired. The chances of either were slim, but if he had another puncture on the road he could at least say that he had tried, and perhaps they would not shoot him.

He switched off the engine and banged on the back of the cab. 'You can get out and stretch your legs if you want,' he shouted. 'We'll be stopped for a while.' He jumped down on to the road and breathed in the cool night air of his home town. But even the air did not smell the same anymore. In his memory it had always been laced with the scent of *nuoc mam*, a pungent fish sauce that smelled foul and tasted wonderful. It was a taste he had not had on his tongue for years.

No sign of the guards. He banged several times on the side of the truck. 'Hey, wake up guys!' When he got round the back he pulled out the pin to drop the loading flap. As it swung down, the naked body of the dead guard tumbled on to the road, and the driver screamed.

Elliot, Slattery and McCue moved quickly through the forest, eyes scanning the moonlit gloom for the tiniest movement, ears straining to pick up the slightest sound. Each held his automatic ready, for everywhere here there were signs of human activity. Many trees had been felled and there was a criss-cross network of footpaths and cart tracks. Much of the undergrowth had been hacked away, creating access for more tree felling. From time to time they came across piles of cut and stripped trunks awaiting transport. The moonlight splashed down through the thinned-out forest in irregular patches, like liquid silver, but they stuck as far as possible to the shaded areas.

They had dropped, one by one, from the back of the truck

as it neared Siem Reap, and regrouped in the trees. Elliot had used his compass and the stars to fix, as best he could, their position. According to the refugees' accounts, the commune where Ang Serey and her daughter were being held lay four to five kilometres north-east of Siem Reap, almost within sight of the temples of Angkor Wat. Beyond the trees, in what had once been open savannah, work had begun on digging a new irrigation network to create more paddies for increased rice production. Further to the east, a new dam was being built to feed the irrigation canals, all part of the Khmer Rouge grand plan to turn Cambodia, now Democratic Kampuchea, into an agrarian Stone Age society based on a self-sufficient rice economy.

They had made steady progress through the woods for nearly an hour when the sound of a vehicle engine stopped them dead in their tracks. It came from somewhere away to their right. At a signal from Elliot they fanned out through the trees, treading cautiously in the direction of the sound. The ground began to fall away, the trees grew more sparse, and they dropped flat as the lights of a truck raked the ground below. A wide open plain stretched ahead in the moonlight, partially flooded and divided into neat rectangles marked out by irrigation ditches under construction. Along the near perimeter ran a winding dirt track, and it was here that the truck bumped and clattered its way over ruts and potholes. Apart from the driver it appeared empty. It passed below within fifty metres.

When it had gone they moved back up into the trees and continued east, following the line of the road. McCue again took up point, moving silently and carefully through the shadowed areas, stopping every twenty or thirty seconds to check out the lie of the land ahead. After a while the ground started to rise steeply and they followed it upwards.

Now Elliot saw McCue crouch down suddenly and signal them to stop. Still crouching, he sidled to his left, then waved them forward again, gesturing that they should keep low. They approached with great care to finally draw level and find themselves looking down on a collection of huts, some raised on stilts, around a small compound. Half a dozen oxen stirred restlessly in a pen beside a large hut raised only two or three feet from the ground. A few metres away was a second, smaller hut, raised to the same level. Facing them across the compound, about a dozen long huts stood high on stilts that rose two or three metres above piles of refuse, sturdy bamboo ladders climbing to small open doorways. The roofs were thatched with dry palm fronds. To the far right, looking out over the fields, and with a view of the compound and the approaching road, stood a rickety watchtower. They could see the silhouette of a guard leaning on the rail smoking.

Elliot checked the layout against the rough map he had drawn based on the refugee accounts Ang had acquired. 'This is it,' he whispered. 'The big hut houses the cadres. There are about half a dozen of them. The one next to it is the guard hut. The civilians are in those long huts across the compound.

According to my information there are ten or twelve armed guards at any given time. As well as the one in the watchtower, there are usually another two on perimeter patrol.'

Slattery whistled softly. 'That's a lot of bodies, chief.'

Elliot said, 'We have an advantage over them. Their function is to keep people in, not out.' He checked his watch. Nearly 0200 hours. There was no sign of life from the cadres' hut, but a thin line of light marked the door of the guard hut, and through the silence came the faint sound of voices. Elliot turned to McCue. 'Check out the perimeter, numbers and positions of guards, and report back.' McCue nodded, took off his backpack, laid it carefully down with the mortar and slipped off through the trees.

'What's the plan, chief?'

Elliot was thoughtful for a moment. 'We can't afford to get involved in a firefight with ten or more guards. We'd be heavily outnumbered, wouldn't stand a chance. We'll have to remove the perimeter guards one at a time and then take out the guard hut in a oner.'

'Mortar?'

Elliot shook his head. 'Can't be sure of a direct hit. And if we miss, we lose the advantage of surprise. It'll have to be grenades.'

Slattery grinned. 'That's for me, chief. No troubles.'

Elliot thought for a moment. Then he said, 'Alright. As soon as you've put them out of commission I'll let off at the cadres' hut with the mortar. I've got four shots at it.' He smiled. 'Bound to get it with one of them.'

They waited nearly fifteen minutes before McCue crept back through the trees. 'Two guards, plus the one in the tower.'

'Can you take them?' Elliot asked.

McCue nodded. 'The guy in the tower's going to be tricky. But, yeah, I can take them.'

'Okay. We'll not move till we see you up there, and you can cover us when we move in.'

They spent another ten minutes going over it all, twice, in detail, then Elliot checked his watch. 'Alright, go.' And McCue slid away into the night, still clad in black pyjamas and chequered scarf.

The murmur of voices from the guard hut drifted across the compound on the warm night air as McCue slipped through the trees and into the shadow of the civilian huts. He ran softly among the stilts, making his way to the east side of the compound where he had seen one of the guards sitting on a woodpile, his AK-47 laid carelessly among the logs beside him. He was still there, striking a match to light a cigarette, and McCue saw his face flicker briefly in the light. The guard drew deeply on his cigarette and sighed, contemplating without enthusiasm the long hours of night watch ahead. He heard the faintest sound, like a whisper in the wind, and a chill ran through him as the long, lethal blade of McCue's hunting knife slid into his heart.

McCue pulled him backwards over the logpile and laid him out in the shadows. He lifted his AK-47, checked that the magazine was fully loaded, and left his own M16 beside the body. Then he crouched for several moments, listening and watching. There was no indication from the tower that the guard there had seen or heard anything.

Bent almost double, McCue took long, loping strides back into the shadow of the huts, and started to work his way round the edge of the compound to the west side where the second guard was posted. He was in his element, high on adrenalin, a born killer working in the dark as he always had in the tunnels. One on one. Always, until just seconds before the kill, he would be almost rigid with tension, and then in those last seconds every muscle relaxed and he felt warm and good, like that moment of letting go when you make love to a woman.

He circled the stinking pile of refuse behind the guard hut, and drifted back into the shade of the trees, moving freely round to the west flank. But the guard was gone. McCue froze, then dropped to his haunches, searching for any sign of movement among the shadows. Nothing. Where had he gone? He heard a twig snap underfoot and turned to find the guard almost on top of him. The man had his rifle slung across his back and was preoccupied with retying the cord of his trousers. The thought flashed through McCue's mind that all these guys seemed to do was piss. The guard did not see him until the last second, would almost certainly have walked into him if McCue had not risen from the ground like a black ghost. The Cambodian had no time to draw breath before McCue's blade slid up through his rib cage. He fell forward, and McCue held him for a moment in an embrace of death, slowly withdrawing the knife before lowering him gently to the ground.

McCue took a moment to steady himself. That had been too close for comfort. He wiped the blade clean and resheathed the knife. Through the trees he saw that the guard in the tower was still smoking. There was no way he could approach the tower unseen or, even if he could, climb to the platform unheard. He took a deep breath, and the tension seeped back into his muscles. He adjusted the scarf at his neck to hide the jungle camouflage beneath the black pyjama top, and walked out from the shade of the trees into the naked moonlight of the open compound.

From their position among the trees above the commune, Elliot and Slattery saw a guard approach the tower. Elliot tensed. 'Where's McCue? Something must have gone wrong.'

Slattery grinned. 'Nothing wrong, chief. You're looking at him.'

Elliot looked hard at the figure crossing the compound. 'Jesus,' he whispered, 'that guy's got balls.'

'Time I moved,' Slattery said. He hesitated. 'Anything goes wrong, chief, it's been nice knowing you.'

'Just make sure nothing goes wrong, you ugly bastard.'

Slattery grinned and slipped off through the trees. Elliot felt the seed of fear growing in his gut. But he knew that fear was not such a bad thing. It was when you stopped being afraid that you would die.

From his platform high above the compound, the remaining guard saw McCue approach. 'What's up?' he called. The figure below merely waved in response. The guard frowned. What was going on? He didn't recognize the approaching guard. The face always seemed to be in shadow. The figure disappeared below the tower and he heard the creak of the ladder. He went to the open trap and watched the figure climb up towards him.

'What is it? What's wrong?' He still couldn't see the man's face. Who was it?

Almost at the top, McCue held up a hand for the guard to help him up. The guard obliged and found himself looking into a strange face that smiled in the dark. The questions that filled his head went unanswered, and death rattled briefly in his throat. McCue rolled him to one side and picked up the cigarette that had fallen from his mouth. It was still wet with the dead man's saliva as he took a single draw and threw it over the side. He unslung his automatic and crossed to the rail that gave him a commanding view of the compound. A stalky, oddly familiar figure was strolling across the open ground towards the guard hut. It was Slattery, McCue realized, humming to himself as he walked, as if he was taking a casual stroll along Bondi Beach. McCue's jaw slackened with disbelief as he recognized the soft strains of Waltzing Matilda. 'Mad sonofabitch!' he whispered.

In the hut, four guards sat around a table playing cards by the light of an oil lamp. The others lay sleeping on bunks around the walls. One of the players lifted his head and frowned as he heard a tuneless voice softly humming a strange melody. They all looked up as the door opened and Slattery stood framed in the doorway, grinning.

'Good day,' he said and rolled two hand grenades into the centre of the hut. He slammed the door shut and took several steps back, hearing the clatter of panic inside before the grenades went off, blowing the door outwards. He felt the force of the blast, but stood his ground before swinging his M16 round and stepping back into the doorway. He emptied the magazine into the confusion of smoke and destruction in two sweeps of the room, quickly banged in another and waited for the smoke to clear. His eyes flickered over broken, bleeding bodies, making a quick professional assessment. All dead.

He turned and ran back out into the compound as the door of the cadres' hut flew open and a man, half naked and still half blind with sleep, staggered out. A burst of automatic fire from the tower cut him down, and Slattery heard the soft whistle of a mortar shell. He threw himself flat and heard the shell explode just behind the hut. The bugger's missed, he thought. But he didn't get up, still pressing himself flat in the dust and listening for the second shell. He heard shouts of fear and confusion from inside the hut, and there was another burst of fire from the tower. Come on, Elliot! He gritted his teeth and covered his head with his arms as the second shell whispered through the warm night and ploughed into the roof of the hut. The explosion sent large splinters of wood singing out across the compound.

The dust hung in the air like silver mist in the moonlight. Slattery got slowly to his feet and looked around him, but could see very little. McCue shinned quickly down from the tower, collected his M16 and joined him.

'Jeez,' Slattery said. 'It's so quiet it's eerie.' He looked towards the civilian huts, but there was no sound, no sign of movement. 'Where is everybody?'

A tall figure walked towards them, through the settling dust, from the other side of the compound. Elliot looked grim. He dropped their backpacks at their feet and glanced round.

'Sure we got the right place, chief?'

Serey had awoken from a shallow sleep with the first explosions of the hand grenades, and wondered if she had been dreaming. Then bursts of automatic fire had sent chills of fear through her. All the women in the hut were awake now, sitting up and staring with frightened eyes in the dark. She had felt Ny move at her side.

'What is it?'

'I don't know.'

Then two huge explosions had rocked the whole commune. Their hut had shaken on its stilts. Ny held tight to her mother's arm. Still no one in the hut moved, and a deep silence followed. Then the sound of voices from somewhere across the compound. Men's voices. Strange voices, speaking in a strange tongue. There was a further silence, then a loud call. 'Ang Serey.' Ny's fingers tightened around her arm and she thought it was the voice of death calling her. 'Ang Ny,' the voice called this time, and Ny's eyes opened wide with fear. Mother and daughter clung to each other, too afraid to move.

'Serey, Ny.' The voice was insistent. 'We have come to take you away. Come out.'

Confusion penetrated the fear. Serey frowned. Now she recognized the words. The man was calling in English. A language she had not heard for four years, a language whose words she had never dared utter for fear of betraying a background that would have meant certain death.

'It's a trick, Mother,' Ny whispered. 'It must be a trick.'

A murmur ran among the other women in the hut, their eyes all on Serey and Ny. 'Go,' one of them said, 'or they will kill us all.' But still mother and daughter could not move.

'Serey, your husband Yuon sent us.' The voice again. And Serey knew for certain it must be a trick.

'Go! In the name of Buddha, go!' the woman hissed. The hands of other women pushed them towards the door.

Ny took her mother's hand. 'We have no choice.' They rose up and the others shrank away. Serey thought, if I am to die, I will die with dignity. But her heart wept for Ny.

The men in the compound looked from hut to hut, searching for a response. Then the shrunken figures of Serey and Ny appeared at the door of one of them, and started down the ladder. When they reached the bottom they stood and looked at the three soldiers in amazement.

'Jesus,' Slattery said. 'They're little more than skeletons.'

Elliot turned to McCue and pulled the chequered scarf away from his neck. 'Get rid of those.'

McCue obliged, slipping quickly out of the black pyjamas

to reveal his jungle camouflage. Elliot walked over to the two women and was stunned by the appearance of the mother. Fleshless yellow skin stretched tightly across every bone, arms and legs flawed by open sores, grey hair thin and matted. A shrunken wreck of a human being. He was reminded of the photographs he had seen of pitiful souls in Belsen and Auschwitz. The girl looked fitter, stronger, a lustre in her hair. Perhaps youth had provided her with a resilience that her mother had lacked. And, yet, while Serey's eyes seemed dead, Ny's burned brightly with something he could not put a name to.

He spoke softly to Serey.

'My name is Elliot. I've been paid by Yuon to bring you out of Cambodia.' He paused. 'Do you understand me?' She nodded, but the eyes were still dead. He looked at Ny. 'And your daughter?'

Ny said, 'I understand.'

Elliot was relieved. A language barrier would have made things difficult. 'We must leave this place quickly. Our guns will have been heard for many kilometres. There will be soldiers here very soon.'

He took Serey gently by the arm and led them across the compound to where McCue and Slattery stood watching. Both were kitted up, ready to go. They too were shocked by Serey's appearance.

'Do you know where your son is?' Elliot asked her, and the first flicker of life appeared in her eyes.

'He is in Phnom Penh,' she said.

Elliot cursed inwardly. 'Then we can do nothing for him.'

There was no emotion in her voice as she said, 'I will not leave Cambodia without him.'

Slattery nudged Elliot and nodded towards the huts. In the moonlight, men and women, young and old, were descending ladders, pathetic figures in ragged black pyjamas. Big dark eyes staring from shrunken heads, bones and joints stretching skin like crepe, blemished by sores and shrivelled by the sun. A hundred, perhaps more, pairs of feet shuffled through the dust of the compound towards them. Slattery felt the sting of tears in his eyes. These creatures were scarcely recognizable as human. 'What the hell have they been doing to people in this country?' His voice was barely a whisper.

'We've got to get out of here,' Elliot said.

'I will not leave Cambodia without my son,' Serey said again.

Elliot strapped on his backpack. 'We'll discuss that when we're safe.'

'What about them?' Slattery nodded towards the eyes that watched them with a dull curiosity and the faint light of hope.

'Well, we can't take them with us, can we?' Elliot snapped. 'They're going to have to take their chances on their own.'

'What chances?' Slattery looked at him. 'They have no chance, Jack.'

McCue suddenly broke ranks and sprinted across the compound. A figure darted through the shadows of the huts, running for his life. McCue caught him before he reached the trees and brought him crashing to the ground. He pulled him, struggling in an armlock, back across the compound. He was a young man, full-faced and well-fed. He wore the black pyjamas and red-chequered *kramar* of the Khmer Rouge. His eyes were black with fear.

Ny's heart skipped a beat as she recognized the young cadre who had come for her every night all these months. 'What do you want me to do with him?' McCue asked Elliot.

'Kill the bastard!' Slattery said and drew out his pistol.

'No!' Ny stepped forward and stopped him. The young man's knees almost buckled with relief. She was going to save him. Ny smiled a strange smile and drew Elliot's knife from its sheath. A look of disbelief flashed across the face of the cadre as she drove it deep into his belly and, with both hands, pulled it up high under his rib cage. The scream choked in his throat as blood bubbled into his mouth, and he fell dead in the dust. Ny stood, pale and trembling, and the bloody knife fell from her hands. There was not a sound as the tears welled up and spilled from her mother's eyes.

And, then, one by one, the ragged creatures that had once been men and women stepped forward to spit on the body of the cadre until it ran with saliva that glowed almost luminescent in the moonlight, like the ghost of all their suffering. Elliot picked up his knife, cleaned and sheathed it. He had seen many men die, but rarely had he felt such a sense of shock. Not for the man who had died, but for this young girl, still little more than a child, whose hatred had robbed her of her innocence, corrupting her in a single act of cold-blooded killing. He thought, she could have been my daughter.

'Elliot.' He turned. McCue's face was very pale. 'We're running out of time.'

Elliot nodded. 'Look after the old woman. I'll take the girl. Slattery, get us out of here.'

Serey glanced back over her shoulder as McCue led her away across the compound after Slattery. How many times she had dreamed of freedom, of escape. But now, with the eyes upon her of all those who had shared her misery and pain, she felt empty and sad, cheated of her moment. She wondered if any of them could ever escape from the memory. She saw the man called Elliot take Ny by the arm and lead her after them. And she turned away quickly. She had done everything she could to protect her, but it had never been enough, and now she was lost.

'Stick close to me at all times,' Elliot whispered to Ny. 'Do everything I tell you, without question.' If Ny heard, she gave no sign of it. He felt her trembling still, but she offered no resistance.

As they reached the trees, Elliot became aware of a shuffling sound that whispered in the darkness and seemed to fill the air. He turned. A hundred pairs of leathery feet padding in the dust. The whole commune was following behind. As Elliot stopped, they stopped too, their eyes upon him. He felt uncomfortable under their gaze, and a sense of shame made him angry. 'For God's sake!' he shouted. 'Don't you people understand? We can't take you with us!' They stared back in silence. Slattery, McCue and Serey stopped at the sound of his voice. Elliot turned to Serey. 'You tell them,' he said. 'Together we are dead. If each goes his own way then at least some of us will survive.'

'Why should I tell them what they already know?' she replied simply. 'You gave them their freedom, so they will follow you.'

Elliot's eyes went cold. There was no time for this. Already there would be soldiers on their way to investigate the gunfire. He drew his pistol and levelled it at the crowd. 'Then tell them that I will shoot anyone who follows us.' And he raised his pistol a little and fired a single shot over their heads. There was an involuntary ducking, a shuffling of feet.

'Hey, steady on, chief.'

Elliot ignored Slattery. 'Tell them,' he said again to Serey, single-minded, insistent.

She looked at him with contempt, then turned to the waiting eyes and spoke a few short sentences in a high, clear voice. And she, in turn, felt their contempt for her. She had betrayed them as surely as the Khmer Rouge had. She turned back to Elliot and spat in his face. 'The Khmer Rouge shamed my daughter. Now you have shamed me.'

Elliot wiped the spittle from his face with his sleeve and glanced at Slattery and McCue. There was no sympathy in their eyes. 'Fucking move!' he barked. McCue took Serey gently by the arm and led her away at a trot after Slattery.

Elliot holstered his pistol and found Ny staring at him. He hesitated a moment under her gaze then, 'You, too,' he growled, and pushed her ahead of him to hurry after the others. As he glanced back through the trees, he saw the dozens of dark figures still standing on the edge of the compound, and knew he had just sentenced them to an almost certain death.

They made slow progress through the forest. Serey and Ny were both weak, and the old woman had to stop and rest frequently, pale and breathless, a dry cough rattling in her throat. McCue gave them both water and a little food. He knew they would not be able to eat much. Stomachs shrunken by the paltry Khmer Rouge rations, conditioned to a daily intake of a few grains of rice, unable to cope with anything richer. It would be some time before they could eat a sustaining meal.

They had stopped to rest for five minutes, squatting in the cover of a dry river bed. Slattery had gone ahead to scout out the lie of the land. Serey looked at Elliot. 'Why?' she said. He frowned, not understanding. 'Why would you risk your lives to save us?'

'Your husband is paying us well.'

Her laugh was without humour, full of bitterness. 'Does he think he can buy us, too?' She looked at Ny. 'Does he think he can buy back his daughter's innocence?' Ny lowered her head, unable to meet her mother's eye. 'What value does he put on our lives?'

'He told me, everything he has,' Elliot said.

She snorted her disgust. 'Except his life and his freedom.' She shook her head. 'Time will mend a broken heart, but does he really believe he can pay for his soul?'

'Frankly, Mrs Ang, I don't know, and I really don't care,' Elliot said. 'He's paying me to do a job and I'm doing it.'

'I have already told you,' she said, 'that I will not leave without my son.'

'If he is in Phnom Penh then he is lost.'

'No. He will wait for us there.'

Elliot sighed. 'So you are going to go to Phnom Penh – on your own?'

'If I have to.'

'And how far do you think you would get?'

Her smile was serene with a fatalism that a Westerner would find hard to fathom. 'Not far, perhaps, but I will die rather than leave him.' She paused. 'But you must take Ny with you.'

'No!' Ny turned on her mother, eyes burning, and spoke rapidly in her native tongue. Then she turned to Elliot. 'I go with my mamma to Phnom Penh.'

Elliot looked at McCue, who shook his head. 'What you gonna do, Elliot? Tie them up and carry them to Thailand?'

A rustle in the undergrowth brought both men sharply back to their present danger. Elliot swung his automatic round as Slattery crawled through the thick bank of ferns overhead to drop down to the river bed beside them. He was breathing hard and sweating. 'Khmer Rouge,' he whispered. 'A dozen, maybe more. Coming this way.'

'Move!' Elliot hissed, and he pulled Ny roughly to her feet. 'Which way?' he asked Slattery.

Slattery nodded up ahead. 'Better stick to the river bed.'

'Okay, we'll follow you.'

Slattery led them, through patches of dappled moonlight, at a half-run, half-crouch, east along the stony bed of the dry stream, ferns and creepers snagging on clothes and hands and faces. Serey stumbled and fell several times, and McCue half dragged, half carried her for several hundred metres before the strain on his arms began to take its toll. He slumped back against the bank, and damp, crumbling earth showered down over both of them. Beads of sweat left tracks in the dirt on his face. Elliot and Ny caught up and stopped. McCue caught the look on Elliot's face. 'Shit, man,' he gasped. 'Got to take a breather. The old lady ain't got the legs for this, and I can't carry her for ever.' Elliot nodded and whistled softly into the darkness ahead. After a few moments, Slattery came back along the stream bed to join them.

'What's up, chief?'

'We're going to have to lie up for a while. Check our position.'

Slattery nodded and slipped over the north bank and melted silently away through the trees. Perhaps two kilometres to the west came the distant sound of automatic gunfire. Eight or ten bursts. And Elliot knew that the killing of those left behind had begun.

Slattery took a wide sweep through the trees, north then west, before crossing to the south side of the dry stream and turning east again to head back towards the others. There was no sign of the soldiers he had seen earlier. Perhaps they had headed west, back towards the commune in an attempt to cut them off. He heard sporadic fire from that direction and felt sick at the thought of those poor shambling creatures, unarmed and defenceless, being cut down as they made their hopeless breaks for freedom. They had not asked to be set free. They had not deserved to be enslaved. Perhaps death was now the only freedom they would ever know, their only possible escape.

Slattery's few moments of lapsed concentration were fatal. He missed the shadows that slipped darkly through the trees away to his left. The snap of a twig crashed into his thoughts, through the haze of pain that came from the ache in his gut. But that split-second warning was not enough. He turned just in time to see the flash of an AK-47 and feel the pain of its burst of bullets as they tore through his left thigh and knee, shattering bones and arteries. The leg buckled under him and he fell face-first into the damp earth and humus. And he thought he smelled death in its bitter odour. The pain, at first, was crippling, and he found he could not move. He heard footsteps approach cautiously through the undergrowth. He cursed his careless stupidity, his lack of professionalism. His cancer seemed such a small thing now, and he thought, in that moment, that he loved life more dearly than he had ever done before.

The initial, all-consuming pain receded now before a wave of warmth that spread upwards through him from his shattered leg. He raised his head a little and saw his automatic lying two feet away, where it had fallen. He reached forward to grasp it, but only in his mind. His body would not respond. He managed to incline his head to his left and saw six or seven figures in black pyjamas approaching, AK-47s held at the ready, dark eyes burning with a triumph fuelled by fear and confusion. They stopped, no more than two or three metres away, and looked at the prone figure on the ground. One of them stepped forward and raised his automatic. Slattery watched the barrel lift to point at him, like the finger of God passing judgement. And the sentence was death. Even in these last seconds it struck him as odd that he should think now of God, when he had not thought of God in all the years of his life. He closed his eyes as the sound of automatic fire exploded in the dark.

So this was death. He felt confused. It seemed no different from life. The pain, the heat rising in his body, the smell of the forest. He opened his eyes to see four Khmer Rouge soldiers lying dead and bleeding only a few feet away. In his confusion he thought he saw others running away through the trees. Another burst of fire brought two of them crashing down. A third swung around, returning a swift burst, before vanishing into the night.

A hand pulled Slattery gently over on to his back, and he found himself looking up into Elliot's grim, smeared face. Slattery grinned feebly. 'Strewth, chief,' he whispered, 'you took your bloody time.'

*

Elliot jumped down between McCue and the two women, and lowered the now unconscious Slattery from his shoulder into the bed of the dry stream. 'Tourniquet, quick!' There was an urgency in his voice that McCue had not heard before. His face and shirt were dark with Slattery's blood, and McCue wondered, briefly, if it was tears that glazed his eyes. But the thought did not linger. He unsheathed his knife and expertly cut away the blood-sodden trouser leg above the wounds, peeling it slowly back to reveal the shattered flesh. The full extent of the damage became apparent. He glanced at Elliot, and the look that passed between them left no room for words. He cut a strip of cloth and tied it round Slattery's upper thigh, tight enough to stop the blood that was still gouting from the wounds. Then he took out a plastic bottle of spirit and several gauze pads from his backpack to wash away the blood and clean out the wounds.

Serey and Ny watched, transfixed with horror, as McCue clipped and then tied off the severed arteries as best he could, and the fleeting security they had felt with these men evaporated into the night.

Elliot, working in fevered silence, unravelled a roll of lint and wrapped it tightly around the pads that McCue placed over the wounds. He tore the ends, running one back around the leg to join with the other and tie the bandage in place below the knee. The whole process took less than two minutes, both men ignoring the frequent bursts of gunfire that seemed increasingly nearer. Slattery's face was chalk white, his breathing shallow.

Now they could hear voices and many feet tramping through the undergrowth, not more than three or four hundred metres away. Elliot pulled Slattery into a sitting position then heaved him up over his shoulder. McCue lifted his own and Slattery's backpacks and jerked Serey to her feet. 'Listen, lady, you're going to have to run or we're all dead.'

'I help her,' Ny said, and she held and squeezed her mother's hand.

McCue nodded to Elliot. 'Go.' And they started to run, along the bed of the dry stream at first, then up over the bank and through the trees, away from the sounds of the approaching soldiers. Ny put her mother's arm around her neck and her own arm around her mother's waist, and half-dragged her after Elliot. McCue came behind, automatic held in one hand ready for use, frequently turning to glance back, eyes searching the darkness on either side. Elliot's long strides took him quickly through the forest, bending at the knees, transferring the strain of the extra weight he carried to his thighs. Within a few minutes his shoulder, arm and neck were aching. But there could be no stopping. Pain at a threshold of intensity. If you passed through it, then it became bearable, and you could live with it a little longer. His sweat almost blinded him, salt stinging his eyes. But he found a rhythm, of stride and of breathing, that carried him on for ten, perhaps fifteen minutes before his knees began to buckle and gradually his rhythm was lost, becoming a stuttering, staggering stumble.

He barely noticed how the trees had grown sparse, and was

almost surprised to emerge from the darkness on to a bright moonlit track rutted by cartwheels and pitted by the hooves of many oxen. He lost his footing and dropped to his knees, acid rising in his throat. With leaden arms, he lowered Slattery to the ground, lungs pumping hard to feed oxygen to starved and aching muscles.

He felt light-headed and sick as he heard Ny and Serey stagger up behind him. Breathless sobs caught in Serey's throat as she fell down beside him, utterly exhausted, unable to take another step. Ny was pale, her face stained and glistening with tears and sweat. Elliot looked up and saw pain in her eyes, but also courage there. McCue's whisper seemed to fill the night. 'We can't stop here!'

Elliot nodded. He took a few more seconds to catch his breath. 'How far behind us are they?'

McCue shrugged. 'Difficult to say. We may have lost them – for the moment. But we gotta keep going. I'll take the Aussie.' He stooped to heave the dead weight of Slattery on to his shoulder, and visibly buckled under the strain. Elliot dragged himself wearily to his feet, wiping sweat from his eyes, and lifted Slattery's discarded backpack. He took Serey gently by the arm and raised her upright, slipping an arm round her waist to support her. He looked at Ny, whose face gave no clue as to what was going on behind it. She reached across and took the backpack from his hand and slung it over her shoulder.

The stricken group stumbled east along the rutted path, at little more than walking pace, for ten to fifteen minutes. The path grew wider, the trees receding on either side, quite suddenly and unexpectedly opening out to reveal a large moon reflected in black water. And from myriad lakes and waterways, awesome and dark, rose the lost temples of Angkor Wat.

Serey dropped at once to her knees, pressing her palms together and bowing towards the sacred ruins. The sheer scale of the wat filled their eyes and minds, gathering itself in the distance, rising above a long, low-lying portico, its lotus-broken reflection carried on the still waters of the moon-silvered lake. Elliot glanced back through the trees, watching for movement, listening for sounds of pursuit. But he saw nothing, heard nothing. The Khmer Rouge must have assumed they would head north, rather than south towards the Wat and the dead-end shores of the Tonle Sap. The silence was broken only by the mumblings of Ang Serey as she offered prayers to the Lord Buddha. Slattery's face was a waxen, grey mask shining with sweat. His grin was a grimace as he raised his head to look out across the waters at the temples.

'Shit, chief,' he said, 'it don't hold a candle to the Sydney Opera House.'

Serey was weeping now. Ny knelt beside her, an arm around her. 'What is it, Mother?'

Slowly Serey raised her head, drawing her daughter's eyes to where a red flag hung limp in the still night air above the temples.

CHAPTER TWENTY-THREE

Elongated slats of bloodless light, like the bars of a prison cell, fell across the floor, distorted by the debris that littered it, extending upwards across a wall daubed with revolutionary slogans. They had no substance, these bars. The light of the hidden sun reflected on earth by the moon and casting only shadows. And yet they locked Hau in, as securely as if they were steel. Like fingers reaching through the darkness, they held him in their grip. It was his fear that gave them their power. The power to back him up against the wall, knees pulled into his chin, arms folded around his shins. He pulled his legs in tight as though he might somehow be able to make himself so small as to be invisible.

The night was hot and humid, but still he shivered. A broken shutter hung down across the window in the breathless dark, swinging slowly back and forth. At first he was puzzled by its motion. There was not a whisper of movement in the air. What magical energy was there at work, what hidden fingers tipping the shutters to and fro on rusted hinges? The breath of what invisible demon stirred the still night air? He wanted to scream. To shatter the fragile peace of the night. But he could raise no sound in his throat. He closed his eyes and felt hunger gnawing at his stomach like some devil eating him from the inside out. The whole room tilted towards him now.

He had found his old home as dawn broke. A pale misted dawn that allowed the world to etch itself with only a pastel imprecision upon the day. A tracery of cracks had opened up across the suburban streets, grass and weeds poking up through broken kerbstones. Once grand villas, set in secluded grounds, lay dilapidated as the first tendrils of primeval jungle reached up through devastated gardens to reclaim what man had so recently stolen and now abandoned. The house seemed only faintly familiar, a dream of a previous life. Windows and shutters had been smashed, doors ripped off. Everything of value had been taken, everything else destroyed. Every conceivable hiding place had been sought out, floorboards torn up, walls smashed. And then this broken monument to defeated imperialism had been left to rot.

Hau had shuffled despondently through the rubble, from room to room, trailing his automatic rifle on the floor behind him, hope draining from him with every step. Home – that place he had always held in his memory safe and inviolate, nourished with thoughts of his mother and father and Ny, the one place in the world he could escape to – no longer existed. Home, he realized as he stumbled through the devastation, was not a place. It was the people who filled it. And the emptiness he now found in what had once been his home cut deep into his soul, like the jagged edge of a blunt razor, bringing the searing realization that he had no home, no family, no place to go.

Now, he opened his eyes in the dark, heart pounding, the room still tilting him this way and that. And he realized that it was not the room that tilted back and forth. Nor the shutter swinging in the still air. It was his own movement as he rocked gently from heel to toe. And, suddenly, it seemed a warm, comforting movement.

He saw his AK-47 lying abandoned on the floor where he had dropped it. It seemed a strange, hard, metallic thing. A toy in a catalogue. How could such an inanimate object take life? Of course, he knew, it couldn't. Not on its own. It took him, or anyone with a will, to pull the trigger. It took intent. It took malice or jealousy or fear or greed. And he had had such intent. At once he felt shame and anger and hurt at this knowledge, and he kicked out at the rifle, sending it clattering across the room. But he could still see it in the moonlight, staring back at him, reproachful, accusing.

He picked up the dusty, threadbare teddy that lay beside him and clutched it to his breast. He'd found it lying torn and broken in a corner of what had once been his bedroom. It brought an instant comfort. It shared all his secrets, all his fears. He buried his face in its fur and immediately smelled something disturbingly familiar. It took him a moment to realize it was himself that he smelled. A smell so familiar it frightened him, unlocking a door on the past, on a lost innocence, on the boy he had once been. Who was he now? He squeezed the teddy tight. Tears sprang from his eyes, salty and stinging, and he wondered how long it would take him to die.

CHAPTER TWENTY-FOUR

Four tiny figures moved with the infinitesimal speed of crippled time along a stone causeway flanked at exact intervals by pairs of seven-headed serpents. Above them rose the towers of the wat, the moon casting their shadows long and deep, the still mildewed lakes spanned by the causeway drowning their reflections. Elliot carried Slattery over his shoulder. He felt blood soaking through his fatigues, life ebbing from the dying weight. Behind him, the smack of bare feet on cool stone, Serey leaning heavily on the arm of her daughter. The gentle clatter of McCue's webbing as he moved slowly backwards, eyes focused into the dark of the trees whose shelter they had left, seemed to fill the hot damp air. Behind them lay only darkness and silence. Ahead lay the towering emptiness of the wat, and beyond that the watery vastness of the Tonle Sap. The sheer size of everything that lay around them, that was against them, reinforced their sense of smallness.

'We shall be safe in the temple,' Serey had said. 'The Lord Buddha will protect us.' Ny wondered why the Lord Buddha had failed to protect them from the Khmer Rouge for four years.

But Elliot felt drawn to the temples, felt an unaccountable sadness at the imminent loss of his friend. At the loss of all the lives he had taken. Of all the deaths he had encountered in a life that was more about dying than living. As they at last reached the end of the causeway and mounted the steps into the black and cavernous mouth of the temple, he wondered why he should feel now, for the first time, what he had not felt in all those years. Was it the proximity of death? And yet he had been close to death many times. Perhaps, as the wat swallowed them into its darkness, so hell would swallow him into eternity. And the seductive allure of death stirred somewhere deep inside him. Perhaps all his life had led him to this place only to die.

In the blanket of darkness that enveloped them, the faintest sound rustled and echoed off invisible surfaces. Elliot eased Slattery gently on to the icy slabs and a soft grunt escaped his lips in a breath. McCue knelt beside him.

'You okay, buddy?'

'No troubles.'

And McCue heard him grin in the dark.

Elliot struck the flint of his lighter and held a small flame up above his head. A tiny halo burgeoned into the almost tangible darkness that engulfed the flame and snuffed its light. Elliot's sweat grew cold on his skin. He shivered, taking several steps into the void, seeking a surface that would reflect his light. Faint grey images flickered back at him. Thick-limbed peasants with coarse, clownish faces; the bodies of the damned trodden underfoot by horsemen and torn by wild beasts; aristocratic faces smiling beatifically from long boats, secure in the knowledge that, sooner or later, they would appear in the honours lists as minor gods. A cockfight seemed to reflect the futility of their own struggle. Elliot stepped closer to run his hand lightly over the cold carved stone and feel its slimy humidity. For a moment, a memory of the tiny engravings on Grace's silver necklace and bracelet, crafted by Sihanouk's own silversmith, flickered through his mind. A memory from another world. He put his hand to his neck and found that the thong was broken, the ring she had given him gone – the only part of her that would ever return to the soil of her birth. His fingers found only his own St Christopher.

'Hey, Elliot. We gotta do something for Mikey.'

Elliot turned back, the lighter now burning his fingers. Ny and her mother squatted on the floor beside the prone figure of Slattery and the kneeling shadow of McCue. Faces glowed palely in the light of the searing heat that grew from his hand. All turned towards him. Looking for answers. From him. His responsibility. Hadn't it always been that way?

'Better light a fire.' He wondered for a moment where this strange voice had come from, metallic and soulless, echoing out of nowhere – before he realized it was his own.

McCue took less than half an hour, returning several times with armfuls of dry wood, to get a fire burning. Elliot laid out a sleeping mat, eased Slattery on to it, and covered him with another. The Aussie's face was so pale it almost glowed, drained of blood and life. Elliot fingered the sticky warmth of the blood that oozed around the tourniquet on Slattery's leg. He knew that if he took it off Slattery would bleed to death. If it stayed on much longer he would lose the leg.

The flames of McCue's fire licked up around the small group, yellow light flickering across faces lost in fatigue and hopelessness.

'Sleep,' Elliot said. 'I'll take first watch.'

The shadows of lions couchant and many-headed serpents rose up around him. He walked slowly through the slabs of silvered light that fell between the tall stone columns guarding the hideously carved outer walls of the wat. People devoured by crocodiles, butchered by swordsmen. Elliot wondered if this barbarous culture had somehow proved a breeding ground for the horrors of the Khmer Rouge to come.

He glanced back along the length of the causeway, across the long grass and the still lakes, to the distant line of the outer walls and the jungle beyond. Not a sound, nor a move-ment, stirred the night air. It did not seem natural. McCue had pumped Slattery full of painkillers and the Aussie had fallen into a restless slumber. McCue himself had been asleep almost before his head touched the floor, curled up in a curiously foetal position close to the fire. A sleeping child. Elliot had left Ny wide-eyed and sleepless watching over her mother. 'Don't let the fire go out,' he told her.

The scrape of a foot on stone brought his thoughts to an

abrupt halt. He turned to find Ny staring up at him out of the gloom, dark eyes turning black. 'You should be sleeping,' he said curtly.

She shrugged. 'No can sleep.'

He took in her slight, fragile frame, and for the first time realized just how small she really was. Like a child half her age. And yet there was a maturity and experience in her eyes that might have belonged to a woman of twice her years. In her gaze was a sense of knowing, as if she had known him all her life. As if she knew him all too well, as only he did. The idea discomfited him. He rested his M16 against the wall and squatted down on the top step, leaning back against a pillar and taking out a cigarette. He lit it and felt the smoke, dry and acrid, burn his mouth, and he sucked it deep inside him and felt the tightness across his chest relax.

'Smoke?' he asked, and held out a cigarette.

She shook her head. 'When cadres smoke it smell bad. Bitter. Like . . .' she searched for the word '. . . privilege.'

He smiled. 'You're too young to have thought that one up for yourself. You hear it from your mother?'

She tilted her jaw defiantly. 'My mamma clever. She keep us stay alive.'

Elliot nodded seriously. 'Sure.' He drew again on the cigarette. 'Weren't you ever curious? For yourself?'

'About what?'

'Smoking.'

She met his look with the same directness, mirroring his

seriousness, unaware that he was laughing at her. And at once he regretted his flippancy.

'I remember see ladies smoke, Phnom Penh. It make them look like bad woman.'

'Sounds like your mother talking again.'

'You no laugh me, Mistah Elliot.'

He heard, with something like shock, her father's voice in hers. The way she said his name. And he remembered she was somebody's little girl who'd grown up without a father.

'You no – curious?' she asked, rolling the word around her tongue, savouring its newness.

'About what?'

She looked at his blankness and wondered if it could be real. A little half smile. 'You no curious.'

'If you mean about what happened to you and your mother, to this whole godforsaken country, I'm not paid to be curious. Just to get you out.'

'You only thinking and doing what you paid to.'

'Yes,' he said. And he remembered the heat and the white blinding brightness, and then the sightless dark, the smell of sweat and fear. And after, through the red mist, smoke clearing, eyes adjusting, the broken bleeding bodies. Children, like Ny, and younger. 'It's an old army trick I learned years ago. Otherwise you end up drunk somewhere, or shooting junk.'

She didn't speak for a long time, sitting on the edge of the stone balustrade watching him. He let his head fall back against the pillar, the cigarette easing his tension. And as the tension eased, so he felt the first seductive waves of fatigue. His eyes were gritty and sore and he closed them for just a moment. And saw himself standing beneath the stark winter trees in the rain watching the stranger in black who was his daughter being led away by another stranger – a young man with red hair. He knew she'd seen him. But of course she had no idea who he was. A stranger at her mother's funeral who was her father. She commented on him to the young man with red hair who flicked angry eyes in his direction before steering her away toward the line of cars.

'Will your friend die?'

Ny's soft, stilted voice startled him. He opened his eyes and saw her still sitting on the balustrade. Birds fluttered around in his chest and stomach. He saw that his cigarette had burned down to the filter and gone out. 'What?'

'Your friend who is shot. He will die?'

The blunt, emotionless quality of her question was unnerving. She accepted death with the same ease she accepted life. But, then, hadn't she known as much of one as the other? 'I don't know,' he lied.

She seemed to accept this, nodding thoughtfully. Then, 'My mamma mean what she say.'

'Uh-huh.' Elliot searched his pockets for another cigarette.

'Will you take us Phnom Penh?'

He found one and looked at her irritably. 'You ask a lot of questions, don't you?'

'No answer without question.'

He lit his cigarette and got to his feet. He was getting tired of her fatalism. 'Sometimes the last thing you want to hear is the answer, so you don't ask the question.' And he walked back into the temple to the glow of the dying embers of McCue's fire. He heard Ny's bare feet behind him. 'I thought I told you not to let the fire go out.'

Without a word she padded towards the circle of light and picked up a log to poke among the ashes before piling on fresh wood. McCue sat up, instantly awake. His eyes shone like polished coals, fastening on Elliot as he stepped into the flickering light. 'My watch?'

Elliot nodded. 'Wake me at first light.'

The blood drained out of the dawn sky leaving it a blue so pale it was almost yellow. A mist lay across the water like gently undulating gauze slowly smoking into the morning haze as the sun rose to scorch the air. McCue and Elliot stood, silent statues, staring out across the causeway towards the jungle. With the light, they realized how vulnerable they had been through the night. The wat was surrounded on three sides by flat swampland, tall trees growing sparsely through the swollen waters of the Tonle Sap. They had limped up a blind alley without knowing it. Had the Khmer Rouge picked up their trail the night before, they would have been trapped. As it was, they were still in danger, and Elliot wanted them out of here fast.

'Do we go north or south?' McCue asked without looking at him.

'North.'

'What about the old woman?'

'She'll have to be persuaded.'

'That will not be possible.' They turned, startled, to find Serey there, calm, almost serene, Ny standing a respectful distance behind her. 'And I am not such an old woman. Even if I look it.'

'Lady, I'm sorry for calling you old, but we got no choice but to head for Thailand.'

Serey remained implacable. 'Perhaps you do not. I do. My daughter and I are going to Phnom Penh.'

'Shit!' McCue glanced at Elliot. 'What's there? There's nothing there, is there? No hospital, no doctors, nothing. They emptied the goddamned place, didn't they?' He shook his head. 'Mikey'd never make it.'

Elliot was impassive. 'He'll never make it to Thailand either.'

McCue regarded him with disbelief. 'Shit, man, you're not going along with this crap? Phnom Penh! That poor bastard ain't got a chance! Be like putting a gun to his fucking head – never mind ours!' He turned towards Serey. 'You want that, do you, lady? You want the man's blood on your hands? Maybe ours, too?'

'I didn't ask you to come,' she said simply.

'We'd better move,' Elliot said.

McCue grabbed his arm, frustration boiling over. 'Where to? Phnom Penh?'

Elliot's silence was his confirmation.

'Why, for fuck's sake? Why are you doing this?'

'Because we can't make them go north with us, and they haven't a hope if they go south on their own.' He paused. 'Then Slattery would have died for nothing.'

McCue ground his anger out through clenched teeth. 'He ain't dead yet.'

'Only a matter of time,' Elliot said, and he pulled free of McCue's grip and walked into the cold grey gloom of the temple.

McCue shouted after him, 'You're a callous fucking bastard, Elliot, you know that!'

Slattery's face was a mask. He raised himself on one elbow with difficulty and grimaced at Elliot. 'Not like Billy boy to go shooting his mouth off. What's the trouble, chief?'

'No trouble,' Elliot said. 'Time to go.'

The constant but irregular bumping jarred his whole aching being, sending pain in random waves through a hazy consciousness that was clearly focused on only what hurt. And that clarity centred upon his leg, a leg that seemed to have swollen larger than anything in his forty years' experience, enveloping everything, filling all of time and space. It left him feeling like some infinitely small being attached somehow to one of its vast curved surfaces. But even that infinite smallness was full of pain. His throat was swollen so that he could barely swallow and his head was filled with a fire that burned and raged.

He was only vaguely aware of Elliot and McCue taking turns to drag his crude bamboo litter through this eternal landscape. Overhead, light flitted erratically through the broken canopy, drifting in and out of focus. And from time to time a face would swim into his field of vision, disembodied concern, eyes that blinked to hide their hopelessness. He wanted to say, Stop! Enough! His lips moved, but there were no words.

Elliot looked into Slattery's clouded eyes and knew he didn't have long. He brushed flies from dried cracked lips that tried to move and he heard the breath that rattled in his throat. Then suddenly the dying man's hand clutched Elliot's wrist, every last ounce of his strength pressed into the grip. And his eyes opened wide, burning with a diamond-sharp blue-grey intensity. For a moment Elliot thought it was death that gave them their brief, bright life, before he saw, with a sudden shocking clarity, that it was not death itself, but an appeal for it. And he felt a sack of bile knot in his stomach.

McCue was on point. He came quickly back through the trees. They had been circling south-east around the top end of the Tonle Sap, avoiding the small towns of Roluos and Kompong Kleang, trying to reach the shores of the great lake. The one thing Elliot and McCue had agreed on was that the only way they were likely to reach Phnom Penh was by boat. It would be the fastest, most direct route, south-west across the Tonle Sap, eventually feeding into the wide, slow-moving, southbound waters of the Mekong, a great river highway that led past the city and on down through Vietnam, before finally

PETER MAY

debouching, through the nine dragons' mouths of the Mekong Delta into the South China Sea. McCue crouched breathless beside Elliot.

'We're about quarter of a mile from a small fishing village on the lake shore. Half a dozen huts on stilts. It's partially flooded and looks deserted.'

Serey and Ny squatted silently in the grass, gnawing on small hard biscuits that Elliot had taken from his pack. The heat was devastating, stealing away all their energy, sapping their strength and will to move. The air chirred with the sounds of countless insects, while high above strange birds cawed and screamed in the canopy. Elliot wiped the sweat from his eyes with his sleeve and nodded. 'Okay.' He inclined his head towards the two women. 'We'll give them five.'

McCue looked at Slattery. 'How is he?'

'Do you need to ask?'

A moment of contempt flickered in the American's eyes, but he said nothing. He stood up and turned away, only to stop as the incongruous sound of voices in idle chatter reached them through the trees. Three Khmer Rouge soldiers walked into the clearing. Stunned by the sight of the two women, they stopped abruptly as McCue and Elliot snatched weapons, the clatter of gun metal on webbing, to cover them. Taken completely off guard, they reacted too late. One swung his AK-47 from his shoulder and fell in a burst of fire from McCue's automatic. The other two stood in frozen horror, staring in near-disbelief at the Western faces.

'Mrs Ang, tell them to put their weapons on the ground, very slowly,' Elliot said. Serey was scared but hiding it. She and Ny were both on their feet, Ny breathless with fear, holding her mother's arm. Serey glanced at Elliot then uttered a few halting words to the Khmers. They hesitated, just boys with frightened faces. And then the snap of a safety catch from behind forced Elliot into a half-turn. A fourth Khmer was standing over Slattery with a pistol pointed at his head. The soldier's face was distorted by fear as he shouted a cryptic command.

'He says if you do not throw down your weapons your friend will die,' Serey said.

'Fucking ironic, isn't it.' Elliot half-smiled. 'Keep those bastards covered, McCue.' And he dropped his M16 and drew out his service pistol.

McCue shifted uneasily. 'What the fuck are you doing!' Elliot raised the pistol, levelling it at the soldier's head. 'Elliot!' McCue shouted. And with the fear there was now confusion in the Khmer's face.

The air hummed with the silence that had fallen after the first shots. Elliot's eyes met the Khmer's, and the Khmer could not understand the gratitude he read in this alien face. Then Elliot's eyes dropped to where Slattery lay on the stretcher. And in a single swift movement he lowered his revolver and shot Slattery through the temple. A small fountain of blood looped briefly through a patch of sunlight. The sense of disbelief was paralysing, the Khmer standing pointing his gun impotently at a corpse. His mouth gaped as he stared at the body then looked up to see Elliot as he raised his pistol to shoot him in the face. A bloodcurdling scream filled the air as McCue squeezed the trigger of his M16, venting his anger and confusion on the other two soldiers, bodies torn apart by two dozen bullets as they fell broken to the ground. Then he spun round, cracking the butt of the rifle across the side of Elliot's head, knocking him over. Specks of spittle frothed at the corners of his mouth. He pointed the weapon at Elliot's chest and screamed, 'You bastard! You fucking bastard! I'm going to fucking kill you!'

Elliot shook his head to clear it, and felt blood running sticky down one side of his face. He stared back into McCue's fury for several long moments, then he pushed the hot, smoking barrel aside and got back to his feet.

'We'd better get out of here.' He wiped the blood from his face and picked up his M16.

CHAPTER TWENTY-FIVE

The freshly watered grass was cool and crisp under her feet. She felt vulnerable barefoot, wrapped only in a flimsy silk dressing gown, but was comforted by the hand of the girl in the yellow dress who held her lightly just above the elbow, guiding her from the dark interior and into the glare of the garden. The air was velvety warm, cooled by the fine spray that filled the air and carried the scent of winter blossoms across the lawn. A gardener, dressed all in black, played a hose liberally over flower beds across a haze of green, while in the centre of the lawn a sprinkler sent millions of tiny droplets flickering through the morning sunlight, making perfect little rainbows.

Under the shade of a large tree Tuk sat at a white, circular table eating breakfast, a morning paper folded beside his plate. He looked up and smiled across at her and stood as she approached.

'Good morning, my dear. And how are you feeling today?'

'Confused,' she said, and was suddenly aware that the girl in the yellow dress had gone, a glimpse of pale lemon melting into the cool darkness of the house. Tuk pulled out a chair for her and she sat down.

'But of course,' he said. 'I understand. You must have many questions.' He paused. 'And perhaps a few answers.' He regarded her speculatively for a moment, then he waved his hand dismissively. 'But there will be plenty of time for both. First you must have a little breakfast. Juice?' He sat down, about to pour her some freshly squeezed orange, but stopped, inclined his head a little and reached out to run his fingers lightly down one side of her face. She winced and drew back from his touch. 'Such a nasty bruise,' he said. 'That man must have been an animal. Such beauty as yours should be treated with reverence.'

She had seen her own face earlier, when the girl in the yellow dress had come to wake her. An ugly purple bruise extending from her swollen upper lip across her cheekbone. One eye, too, was bruised and swollen and almost closed. Her whole body ached, and she was surprised not to find its creamy whiteness covered by bruises. The girl had not spoken to her, only smiling as she led her gently into a lilac-tiled shower room. There, to Lisa's embarrassment, the girl had washed her down with a large soapy sponge under a stream of steaming hot water that relaxed her so that her legs felt weak and almost buckled. Then she rubbed her down with a big soft towel before holding the silk robe for her to slip into.

Lisa felt better now, seated in the soft drowsy shade, and only realized how hungry she was when the sharp sweetness of the orange juice nipped her tongue. Over his paper, Tuk watched with a half-smile as she tucked into slices of freshly toasted bread running with melted butter and honey. He sighed with satisfaction when the girl with the yellow dress brought a fresh pot of scented tea and poured them a cup. Lisa flicked uncertain darting glances at him when she thought he wasn't watching her, building up a series of tiny snapshot impressions to sketch in the detail she had failed to take in at first sight. His freshly starched white shirt and trousers bore creases like razors. You could cut yourself just touching him, she thought. And she smiled to herself as it occurred to her that he brought new meaning to the phrase sharp dresser. And with that, she realized how much better she was feeling.

His short dark hair was oiled back. Dyed, she guessed. It was too uniformly black for a man of his age. He had a not unpleasant face, brown as a nut, smooth and unlined. But his eyes, she noticed, dark unyielding eyes, never reflected the smile that played constantly about his pale lips. She took in the manicured nails, the three gold rings, and the diamond on his little finger, and smiled up at him from the last of her tea.

'Better?' he asked.

She nodded vigorously. 'Much.'

He folded his paper and put it aside, clasping his hands over his crossed knees. 'So,' he said. 'Shall we exchange a few confidences?'

'You do know my father?' she asked.

'Oh, yes, I know him well. In fact, he was seated here with me at this very table less than a week ago.'

Her heart leapt. 'You know where he is, then?'

'Yes, I do.'

She felt both excitement and relief in a single emotional response. She had found him, finally, after all these weeks. And, yet, now that he was within reach, she felt an involuntary drawing back. Fear. Perhaps, after all, he would not want to see her. 'When will I be able to see him?'

Tuk smiled. 'I'm sorry, my dear, I really don't know.'

'But you said you knew where he was.'

'Oh, I know where he's gone. But not when, or even if, he'll be back.'

She frowned. 'I don't understand.'

He leaned on the table and put a hand over hers. 'How well do you know your father?'

She hesitated, then drew her hand away, and felt herself withdrawing inside, suddenly aware that she knew nothing about this man, or how she came to be in his house.

'Enough,' she said, and felt clumsily defensive. 'Where is he?'

'Kampuchea.'

'Kampuchea?' She had heard of it, of course, but her grasp of south-east Asian geography and current affairs was sketchy.

'You have heard of Cambodia?' Tuk asked.

'He's gone there, too?'

Tuk grinned, genuinely amused. 'They are one and the same, Miss Lisa.' And he paused long enough for her to feel foolish. 'Cambodia is bordered on the north by Laos, to the north and west by Thailand and the Gulf of Thailand, and to the east and south by Vietnam. She was a casualty of the war in Vietnam. A bystander caught in the crossfire between the Americans and the communists, and has now fallen prey to a kind of political cannibalism that we call the Khmer Rouge.'

Lisa knew little of the war in Vietnam, but she had heard of the Khmer Rouge, a vague memory of obscure reports on the evening television news bulletins. They had never seemed relevant and she had never got interested.

Tuk said, 'Your father has been paid a great deal of money to go into Cambodia to try to rescue a woman and her children who, like everyone else in the country, are prisoners of the Khmer Rouge. He came to me for' – he picked his words carefully – 'equipment and supplies. But of course, you already knew that.' He raised an eyebrow and she realized it was a question, not a statement.

She shook her head. 'No. I had no idea who you were.'

'Your father didn't say?'

She avoided his eyes. 'No. He doesn't know I'm here.'

'Then who gave you my name?'

Lisa ran her hands back through her hair. 'I'm beginning to feel tired, Mr Tuk.'

'Of course, Lisa,' Tuk said, full of ersatz sincerity. 'But it is important that we know certain things about each other, don't you think?'

'I suppose,' she said reluctantly. She felt herself being inextricably drawn into a question-and-answer session in which she really did not want to participate. 'But I'm not sure I should say.'

'Oh, come now, my dear, it's not a secret, is it?' His patient amiability was very persuasive.

'I suppose not.' But still she hesitated.

'Well?' There was just the hint of an edge in his voice now. She could see no polite way out. 'It was Sam Blair.'

'Ah,' Tuk said, apparently satisfied by this. 'Mr Blair. Of course.' He thought for a moment. 'So your father was not expecting you?'

She hesitated for a long time before she decided, finally, to tell him the truth. After all, she thought, there could be no harm in it, could there? 'Mr Tuk, all my life, until just a few weeks ago, I thought my father was dead. As far as he knows, I still do.'

If Tuk was surprised it registered for no more than a fraction of a second on his smooth, smiling face, and Lisa could not be blamed for missing the gleam of malice that burned briefly in his dark eyes. His smile broadened. 'Then he has a surprise in store when he returns,' he said. He rose to his feet and offered her his arm. 'But now you must get dressed. You have a visitor coming very soon.'

'Do you remember any of the numbers on the plate? Or the licence number of the cab?' The captain of police asked his questions wearily, as if he wasn't really interested in the answers.

Lisa shook her head, frustrated and angry. 'Why don't you ask the man outside the hotel? He spoke to him. I'm sure he knew him.'

Captain Prachak glanced across the room at Tuk. 'We spoke to several of the touts outside the Narai. No one even remembers you.' His eyes met Lisa's briefly, then flickered away.

'You're not going to get him, are you?' she said angrily. 'You don't care whether you do or not!'

The police captain had an unpleasant face, streaky brown like a badly stained piece of wood, flat, high cheekbones, with narrow suspicious eyes. His patience was wearing thin. Tuk intervened. 'You must understand, Lisa, that Bangkok is a city of five million people. Many cabs operate illegally on the streets without a licence. Without something more for the captain to go on it is very difficult.'

Lisa was on the edge of tears. 'I told you! His name is Sivara, and he's got a brother who . . .'

The captain cut her off. 'Yes, you did,' he agreed. 'Several times.'

'And what about my passport? He took my passport! How am I supposed to get home?'

'Don't worry, my dear.' Tuk put a comforting hand on her arm. 'I've already been in touch with the British Consul. Everything is in hand.' He turned to Prachak. 'I think we could finish this another day, Captain. The girl has had a bad time.'

'Of course.' Prachak looked relieved. 'I'll be in touch.' He opened the door to the hall.

'I'll see you out,' Tuk said, and the two men left Lisa sitting in a tearful silence under the downdraught of the ceiling fan. Her throat felt swollen and her head ached. She was depressed and frustrated and afraid.

When Tuk had led her in from the garden he had sent her upstairs to dress. He'd had her bags sent round from the hotel and paid her bill. As well as her passport, Sivara had

also taken her money. She was grateful and embarrassed and
a little ashamed of the niggling doubt she'd had about Tuk – a
grain of uncertainty that had lodged itself somewhere in her
unconscious. She protested when he said that, of course, she
must stay – at least until she got things sorted out. He had
shrugged and said, 'Where else would you go?' And she had
known he was right. But she disliked the thought of being so
totally dependent upon him. Her brush with Sivara had shaken
much of her young faith in her fellow humans, and in herself.

She wiped the tears from her cheeks and became aware of
the murmur of voices from the hall. Tuk and Prachak were still
engaged in conversation, hushed and barely audible. The door
lay slightly ajar, and through it she could see the dark reflection,
in a tall mirror, of the two men standing in the doorway. She
saw Prachak hand Tuk something that he slipped into his inside
jacket pocket. Her vision of them was still blurred by tears,
and she rubbed her eyes and strained in the gloom to see more
clearly. She wished that all the shutters were not closed against
the heat of the day and that there was more light to see by.

The two men shook hands now and Prachak left. Tuk moved
out of sight but did not come back into the room. She heard
soft footsteps above the hum and rattle of the fan, a phone
being lifted and a number dialled. Then Tuk's voice talking
softly to someone on the other end. She gave up trying to
hear and looked around this large impersonal study with its
cold, tiled floor and marble ashtrays on glass tables. Shiny
hard surfaces, austere and lacking in comfort or warmth. Even

the chairs were unyielding. She wondered what kind of man Tuk really was, and in what way the truth was reflected in the nature of this room. Despite the temperature outside, she shivered. Cold, she thought. In spite of all his smiles and words of comfort, he was cold. Like the room.

She heard the receiver being replaced and then soft footsteps again. Tuk appeared, smiling, in the doorway. 'Good news,' he said. She raised an eyebrow. He came and sat beside her and took her hand in both of his. 'I know you are uncomfortable with the idea of staying here. A young woman living alone in a house with a man she barely knows . . .'

She began a half-hearted protest which he brushed aside.

'No, no. I understand. And so a very good friend of mine has agreed to take you in for a few days, just until we get things sorted out. You'll like her, I'm sure. She knows your father quite well, I believe.'

After she had gone up to her room to lie down for a few hours, Tuk sat for a long time in satisfied contemplation. From his inside pocket he took out the small black book Captain Prachak had given him. He looked at the elaborate gold crest on the cover and thought how pretentious the British were. Inside, Lisa's innocence stared back at him from a cheap colour photograph. A very pretty girl, he thought. When the bruising was gone . . .

He snapped the passport shut, held it for a moment, then crossed the room to lock it away in his desk drawer.

CHAPTER TWENTY-SIX

Lisa awoke to the gentle touch of fingers on her bruised cheek. The room glowed with the muted light of the early morning sun, shutters still drawn, sunlight burning in bright sharp lines around their edges, trying to insinuate its way inside. She turned, still cloudy with sleep, to look up into Grace's soft smile.

'The swelling is down a little this morning,' Grace said.

And Lisa remembered arriving the night before on Tuk's arm, delivered into this sumptuous colonial villa in East Bangkok, still bewildered, a little frightened. The gentle warmth in the sympathy and welcome of this woman who knew her father had comforted her. Fear melting with the reassuring touch of her hand, the gentle kiss on her forehead. 'Poor child,' she had said, and led her into a soft-cushioned room that seemed heady and seductive after the cold austerity of Tuk's house.

'It's very good of you,' Lisa had mumbled.

Grace, smiling, had brushed the hair back from Lisa's face with delicate fingers and tilted her jaw, turning the bruising to the light. Shaking her head, she'd said, 'Men can be such animals.' And Lisa had caught the look that flashed darkly in her eyes as she glanced at Tuk.

When Tuk had gone Grace had given her a hot sweet drink laced with the taste of alcohol, and sat with her for what seemed like a very long time, holding her hand in one of hers, gently stroking the back of it with the fingers of her other. The soft murmur of her voice, the silky quality of her touch, had been reassuring. Lisa had heard the words without listening. Instead she let the alcohol and the gently undulating waves of fatigue wash over her with a grateful relief. And, now, as she gazed up into the delicate oriental beauty in the face of this older woman, she had no recollection of having come to this room, or of falling asleep in this bed. But there was something safe in the smile, comforting after all the uncertainty of the past few weeks and the traumas of the last few days. She returned the smile. 'What time is it?'

'Early. I thought a little waterborne breakfast might restore you. The floating market gets up early. And so must you if we are to catch it at its best.'

Grace's car took them to the landing stage at the Oriental Hotel, and Lisa was surprised to find it driven by an attractive young girl in uniform. She glanced at Grace, realizing how little she knew of her. Although clearly many years older than Lisa, old enough possibly to be her mother, her beauty was still startling. She was dressed casually in a long white wraparound skirt and white blouse, cool and radiant in the early morning heat, her skin the colour of milky coffee. Her gleaming dark hair was drawn back in a white-ribboned bow. She caught Lisa looking at her and smiled. 'We should get you some clothes,' she said. 'Perhaps when we get back from the market.'

'I've got clothes with me,' Lisa said, a little uncertainly.

'Hardly a wardrobe for every occasion,' said Grace. 'And who knows how long you might have to wait for your father's return. There are places I should like to take you where you might feel a little out of place in jeans.'

Lisa found Grace's self-assurance intimidating. 'The truth is,' she said, 'I don't have any money. It was all stolen.'

Grace laughed. 'That's no problem, Lisa. You're my guest.'

Lisa blushed. 'I couldn't possibly let you . . .'

'I insist.' Grace cut her off. 'And that's an end to it.' Lisa felt like a schoolgirl who has just been rapped on the knuckles for a breach of etiquette, and she lowered her eyes. Grace laughed again and put a hand over hers, giving it a tiny squeeze. 'My child, forgive me if I bully you, but your father would not be happy with me if I failed to look after his little girl.'

Lisa met her eyes again and wondered if she detected a hint of mockery in their laughter. 'Do you know my father well?'

'Well?' Grace smiled reflectively into the middle distance. 'No, I should not say I know him well.' She turned to meet Lisa's gaze again. 'But do I know him intimately.' Again that sense of mockery in the eyes that left Lisa feeling unsettled. And the deliberate manner in Grace's choice of words had an ambiguity calculated apparently to leave her guest confused and insecure. Lisa drew her hand away from Grace's and locked it together firmly with her own in her lap. She felt Grace's eyes still on her, but kept hers averted, pretending that something on the street had caught her interest. She wanted time to sort out her feelings, to know how to respond. Sivara had shattered her young innocence. She would not be taken in so easily again. 'You will like the floating market,' Grace said. 'It attracts many tourists.'

'I have been before,' Lisa replied, and she did not need to look to know that Grace was surprised.

They waited by the car at the landing stage while the chauffeur went to hail a water taxi. Crowds thronged the pier waiting for one of the many motor launches that criss-crossed the river. Pop music blared from the speakers of a ghetto-blaster on the shoulders of a young man dressed in peasant black pyjamas and wearing a reed-woven sunhat. Lisa searched vainly among the many faces for one that might be familiar. Eyes full of mischief that had turned to lust. But one in five million, she knew, was long odds. A small boy in shorts and a khaki-green shirt several sizes two large for him pushed through the crowd with a large, circular bamboo tray on his head. Coloured ribbons hung down around its edges. He turned this way and that, arms up holding his tray steady, appealing to each face he encountered.

'What's he doing?' Lisa asked.

'Selling jasmine-blossom garlands,' Grace said. 'The blossoms are associated with good fortune. They can be left at temples as offerings, or kept by the purchaser for good luck – or presented to friends as gifts.' She waved her hand and called him over. He ran up to them eagerly. Grace haggled over the price. Several exchanges in bursts of staccato Thai. At last the boy shrugged and handed her one of the garlands in return for a few coins. He melted away into the crowd again, disgruntled with his sale. Grace crushed the blossoms gently in her hand and inhaled the heady fragrance with satisfaction. Then she turned to Lisa, smiling, and placed the garland around her neck. 'For good luck,' she said. 'And such a pretty child as you deserves a pretty fragrance.' Her fingers brushed Lisa's bruised cheek. 'Such a shame,' she said. 'But it won't last long – like the blossom.'

Or like my luck, thought Lisa. She felt sure now that she was being mocked. And her initial feeling the previous evening of security, and gratitude towards Grace, was being replaced by a growing sense of unease.

The long, narrow *hang yao* knifed its way through the choppy waters of one of the larger *klong*s, weaving between the rice barges and water buses and sampans. And for a time Lisa forgot her misgivings, enthralled again by the sights and sounds of this exotic waterborne culture that engulfed the senses. Women hung from their reed-woven lampshades like fat black light bulbs, squatting in tiny sampans. A canoe, groaning under the weight of a huge load of golden hay, turned into one of the many smaller *klong*s, heading east to feed the buffalo that ploughed the neighbouring paddies. Grace pointed out the flotilla of Royal Barges housed in a special pavilion along the canal, and Lisa's gaze strayed up to the giant statues guarding the entrance to the Wat Arun, whose central porcelain-studded tower flashed in the morning sunlight.

The sun had risen mercilessly high in the pale blue sky by the time they reached the market itself. It was cooler on the water than elsewhere, but the heat was still oppressive. Their *hang yao* had slowed to less than walking pace, bumping its way gently among the hundreds of bobbing craft. Grace ordered their driver to stop by a boat selling headgear, and she bought them each a wide-brimmed straw hat. 'To protect that pretty white skin,' she said, brushing Lisa's hair back and placing the hat on her head, tilting it forward to shade her face from the sun. Lisa was again reminded of her trip with Sivara. She had bought a straw hat then, too.

All around them clicking Thai tongues bargained and fought over purchases and sales, and Lisa became aware of Grace's eyes on her. She turned boldly to meet her gaze. Grace smiled disarmingly. 'You must be hungry.'

Lisa nodded. 'Starving.'

Grace spoke to their driver and he eased their *hang yao* through the other craft to a sampan selling fresh fruit. They bought a bamboo tray laden with slices of watermelon, papaya, pineapple and halves of lime. As they ate the juicy red flesh of the watermelon and squeezed lime on the papaya, Grace reclined, supporting herself on one arm, and gazed speculatively at Lisa. 'What brings a young English girl to the other side of the world to find a father she has never known?' she asked.

'My mother died,' Lisa said simply. 'Wouldn't you have done the same?'

Grace gave a tiny dismissive shrug. 'It never occurred to me.'

Lisa frowned, unbalanced by this unexpected response. She had thought her question hypothetical. 'I don't understand.'

'My father was a Frenchman in the diplomatic corps. I was the result of a brief liaison with my mother. His name was Jacques. Beyond that I know nothing of him.'

'But weren't you ever curious? I mean, didn't you want to know who he was?'

Grace shook her head. 'No. He had no interest in me. Why should I care about him?'

'That's very sad.'

'I don't think so. I was educated in Paris, you see. My mother thought a great deal of the French, but I never liked them much. I am a Cambodian. Always have been, always will be.'

'Oh.' Lisa realized that she was wrong in yet another assumption. 'I thought you were Thai.'

Grace smiled indulgently. 'In Vietnam,' she said, 'all white men were once French. Then they were American. Now they are Russian. But to the Vietnamese they are all just white. As all the peoples of Indochina were just *jaunes* once to the French. I have long since ceased to be insulted by it.'

'I'm sorry,' Lisa stuttered, wondering how it was that Grace always seemed to make her feel so clumsy.

'Ignorance is hardly a sin, my dear.' Grace paused for a

moment to squeeze more lime on her papaya. 'Than tells me
you believed your father was dead.'

'It's what my mother told me,' Lisa said.

'Why?'

'Because he'd disgraced her. Us. Or so she thought.' Lisa drew
in a deep breath. 'He was court-martialled and sent to prison
for a massacre of civilians in Aden.' A slightly raised eyebrow
was the only betrayal of Grace's surprise. 'Didn't he tell you?'

'No.' The faintest hint of a smile played about Grace's mouth.
'But, then, that's hardly surprising.'

'Why? Because you think he'd have been ashamed to?'

Grace evaded the question. 'Are you ashamed of him?'

Lisa felt a flush rise on her cheeks. It was something she'd
wondered herself many times. How could she answer Grace
when she'd never found an answer for herself? 'I don't know,'
she said at length. 'Maybe that's why I'm here. To find out.'

Grace's smile faded, and Lisa wondered if it was a flicker
of pity she saw cross her eyes. 'He does not give much away,
your father,' Grace said.

Lisa gazed at her speculatively along the length of the *hang
yao* and wondered if she had ever seen such beauty. A beauty
that could in one moment seem warm and enticing, and in
another cold and dangerous. 'What exactly is your relationship
with my father?' she asked.

Grace seemed to consider her answer carefully for some
moments. Then, 'We were lovers,' she said simply.

Lisa felt the shock in her heart sting her face pink. Intimate.

That was the word Grace had used in the car. She had not known him well, but intimately. Lovers. Of course. They had been lovers. This woman, a complete stranger to her, knew her father in ways that she never could. It seemed to explain all the ambiguities. And for a moment Lisa was almost jealous.

Grace sat up suddenly, pushing her tray aside. 'A little coffee, I think. Then we should get you some clothes.'

Sweat glistened on the firm brown bodies in the steamy heat of the dyeing room. The dark-haired boys wore only gloves and sandals, and the flimsiest of shorts, as they worked with dexterous ease, apparently impervious to the heat, dipping the heavy skeins of silk into vats of hot dye. In the glow of the fires, the smoke and steam that permeated the claustrophobic darkness stung Lisa's eyes and caught in her throat. Grace, standing at her side, gently holding her a little above the elbow, seemed oblivious. Lisa glanced at her and saw the gleam that lit her eyes as she ran them across the taut young muscles of the bare-chested boys.

'How can they work in this atmosphere?' Lisa said, almost choking as she spoke.

Grace replied distantly. 'They're used to it.' Then she turned to Lisa and smiled. 'You can get used to almost anything. Come. It's time to choose.' And she guided her back out into the comparative cool of the factory where women moved vast screens back and forth along three-hundred-metre lengths of undyed silk, printing repeated patterns of exotic jungle scenes. Earlier, Lisa and Grace had passed through large rooms resounding to the clatter of dozens of flying shuttle looms weaving great lengths of raw silk. Their guide had explained to Lisa that Thailand's silk larvae spun unusually soft, thick fibres, and that the resultant fabric accepted dyes more readily than silk made elsewhere in the world. He was waiting for them as they climbed the steps to the factory showroom, where huge rolls of printed and dyed silks were stacked one upon the other.

A shrunken man with a bald, brown pate, he bowed and smiled. 'Your friend enjoyed her tour, La Mère Grace?'

'Did you?' Grace turned to Lisa.

'Very much,' Lisa said. She laughed. 'I feel like a child in Santa's grotto.'

'Then let me be your Father, or should I say Mother Christmas – although we are a week or so late.' Grace's smile seemed to conceal a greater amusement at the idea. She waved a hand expansively around the room. 'You choose. But something fine, I think, and self-coloured, and dark to contrast the whiteness of your skin.'

Lisa finally chose a deep, lustrous crimson in a very fine fabric. Grace seemed pleased with her choice, running the material sensuously through her fingers. 'Red for passion,' she said. 'Are you a passionate creature, Lisa?'

Their guide smiled.

Lisa flushed deeply. 'I really don't know,' she stammered. 'Red has always suited me.'

'We'll take five metres,' Grace told their guide. 'On my account, of course.'

'Of course, La Mère Grace.'

In the car Lisa asked, 'Why did he call you La Mère Grace?'

'It is how I am known,' Grace said. 'My business name, if you like.'

'What business is that?'

'Oh, I have many business interests. Property, entertainment, clubs, restaurants.'

Lisa was intrigued. 'And you run them yourself?'

'Of course. You seem surprised.'

'I'm sorry – I just thought—'

'That there should be a man behind it?'

'Isn't there?'

'My business interests were inherited from my mother. When I was forced to leave Cambodia, I re-established myself here. The women in my family have been very singular, Lisa. Men have their place, but not in our hearts or our lives. And certainly not in our business.'

'What other place is there?'

Grace turned a smile of genuine amusement on the young girl beside her. 'You really are very innocent, Lisa,' she said. 'In our beds, of course.'

The House of Choisy was in the Patpong 2 district, an upmarket boutique with the latest fashions from Paris, London and New York. A twittering middle-aged lady fussed and fluttered around Lisa for nearly fifteen minutes in the dressing room, taking every conceivable measurement. 'Beautiful lady, beautiful lady,' she kept saying. 'I make you beautiful, beautiful dress.' She thought, too, that the fabric Lisa had chosen was beautiful. Grace sat smoking and watching the proceedings with idle amusement.

They leafed through a well-thumbed brochure looking at hundreds of designs. Lisa was flustered and indecisive. 'I'm spoiled for choice.' She shrugged helplessly at Grace. In the end it was Grace who chose – a full-length, close-fitting dress, split to the knee at the left side, sleeveless and with a daringly plunging neckline. 'Along traditional Thai lines,' she said, and looked Lisa up and down. 'With one or two concessions to the modern world. You will be stunning.'

Lisa was uncertain. 'I'm not sure it's really me.'

'You mustn't underestimate yourself,' Grace said. 'You have the looks. This will lend you the sophistication. A woman must make the most of herself.'

Grace also chose an off-the-peg short brocade jacket, subtly patterned in deep blue, violet and crimson, to go with the dress. The tailoress tucked and pinched at it when Lisa tried it on. 'Need alteration,' she said.

'This is all going to cost a fortune,' said Lisa, turning to admire the jacket in the mirror. She stopped to look ruefully at Grace. 'I really can't accept.'

'It gives me pleasure,' said Grace. 'You wouldn't deny me that, would you?'

Lisa shook her head in embarrassed resignation. 'I really am very grateful.'

Grace turned to the tailoress. 'You will have it ready by Saturday?'

'Of course, La Mère Grace.'

'Good.' Grace turned a charming smile on Lisa. 'Then Cinderella shall go to the ball.'

Back in the car Lisa asked, 'What ball?'

Grace laughed. 'Not exactly a ball, Lisa. A dinner at one of my clubs. There will be some very influential guests. I hope you will be able to come.'

Lisa was still flushed with the unaccustomed pleasure of her purchases. Her earlier ambivalence towards Grace had mellowed and, although still uncertain about this bewildering and contradictory woman, she felt somehow closer to her now, knowing that she and her father had been lovers. Being close to her was like being close to her father. She took Grace's hand, feeling genuine affection, and squeezed it. 'I hope so, too,' she said.

The south-facing windows along one wall of the dining room were closed against the heat and brightness of the midday sun. But large French windows at one end opened out onto a shaded area of the lush green tropical garden that grew wild behind the high walls that surrounded Grace's villa. The rumble of traffic from the road seemed distant and unreal, like a dream on waking. The hum of insects, and the squawking of tropical birds among the luxuriant greenery of the trees, was the only real intrusion on the peaceful semi-darkness of the room.

Lisa sat alone at the long dining table, drinking strong black coffee under the gentle cooling downdraught of the fan overhead. The girl who had served them lunch had cleared the table, and Grace had left the room a few moments earlier to take a phone call. Lisa could hear the soft murmur of her voice somewhere deep in the house. She drained her cup and got up and walked slowly to the open French windows to stand framed in the doorway, smelling the damp, sweet fragrances of the fleshy-leaved tropical plants and flowers. The garden was a profusion of wild growth, a lotus pool choked with leaves, fruit trees untended, papaya, mango, the fruit of countless seasons rotting in the dark damp soil.

Over lunch, Grace had seemed distracted. She was quiet for a very long time before suddenly looking up and asking Lisa if she was still a virgin. Lisa had, again, flushed deeply. It was something she had never discussed with anyone. Even her mother. Anything to do with sex had been a subject of great embarrassment in her house. It had come from her mother and transmitted itself to Lisa. She had known nothing about the periods that would afflict her in adolescence until the first blood ran from between her legs at school. Then she had panicked, locking herself in the toilets and weeping hysterically in the certain knowledge that she was dying. The brutal truth had been conveyed to her by an unsympathetic form mistress who had sent her home with an angry note for her mother. Lisa's mother had, in turn, been angry, masking her embarrassment by accusing Lisa of stupidity, as though somehow the child should have known without having to be told. In the years that followed, it had only ever been referred to in the house as the curse.

Sex was something she had learned about from giggled tales told by fellow schoolgirls, vulgar jokes provoking raucous laughter. For a long time Lisa had laughed too, without fully understanding why. In retrospect she had often wondered how many of her friends had been equally mystified. True knowledge seemed to rest in the hands of just a fortunate few. She could smile now at her ignorance, but the fear of the unknown, the sense of taboo, had never left her.

'Well . . .?' Grace had inclined her head, amused by her embarrassment.

At first Lisa had denied it. Of course she wasn't a virgin, she'd had lots of boyfriends. Grace had raised a sceptical eyebrow, and her penetrating gaze seemed to see through Lisa's flustered deceit with startling ease. Lisa felt her cheeks burn again. 'Well, one anyway,' she said.

'And he has made love to you?' asked Grace.

'Not exactly.' Lisa stared hard at her hands on the table in front of her.

'Then you are still a virgin.'

'I suppose so.'

Grace smiled fondly at her, marvelling at such innocence. 'Well, don't worry about it,' she said. 'It's not necessarily a permanent condition. There is a cure.'

In spite of herself Lisa smiled. 'Only it doesn't come on prescription.'

'I should hope not!' The idea seemed to shock and amuse Grace. 'The only cure for virtue' – she smiled wickedly – 'is vice. It's delicious. Not a bit like medicine.'

Lisa wondered now, as she gazed out at the garden, if Grace had simply been poking fun again. She knew she must seem very naive to a woman like La Mère Grace, but wondered what pleasure the woman derived from taunting her with it. There seemed no malice in her, just amusement, but it did nothing for Lisa's confidence, serving only to increase her sense of vulnerability.

She remembered that, not so long ago, what she had craved most was safety, the security of her home, her mother, David; and for a moment she almost regretted forcing open the trunk in the attic. It was as if, in that one action, she had closed down her past and opened up a future of bleak uncertainty, where the only light, glowing faintly in the distance, was the know-ledge that somewhere in this hostile world was a man who was her father. She knew that somehow she thought that in finding him she might find herself. But it appeared that the closer she got, the less, rather than more, certain she became of who she really was. What was she doing here? What did she hope to find? And, in that moment, she was almost overwhelmed by a feeling of being completely and hopelessly alone.

A movement in the garden caught her eye. A glimpse of pale lilac caught in dappled sunlight. It was the girl who had served them lunch. She wore a simple lilac shirt over short, baggy, black trousers. Her dark hair was bobbed, cut short high into the nape of her neck, and her feet flapped in open rubber sandals as she padded from the house along an overgrown path. There was something odd in the nervous, secret intent of the girl's carriage that banished Lisa's thoughts of only a moment before, and aroused her curiosity. She stepped out on to the terrace and ran quickly down the half-dozen steps to the garden to follow the girl along the path.

By the time Lisa reached the spot where she'd last seen her, the girl had disappeared and the path seemed to peter out among the fronds that grew in prolific clusters all around. The garden appeared to stretch endlessly away on either side, and Lisa stood on tiptoes trying to catch a glimpse of the lilac shirt. She listened intently in the hot broken shade for some sound to give her a clue, but all she heard were the insects and the birds, and a rustling among the undergrowth that might have been a snake. She pushed quickly on through the fronds and found the garden opening up, suddenly, into a paved clearing.

The paving stones bore all the scars of neglect that characterized the rest of the garden, cracked and broken, weeds reaching up from the rich damp earth below. At the other side of the clearing, the girl in the lilac shirt was sunk on bended knee, sticks of burning incense pressed between palms raised to her bowed forehead. Her discarded sandals lay on the ground behind her. In front of her a large square stone table stood before a jumble of shrines raised on brick pillars, tiny replicas of houses and temples bedecked with flowers and strings of jasmine blossom. Laid all around, pointing upwards towards the shrine, at an angle of forty-five degrees, were a dozen or more red and white cylinders, some of which were four or five feet long. The upward ends were round and elongated like helmets, and Lisa realized, with a sudden sense of shock, that they were giant phalluses, an arrangement of enormous erections directed towards the shrine.

She stood for a moment, then turned, startled by a touch on her elbow. Grace stood by her side, smiling.

'Erotic, isn't it?' she whispered.

'What is it?' Lisa asked.

'The fertility shrine of San Chao Mae Tap Tim. The phalluses represent the Hindu god Shiva. Phallus worship is an ancient tradition in Thailand. But, of course, it originated in my own Cambodia more than seven hundred years ago.'

'It's disgusting!' Lisa hissed, embarrassed by her own arousal.

'Sex is never that,' Grace said calmly. 'It can be the most poignant experience life has to offer, if treated with respect.'

'But what's she doing?' Lisa asked, nodding towards the girl.

'She wants a child. She is praying for success. I pray that she doesn't have it. She is one of the best girls I have. But, then, who am I to stand in the way of the procreation of the human race?'

The girl finished her prayer, arose and turned to slip back into her sandals. She was startled to find Grace and Lisa watching, and a blush coloured her cheeks.

'I'm sorry. Forgive me, La Mère Grace,' she whispered, and she hurried past them, head bowed, back towards the house.

Grace laughed. 'If the girl wants to throw away her life . . .'
She glanced at Lisa. 'Come, take a closer look.' She took Lisa's
reluctant hand in hers and led her across the uneven pavings.
'Shiva is the third member of the Hindu trinity. Although rep-
resented here by the phallus, he is also sometimes known as
the Destroyer. In human form he is portrayed with four arms,
a third eye in the centre of his forehead, and often wearing a
necklace of skulls. Sex, my poor ignorant child, can be very
beautiful, but also sometimes very dangerous.' She turned a
provocative smile on the younger woman. 'Things you will no
doubt learn for yourself, in time.' And to Lisa's acute embarrassment she leaned towards her and kissed her lightly on
the lips.

'I think I should go back to the house,' Lisa said, flustered,
her cheeks burning. And she turned and hurried away across
the clearing.

'Perhaps you should lie down for a couple of hours,' Grace
called after her. 'The afternoons are so hot, and I shall be out
until this evening.'

Lisa didn't look back, but hurried through the tangle of
vegetation until she stumbled into the cool darkness of the
dining room.

Her bedroom, at the top of the house, was hot and humid.
She pulled the shutters closed and undressed quickly to slip
between the cool sheets, then lay a long time in the dark, listening to the rapid beat of her heart. After a while she heard
Grace's voice down in the main hall, then the front door

slamming shut. Somewhere, from the front of the house, came the sound of a car starting, the engine revving as it moved off down the drive. Then a deep silence. Lisa closed her eyes and let drowsiness take her in the airless heat of the room.

'So what do you think?' Tuk sat back in his favourite hard leather chair and sipped at his whisky through large cubes of ice.

Grace waited until the girl in the yellow dress who had brought her iced Perrier left the room. 'I think she's very young, very naive and very beautiful,' she said. Her heel scraped on the tiles as she crossed her legs.

Tuk smiled. 'And English. Such lovely white skin, and a virgin, too. A valuable commodity.'

'Very,' Grace agreed. She lifted the glass to her lips and let the cold, aerated water slip back over her throat. She enjoyed its tartness.

Tuk watched her with pursed lips and a gleam of malicious amusement in his eyes. 'And tempting.'

Grace flicked a darting glance in his direction, then took another sip of the Perrier. 'My interest is entirely commercial,' she said.

'Of course.'

'She could become the most sought-after property in Bangkok – at least for a while.'

'My thoughts exactly.'

Grace studied him for a moment. 'And just what exactly

are those thoughts, Than? I hardly see what you stand to gain from all this.'

'Ah,' Tuk smiled, 'now that's what I wanted to talk to you about. My interest is personal rather than financial.'

'In what way?'

'Who she is, of course. How can I put it . . .?' He tugged gently at the ends of his fingers. 'A little insurance policy.' She raised a quizzical eyebrow. 'In the unlikely event of Elliot returning, a little leverage would not go amiss.'

'And why would you require a little leverage, Than?' Grace was intrigued.

Tuk shifted uncomfortably. 'Let's just say that certain events which occurred last week may be open to misinterpretation.'

'You mean you double-crossed him.'

'That is one interpretation.'

'The one that Elliot is most likely to make?'

Tuk shrugged. 'Who knows? Elliot is a dangerous man. I do not wish to take any risks.'

Grace nodded her understanding. 'Wasn't that exactly what you were doing when you didn't play it straight with him?'

Tuk smiled ruefully. 'The best-laid schemes.'

'So.' Grace relaxed a little now. She had the measure of the situation. 'What exactly is there in it for me?'

'I have my insurance, you have the girl. She is of value to us both.'

'But if Elliot returns?'

'I think that very unlikely.'

'But if he does, you have your insurance. Where does that leave me?'

'She is your insurance also.'

'But as things stand I have no need of insurance.'

Tuk waved his hand dismissively, irritated by her persistence. 'He will not return.'

'How can you be so sure?'

'Do you not read the newspapers, listen to the radio?'

Grace inclined her head, smiling at the foolishness of the question. 'When do I have the time, Than? Or the inclination?'

'You should make a point of it, Grace. These are unsettled times.'

'So what have I missed?'

'The Vietnamese have won decisively in the south. The Khmer Rouge are retreating north. It can only be a matter of days before Phnom Penh falls. If Elliot is hoping to come back out through Thailand he is likely to find himself in the thick of the Khmer Rouge retreat. Unless he makes it in the next forty-eight hours, I think one can safely assume he never will.'

Grace drank all this in thoughtfully. 'And what will happen to the girl, then?'

Tuk showed his teeth, but it could hardly be described as a smile. 'When you have finished with her, I have plans of my own. A small revenge, perhaps, for her father's threats, but there will still be a satisfaction in it.'

A chill ran through Grace's heart.

CHAPTER TWENTY-SEVEN

Shards of reflected moonlight danced on the gently rippling black waters of the Tonle Sap. The thick stillness of the night was broken only by the sound of water slapping softly against the sides of the small wooden fishing craft. Elliot sat in the stern drawing on his last cigarette. It was several hours since the outboard motor had packed in. All day they had been heading south, keeping the eastern shore just in sight. To the west, the great lake stretched to the horizon and beyond. They had seen no one, no other craft. There had been no sign of life all day except, in the mid-afternoon, for an aeroplane flying very high and crossing their bows some miles to the south. A military aircraft.

In the deserted fishing village close to where they had been attacked by the Khmers the previous day, they had found a small abandoned fuel dump, and a number of flimsy fishing boats scuttled on the shore. Two of them were fitted with outboard motors, neither of which worked. Although tension between Elliot and McCue was still high, professional instinct and the cause of their survival had forced them to work as a team. Posting Serey and Ny on lookout, they had laboured in feverish silence to repair the least damaged of the boats and refloat it, before tackling the outboards. They had stripped each down to its casing, before selecting the best parts and rebuilding one sound motor. Black with grease, and running with sweat, they had taken more than fifteen minutes, and a dozen adjustments, before coaxing it to life.

They had loaded the boat with every fuel can it could safely carry, in addition to themselves and their packs, and it was almost nightfall when they finally pushed off from shore, dangerously low in the water. At little more than walking pace, they had headed south, a hundred metres offshore, hugging the shoreline which they could see brooding darkly, first by starlight and then, when it rose, by the pale light of the moon.

McCue and Elliot took turns at the helm in two-hour shifts. The two women slept, curled up in the bottom of the boat, waking up to bale out only when the water they were shipping began to slop about their faces.

At dawn they had been spotted, from shore, and fired upon by a ragged Khmer Rouge patrol. McCue, then at the helm, had gunned the motor and turned the boat quickly out across the lake until the shore was a distant smudge on the horizon. He had then resumed their southbound course and adopted a slower pace to conserve fuel.

As the sun rose through the day, the heat became unbearable, eyes burning in the glare and reflected blaze from the water. Only the faintest relief came from the breeze created by their slow progress south. They improvised headgear by cutting up a sleeping mat, and McCue contrived a makeshift awning to provide a tiny area of shade at the prow of the boat, using a sleeping bag and two crossplanks. They took it in turns to squat, uncomfortably, under its protection.

Slattery was still a presence among them, like a ghost. Although the subject had never been raised, the anger burned deeply still in McCue's eyes. Elliot's sullen silence seemed devoid of remorse. Serey had watched them both for long periods. She had read the anger in McCue's eyes, recognized the hatred that simmered there. It was something she had seen many times before, in the early days of the Khmer Rouge, before all those angry young men with hate in their hearts had forgotten their justification for killing, and death had become an end in itself. It was the dead quality in Elliot's eyes that frightened her most, a chill, emotionless quality that glazed rather than burned – windows without reflection on a man without a soul. Ironically, it was this that had made her decide that, should she ever face a choice, she would side with Elliot. It was with him, she had concluded, that the best chance of salvation lay. Not for herself – she hardly cared any more – but for Ny, if that were at all possible.

She glanced frequently at her daughter, distressed by her brooding silence and outward calm. She had mourned the loss of Ny ever since the girl had plunged Elliot's knife with such ferocity into the soft belly of the young cadre at the commune, severing not only a life, but the last lingering ties between mother and daughter. The shock of it was with her still. She had understood then, as now, why. And with understanding had come guilt, as if she were somehow responsible. Should not a mother lay down her life to protect her child? And yet she had done nothing, said nothing, all those nights when the cadre had come and taken Ny off in the dark.

Once, as she was baling out water with a tin mug, Ny had caught her mother watching her, and Serey averted her face, ashamed to meet her daughter's eye. She had failed her. Nothing could be the same between them again. And she felt tears filling her eyes. Ny watched her for some moments then turned back to her task with a leaden heart. Her mother, she knew, was ashamed of her.

Elliot had been aware of the change of pitch in the engine for some time. It was slight, almost imperceptible, but it rang an alarm in his head. McCue heard it also, raising his head and glancing towards Elliot with concern. Elliot shrugged, and they waited, through what seemed like eternal minutes, for confirmation of their fears. From that initial change in pitch, the rhythm of the engine had begun to falter and choke, like phlegm gathering in its throat. Elliot swung the rudder in and turned the boat in the direction of the shoreline, gunning the engine to carry them faster towards its distant, hazy outline. Serey and Ny were alerted, sitting up and watching with alarm. The outboard finally coughed and spat before choking on its own failure.

In the silence that followed, the sound of McCue clambering

to the stern of the stricken boat seemed unnaturally loud, echoing across the stillness of the water.

With no exchange between then, the two men loosened the clamps and pulled the inert engine on board. McCue made a quick examination. 'Ain't fuel,' he said.

Working with oily, black fingers, he took the outboard apart and reassembled it several times without success. Elliot had watched, with growing despair, as they drifted further and further away from the safety of the shore. McCue tried again, pulling repeatedly on the starter only to hear the engine cough into life and then choke again, like a sick man's dying whisper.

Darkness had gathered quickly from the eastern shore, before finally enveloping them and ending their hopes of repairing the engine before dawn. McCue's face had flickered briefly in the light of a match as he lit a cigarette. 'Shoulda killed us all when you had the chance, Elliot,' he said grimly. 'We're as good as dead now.'

As the moon rose, they drifted, helpless, further out into the watery vastness of the Tonle Sap. Elliot knew that he had finally lost control of his own destiny. If there was a God, then they were all in his hands. He felt no fear, just an inner numbness, as when a man has swallowed a bottle of pills and succumbs drowsily to the onset of the final sleep. His mind turned away from looking back on the wasteland of his life, and there seemed little point in looking forward, since he could see no further than the dark night that surrounded them. He took a final draw on his cigarette and threw the last inch of it away into the night, hearing the briefest sizzle as it hit the water. Fatigue engulfed him. He turned at the sound of a whisper at his side, and found himself looking into Ny's pale, moonlit face.

'We going to die?' Her voice seemed very tiny.

'Sure,' he said. 'We all die sometime.'

She dropped her eyes and shook her head in frustration. 'No, I mean . . .'

'I know what you meant,' he interrupted her.

'Then, why—'

'Because I don't know!' There was irritation in his voice.

A long silence in the dark. Then, 'My mamma is shamed of me,' she said. Elliot glanced quickly at the dark shape of the older woman lying sleeping in the bottom of the boat. 'Because I kill man.'

'Are you ashamed of yourself?' he asked.

'No.' Her voice was hard. 'He deserve to die.'

Elliot shrugged. 'Lot of people do.'

'Like your friend Mistah Slattery?'

A seed of anger grew for a moment inside him, but failed to germinate. 'No,' he said. 'He didn't deserve to die.'

'But you kill him.'

'I've killed too many people to draw distinctions.'

'I no understand.'

He sighed. 'No. Most people don't.'

'But if he no deserve to die, why you kill him?'

For a moment he studied the earnest child's dark eyes that

274

genuinely sought answers, and wondered why it should matter to her. Then it struck him that his daughter would probably have asked the same questions, and he was glad he would never have to face her, never have to tell her the truth, or face it himself.

'If you are a soldier, if you are prepared to kill – for whatever reason – you must be prepared to be killed.'

'And you are soldiers? You and your friend?'

'Yes.'

'I no understand. What is your army?'

Elliot searched for another cigarette, then remembered he'd smoked the last one. 'We have no army,' he said irritably. 'We are soldiers of fortune.' And he pre-empted her '*No understand*' by adding, 'We do it for money.'

'You kill to live.'

Elliot nodded. 'Yeah, I suppose you could put it that way.'

'Why?'

Why, indeed, he wondered. He remembered his pride in donning his first uniform, his determination to excel in training, his aspirations to leadership. And then, the grim reality of action. He closed his eyes and, as the red mist dispersed, saw again the bodies of women and children lying dead and dying in the fly-infested heat. 'Governments train you,' he said, 'to defend your country, they tell you. A proud tradition, a heritage of freedom. War, they say, is about the nobility of one man sacrificing himself for the freedom of another. And so you go and kill people in the name of freedom and you believe you are right. And maybe sometimes you are. But when you find yourself a long way from home, in a strange land where the people see you not as a liberator but as a jailer, perhaps you begin to question who is right and who is wrong. And then all that matters is survival. You kill in order not to be killed. If you stop to think about it, you die. So you stop thinking. And then you just kill. After all, it's what they trained you for.'

A shiver ran through him, a quick unaccountable chill in the heat of the night.

'And when they have no further use for you, you find it hard to stop. It's what you know, it's what you do best. It has become a habit. So you sell yourself to whoever will buy. No proud tradition, no heritage of freedom.' He paused. 'No hypocrisy.' He smiled without humour, a heavy irony in his chuckle. 'For what we do we would once have been heroes. Now we are despised.'

'Despised?' Her brow crinkled in a frown of confusion.

'Hated.' He wondered how much she had really understood, wondered what it mattered how little she did.

'And you no mind?'

He smiled at the absurdity of her question. 'What's to mind?'

'If you choose be hated,' she said solemnly, 'then no one love you.'

Elliot's smile faded. 'That's right, little girl,' he said. 'No one loves you.'

They sat in silence for a long, long time, and Elliot thought how comforting the night was, the dark wrapped around them a cloak of safety, all things hidden from the world. Ironic that they should be safe in the dark, the stuff of most men's nightmares. It was with the light, he knew, that danger would come, perhaps death. He glanced at the child's face beside him and felt awkward in the presence of such innocence, an innocence that could kill, incorruptible in its silent accusation. And yet, he knew, it was not her innocence that accused, but his guilt. 'You should sleep,' he advised.

Her eyes were unflickering as they gazed off into the blackness. 'Every time I close eyes I see his face,' she said. 'He was so – surprise. Did he really think I love him? Did he think I choose to go with him all those time?'

And now Elliot realized why she had done it, and he too wondered at the cadre's surprise. He was aware of the turn of her head, her eyes watching him for a long moment, almost as though she knew what had gone through his mind.

'You see your friend when you close eyes?' she said.

His face stung, as if she had slapped him. His mouth and throat were dry and he wished like hell he had another cigarette. 'He was dying,' he said, his voice little more than a whisper.

'Mistah McCue don' think so.'

'Mr McCue didn't know.' He turned to see confusion in her frown. 'It wasn't his wounds,' he said. 'You see . . .' He searched for the words. 'Mr Slattery came here to die. He had stomach cancer.'

'Cancer?' The word meant nothing to her.

'A sickness,' he said. 'Something bad that grows inside you and kills you. Even if he had survived his wounds, the cancer would have killed him. He only had a few weeks left, maybe months.'

'And you would have not kill him if he had not this – cancer?'

It was the question that had filled his own thoughts for the last two days. One he could never answer. 'I don't know,' he said simply, and stared hard at his hands clenched together on his knees in front of him. She reached out and placed her small hand gently over his. He tensed, her touch like an electric shock. And suddenly all tension seeped away, like a burden lifted. For the first time in as many years as he could remember, he had lifted a self-imposed embargo on himself. He had shared a part of himself with someone else. With the sharing came relief. But it also brought a feeling he had not known since childhood. Of vulnerability. And with that, fear.

He withdrew his hands from her touch and glanced down the length of the stricken craft. Serey still slept in the bottom of the boat and, at the far end, McCue dozed lightly, his mouth gaping a little. Moonlight reflected on the water seeping slowly but insistently through the boards of the hull. Elliot handed Ny a tin mug and lifted one himself. 'Better start baling,' he said. 'We're shipping more water.'

The dawn took them by surprise. The darkness lifted suddenly, receding west as the first rays of early morning yellow light fanned out from the watery horizon. McCue stood bleary-eyed scanning the endless expanse of Tonle Sap that surrounded them. He flashed a grim glance in Elliot's direction and shook his head.

'How's our water?' he asked.

'About one more day.' Elliot arched his eyebrows, creasing his forehead. 'If we go easy.'

'Is there any point?' Serey glanced wearily from one to the other. 'We are going to die out here anyway, are we not? And without food or water, it will be a very slow death.'

'Not if my buddy here put a bullet through our heads. Then it could be quick and easy, just like it was for Mikey. That right, Elliot?' McCue's smile was a humourless grimace.

Elliot moved towards the stern. 'I suggest we try and get this outboard working,' he said as though McCue had not spoken. Ny watched him, concerned. Why didn't he say something to defend himself? Why didn't he tell the American the truth?

McCue moved to the back of the boat to join him, and the two men crouched over the motor to resume the hopeless task of stripping and reassembling. Ny turned to her mother. 'We're not going to die,' she said in a high, almost hysterical voice. 'We're not!' Serey sat unmoved, staring across the water, her face grey and gaunt. She gave no indication that she had even heard.

By mid-morning, after repeated failure to restart the out-board, McCue and Elliot gave up and collapsed into the bottom of the boat, running with sweat, gasping in the heat. Serey watched them expressionlessly from the shade of McCue's makeshift awning. 'Goddam!' McCue shouted in sheer frustration. 'Goddam this fucking country!'

'Shhhh!' Ny waved a hand to silence him. She had moved up to the stern when the two men had given up on the outboard, and was staring intently out across the lake.

Elliot pulled himself quickly on to his knees and followed her eye line. He could see nothing. 'What is it?'

'A sound,' she said. 'Listen.'

McCue sat up, too, and strained to hear. 'I don't hear nothing.'

But Elliot was still listening. 'It's an engine,' he said, and his eyes raked back and forth across the horizon.

McCue focused all his attention on the apparent silence before he too picked up the distant growl of a motor. 'Got it,' he said.

'There!' Elliot pointed suddenly to the south-west. And out of the blur of blue, shimmering heat, a tiny dark speck seemed to grow on the horizon.

'A boat,' McCue whispered.

The power launch had once been the property of a wealthy Phnom Penh businessman who kept it moored at an exclusive marina outside the city, using it for weekend fishing trips and pleasure cruises on the Great Lake. It had been lavishly appointed with six berths and a small galley finished in rich mahogany and polished brass. Since 1975 it had been used to ferry important Khmer Rouge cadres and officials back and forth across the Mekong, between Phnom Penh and the Royal Palace, with occasional trips up the length of the Tonle Sap. As it powered its way north yet again, across the endless expanse of the largest body of inland water in Indochina, it had changed hands once more.

Hou Nim stood at the helm, a short wiry figure in his late thirties. His black tunic and trousers hung limp on his lean frame, and a little of the tension that had held him like a clenched fist these last hours had begun to ease. His eyes were dry and gritty, and screwing them up against the reflected glare from the water he felt a wave of fatigue wash over him. He blinked several times, striving to refocus his wandering concentration. The cabin was stifling. A small fan mounted above the dashboard followed an erratic path from left to right and back again, barely ruffling the oppressive airless heat.

He had been at the wheel for nearly six hours since he and his two younger companions had slipped stealthily through the midnight shadows of the deserted Phnom Penh docks to board the vessel in which he had so often ferried the leaders of the revolution: the pompous, self-important Pol Pot, with his fat face and fish eyes; the shrewd watchful countenance of Khieu Samphan; even, once, the darting, frightened, rabbit eyes of Prince Sihanouk himself, unwilling accomplice and virtual prisoner of the Khmer Rouge – a diplomatic sop to the constant stream of wary Chinese advisers in Western suits without whose backing the revolution could never have survived. And, in these last months and weeks, he had seen the corrupt confidence of absolute power gradually vaporize, replaced in his passengers' eyes by a growing panic, that only fuelled their toxic fanaticism.

Fear stalked the empty streets of the capital now like all the ghosts of the Cambodian dead come back to haunt their murderers. The tattered remnants of the Revolutionary Army of Kampuchea were heading north in disarray. Phnom Penh was being abandoned to its fate, though the leadership were still there, clinging insanely to the hope that the Vietnamese, less than fifty kilometres to the south, could yet be stopped. Only hours before Nim had taken his fateful decision to escape the city, he had listened to Pol Pot announcing over Radio Phnom Penh that the Revolutionary Army of Kampuchea would achieve certain victory over the Vietnamese invader. But the procession of Chinese diplomatic personnel, technicians, military advisers, and dependants, heading for the airport, clearly demonstrated that the Chinese thought otherwise.

Nim, like his companions, had been a fisherman before the revolution – the *old people* as they had been called, as opposed to the *new people* from the cities. It was his knowledge of boats that had saved him from a wretched existence digging endless canals or toiling in the paddies. Their relatively privileged position, maintaining and operating the launch for the Party hierarchy, had meant they were well fed and well billeted in almost civilized conditions. But they were now under no illusion that the period of comparative security they had enjoyed in the last four years was drawing to an end.

It had been Nim's idea to take the launch and head north across the Tonle Sap. Rath, the son of a former village chief and friend of Nim, and his cousin, Sien, had taken little persuading. They looked up to the older man who had promised Rath's father that he would keep them safe. They had survived the years of horror virtually unscathed, and were ready to trust him again. The lake, Nim had argued, was their safest means of escape. It would be fast and, since the Khmer Rouge had little in the way of waterborne transport, once they were out on the Great Lake there would be virtually no danger. The riskiest part of the plan was sneaking the boat out of the docks, and the first stage of their journey up the short stretch of the Mekong into the river that flowed out of the Tonle Sap itself. Which was why they had decided to make their break during the hours of darkness. And in the confusion and slack security of the besieged city it had, in the event, proved surprisingly easy. Now they were heading for a small village on the north-eastern shore of the lake. They had no idea what might await them there, but it was home – and they hadn't seen home for a very long time.

Rath was asleep down below on one of the bunks. Sien was on the roof of the cabin, supposedly keeping watch and manning the six-barrelled machine gun that had been mounted there four years earlier. But he was probably asleep, too. Nim glanced at the large compass set into the mahogany fascia in front of him, checked his bearing, then looked up again, beyond the fluttering red flag at the bow of the boat, sweeping his gaze across the unending horizon ahead. For a moment he thought he must have been mistaken, a brief dark speck in his peripheral vision. His eyes flickered back in its direction, and he frowned into the glare. A boat? It was still too far away to be certain. It might be debris of some kind, a tree perhaps. He was tempted to give it a wide berth – it was very small, whatever it was. But he was curious. If it was a boat, what was it doing out here in the middle of the lake? He changed course, tilting them to the east, and the bow of the launch knifed its way towards the distant object.

As he drew closer, within half a kilometre, Nim saw that it was indeed a boat. A small, open fishing craft, little more than a canoe. He pulled back on the throttle, slowing their approach, and banged on the roof.

'Hey, Sien, wake up! Boat ahead!'

Sien was awake instantly, uncurling from his foetal position and springing to his feet. He blinked several times in the flashing sunlight before focusing on the small fishing boat bobbing aimlessly on the water a few hundred metres away. Rath, roused by Nim's voice and the sudden change in the pitch of the engine, emerged sleepily on to the deck.

'What is it?'

Nim pointed ahead and Rath turned his gaze in the direction of the fishing boat. Quickly he ducked back into the cabin and re-emerged clutching an AK-47. Nim had reduced their speed to a crawl, and he approached cautiously.

'Any sign of life?' he called up to Sien.

'Nothing yet,' Sien shouted back. He clasped the grips of the heavy machine gun and swung it on its mounting to point at the small craft as they approached, hooking a nervous finger around the trigger. Rath moved warily along the rail towards the prow of the launch, keeping his eyes fixed on the gentle motion of the fishing boat.

As he was almost upon it, Nim swung the wheel hard left and careened to a stop, side on, towering over the stricken craft and causing it to roll dangerously. He moved out of the cabin and joined Rath at the rail to find himself looking down into the leaking hull of the tiny vessel and raising astonished eyebrows at what he saw.

A sheet of torn and dirty matting had been draped across two planks to create a makeshift shelter at one end, and huddled in its shadow among a pile of canvas packs were an old woman and a young girl. The stern was strewn with the pieces of an unserviceable outboard, and two tin mugs bobbed in the water sloshing back and forth in the bottom of the boat. It was clearly leaking badly and would not stay afloat much longer. From the skin hanging loosely around her neck, the cadaverous cheeks pitted with sores, and the skull that stretched the skin of her shrunken face, Nim saw with a shock that the old woman was barely alive. Her dead eyes stared listlessly up at him from the shadows. The girl, though strained and frightened, looked in better shape. Her eyes burned black with fear.

'Runaways,' Sien called from the roof of the cabin, the relief audible in his voice. And he relaxed his grip on the machine gun and laughed. 'I don't fancy yours much, Rath.'

Rath grinned. 'I don't know,' he said. 'You always did go for older women.'

But Nim was still tense. 'What have you got in there?' he called to the women.

'We need help.' Ny's voice was quivering. 'We are sinking.'

'We have no room,' Nim said.

Rath turned to him. 'Of course we have. We've no use for the old one. But the girl . . . When was the last time you had a woman, Uncle Nim?'

Sien jumped down from the roof to join them and leered over the rail. 'She's a pretty little thing, that one. I'll get her.' He swung a leg over the rail, but Nim grabbed his arm.

'No,' he said firmly. 'I don't like this. What are they doing here – two women on their own?'

'Runaways, like Sien said.' Rath glanced back at the girl and felt the stirrings of lust between his legs.

'You've just forgotten what it's like, old man,' Sien snarled, pulling free of Nim's grasp. 'Me and Rath, we're younger, we've got needs.'

'The only thing we need is to survive,' Nim snapped. 'There's something not right about this. Where did they get these?' He pointed to the canvas packs under the awning.

'Who knows, who cares?' Rath sneered. 'How can an old woman and a young girl be a danger to us?'

'I'll check it out,' Sien said, and he skipped over the railing before Nim could stop him, and clambered down into the boat.

Ny's grip tightened around the butt of Elliot's revolver hidden below her tunic.

On the far side of the launch, Elliot and McCue slipped quietly out of the water and pulled themselves noiselessly aboard. Elliot pointed to the machine gun on the cabin roof. McCue nodded and climbed, catlike, up the side of the cabin, hidden from the view of the three Khmers whose attention was still focused on Serey and Ny. Elliot drew a long hunting blade from his belt and crouching low, inched his way around the forward side of the cabin, bare feet leaving soft wet footprints in his wake.

Sien grinned lecherously at Ny. He pulled one of the canvas packs out from the awning and, squatting in the bottom of the boat, started rifling through its contents. He arched his eyebrows in surprise. Maps, a shortwave radio, various foreign provisions. He looked up at the two women and frowned in suspicion.

'Where'd you get this?'

'What is it?' Nim called.

But Sien paid no attention. Instead he drew a knife from his belt and moved towards Ny. 'I asked you a question!' he hissed.

Ny stiffened with fear, and almost involuntarily started to draw the revolver. But her clumsy movement alerted Sien and he grabbed her wrist, twisting it backwards so that the revolver swung up and then fell harmlessly from her grasp. 'Well, well,' he said grinning, 'a dangerous little thing, aren't you?' And he glanced at the revolver, his expression hardening. 'Now where would you get something like that?' His body partially masked the view from the launch, and Nim leaned nervously over the rail.

'What's going on?'

Sien barely registered the movement beside him, turning instinctively to find himself staring into the barrel of McCue's revolver clutched between Serey's trembling hands. For a moment he tensed, then relaxed and stretched his lips across yellowing teeth in a humourless grimace as Serey jerked the trigger. The explosion was deafening in the confined space, and Serey and Ny felt a singeing flash of heat. Warm blood spattered across their faces as the bullet punched a hole through Sien's face, hurling him backwards into the bottom of the boat.

There was a second of startling confusion in Rath's mind before he swung his AK-47 towards the women in the boat below. But his finger never reached the trigger. A burst of fire sprayed half a dozen bullets into his lower back, cutting him almost in two and launching him over the rail to sprawl across the corpse of his cousin below.

Nim threw himself backwards, instinctively, against the wall of the cabin and out of the line of fire from above. Fear and confusion tumbled together through his mind in a moment of blind panic. There were weapons below. He turned towards the hatch and literally ran on to Elliot's blade, gasping in pain and surprise as the cold steel ruptured his spleen and slid upwards through his stomach towards his heart. Elliot's cold blue eyes met his, and he knew in that moment that he would never see his home again.

Elliot withdrew his knife and let the dead weight of the lifeless Khmer drop to the deck, a pool of dark red spreading quickly across the boards. He crossed to the rail and looked down into the boat below. The bodies of the two younger men lay in a grotesque embrace. Ny clutched her mother's head to her breast, the older woman sobbing uncontrollably, McCue's revolver lying at her feet where she had dropped it.

'Elliot!' There was an urgency in McCue's voice.

Elliot turned to find McCue standing with the machine gun trained on his chest. His face was tight and pale. The two men stared at each other for a long moment.

'Get the women on board,' Elliot said. 'I'll check out the rest of the boat.' And he moved towards the hatch, and swung himself down the steps below deck and out of sight. McCue remained motionless for a few seconds longer, still rigid with unresolved tension, before pushing the machine gun aside and jumping down from the roof.

CHAPTER TWENTY-EIGHT

In the deserted streets the clatter of the bicycle, flat tyres shredding rubber on cracked tarmac, echoed back from the long abandoned blocks of flats. Its rider, in tattered black trousers and ragged tunic, seemed unaware of the devastation around him. Metal security grilles, once drawn across shop doorways, hung smashed and rusting from broken hinges. The carcasses of cars and motorbikes and *cyclo-pousses* littered the streets and pavements like the rotting corpses of wild game killed for sport. In the heat and glare of midday, the shattered remains of Phnom Penh were silent and unmoving, like death itself. Only the distant and occasional rumble of heavy artillery stirred the silence, unheard or disregarded by the cyclist. The rider turned left, along a broad boulevard lined on either side by palm trees. Banknotes fluttered briefly along the gutter in the breeze of his passing. A torn teddy hung from the handlebars, spinning slowly, eyes as sightless as the boy's.

Hau's AK-47 was slung across his back. His hands and face were sticky with the juices of the fruit on which he had earlier gorged himself – wild tropical fruits growing in profusion in the overgrown gardens of the villas near his home. He felt again the fierce cramps in his lower stomach, signalling yet another emptying of his aching bowels, and he began to sing to take his mind off the pain. A tuneless rendering of the Khmer Rouge national anthem. He did not think about the words he sang. They were a reflex action, almost instinctive, dinned into his impressionable young mind at countless compulsory national culture meetings at the commune.

Bright red blood which covers our fields and plains,
Of Kampuchea, our motherland!
Sublime blood of workers and peasants,
Sublime blood of revolutionary men and women fighters!
The Blood changing into unrelenting hatred
And resolute struggle,
On April 17th, under the flag of the Revolution,
Free from Slavery!

The dark shadow of a vulture swooping overhead flashed across the road ahead of him. Its claws rattled on a corrugated iron roof as it landed on a building opposite, its beady black eyes watching with intense interest the figure on the bicycle below. But Hau didn't notice it. His singing faltered as the cramps in his belly increased in intensity. He pulled up and climbed stiffly off the bike, letting it fall to the road in his haste to wrench down his trousers and squat in the gutter. A stream of foul brown liquid squirted from under him to splash into the dust. After a few moments the cramps subsided and he pulled his trousers up and picked up his bike. He felt weak, a little giddy, his mouth parched and dry, a hungry knot in his stomach. He remounted the bike and pushed off, the strain of regaining momentum taking its toll on the wasting muscles of his legs. For a while he tried to remember the song he had been singing, but it seemed strangely elusive, and he soon gave up to let his mind wander as aimlessly as his bike.

He passed a dilapidated petrol station, its pumps long since torn away, the charred remains of vehicles behind the barbed wire of what had once been a second-hand car lot. A yellow SHELL sign still rose high on a pole above the smashed building, an oddly potent reminder that life here had once been very different.

A pall of midday heat hung over Monivong Boulevard, very nearly tangible in its humid intensity. The dirty rag wrapped around Hau's head, to keep the mat of tangled black hair out of his eyes, was sodden with sweat, and tiny rivulets of sweat ran through the grime that clung to his smooth round young face. He was finding it hard to breathe, and he stopped amidst the rubble on the pavement outside the towering Monorom Hotel. This time he leaned the bike against the wall and clambered over the splintered timbers and broken glass into the semi-darkness of the lobby. Shattered glass and the remnants of smashed furniture lay everywhere, a dusty cool in the air.

He shuffled past the elevator to what had once been the reception desk and smacked his hands, palms down, on top of it, raising a thick white stour in the stillness, almost as if to summon the desk clerk with his room key. Only silence greeted him. He picked his way through the upturned tables and chairs in the main dining room, to where double swing doors leading to the kitchen had been torn from their hinges – doors that had swung back and forth countless times as the food prepared by Cambodian chefs had been carried out by Cambodian waiters to feed the voracious appetites of the Americans, and the French *colons* before them.

The kitchen was largely intact, although the tiled floor was thick with broken crockery. Blackened pots and pans lay about where they had been pulled out of cupboards or torn from hooks. Two enormous refrigerators stood in the dark with their doors hanging open. Hau hurried across the kitchen with a quickening heart and the false hope that there might still be food in them. But they were empty, shelves ripped out, a cracked ice-tray lying on the floor. It was nearly five years since electricity had powered these icons of Western decadence, inducing them, improbably, to produce ice from water in tropical temperatures. In a fit of temper he kicked out at one of them, then thumped into it with his shoulder, rocking it back and forth till it crashed on to its side, rupturing the network of pipes at the back of it to release a trickle of milky white chemical on to the floor.

The noise of the crash still reverberating in his ears, Hau turned away in disgust and stumbled over a small round metal object beneath his feet. He stooped to pick it up and found himself holding a tin little larger than a hand grenade, its label blackened by time and dust. He wiped it furiously on his sleeve then crossed to the door to examine it in the light. A faded blue-lettered *Nestlé Milk* was just discernible. The words themselves had no meaning for Hau, but there was something vaguely familiar about them, evoking a misty childhood memory of his mother's kitchen and something sweet. With a rising excitement, he realized that it was food, and he turned the tin round and round in his hands, staring with sparkling eyes. He ran his tongue across parched lips and squatted on the floor, drawing his knife from his belt. He stood the tin in front of him, took the knife in both hands and drove it several times into the lid, causing a thick white substance to ooze from the punctures. He collected a little on the tip of a finger and raised it tentatively to his tongue. The sweet taste almost burned his mouth, and in an instant he had snatched the tin from the floor and lifted it to eager lips that sucked fiercely at the cloying sweetness. When the tin would yield no more, he placed it once again on the floor and stabbed at it repeatedly with his knife until he could force the jagged lid out and dip fingers inside. Again and again he ran them around the inside of the tin and sucked at them hungrily until he had cleaned out every last drop. Then he threw the tin away and turned back into the kitchen, eyes probing each dark corner in search of more.

For half an hour he tore the kitchen apart, ripping units from the wall, searching on hands and knees among the debris on the floor, before slumping, unrewarded and sweating, against an upturned table in the centre of the room.

He sat in the semi-darkness for a long time until his

breathing and his disappointment had subsided, and he realized that he was thirstier than ever. But now he felt weak again too, the sweet taste of the Nestlé milk already a distant memory, almost as though he had dreamt it. He closed his eyes and felt himself swimming backwards through space. Faces ballooned at him through the darkness and he saw his own hands reaching out to pull plastic bags tight over their heads, holding them in place, ignoring the frantic fight for breath that came from within. Hands reached out towards him like claws, fingers grotesquely curled in a last desperate attempt to hold on to life. He felt them tug at his trousers, at his tunic and, finally, at his face, sharp nails drawing blood.

He awoke with a yell and felt scurries of movement all around him. His cheek still hurt where the nails of the hand in his dream had scratched him. When he put his hand to his face he drew back bloodied fingers. The floor had come alive and seemed to be moving beneath him. He drew in his knees and found himself staring into hundreds of tiny black eyes, twinkling with pinpoints of light. For a moment he thought he must still be asleep before he realized that the floor around him was indeed alive – with rats. He heard himself scream as he leapt to his feet, swinging the Kalashnikov from his back and firing wildly at the floor around him, raising clouds of choking dust and sending splinters of tile and crockery spanging off in all directions. The rodents scattered in a squealing panic, several exploding in a bloody mush, caught in the spray of bullets as they fled.

Hau stopped screaming as he stopped firing and found himself breathless and shaking uncontrollably. He didn't wait to count the rats he had killed, but turned and ran from the kitchen, through the dining room, crashing into tables and chairs as he went, oblivious of the pain. Into the gloom of the lobby, back past the elevator to stumble over the rubble in the doorway and out on to the street, where the heat and glare of the afternoon sun hit him like a wall. He screwed his smarting eyes against the light and snatched his bike from the wall, mounting it and pedalling blindly away along the boulevard.

When, finally, Hau became aware that his progress had slowed almost to a halt, he had no idea where he was. He had pedalled furiously through a dozen or more deserted streets, unseeing, uncaring, driven only by the desperate desire to escape the nightmare presence of the rats that had crawled over his sleeping body to tear at his face in the dark empty kitchen of the Monorom Hotel. He swung his leg over the saddle and staggered to a halt, the hot pavement burning the leathery soles of his feet. His fitful gasps for air seemed to scorch his lungs.

He glanced around at the crumbling buildings with all their broken windows, the trees and bushes that grew in thick profusion in deserted yards. And his eyes came to rest, across the street, on the high walls and open gates of the deserted Phnom Penh High School. Beyond the walls, and the desolation of the empty playground, stood three plain buildings built in the early Sixties by the Sihanouk government to serve as one of the city's principal high schools. Hau could not, at first, identify what it was about these buildings that seemed odd, until he became aware that all their windows were intact. But more than that, a dreadful silence seemed to emanate from the very heart of the school, smothering all sound around it. Nothing moved, nothing stirred. There was no birdsong. A pall of something you could almost touch seemed to hang over it, drawing Hau's curiosity, yet at the same time provoking a dread that he could not identify.

He leaned his bike against a tree and very slowly crossed the road, watching keenly for any sign of movement. As he passed through the gates and beyond the walls he stopped, suddenly, and listened. What had seemed like silence was developing into a deep, distant hum, a vibration like the sound of a motor or a high-tension electricity pylon. Although ever-present, it was not a constant sound, but rose and fell in unusual cadences. And as Hau neared the main entrance, the intensity, though still muted, increased. It had a disquieting effect, and for a moment Hau hesitated, and considered turning back. But something compelled him on, to push open the door and step inside.

The stench of decay closed around him, sickly sweet, almost overpowering in the heat, and his ears filled with a buzzing that roared in the stillness. The air was black with flies. Engulfing, smothering clouds of them. He struck out blindly as if he could somehow fend them off, and quickly ripped the cloth from around his head and clamped it to his nose and mouth. The door he had entered by swung shut behind him, and in his panic he stumbled towards the light shining through another to his left. He found himself in a long corridor divided into cubicles by crude brick partitions. Sunlight slanted through the windows all along one side, almost obscured by the flies. His entrance seemed to infuriate them, their rage redoubled to a pitch that was almost unbearable.

The air was virtually unbreathable, and Hau choked behind the filthy rag he clutched to his face. His only thought was to get out. But the heat, his fever, the gnawing in his gut, combined with the stink and the flies, had a disorientating effect. Afraid to go back, uncertain now of which way he'd come in, he stretched out a hand to support himself against a brick partition and staggered forward to reach an opening. Turning into the cubicle, he tripped over a petrol can, falling and spilling an acrid yellow liquid across the floor beside him. Bile rose in his throat as he reached up to grasp the skeleton metal frame of a bed without a mattress, and found himself staring into eyes that gaped back at him from a half-decayed face – a face that seemed almost animated by the flies that crawled over its putrid flesh. The nose had gone. Black and broken teeth protruded from a mouth that gaped in a hideous grimace. Hau screamed in terror and fell back against the wall. The corpse was tied to the bed frame, hideously mutilated, still straining against the agony of a death that had not come soon enough. An empty chair sat by the side of the bed, and beyond it a blackboard still bore a bizarre list of instructions:

You must immediately answer my questions without wasting time to reflect.

During the bastinado or the electrisization you must not cry loudly. Don't be a fool, for you are a person who dares to thwart the revolution.

If you disobey any point of my regulations you will get either ten strokes of the whip or five shocks of electric discharge.

The walls were plastered with grotesque black and white photographs of hundreds of dreadfully tortured faces and mutilated bodies.

Hau was shaking uncontrollably now, and he heard his screams like some disembodied sound from another world. He slithered across the fly-infested urine he had spilled on the floor, and ran down the corridor. More faces leered at him from every opening; twisted fingers, their bones poking through fetid flesh, grasped at him from beyond the grave, as they had done in his dream. Only this was no dream. Through a door to a classroom, all light nearly obliterated by the flies, Hau stumbled and fell. Stinking corpses piled up in the dark clasped him to their bosoms, a nightmare of arms and legs whose rotted flesh fell away in his hands. Accusing eyes stared in the gloom, open mouths breathing death in his face. Somehow, for he no longer acted with any will, he pulled free of their embrace and tumbled back through the door and along the corridor, flies in his ears and nose and mouth, tears blinding him. Through another door, and another, until suddenly he collapsed down a short flight of steps into bright afternoon sunshine and lay retching in the yard.

Still crawling with flies, he tore away his ragged calico tunic and trousers and ran naked across the yard, out through the gates and across the street. He grasped his bike, still racked by the sobs that tore themselves painfully from his chest, and ran pushing it up the street, almost unaware of his nakedness, certainly unashamed by it. For he knew now that there could be nobody left alive in this world but him.

The speeding black American saloon car wove its way through the debris-littered streets; the charred, rusted remains of civilian and military vehicles, the belongings of a lost population dragged out on to the street and left to the ravages of time. Its driver wore a *kramar* over his black tunic and trousers, but his three passengers were incongruous in their dark Western suits: two expressionless Chinese and a small, ageing Cambodian with a sad round face and deeply ringed dark eyes.

Sticky and uncomfortable in the airless heat of the car, they were jolted again and again by wide cracks and potholes in the road. The Cambodian gazed out at the ruins of his city. The desolation of what he saw was reflected in his heart. Pol Pot and the others had left ahead of him, no doubt in futile resistance to the invader, but still the Chinese adhered to their ally, insisted on providing his safe passage out of the country. He was after all, as the legitimate ruler of his beloved Cambodia, their last vestige of international credibility, as he had been since the Khmer Rouge victory in 1975. He himself had been powerless, clinging despondently to the hope that the madness must end sometime, and that he could play a part in the rebuilding. But now he knew that for him it was over.

His thoughts drifted back to the past, how it had all once been – in his mind an enchanted, happy time; court dancers performing to the music he himself had written, extravagant royal banquets, the gatherings of joyous, colourful crowds on the river to witness the *Fêtes des Eaux*. And he frowned as he recalled the tide of events, his attempts to keep his country out of the war that raged between America and Vietnam. And then the bombs and the coup, conspiracy and betrayal feeding the cause of the Khmer Rouge. And finally the murder of his people, and now his own enforced exile. He wondered what the future could possibly hold for him.

As they sped past the Phnom Penh High School he shuddered inwardly. He had built it to educate. The Khmer Rouge had used it to re-educate. Such an innocent word to describe the torture and murder that raged inside S.21, the Tuol Sleng extermination centre. All in the name of a people who had been brutalized just as savagely. The madness, he knew, had no parallel. Even Hitler had not enslaved and destroyed his own people.

At the top of the street, the car turned north towards the airport where they would catch the last flight out to Peking. A movement caught the Cambodian's eye, and he turned with amazement to see the naked figure of a small boy pushing a bicycle and running away down a side street. Their driver braked hard, slamming the car to a halt with a squeal of tyres.

'What are you doing!' Prince Sihanouk demanded.

'Deserter!' spat the driver, and swung himself out of the car. He drew his pistol, steadied it at arm's length on the roof, and levelled it at the back of the running boy.

'Leave it!' snapped one of the Chinese. 'There is no time!'

The driver cursed. The boy was out of range anyway. He holstered his pistol and jumped back into the driver's seat, his lips curled in annoyance.

'Go,' said the Chinese. 'We are already late.'

As the car screeched away with spinning tyres, Sihanouk saw the naked boy turn safely out of view to be swallowed up by the doomed city. It was to be the Prince's last sight, he knew, of his beloved Phnom Penh. And it filled him with a deep despair.

CHAPTER TWENTY-NINE

Serey and Ny squatted on facing bunks by the light of a small oil lamp, gorging on large bowls of steaming rice. Outside, the rumble of thunder sounded ominously in the black night sky, and warm rain battered on the deck above. Ny glanced nervously at her mother. They had not spoken in the hours since the shooting on the boat. The initial tears had dried up. The warmth of their embrace, as Serey clung to her daughter in the moments after the shooting, had turned cold, and that brief vulnerability had dissipated, leaving her brittle and aloof. Ny's burden of guilt seemed greater now than ever.

She looked at the frail, shrunken figure in peasant pyjamas and longed simply to hold her. Through all the silent years, when family loyalties and affections had been dangerous, banished by the higher demands of Angkar, they had grown apart. Confidences had become almost as rare as conversation. Increasingly, all that had tied them was the umbilical cord of the past, memories, how they had once been. Mother and daughter. They were like strangers now, embarrassed by the knowledge of what each had done, what each had become.

They had no secrets. Whatever Hau had done or become, only he knew. And he knew nothing of their shame. Perhaps Hau would be their only salvation. *I have done things. They made me do things*, he had told her that night beneath the hut at the commune. She hadn't wanted to know then, didn't now. She wanted never to know. She remembered his small, boyish face with its old eyes, and the tears that had run down his cheeks as he left. *I will go to our home in Phnom Penh. If our country is freed tell my mother to look for me there.*

'Do you think Hau will be in Phnom Penh?' she asked suddenly.

Her mother's sad eyes flickered slowly up to meet hers. 'There is no point in asking questions that cannot be answered.'

It was like a slap in the face, and the old woman turned back to the last of her rice, unaware of the tears that filled her daughter's eyes, blinking hard to hide her own.

Directly above them, in the cabin, Elliot was slumped in a fixed swivel seat by the wheel watching the rain run down the windows. His cigarette glowed in the dark as he sucked deeply at the hot burning tobacco. Along with the sacks of rice in the galley, they had found other provisions: tinned foods, cartons of cigarettes, a crate of beer. They had eaten their fill, then taken a course south across the deserted wastes of the Great Lake. As the sun set, they had reached the southern end of the lake and navigated slowly through numerous waterways before debouching into the wide, chocolate-brown waters of the slow-moving Mekong. These had been tense moments, exposed as they were to attack from either bank. But they had seen nothing, no sign of human activity or habitation. An eerie calm blanketed the land, unnatural in its stillness.

'Where is everyone – *anyone*?' McCue had muttered under his breath. He was unsettled by the pall of silence, broken only by the gentle put-put of their engine, that hung over them.

With the ending of the day, the heat and humidity had intensified, great dark clouds rolling in from the west to blot out the sky before night fell to cloak them in darkness. Elliot reckoned they were less than an hour upriver from Phnom Penh itself, and they had decided to drop anchor in the lee of the west bank and wait until just before dawn to make their final approach to the city. The rain had started not long after.

Elliot took a slug of beer and checked his watch. Almost half-past ten. It would be a long night, through which the fear of tomorrow would deny him sleep. He was annoyed by the fear that knotted in his stomach and held all the muscles of his body hard and tense. It was unaccountable. Less than eight hours earlier he had accepted, without fear, that death was inevitable. And now, the hope that glimmered feebly in the promised light of dawn had made him fear again. Perhaps, he thought, it wasn't death he was afraid of, but life.

The sound of bare feet slithered across the roof and McCue dropped lightly down in the open doorway. Elliot could see his dark form faintly silhouetted against the sky beyond. The American stepped in out of the rain, dripping on to the dry boards. 'No point in keeping watch. We can't see and we can't be seen in this rain.' He spoke quietly, but his voice seemed very close.

'Sure,' Elliot said.

'D'you get anything on the radio?'

'Voice of America, Radio Moscow, World Service.'

'And?'

'The Brits and the Yanks say the situation is confused. Moscow says the Khmer Rouge have abandoned the city and are fleeing north. The Vietnamese are expected to take Phnom Penh tomorrow.'

McCue shifted uneasily in the dark. 'What do you think?'

Elliot took another draw on his cigarette. 'I think things are bound to look confusing from a Bangkok massage parlour, which is where most of the American and British correspondents will be right now. The Russians'll be getting their briefing from the front line.'

'You still plan to go in before dawn?'

'Have you got a better idea?' The tension between them crackled like electricity in the dark.

'You know the kid won't be there.'

'Sure.'

'So what then?'

Elliot sighed and brushed the sweat from his eyes. 'I don't know.' He sounded weary. 'The woman and the girl shouldn't have anything to fear from the Vietnamese.'

'You ain't suggesting we give ourselves up?'

Elliot raised a bottle to his lips and let warm flat beer run back over his throat. 'Can't say I particularly fancy an extended stay at the Hanoi Hilton.'

The Hanoi Hilton was the name given to the re-education centres in Hanoi where hundreds of American servicemen captured during the Vietnam war had been imprisoned and tortured, brainwashed into making public denouncements of their country's involvement in the war. Many had eventually been released, but it was rumoured that many more still languished there.

'So what are you suggesting?' McCue's voice was cold.

'Seems to me,' Elliot said, pulling the last lungful of smoke from his cigarette, 'that our best hope is to reach the coast, try and get across the Gulf of Thailand.'

'Shit, man! How are we gonna do that with an old lady and a young girl in tow?'

Elliot shook his head. 'We can't.'

There was a long silence. When at last he spoke, McCue's voice was brittle and flinty. 'You're saying we dump them.'

'Even if we could take them with us, they wouldn't go. Not without the boy.' Elliot's voice was calm and even. There was no hint of defensiveness in it. He was simply stating the facts as he saw them. He wasn't prepared for McCue's lunge across the cabin, the hands that grabbed him in the dark. Hot breath hissed in his face.

'You bastard, Elliot! If you were ready to dump them, what the fuck are we doing here? What did Mikey die for?'

For the first time in many hours all Elliot's tension fell away.

'I don't know,' he said. 'I really don't.' And somehow the words relieved him of the burden. 'Things just didn't work out the way I planned.'

'Fuck you!' McCue raised his eyes to the ceiling in frustration and he let go of Elliot to slump back into the chair. He thought about Lotus, and his baby who would be asleep now on the rush mat in the back room of his *klong* house. Tears welled in his eyes with the realization that the boy would never know his real father, that Lotus would probably take another husband. That he was, after all, going to die. He sat limp, his arms dangling loose at his sides. 'When I don't need you any more, Elliot,' he said softly, 'you're a dead man.'

Elliot's face glowed red, briefly, in the flare of the match he struck to light another cigarette. 'You're too late Billy,' he said, his voice tight with emotion. 'I died a long time ago.'

CHAPTER THIRTY

'Have you known La Mère Grace long?' The fat smiling face of the General leaned closer beside her at the table, a confidential air in his voice. His attentive eyes twinkled into hers.

'No, not long at all,' Lisa said. 'Less than a week, in fact.'

'Ah,' the General said, as if this was deeply significant and he was being made privy to a secret. 'She is a fine woman,' he added.

Lisa nodded. 'Yes, she's been very good to me.'

The General was a large man, tall by Asian standards, overweight but impressive in his army dress uniform. He had a fine head of thick steel-grey hair and black, bushy eyebrows above smiling eyes. His lips were a little too thick, purplish and wet. In his mid-fifties, he was not an attractive man, but full of charm, Lisa thought. He had been particularly attentive and put her at her ease in this gathering of strangers. She heard the sound of Grace's voice raised in laughter and she glanced down the table to see her in animated conversation with a small, ugly man in an expensive-looking grey silk suit. There were twenty round the long table, silver cutlery and cut crystal glasses sparkling in the candlelight. Much wine had been consumed with the meal and the conversation was lively, punctuated by frequent bursts of laughter.

Most of the men were middle-aged or elderly; politicians, high-ranking army officers and senior policemen, Grace had told Lisa. Influential friends. Their female companions were all very young, Lisa's age and a little older. Dazzlingly beautiful, delicate oriental girls, demure in traditional costumes of patterned Thai silk, or in long figure-hugging Vietnamese *ao dai*.

Lisa's dress, when it had been delivered that morning, had delighted her, the deep crimson complementing the hint of strawberry in her rich blonde hair, the daring cut exposing a wide slash of creamy white skin across the swell of her breasts. Grace had regarded her with obvious pleasure, nodding, satisfied, and said, 'You'll be the belle of the ball, my dear.'

But when she first arrived at the club, Lisa had felt very conspicuous, tall and big-boned and rather clumsy beside these sylph-like Thai girls. Her skin, she thought, seemed an ugly, blue-veined white compared with the smooth golden brown of these lovely creatures. She felt very unattractive. So she had been surprised, and then flattered, when very quickly she had become the centre of attention, eyes dwelling on her with undisguised admiration. She had caught the jealous glances of several Thai girls and felt her confidence returning, taking a heady delight in the attentions of such important people. Once or twice she had caught Grace's eye, and Grace had nodded, smiling encouragement.

The General introduced himself early, fetching her a drink and telling her that she must sit beside him at dinner. A young white girl, particularly one as beautiful as Lisa, must take great care in a city like Bangkok to choose carefully the company she keeps, he had told her. His mischievous smile had instantly endeared him to her. She had laughed. But still she remembered Sivara.

The meal was served discreetly by white-jacketed waiters who flitted soundlessly among the guests like ghosts. Seafood platters on beds of rice, tender beef curry and coconut in scooped-out pineapple shells, cellophane noodle salad and sticky rice with coconut cream. For the most part the men drank Thai whisky and the women sipped at glasses of expensive French wine. At the other side of a small, dimly lit dance floor, a quartet of musicians played lazy American jazz music that drifted across the conversation.

Lisa felt warm and relaxed, and was gently tipsy from too much soft, fruity, red wine.

'Grace tells me your father is in Cambodia.' The General's simple statement startled her. In the days she had spent lying around reading, lazily flipping through Grace's huge collection of books on erotic art, accompanying Grace on occasional shopping trips, she had almost forgotten why she was here. The nightmare of the attack by Sivara had retreated from her memory like a bad dream, and for the first time since her mother's death she had begun to relax, succumbing to the warm somnambulant comforts of Grace's sumptuous villa with its pretty maidservants and good food.

'Yes,' she replied, and she felt her face flush with guilt. Why did it seem so much less important now that she find her father than it had only a week ago?

The General shook his head sadly. 'It's a bad business.'

'What do you mean?' A stab of fear pierced Lisa's complacency.

'Have you not read the newspapers? Refugees from Cambodia and many deserting Khmer Rouge are flooding over the Thai border in their thousands. The Khmers have been well beaten in the south and are retreating north into country which, by all accounts, is now ravaged by famine. And the Vietnamese seem poised to take Phnom Penh any day.'

'But what does that mean for my father?'

The General put a comforting hand over hers. 'I'm afraid, my dear, that any Westerner caught up in events south of the border has little or no chance of surviving them.'

'It will be a difficult time, too, for Thailand.' A dapper, middle-aged member of the government sitting opposite poured himself another whisky. 'Just when we thought we had the communists under control at home, there could be anything up to half a million of them flooding over the border.'

'Frankly,' an earnest middle-aged journalist cut in, 'I see a bigger threat from having the Vietnamese along our border. At least the Khmer Rouge kept themselves to themselves. The Vietnamese are well known for their territorial ambitions.'

The General lit a fat Havana cigar. 'There are already several divisions of our troops on their way to stiffen border security,

Lat, as you well know. It would be very unhelpful of you to print such scaremongering speculation in your newspaper.'

The politician added, 'We also have the full financial and political backing of the Americans.'

The journalist curled his lips in a sardonic smile. 'A lot of good that did Thieu in Saigon or Lon Nol in Cambodia.'

'You mean there could be a war?' Lisa felt nonplussed by this exchange on a subject of which she had so little grasp.

'Oh, I doubt that,' the General smiled. 'A little sabre-rattling, perhaps.' He patted her hand reassuringly. 'I'm sorry to alarm you about your father, my dear. Perhaps he will survive. He is a soldier, after all, is he not?' Lisa was shocked by how much he seemed to know. He leaned closer and whispered, 'La Mère Grace has told me everything. She thought I might be able to help.' She smelt the whisky and cigar smoke on his breath.

'And can you?' Her voice seemed very tiny.

'I will certainly do whatever I can. My people on the border have been well briefed. If your father succeeds in crossing back into Thailand he will be in safe hands.'

If she'd had a little less to drink, Lisa might just have detected the subtly ambiguous stress placed by the General on the word safe. She might also have noticed the envy in the eyes of his companions across the table. But as it was, she felt nothing but gratitude towards this benevolent father figure who had steered her with such gentle assurance through the evening. He pushed his chair back and rose to his feet, holding out a hand towards her. 'Dance?'

Startled out of her reverie, brief thoughts about her father and why she was here, Lisa glanced towards the dance floor and saw that several other couples were already dancing. 'Yes, of course.' She took his hand and he led her on to the floor. He held her firmly, but formally, not too close, and guided her in a slow shuffle around the floor to the dreamy music of the small jazz band. Lisa noticed that most of the other couples danced with bodies pressed close, hands and arms entwined, and felt that she and the General seemed very out of place.

'Are you not married?' she asked suddenly.

'Oh, yes,' he said. 'I was married for nearly twenty-five years. My wife died eighteen months ago. Cancer of the throat.'

'Oh, I'm so sorry.'

The General smiled sadly. 'We had not been close for many years. It was important to me that she give me sons. We tried for a long time. Then the doctor told us she could not have children and gradually we grew apart.' He stared off somewhere over her shoulder, eyes glazed. 'My fault really. I suppose I blamed her. As I blamed her for dying and leaving me, finally, on my own.'

It was a sentiment Lisa understood only too well, and she gave the General's hand a squeeze of sympathy. 'But if you weren't close . . .'

'It is strange,' the General mused, 'how we grow to depend on people. Just her presence had always been a comfort to me. Now my house seems cold and empty without her. Even yet.' He seemed to return from some distant place, and he smiled as his eyes flickered back to meet hers. 'Of course, my life, as it always has been, is consumed by the army. And these are demanding times. Although in my few moments of relaxation I always have my ...' he hesitated a moment '... my books and my pipe.'

Lisa laughed. 'Your pipe?'

The General acknowledged her misunderstanding with a small secret smile. 'Not as you understand it, my dear.'

It was a moment before realization dawned. 'You mean opium?' she asked, horrified.

'A small vice, commonly practised in the East. Harmless in moderation and wonderful therapy for a troubled spirit.'

Lisa remained unconvinced. 'But – isn't opium just like heroin?'

The General laughed. 'Heroin is merely a derivative, processed for Western tastes, cheap and nasty like American junk food. The experienced smoker uses his opium, is not used by it.' He glanced around the room. 'I doubt if there is a single one of my colleagues here who does not enjoy the occasional pipe.'

'Isn't it illegal?'

But the General's smile only widened. 'You have, I think, a lot to learn, my pretty little English rose.' Which left Lisa feeling very foolish and very young.

She turned at a touch on her arm to find Grace there, radiant and with a little smile of apology. 'I'm sorry to interrupt,' Grace said. 'I'm afraid I have been called away to attend to some business. I don't want to break up the party, so please carry on for as long as you wish.'

'When will you be back?' Lisa asked.

'I shall go straight back to the house,' said Grace. 'I have invited a few of my guests there for drinks. General, could you see that Lisa is delivered safely home?'

'It would give me great pleasure, La Mère Grace.' The General made a formal bow of apology. 'Unfortunately I have to return home. I am expecting an important phone call around twelve.'

'Then perhaps Lisa could go with you, and you could bring her to my house after your call. I am sure the midnight curfew does not extend to army generals.'

'Well, of course. I should be only too happy to oblige.' He turned to Lisa. 'Assuming you have no objections, my dear.'

'No. No, of course not,' Lisa said a little uncertainly.

'Good, that's settled, then. Thank you, General.' Grace beamed and kissed Lisa on the cheek. '*À toute à l'heure, ma chérie.*' And she drifted away through the dancers towards the table, where a waiter hovered with her shawl.

'Well,' said the General as Lisa turned back to him, 'at least I shall have the pleasure of your company for a little longer than I expected.' He raised his arm to look at his watch. 'We should leave soon. My home is on the other side of the city.'

The General's house lay at the end of a dark *soi* off Rama I Road, next to the Klong San Saep. It was built in traditional Thai style, mostly from teak, and was set in beautiful floodlit gardens. The General had to negotiate an elaborate security system to let them in. He clapped his hands and called for his houseboy to fetch drinks, and then switched off the floodlights in the garden. The houseboy – he could have been no more than fifteen – brought warmed rice wine, and Lisa sank back into a comfortable settee and let her eyes wander over the collection of Asian art and artefacts that filled the sitting room: Japanese watercolours, a series of paintings depicting scenes from the Buddhist Jataka tales, Chinese and Thai porcelain, and literally dozens of Buddha images from all over south-east Asia. She sipped the warm, slightly bitter wine. 'You have quite a collection,' she said.

'It was my wife who collected,' said the General. 'Something to fill her days.' He sighed, a touch of melancholy in his smile. 'Oddly, I get more pleasure from it all now than I did when she was alive.' He followed her gaze to the collection of Buddhas. 'You like the Buddhas?'

'They're beautiful,' Lisa said. 'Are you a Buddhist?'

'A very bad one,' he said with a rueful grin. 'I suppose there are bad Christians, too.'

Lisa returned the grin. 'You're talking to one.' She rose and crossed to a tall, slender and pensive image sitting cross-legged on a stone pillow. She reached out a hand to touch it, 'May I?'

'Of course.'

It felt smooth and cold to the touch. 'So many images to worship.'

'The images are not for worship,' he corrected her. 'One worships Buddha, but merely venerates the image.' He paused to sip his wine and watch her contemplatively. 'Do you know anything of our religion?'

'Nothing,' Lisa said. 'I'm afraid I'm really very ignorant.'

The General eased himself out of his chair and wandered across the polished teak floor to join her. 'Buddha,' he said, 'gave us Four Noble Truths. Life is subject to sorrow; sorrow is caused by ignorance, which leads to desire; sorrow can be eliminated by eliminating desire; desire can be eliminated by following the Noble Eightfold Path.'

'What is the noble eightfold path?'

He laughed. 'No doubt as a child you learned the books of the Old Testament, or the Catechisms. Do you still remember them?'

'No.' She returned his laugh. 'Probably not.'

He shrugged. 'My problem has always been in eliminating desire.' And he reached out and ran his hand through her thick, short, blonde hair. She took a step back, alarmed by the unexpectedness of his touch. 'You mustn't worry, my dear,' he smiled. 'It would be unnatural, even for an old man like me, not to have his desire aroused by your beauty.'

For the first time, Lisa felt a stab of doubt, followed by an acute sense of vulnerability. Was it a mistake to have come here alone with this man? And yet he was a friend of Grace. She searched for something appropriate to say, but nothing would come.

Somewhere in the depths of the house a phone rang. 'My call,' the General said. 'Please make yourself comfortable, have some more wine. I should not be too long.' And he hurried away to disappear down a dimly lit passage at the far side of the room.

Lisa took a deep breath and told herself she was in no danger. How could she be? She took another sip of wine and crossed back to the settee and perched herself gingerly on the edge of it. In a short while they would be heading back across the city to Grace's house.

She sat for what seemed like a very long time looking idly around the large sprawling sitting room, oriental rugs scattered across the polished teak floor, black lacquer tables laden with ornaments, several beautifully painted lacquer screens. She was startled when the fan overhead suddenly hummed into life and began turning lazily. She glanced round to see the General's houseboy emerge from the passageway and climb the open-slat staircase to the upper floor. He did not look in her direction. After a while she grew restless and more nervous. Her wine was finished and she laid her cup on a table and stood up to wander round the room, touching things distractedly.

'I'm sorry to have kept you, my dear.'

She turned and saw, with a sense of shock, that the General was dressed only in a black silk robe with red trim and a red belt. On his feet he wore soft open slippers.

'What are you doing?' she asked, with a sudden foreboding. But he remained relaxed and smiling.

'I'm afraid I must wait for a further call. Thirty, forty minutes, no more. I have asked my boy to prepare a couple of pipes while we wait.'

Lisa picked up her purse, panic rising in her chest. 'I think I'll just get a taxi.'

'I regret that will not be possible. It is already after twelve and the curfew is in force.'

'I should phone Grace and let her know, then.'

The General smiled. 'I have already done so.' He held out a hand towards her. 'Come,' he said. 'Think of it as an education. The broadening of your experience.'

'I don't think so,' Lisa said.

'Nonsense.' He crossed the room and took her hand. 'You cannot come to the East without experiencing a little of its magic. You must grow up sometime.'

Reluctantly, because she did not know what else to do, she let him lead her to the stairs, and as they climbed slowly to the upper floor he said, 'The Noble Eightfold Path leads to the abolition of suffering.'

'I thought you'd forgotten.' She was startled by this unexpected tangent.

'I looked them up. For my own enlightenment as well as yours. Shall I go on?'

She nodded mutely as they reached a landing and turned down a narrow hallway with concealed lighting.

'Right understanding,' he said, 'meaning an intellectual grasp of the Four Noble Truths; Right intention, meaning the extinction of revenge, hatred, and the desire to do harm . . .' He opened the door into a large study bedroom. A bed draped with mosquito netting, a polished mahogany desk and leather swivel chair, two leather armchairs, a lacquer coffee table. One wall was lined with books, on another hung a huge map of

South East Asia. Soft, deep-piled rugs covered the floor, and the only light came from a brass desk lamp with a green glass shade. The room was filled with a peculiar stale, musty smell, and the General's houseboy knelt over the naked flame of an oil lamp on a low bedside table. In his hands he held the General's pipe – more than two feet of straight bamboo with carved ivory at each end. About two-thirds of the way down, a small bowl was set into the bamboo, dark and polished by the frequent kneading of opium.

Lisa concentrated hard on the General's words to still the fear that was growing in her. 'Right speech,' he droned on, 'meaning telling the truth, avoiding rumours, swearing and conceited gossip; Right action, meaning the decision not to kill or hunt any living thing, not to steal or to commit adultery . . .'

The houseboy was kneading a little ball of hot paste on the convex margin of the bowl, and Lisa smelled for the first time the pungent sweet odour of fresh opium.

'. . . Right effort, meaning the conscious choice of good over evil; Right mindfulness, meaning the awareness of the divisions of contemplation: the body; sensation, the mind, and the Dharma . . .' The General guided her to one of the leather armchairs and indicated she should sit. She sat uneasily as he crossed to his desk and poured them each more wine from a small porcelain jug. 'And Right concentration, meaning the mental absorption on actions to be performed rightly.' He handed her a cup and paused. 'Was that seven or eight?'

'I lost count,' Lisa said nervously

The General laughed. 'So did I. I think I may have forgotten one. But, then, forgetfulness is one of the privileges of old age.' He turned to his boy and barked something in Thai. The boy nodded and the General drained his cup in one draught before crossing to the bed. 'Excuse me, my dear. I like to make myself comfortable.' He arranged himself on the bed, propping himself up with several pillows. Lisa watched with a fascinated horror as the houseboy plunged a needle into a tiny cavity in the centre of the bowl, and with a practised flick of the wrist released the opium and reversed the bowl over the flame. He held the pipe steady as the General leaned forward and took the end of it between his lips. The bead of opium bubbled gently as he inhaled in one long smooth pull before lying back on the pillows, slowly releasing the smoke from his mouth and nostrils. He sighed with a deep satisfaction and visibly relaxed. He barked something again in Thai and the houseboy immediately began preparing another pipe. 'I have asked him to prepare you a pipe,' he said without looking at her.

Lisa sat frozen in her chair. 'I don't think so,' she said. But there was uncertainty in her voice, something seductive in the sweet smell of the smoke. Her head swam with confusion and alcohol and the temptation of something forbidden. She took a mouthful of rice wine.

The General rolled over on to his side, propping himself on one elbow, his fat smiling face almost beatific. 'But you must. We are on this earth for such a short time. It would be criminal not to taste the fruits that it offers at least once. And once

tasted, never forgotten. You will not regret it, I promise you.'
But still she hesitated. He shrugged, arching his eyebrows in
a gesture of regret. 'Of course, I cannot force you.' He spoke
again to the boy, who plunged the needle for a second time,
flipping the pipe over the flame and holding it steady for his
master. The General sucked long and deep and lay back again,
eyes closed, as the smoke drifted up from his open mouth.

Lisa finished the wine in her cup and rose unsteadily to her
feet. Her resolve seemed to ebb away, her throat constricting
in anticipation. She seemed drawn, irrevocably, to the pipe,
sudden desire overcoming all doubts. 'Alright,' she said, her
voice barely a whisper.

The General uttered a short command to the boy and rolled
over on to his side once more. His eyes, though dark and
strangely glazed, shone brightly. He held out a hand. 'Come.'

She crossed to the bed and sat on the edge of it, watching
fascinated as the houseboy kneaded a third ball of the hot
paste on the convex margin of the bowl. She was aware of the
General shifting on the bed beside her, of her shoulders being
taken gently in his hands. The room seemed darker than when
they had entered it. All fear, all doubts had gone, as though
somehow she had left her will to resist downstairs among the
Buddha images. Her mouth was dry and her face flushed hot. The
General's voice was soft and breathy, very close to her. 'Do not try
and draw it all in at once. You will find it hot on your throat at
first. You may choke. Try and draw as much of it into your lungs
as you can and release it slowly. The second pull will be easier.'

The boy plunged the needle, released the opium and flipped the bowl over the flame. The General eased her gently towards the outstretched pipe till her lips touched the ivory mouthpiece. The boy held it patiently as she took her first tentative draw, breathing it in as the General had told her. At once the smoke burned the back of her throat and she choked in a fit of coughing. The General held her firmly. 'Again. Don't be afraid, it will be easier this time.' Her mouth and nostrils were filled by a musty, sweet taste, her throat still burning. She drew again and this time felt the smoke filling her lungs. And as she slowly exhaled, a soft relaxing wave seemed to break over her. 'Again,' the General's voice was softly urging. She drew a third and fourth time before exhausting the opium and lying back, filled with a wonderful warm sense of euphoria. She closed her eyes, hardly aware of the General gently lifting her to lay her out along the length of the bed. Weightlessly she drifted back through space. Falling. Flying. Free.

When, finally, she opened her eyes the room seemed oddly cool. She shifted her head a little to one side. The oil lamp had been doused and the houseboy was gone. A hand turned her head back to face front, and soft wet lips pressed against hers, a tongue forcing them apart, flicking into her mouth. Panic rose in her throat. 'No,' she said, turning her face to one side, and the sound of her refusal seemed to come from very far off. She tried to push the General away, but her arms had no strength. 'No,' she said again, hearing the urgency in her own voice now. But it was all too late.

CHAPTER THIRTY-ONE

The rain raised a fine spray like mist from the river in the first grey light of dawn. It battered on the tin roofs of the buildings all along the wharf, filling the air with a constant drumming, drowning the slow chug-chug of the launch as it nosed its way gingerly into a deserted berth. The docks had a haunted air, eerie in the half-light, devoid of any sign of human existence.

McCue crouched, dripping, on the roof of the cabin, supporting himself on the machine-gun mounting and peering keenly through the saturated gloom. For a moment he tensed as he thought he saw a movement beyond the dark shadows of the empty sheds, then relaxed as he realized it was only a skinny scavenging dog nosing its way through the debris in search of food.

There was a jarring bump, and a grinding of wood against concrete, as the launch came to rest against the wharf. The engine coughed and was silent, and McCue saw Elliot emerge from the cabin, crouching as he ran through the rain to the forward section of the boat to gather up the coiled painter. The Englishman glanced back at McCue, who nodded once and watched as Elliot leaped on to the quay and quickly wound the painter around a rusting metal capstan. Elliot now dropped to a crouch, swinging his M16 into readiness, and glanced around him. McCue jumped down on to the deck. Two pairs of frightened eyes peered back at him out of the gloom of the cabin.

'Right,' he whispered. He heaved his pack on to his shoulder and lifted a second. Ny already had Slattery's pack firmly strapped to her back. They were heavy, stuffed with as many of the boat's provisions as they could carry. McCue flicked his head towards the door. Supporting her mother on her arm, Ny moved out into the rain and headed forward towards the sodden red flag of the defeated Khmer Rouge.

Elliot waited with outstretched arm to help the two women on to the quay, M16 pointing up toward the leaden sky. Ny looked around in the growing light. She remembered the last time she had stood on this quay, with her mother and father and Hau, one family among thousands waiting to board the boats that would take them across the river to the Royal Palace to celebrate the *Fêtes des Eaux*; a colourful happy crowd, noisy and excited. Elliot touched her arm. 'We'll follow you.'

She nodded. He swung his pack on to his back, gripping her upper arm firmly, and the four moved off through the falling rain, passing beyond the vacant, dripping sheds, west towards the centre of the city, unaware that less than ten kilometres to the south the leading Vietnamese divisions were already on the move and would be here in a matter of hours.

Serey hobbled along behind, struggling to keep up, clinging

to McCue's arm, half dragged, half carried by him. The hard paving felt odd beneath her feet after the years of soft mud squelching between her toes in the paddies. Even the smell of the city seemed strange, though it was different now – not as she remembered it. There was a stink of decay carried in the air by the rain, like stale cooking and rusted metal. All around them lay the carcasses of war: tanks burned out by the victorious Khmer Rouge in '75, jeeps overturned, APCs with noses buried in the walls of buildings. Drab, rain-streaked apartments loomed overhead, gaping windows staring down like sightless eyes, doorways smashed in like so many missing teeth in a sad smile.

She hardly knew where they were. Up ahead she caught glimpses of Ny pointing uncertainly, the tense figure of Elliot urging her forward, clinging to the shadows of empty buildings, hesitating at every junction. And always, the voice of the American whispering close to her ear, coaxing, encouraging. On, on. Somewhere, far off to the west, the distant crump of an artillery shell increased the urgency. Serey found it difficult to breathe, a pain tightening across her chest, legs buckling as her head swam. Daylight had grown around them almost without their noticing, the ghost of the city emerging from the shadow of night to reveal its full horror. It was unreal, like some flickering monochrome image from an old movie. This was not her home. She didn't know this place.

Almost as suddenly as it had begun, nearly twelve hours before, the rain stopped, and the tropical sun rent a great chasm in the dark sky, lining black clouds with gold. The streets were immediately awash in soft light shimmering and reflecting from every wet surface to create the illusion of a newly painted world in which the paint had not yet dried. The sticky humidity gave way to a scorching heat that burned their skin, and they felt naked and exposed. Steam rose like smoke from the wet streets, and from their sodden clothing.

They emerged into a large, empty square, and Serey gasped as though struck by a blow. On one side, the station towered above them, an imposing facade crumbling from years of neglect. A row of tumbledown apartment buildings led her eyes to a vast open space the size of a football pitch, incongruous, like a piece missing from a jigsaw. Mist rose in clouds from rainwater gathered across it in great pools. McCue put an arm round her waist to keep her on her feet.

'What is it?' But she could not speak and he followed her gaze.

'The cathedral,' she whispered at last. 'It is gone.' She remembered seeing it as a child, vast and imposing, a monumental stone edifice to a strange God. It had dominated the centre of the city, built by the French *colons* in the Thirties, the symbol of civilizing Catholic colonialism. How could it be gone? It had seemed for ever. And yet not a stone remained.

Serey's head dropped. If the cathedral was gone, what hope of finding her son in this bedevilled place? She had known all along that he would not be here. Hope had remained alive only for as long as Phnom Penh had seemed an impossible goal.

She felt her heart wither inside her. A soft hand on her arm raised her eyes to see a reflection of herself twenty-five years ago, and she recognized the same hopelessness in the eyes. 'We are almost there. We must not give up now.' The hope in Ny's voice belied the desolation she felt.

The crump of artillery shells came again from the west, but closer now. Somewhere out towards the airport.

Elliot's voice was strained. 'We must keep going.'

Ny led them on past the site where the cathedral had stood, along a tree-lined avenue leading to a tree-covered hillock, Le Phnom, from which the city had taken its name. They hurried by a tall, crenellated building that had been the country's most famous and celebrated hotel, Le Royal, renamed Le Phnom after the Lon Nol coup in 1970. Once, French *colons* and their *stagiaires*, planters and tourists, had sat on its grand terraces sipping Chablis and dining on fabulous fish from the Mekong. Now those same terraces gazed out on the avenue with dilapidated indifference as the stricken group limped by: an Englishman and an American, and two Cambodians who were survivors of a holocaust even the Nazis could not have imagined. Fleetingly, Elliot wondered if the French colonizers on their mission to 'civilize' this country a century before could ever have dreamt of such things. History had a power and will of its own which could not be predicted. Only in retrospect could understanding be found, and sometimes not even then.

As they trailed through empty suburban streets the sky

swallowed the sun and began again to spit fat drops of rain. It was impossible now to tell whether it was artillery they heard in the distance or the rumble of thunder. Crumbling villas sat in silence behind high walls and fleshy-leaved trees. Elliot carried the semi-conscious Serey in his arms. At first she had seemed feather-light and fragile, as if she might break if he handled her roughly. But now she was a dead weight, his arms aching with the strain, his khaki T-shirt black with sweat. McCue's rifle hung down at his side, an admission of impotence in the face of overwhelming odds. He turned his face upwards to let the warm rain splash down on his burning skin. They had not seen a soul.

The city was empty, abandoned to history and the Vietnamese. Ny walked mutely ahead, glazed eyes registering the familiar landmarks of her childhood – a time that belonged to another life in another world a million years ago. She heard the faint echo of children playing in the street. Some of the faces she saw quite clearly. Others remained obstinately obscure. Her mother's voice rang out in admonishment, scolding. They must stay in the garden. It was dangerous in the street. Such simple dangers, so easily avoided.

'What's wrong?' Elliot searched her face with concern. She had stopped, suddenly, in the middle of the road, trembling fingers toying tentatively with each other.

'We're here,' she said simply.

Elliot's eyes strayed past the broken gates to the streaked facade of the villa beyond. Its smashed shutters hung from windows opening into a gloomy interior. Gently, he put Serey back on her feet and held her arm as she wobbled unsteadily, blinking to focus on the house she had thought she would never see again. 'You're home, Serey.' His voice was husky. A mighty crack of thunder broke overhead and the heavens opened. Elliot could not tell if it was the rain or tears that streaked Serey's face.

Slowly he led her through the rain up the broken driveway, past the buckled remains of an old bicycle, up a short flight of steps and through the open door. The house was a shambles of dust and debris, the air hot and rancid, and thick with the smell of human excrement. Flies clustered around them, filling the stillness with their incessant whine.

McCue stepped quickly past them and into a front room, stooping to pick up an AK-47 from amongst the rubble. He shook the dust from it and checked the magazine. He looked up at Elliot. 'Half full.'

Both men turned as a tiny cry escaped from Serey's lips, and she shuffled through the darkness of the hall to pick up a threadbare teddy lying abandoned in the dust. She clutched it to her chest and dropped, sobbing, to her knees. Elliot glanced at Ny. She shrugged helplessly, almost overcome by emotion.

'It belong Hau.'

Elliot went forward and crouched to put his arms around Serey. She was shivering and let her weight fall against him, her body racked with sobs. Her thin grey hair clung to her wet face as he pressed it gently to his chest. He could find no words of comfort or hope, and for a moment thought how strange it was that he should even try. Facing him, a door torn off its hinges lay on the floor, thick with a dust broken only by the tracks of small, bare feet. His eyes flickered up, penetrating the darkness of the room beyond. There, crouched against the wall, the naked figure of a small boy, knees pulled up under his chin, stared back at him. Time hung suspended, like the dust, for long seconds. The boom of artillery, the crackle of small-arms fire and the roar of trucks and tanks carried on the rain from the distant edges of the city. 'Serey,' Elliot whispered. And, again, more urgently, 'Serey!' Something in his voice made her lift her head from the depths of despair. She saw light reflected in his eyes and turned to follow his gaze.

A cry of anguish tore from her throat and she broke free of him, scrambling over the door and into the room.

'What is it?' Ny's voice came from the other end of the hall. Her bare feet padded through the gloom. She stopped in the doorway, her eyes filling with tears at the sight of the skinny, naked figure rocking back and forwards in Serey's arms on the floor, clutching at her soaking black tunic. Wordlessly, she walked into the room and knelt to put her arms around her mother and brother and bury her face in theirs.

Elliot slumped back against the wall and lit a cigarette, his eyes gritty and stinging from lack of sleep. He heard footsteps crunch across the debris and looked up as McCue turned his eyes from the room to meet his. They held each other's gaze for a long moment, then Elliot looked away. He had nothing to say.

CHAPTER THIRTY-TWO

Sunlight slanted through the shutters in long yellow stripes, cutting through the dark interior to zigzag across the contours of the bedroom and the bed. Lisa's slender white body lay twisted among the sheets, frozen in the final turn of a restless sleep as though bound there by the strips of light. She seemed caught in time, like the dust suspended in the still air. Somewhere, far off in the depths of the house, the faint sound of breaking glass disturbed the silence, seeping into her troubled dreamland to force her up through unfolding shrouds of darkness to the waking light of day.

For several drowsy moments she lay still, feeling nothing but a vague awareness of the slats of light that lay across her like hot fingers. She turned her head a little to the side and saw the oil lamp on the bedside table. A blurred memory pricked her consciousness, fighting to find focus. And then it all flooded back in a sudden shocking wave of recollection, horrifying in its clarity. She sat bolt upright, a fluttering in her chest, a sick feeling in the pit of her stomach. She tasted the choking, cloying smoke of the opium, saw the face of the

General hovering over hers, twisted to ugliness by the force of his passion.

She looked around her, suddenly anxious that he might still be there, but the room was empty. Only the stale smell of the opium lingered. For a moment she wondered if perhaps it had all been some kind of nightmare induced by the drug. Then she saw the stain of her blood on the sheets and let out a cry of shame and hurt. She turned quickly on to her side as bile rose from her stomach, burning her throat and mouth to spew out on to the pillow. Her eyes blurred as they filled with tears.

She lay for several minutes sobbing painfully, increasingly aware of the raw, tender feeling inside her. Then, slowly, she eased herself from the bed and rose unsteadily to her feet. Still trembling, she picked up the General's black gown from where it had been dropped on the floor. She slipped into it, hugging it tightly around her, and crossed to the door, each jarring step a painful reminder of her lost innocence. The hall was dark. She made her way along it, pushing each door open until she found the bathroom. The light switch yielded a hard bright light that glared back at her from white-tiled walls. Light-headed and on the point of fainting, she staggered to the washbasin and was sick again, a dry, retching sickness. She looked up and saw, with a shock, her face staring back at her from the mirror. It was a face she barely recognized, eyes swollen and puffy from tears she had no recollection of spilling. She saw the disgust in her expression and turned quickly away to run back along the hall to the bedroom.

Her clothes lay strewn across the floor at the end of the bed. Hurriedly, she gathered them together and slipped into her red silk dress with fumbling fingers. She felt soiled. Dirty. But her desire to get out of this house was even greater than her desire to wash – if it would ever be possible to wash away the shame.

She hurried down the stairs as the General's houseboy emerged from the kitchen winding a strip of lint round a bloodied hand. He grinned. 'I break glass,' he said. 'Cut myself.'

'Where's the General?' Lisa heard herself asking.

'Gone,' said the boy. 'Early.'

Lisa fought to remain calm. 'Would you call me a taxi, please.'

'Sure,' said the boy. 'You want breakfast first?'

'No!' Lisa heard the panic rising in her voice. 'Just call me a taxi.'

With a little bow, the boy disappeared back into the kitchen. Lisa saw her purse lying on the settee where she had left it. She picked it up and looked inside. Her heart sank. No money. She put a hand on the back of the settee to steady herself. Think! Think! Grace would pay for the taxi when she got there. Wouldn't she? Of course she would. She perched on the edge of the settee and waited for what seemed an age. The General's collection of Buddhas stared at her from shelves and plinths, something mocking in the serenity of their gentle, smiling faces. She found herself shivering, and had to concentrate to stop her teeth from chattering.

Eventually the houseboy came out from the kitchen. 'Taxi here.'

She almost ran to the door, flinging it open to run down the steps to the waiting car. She slipped into the back seat and pulled the door shut, and only when she saw the driver's inquiring eyes in the mirror did she realize that she did not know Grace's address. Again she fought to stay calm. 'Do you know La Mère Grace?'

'Everybody know La Mère Grace,' the driver said with a grin.

'Can you take me there, please?' She was surprised at how controlled she sounded.

'Chez La Mère Grace?' said the driver. 'No problems.' And Lisa let her head fall back, weak with relief, as the car drew away from the house, out into the *soi* and away from the Klong San Saep towards Rama I Road.

'La Mère Grace, La Mère Grace! Is Miss Lisa!' The girl's shrill Thai voice pierced the brooding silence of the villa, her pale feet pattering across the cool, tiled floor.

Grace emerged anxiously from the dining room wrapped in a white bathrobe, hair pulled back from her drawn face. There was shock in her eyes as she took in the pale, bedraggled figure of the English girl standing awkwardly just inside the door, her new red dress creased, and torn at the shoulder. 'Good God, child! Where have you been? I've been worried sick about you!' She hurried across the hall to take her arm as Lisa almost fainted. Grace barked an instruction in Thai and the housegirl moved quickly to take Lisa's other arm. But Lisa took a deep breath and shrugged them aside.

'I'm alright.' All the way across the city in the taxi she had wanted only to throw herself into Grace's arms, to tell her everything, to feel her warmth and sympathy. But now that she was here she felt trapped by her own secret; guilty and ashamed. 'The taxi is still in the drive,' she said. 'I had no money.'

Grace nodded to the house girl, who hurried away to see to it.

'I'd like a bath,' Lisa said.

'Of course, child. Have you eaten?'

Lisa shook her head.

'Then I will see there is some breakfast waiting for you when you come down.' Grace watched with concern as Lisa walked to the foot of the stairs. As she climbed the first step, Lisa hesitated, half-turned, and looked back as though about to speak. Grace felt a chill run through her at the penetration of those sad blue eyes. She wondered, with a tiny stab of guilt, if it was accusation she read in them, but whatever it was that Lisa had thought to say, she changed her mind, turning away again to walk stiffly up the stairs. Grace stood for a long time in the hall after Lisa had gone. She was disturbed, confused by the powerful and unfamiliar feelings of guilt that the girl had aroused in her. It was as if some half-remembered conscience had returned from a half-forgotten past to haunt her.

She wandered back through to the dining room and sat listlessly at the long table. A great wave of fatigue broke over her and she let her head fall into her hands. It had been such a long, sleepless night, an agony of waiting. Each time she had closed her eyes, Lisa's trusting face had materialized in the dark, and she had been forced to open them quickly to dispel the image. She had lain wide-eyed, remembering the touch of the girl's father. The thought that he might now be dead had only increased her sadness. She heard the faint sound of water running, the bath being filled, and she felt her eyes filling, too. Unaccountably. She shook her head. It was madness! Had she survived a life of corruption, actively pursued it, only to fall victim to the insidious innocence of a young girl? Such feelings, she knew, were a weakness, stealing away her strength and independence. And that could only be dangerous. For the first time she felt a seed of fear germinate deep inside her.

Grace was still sitting at the table when Lisa came down, wrapped in a thin cotton robe, her hair still wet and brushed back from her face. There was something almost shocking in the whiteness of her skin, more naked than naked. With all trace of make-up washed away she looked very young. Her eyes were red and still puffy. She cast a listless eye over the fresh fruit that had been laid out.

'Help yourself,' Grace said.

'I'll just have some orange juice.' Lisa leaned over to pour herself a glass. She sipped at it pensively. There was something dead in her expression, something very far away.

Grace watched her apprehensively. 'Sit down.'

But Lisa turned her back and drifted slowly across to the French windows where she stood in the open doorway gazing out at the sun-dappled garden. 'I'm sorry,' she said at length, without turning. 'I'm not very good company.'

A brightly coloured bird flitted among the dense green growth, screeching some secret signal to a mate. Lisa felt Grace's hands on her shoulders, warm lips on her neck, and a shiver ran through her. 'Do you want to tell me about it?'

Lisa did. But she couldn't. 'I don't think so,' she said.

Grace moved round to her side and took her hand. 'It might help. Whenever you feel you can.'

Lisa turned to face her and was struck anew by her perfect beauty. Fine, dark, almond eyes, the curve of her cheekbones, the full sensuous lips; lips that had kissed her father's. And for a moment she was almost tempted to lean forward and brush her own lips against them. But the moment passed and she took a step away, turning back to the garden. 'My father's dead, isn't he?'

Grace was shocked by the cold fatalism in her voice. She hesitated too long. 'I don't know,' she said.

Lisa glanced at her. 'He should have been back by now. They were talking at the table last night about the Vietnamese, how they have defeated the Khmer Rouge. How things are in Cambodia. Even if he has survived till now he doesn't stand much chance, does he?'

Grace lowered her eyes and shook her head sadly. 'I suppose not.'

'I think I want to go home,' Lisa said.

'You're in no state to travel.' Grace wondered why the

thought of Lisa going induced in her a feeling close to panic. 'In a day or two, perhaps. You need to rest.'

Lisa nodded distantly. 'Is there any word of my passport?'

'I haven't heard anything. I'll speak to Tuk.'

Lisa stepped out on to the terrace. 'You know, when I first arrived here, I thought Bangkok must be the most exciting place on earth.' She drew a deep breath. 'Now I just want to go home. I should go to the embassy and see if they have news of my passport.'

'Tomorrow.' Grace moved on to the terrace beside her. 'I'll take you tomorrow.' She ran her long, brown fingers through Lisa's still damp hair. 'Perhaps you should try and sleep now. Maybe later you'll feel like talking.'

Lisa was silent for a very long time before she turned to face her, and Grace saw that her eyes were filled with tears. 'I just feel so dirty,' Lisa said. And she turned and ran back through the cool of the dining room and disappeared into the hall. Grace heard her bare feet on the stairs.

'So do I,' she said softly to herself.

The day passed in a tormented twilight world, somewhere halfway between sleep and waking Even with the shutters closed against the heat of the day, the room was still hot and airless. Lisa twisted and turned, naked on the double bed, tangling and untangling the sheet around her legs, clutching a pillow to her breast for comfort. Her head felt fuzzy, filled with cotton wool. Her throat was swollen and she found it difficult to swallow. For a long time she thought she would never sleep. Her thoughts were vague and curiously elusive. Faces swam before her eyes. Sivara, good-looking, smiling, seductive; and then ugly and twisted, filled with malice. Tuk, with his smiling lips and cold fish eyes. The General, smiling eyes creasing his round, gentle face, then burning with a dark, heartless passion. And Grace. Something in her eyes Lisa didn't understand. Something disturbing. And always her father, his features unclear except for the livid scar across his cheek, the missing earlobe, the short dark hair greying at the temples. He stood in the rain watching her from a distance. She strained to see his face more clearly, but somehow it remained obscure.

A voice growled close to her ear. You fool! You stupid little fool! How can he be your father? Your father is dead! Dead! She turned to find herself looking into David's pale, angry face. His mouth was curled in contempt. Do you think he cares? Why should he care? You're nothing to him! I'm all you have now. She turned to look back at the man standing in the rain, but he was gone. You see, I told you, he's dead! No, she screamed. No! No! No! And she awoke with a start to find that the room was in darkness, the echo of her voice fading into stillness.

She lay for a moment, breathing hard, disorientated by the unexpected passage of time. She must have been asleep for hours. Gradually her eyes adjusted to the pale moonlight that filtered through the shutters. Shapes and shadows took form around her. A movement caught her eye.

'Don't be alarmed. It's only me.' Grace's voice was soft,

almost a whisper. Lisa could see her only in silhouette. She moved away from the window towards the bed and sat on the edge of it.

'How long have you been in the room?' Lisa asked.

'A while. I was worried about you.'

'I'm sorry,' Lisa said. 'You must think I'm very stupid.'

Grace reached out and ran her fingers lightly down the side of Lisa's face. 'Not stupid. Just innocent.'

'I never thought . . .'

Grace placed a finger over the girl's lips. 'Shoosh. I know. I've spoken to the General.' She paused. 'I'm afraid there's really nothing we can do. I'm sorry.'

Lisa nodded in mute acceptance. Then, 'But don't be sorry,' she said. 'It wasn't your fault.'

Her words turned the knife in Grace's wound, and the older woman was glad the girl couldn't see the guilt in her eyes.

'I feel as if I've been robbed,' Lisa said. Her voice cracked in the dark. 'Of something I can never get back.'

'You have, child. It should have been yours to give. It should have been a wonderful experience.' A long silence. 'I feel so responsible. It was me who introduced you to the General.'

'You weren't to know.' Lisa's innocence was still painful to Grace, and she wondered why she continued to allow herself to be hurt by it, almost sought it, as if somehow the pain could atone for her guilt.

'It was horrible.' Grace saw a silver tear roll down Lisa's cheek. 'I'll never sleep with a man again.'

'Of course you will.' Grace lay down beside her, propping herself on one elbow and brushing the hair lightly from Lisa's forehead. 'It's the most wonderful thing in the world. With the right man.'

'I wish . . .' Lisa said.

'You wish what?'

'I just wish that I could have known my father.'

'You mustn't give up hope, Lisa. You mustn't ever do that.'

'You can't hope for the impossible. He's dead. I know he is.'

'Oh, Lisa.' Grace took her in her arms, holding her head briefly to her breast, before rolling slowly away to swing her legs out of the bed.

Lisa caught her arm. 'Don't go. Please.'

But Grace only shook her head. And Lisa realized, with a start, that there were tears in Grace's eyes as the older woman turned toward the door.

CHAPTER THIRTY-THREE

I

Watery blinks of sunlight punctuated fierce flurries of rain driven down from the north on the edge of an icy January wind. David hurried along the Strand from Temple tube station, collar pulled up against the cold and wet. Sparse mid-afternoon traffic splashed through the shiny London streets, belching fumes into the wind that whipped at the faces of passers-by. On Fleet Street he passed El Vino's, catching a glimpse, in the smoky interior, of journalists researching stories only to be found at the bottom of beer glasses. A little further on, he swept past the commissionaire at the door of a large, modern office block, barely acknowledging the nod of recognition.

The newsroom was busy, green phosphor screens flickering under fluorescent lights, the hubbub of voices engaged in a dozen telephone conversations, lights winking at empty desks. The heads of department were in with the editor for the editorial conference.

David threw his coat across the desk and slumped into a seat to face his terminal.

'What you doing in at this time, Dave? Thought you were still on nights.' The reporter opposite glanced incuriously across the desk.

'I am. Got some calls to make,' David said.

The reporter shrugged. 'Real go-getter, aren't you?' He watched David start up his terminal and search through a drawer for his contacts book. 'Still bucking for a job on features?'

David made no response. He picked up his phone and flicked down a switch for a line. He punched out a long number and waited.

'Still no word from your girl?'

He glanced up grimly and shook his head. The ringing tone sounded in his ear, and he tensed as his call was answered six thousand miles away on the other side of the world. He checked his watch. Three o'clock. It would be ten in the evening there. 'Narai Hotel.' The tinny voice crackled in his ear.

'Could you put me through to Lisa Elliot's room.'

'One moment, please.' There was a long delay before the voice returned with the familiar response. 'Sorry, no one of that name stay here.'

'Look, I'm calling from London.' David had difficulty keeping his frustration in check. 'She was supposed to check in nearly two weeks ago. She promised to call and I've heard nothing. I've called the hotel several times already, and you keep telling me there's no one of that name staying there. I wonder if you could check if she ever booked in?'

'Sorry,' said the voice. 'No one of that name stay here. Very busy now. Thank you. Goodnight.' And the line went dead.

'Fuck!' David slammed the receiver back into its cradle.

'The Vietnamese have taken Phnom Penh,' the reporter opposite said.

David frowned at him. 'What?'

'Came in on the wires early this morning.'

'So what the hell's that got to do with me! She's in Thailand, not bloody Cambodia!' The reporter shrugged again and turned back to his screen as David lifted the phone and dialled an internal number. He waited impatiently.

'Library.'

'David Greene, reporters. I'm looking for a file from nineteen sixty-three.'

The pages of history, enshrined in celluloid, jerked across the screen in a blur as David turned the microfilm impatiently through the plate. Increased American involvement in Vietnam; 16,000 US military 'advisers' now attached to South Vietnam ARVN forces; Soviets withdraw nuclear missiles from Cuba; Buddhist monk sets himself alight in Saigon street; Beatlemania. He paused momentarily. November 22 – Kennedy assassinated in Dallas.

He had a vague recollection of squatting in short-trou-sered uniform in a seedy scout hall, a boy running in flushed with excitement, shouting, 'The President's been shot! The President's been shot!' He had been eight then. He turned the film through more pages, days, weeks. Then, 13 December 1963 – Aden Massacre: Court Martial Opens. He stopped, adjusted the focus, and squinted down the tight columns of copy looking for names. But his mind wandered again.

There was another name that hovered, infuriatingly out of reach, somewhere in the back of his mind. A name Lisa had told him the night she flew out to Bangkok, one that the sergeant had given her. An odd name. But he hadn't paid much heed at the time, and now it simply wouldn't come back. Tun, Tan, Tok – for a moment he wondered why the hell he was bothering. If Lisa had wanted to phone him, presumably she could. Perhaps she'd lied to him. But he discounted that, and for all his increasing ambivalence, he couldn't shake off the feeling that something was wrong, something bad must have happened to her.

He turned his gaze back to the screen. There were several references to the young Lieutenant John Elliot who had ordered his unit into the village. The full list of the accused didn't appear till further down the story. David ran his finger lightly down the screen to stop at the name of Elliot's NCO. Sergeant Samuel Robert Blair. He drew a deep breath of satisfaction and wrote the name down in his notebook. If Lisa could find him, then so could he.

II

The lights from across the river, reflecting on the water, danced brokenly on its wind-ruffled surface. Blair gazed out beyond his dark reflection in the glass and heard the wind among unseen trees on the embankment. Behind him, a tiny reading lamp lit a corner of the room. Newspapers detailing the triumphant progress of the Vietnamese army in Cambodia lay strewn across the floor. He sipped pensively at a glass of iced water turned faintly amber by the merest splash of whisky. His mood was one of melancholy, laced with a hint of anger. Anger at himself. He could, he knew, have done more to discourage Elliot from his Cambodian enterprise. It was madness and he had known it. But then, so had Elliot. Would he even have listened? Blair smiled a humourless smile and shook his head. He doubted it.

He turned back into the room and eased himself down into his well-worn armchair, then placed his glass on the floor and lifted a gnarled and blackened pipe from an ashtray balanced on the arm of the chair. He tapped out the dottle from the bowl, and began refilling it from a soft leather pouch.

Elliot was a resourceful man, he told himself. If anyone could pull it off, it would be Jack. He paused suddenly, catching his thoughts, and sighed. He knew it was a false optimism he was trying to kindle, and there really was no point. He struck a match and sucked several times at the stem of his pipe, drawing the flame down through the tobacco. He listened to it crackle and then tamped down the glow with a blackened, calloused forefinger. Thick blue smoke drifted lazily upwards through the light cast by his reading lamp. His only regret was that Elliot hadn't taken him along. If he had been ten years younger . . .

The sound of the doorbell startled him. With a tut of annoyance, he laid his pipe in the ashtray and heaved himself stiffly out of his chair. He flicked a switch in the hall and blinked in the cold yellow light that invaded the peaceful gloom of the early evening. It was chilly out here, and he shivered as he opened the door to find a tall young man with a startling mane of windblown red hair standing on his doorstep. His face, in the reflected light of the hall, was pale, almost pasty. His eyes, screwed up against the sudden flood of light, had a hunted look. He wore a dark suit under a long beige overcoat, the knot of his tie pulled down from an open collar. Blair cast a wary eye over him.

'Yes?'

'Samuel Blair?' the young man asked. 'Sergeant Samuel Blair?'

Blair tensed. 'Who wants to know?'

'My name's David Greene. I'm a friend of Lisa Robi—' He paused to correct himself, 'Elliot.'

'Never heard of her.'

The young man's mouth set. 'Look, Mr Blair, I don't have time to play silly buggers. I know all about your part in the Aden Massacre, your subsequent career as a soldier of fortune, and latterly your role as a kind of freelance quartermaster for other mercenaries. Now, either you invite me in and we talk sensibly, or you can read all about it in the national press.'

Blair looked back at him steadily. 'You're playing a dangerous bloody game, laddie.'

A little of David's confidence evaporated. 'Only because the stakes are so high,' he said.

'What stakes?'

'A girl's safety, maybe even her life. A girl you sent to Bangkok to look for her father.' He ran out of steam. 'Look, she's been there for well over a week. She hasn't called, she's not at the hotel she was booked into, and they claim they've never heard of her.'

Blair made a decision. He stood to one side and flicked his head towards the interior. David stepped into the hall and turned as Blair closed the door behind him. His initial impression of a shambling, rather frail-looking old man completed its transformation. Beneath the shock of white hair, Blair's eyes were flinty hard, his old jumper and baggy trousers disguising a lean, fit physique. He was a powerful presence in the confined space of the hall and David felt intimidated by him. 'You some kind of newspaper man?' Blair asked.

'It's what I do for a living. But it's not why I'm here.'

'Then a piece of advice, laddie, and it's yours for free. Don't ever threaten me unless you mean it. And if you do, be prepared for the consequences.'

'I'm sorry,' David said feebly. 'I didn't know what else to do. I'm worried about her.'

Blair waved an arm towards the sitting room. 'Go through.'

David walked uncomfortably into the room and stood nervously as Blair crossed to his chair and picked up his pipe. It had gone out, and he dropped it back into the ashtray with annoyance. He stooped to pick up his drink. 'You'd better tell me, then.'

David shrugged uncertainly. 'Well – I already have.'

'When did she leave?' Blair was clearly impatient.

'About ten days ago. I saw her on to the plane myself. She was booked into the Narai Hotel, Bangkok. She said you'd given her the name of a contact.'

Blair pursed his lips. 'And you haven't heard anything?'

'She was supposed to call when she arrived.'

'And she didn't?'

David shook his head. 'It's warm in here. Do you mind if I take off my coat?'

'You're not staying,' Blair said. 'Why didn't you call her?'

'I did. Well, after a couple of days. I thought maybe she . . .' His voice trailed away. 'I don't know what I thought. But I did think she would call eventually.'

'So, finally, you phoned the hotel yourself and she wasn't there.'

'That's right. They said there wasn't anybody called Lisa Elliot registered. I called a few times, but always the same response.'

'And she didn't even book in the day she arrived?'

'Well, I don't know. They weren't very forthcoming. It's

difficult getting information when you're six thousand miles away.'

Blair seemed thoughtful, gazing away through the window across the river. Finally he looked back at David, almost as though surprised to find him still there. 'And?'

David shrugged. 'And – that's it? I thought maybe since you'd given her a contact there . . .'

'I didn't encourage her to go,' Blair said. 'She's a very determined young lady.'

'I know,' David said with some feeling.

'Give me your card.' Blair held out his hand. David fumbled in his pockets before finding a tattered business card and handing it to the Scot. Blair glanced at it. 'I'll make some inquiries and give you a call.' He drained his glass, placed it on a low coffee table and strode out into the hall. David hurried after him.

'When?'

'When I hear anything. *If* I hear anything.' He opened the door to let in an icy blast of night air. 'Goodnight.'

David looked at him, clearly unhappy. 'I suppose that'll have to do.'

'Aye, it will.'

David stepped out into the dark January night.

'And stick to chasing ambulances in future, son. It's a lot safer.' The door slammed, closing off the light that had spilled out across the front lawn, leaving David frustrated and dissatisfied.

He walked up the path to where his car was parked under a street lamp, and cursed his own inadequacy. His initial confidence in his researches, his concern over the lack of contact with Lisa, had made him almost arrogant on the doorstep, until the unexpected force of Blair's response had left him floundering like a novice poker player who shows his hand too early. The rest had been humiliating. Why, then, he wondered as he slipped behind the wheel, did his cocktail of emotions include a substantial quantity of relief?

He sat for a moment, toying idly with his key ring, not wanting to admit to himself what deep down he already knew. That somehow he had passed on the responsibility. If Lisa wanted to go running off to the other side of the world on a wild goose chase, then he could hardly be held to blame if she got herself into trouble. He'd put responsibility firmly back in the hands of the man responsible for her going off in the first place. There was nothing else he could do. He checked the time and realized he would be late for his shift.

From the darkness of his front room Blair watched David's car drive away, then he drifted through again to the back of the house. Automatically, almost without thinking, he sank back in his armchair and relit his pipe. He pulled on it several times, letting smoke drift lazily from his nostrils and the corners of his mouth. For a long time he sat wrapped in a black cloak of winter depression. He felt the burden of guilt weigh heavily upon him. He should have tried to talk Elliot out of going in the first place. He should never have told Lisa where her father had gone.

Quite suddenly he laid down his pipe and rose to cross to

his bureau and search among an untidy pile of paperwork for a number scribbled on an otherwise blank sheet of paper. He sat down, pulled on a pair of wire spectacles, and lifted the phone. The number took for ever to dial but rang only three times. A girl's voice sounded in his ear, shrill and staccato.

'Sam Blair,' he said. 'I'd like to speak to Tuk Than.'

He waited impatiently for half a minute before he heard Tuk's oily voice on the other end of the line. 'Mister Blair. Good to hear from you.'

'Didn't get you out of your bed, did I?' Blair glanced at his watch. It would be nearly one a.m. in Bangkok.

'No, no. I am in a business meeting.'

'Strange hours you keep, Tuk.'

'Was there something you wanted, Mister Blair?' There was irritation in Tuk's tone.

'Just thought I'd check on that job we discussed a few weeks back.'

'No problems. Your friend was very pleased with the merchandise.'

'He got away alright, then?'

'Oh, yes. Two weeks ago. No problem getting away. Problem getting back, I think.'

'Yes, I think so, too. The news is not good.'

'Not good.' Tuk sighed audibly.

'You haven't heard anything, then?'

'Nothing. And I'll be honest with you, Mister Blair, I don't expect to. You must excuse me now, I'm very busy.'

'Sure.' Blair was working hard at keeping his voice casual. 'Just one other thing . . .'

'Yes?'

'You haven't had any contact with his daughter?'

'His daughter?' Tuk sounded surprised.

'Lisa. She was trying to reach him. I gave her your address.'

'That was not very discreet, Mister Blair.'

'Perhaps not. She hasn't contacted you, then?'

'No.'

Blair waited for something further, but nothing came. 'Okay,' he said. 'That's fine. You'll let me know if you hear anything? About my friend – or his daughter?'

'Of course. Goodnight, Mister Blair.' The line went dead.

Blair put down the receiver thoughtfully and took off his spectacles to rub his eyes. He shook his head. Tuk was lying. The tension in his voice had been unmistakable. All the usual ersatz bonhomie absent. He replaced his spectacles, opened a small drawer on the left of the bureau and lifted out a well-thumbed passport. He flipped it open and a younger version of himself stared back at him. He turned another page. Still valid for two more years. Another drawer yielded a London telephone directory and he made a call.

'British Airways.'

'I'd like to reserve a seat on the first available flight to Bangkok.'

CHAPTER THIRTY-FOUR

Grace sat on the edge of a hard leather chair, gazing bleakly around Tuk's spartan study. There was no warmth in the room, even in the light of the reading lamp on the desk. She was tired, her eyes gritty. It was almost forty hours since she had last slept. The desire to lie on, pressed close to Lisa's warm young body, had been almost irresistible. But she had forced herself to leave the temptation of the girl's room, knowing that she had to act fast if she was to save Lisa's life.

She had heard Tuk speaking on the telephone in the hall, but it was several minutes since he had hung up and still he had not reappeared. The call had come at an infuriatingly inopportune moment. When she arrived, Tuk had been mellow and relaxed, and she guessed that he had been smoking – there had been that glaze about his eyes. He had listened to her, sipping an iced whisky, gazing off into the distance, his mind on other things. The fate of Elliot's daughter seemed unimportant. His interest lay elsewhere.

The girl was unaware, Grace told him, that the General had bought her virginity. She thought she had been raped. She had no idea of Grace's role, or Tuk's, so she posed no threat to either of them. What harm would it do if they let her go, gave her back her passport and put her on a plane? She was only a child, after all.

And then the call had come, and Tuk's indifference had shifted at the mention of the caller's name. It had meant nothing to Grace. Sam Blair. English – or American perhaps.

She looked up as Tuk re-entered the room. His face was creased by a deep frown, his eyes black and thoughtful. Grace grew more tense. It did not augur well. He wandered to his desk without glancing in her direction and lifted his drink. For a long time he stood just holding it, staring into its amber depths, frozen in thoughtful contemplation. Then he turned a speculative gaze in her direction.

'What I don't understand, Grace,' he said, 'is your motivation. What is this girl to you?'

Grace gave a tiny shrug. 'An innocent,' she said.

Tuk showed his teeth in a nasty grin. 'Have you slept with her?' Grace made no reply. 'A week ago you saw only money to be made.'

'The General paid well.'

'As will many others.' Tuk emptied his glass and crossed the room, still holding it. He smiled down at her and reached out with his other hand to hold her jaw, gently squeezing her cheeks between his thumb and forefinger. Grace resisted the temptation to recoil from his clammy touch. 'You are a very

357

beautiful women, Grace.' He shook his head. 'You like girls, don't you?'

'Not exclusively.' Grace's voice was steady. 'Unlike you and your boys.'

His pincer grip tightened at once and his smile curled into a sneer. 'You know what I think?'

'No, Than. What do you think?'

'I think you've gone soft in your old age, Grace. I think you've fallen for that girl.'

'Don't be ridiculous, Than!'

He snapped her head back in a sudden, vicious movement and leaned to push his face very close to hers. She made no attempt to struggle, but held herself rigid and still. 'Don't ever call me that!' She smelled the whisky and opium on his breath. 'You didn't think I was ridiculous when I set you up here in Bangkok! When all you had was a reputation and a few thousand baht! I made you, I can break you.' And he smashed the top of his glass on the arm of her chair and thrust the jagged edge at her face. He felt her trembling in his grip and was pleased by her fear. 'And I could mark that pretty face of yours so that no man' – he chuckled – 'or woman, would ever want to look at you again.' The light in his eyes reflected the exultation in his power.

'I'm sorry, Than. I didn't mean any disrespect.' She heard the shake in her own voice.

He jerked her head free and stepped back. 'Good,' he said. She raised a hand to her cheek and felt blood oozing from

PETER MAY

the wound where the glass had pierced her skin. He strode back to his desk and banged down the remains of his glass.

'Anyway, I have no choice now. I must dispose of her.'

Grace felt sick. 'Why?'

'That call.' He gestured towards the hall. 'It was from an associate of Elliot's. He was the one who gave the wretched girl my address. I told him I hadn't seen her.' He shrugged and held out his hands. 'So there you have it. If I let her go he'll know I lied. I can't take that risk.' He seemed annoyed that the decision should be forced upon him.

Grace sought desperately for some kind of reprieve. 'But surely, she's still worth preserving as insurance – against Elliot's return?'

'Elliot's dead,' he snapped. 'We both know that.' Then he relaxed again into his habitual humourless smile. She could not raise her eyes to meet his. He watched with satisfaction as tears fell in dark splashes on the white cotton of her dress.

CHAPTER THIRTY-FIVE

The embers of the fire glowed faintly in the dark, gathered in the small ring of stones McCue had arranged in the centre of the floor to form a makeshift hearth. He squatted cross-legged in front of it, working his needle by the dying light, a crude pattern cut out of canvas with his hunting knife. A pair of shorts for the boy who lay sleeping curled up with his mother and sister.

Elliot glanced at the sleeping bodies of mother and children lying as one, arms and legs entwined. Their first physical contact in nearly five years. Hau's face was buried in his mother's withered breast, McCue's sweat-stained T-shirt drowning his nakedness. Tears had dried, bellies were full. They were at peace, even if only for a few hours. Serey seemed to have drawn strength from the tearful frailty of her son, a redis-covered sense of purpose. Just as Elliot had lost his. She had taken charge of boiling the rice in a pot she had salvaged from the wreckage of her kitchen. She was a mother again, all her maternal instincts driving her to feed and protect her family.

Throughout the day they had heard the distant sound of

sporadic gunfire, as Vo Nguyen Giap's Vietnamese army secured the city. Closer, they had heard the rumble of trucks carrying troops toward the city centre, the roar of tanks moving into strategic positions. It was not a time to be on the streets, and they had stayed hidden and secure in the wreckage of the Angs' once elegant villa. Elliot knew, however, it would not be long before the people from the countryside, freed from the Khmer Rouge yoke, would start drifting into the city in search of food, families, friends. The situation would be confused, the Vietnamese as yet without controls, or any kind of temporary administration. The fighting would continue in the north. If there was to be any escape it would have to be soon, while the country was still in a state of chaos.

Escape, Elliot reflected, was all that was left. An admission of failure. He wondered what there was to escape to. The life he had known? Hadn't the acceptance of this job been an escape in itself – from a life that was going nowhere, a past that had effectively destroyed the future? Escape had become a way of life, a mechanical act, accompanied always by the one person he liked least in the world – himself. And always, as a snowball gathers snow, the burden of his past had grown with the years; a burden that was becoming intolerable.

He shifted his focus back to McCue's needle as it worked dexterously back and forth through the tough canvas. There was something incongruous in his gentle domesticity. 'You're full of surprises, Billy.'

'Like life,' McCue said without raising his eyes from the

needle. 'Like finding the kid. Like you killing Mikey in cold blood.' He raised his eyes slowly to meet Elliot's. 'Like any of us still being alive.'

Elliot nodded toward the canvas that was beginning to take shape as a pair of shorts. 'Where d'you learn to do that?'

'You learn to do a lot of things when there ain't no one else to do them.' He turned back to his needle, the taut muscles of his bare chest reflecting the last glow of the fire. 'What's your plan?'

'We'll head east tomorrow night. As soon as it gets dark.'

'We?'

Elliot shrugged. 'Do what you like.'

'And them?' McCue flicked his head towards the two women and the boy sleeping against the wall.

'We are no longer your concern.' Serey's voice, soft in the darkness, startled them. 'Our lives are in no real danger here. And we are together again. If Yuon wants us he can come and get us himself.' The acrid wood smoke and the darkness obscured her face from them. 'You have brought my family together. It is you who are in most danger now. If you can escape with your lives then you must try.'

McCue looked at Elliot. 'So we're just going to leave them to the tender mercies of the Vietnamese?'

'Whatever the Vietnamese might be,' Serey said, 'they cannot be worse than the Khmer Rouge. If they can rid my country of such an evil then I welcome them with all my heart.'

But McCue shook his head. 'We came here to get them out,

PETER MAY

Elliot. We can't just leave them. A couple of kids and an old woman.'

Serey's shrill voice silenced him. 'Mistah McCue, do you know what age I am?'

McCue sighed. 'No, lady, I don't know what age you are.'

'I am thirty-eight.' She said it proudly.

And Elliot realized, with a shock, that she was two years younger than himself.

'I may look old to you. Withered, perhaps. But I still have a mind, and a free spirit. I am not stupid. Which is why I am still alive.' They heard her shift in the dark, but gently so as not to disturb her children. 'I survived the slaughter of the educated and intelligent by virtue of my education and intelligence. You cannot for one minute imagine what life was like under the Khmer Rouge. To remain silent when all around you saw only senseless destruction. And yet only in silence was there safety.'

Elliot was surprised by her sudden and unexpected clarity of mind. She had barely spoken in the days since the raid on the commune, except to pursue her dogged insistence that she would not leave Cambodia without her son. There was something compelling in her voice now, a power and intelligence that Elliot had never suspected.

'In the first year after the Khmer Rouge victory, we were moved around from village to village. We were the new people, those from the cities, regarded with suspicion and often disliked by the ancients, the peasants in whose name the revolution had been made.' She paused to brush stray wisps of grey hair from her face. 'After several weeks building small-scale irrigation ditches in the paddies, we were assigned to build a larger canal to bring water from a nearby lake.' Her remembered frustration was audible in a deep sigh. 'They made us sleep in the open on mats, without tents, close to the site. We were forced to huddle round fires at night to stay warm and keep away the mosquitoes. Every hour of the day was spent digging. Thousands of us digging – a canal that ran uphill.'

The sarcasm in her tone was acid.

'The site had not been surveyed, there were no plans, no records. The Khmer Rouge appeared to believe that revolutionary fervour could defeat the laws of physics.'

McCue had ceased sewing, his needle held suspended.

Serey's voice continued to rise and fall in an oddly monotonous cadence, the hint of an American accent in her nasal tone. 'The banks of the canal were constructed from loosely piled earth. In the unlikely event that water would someday defy gravity and actually run through it, the banks would simply be washed away. If men and women and children had not been dying all around us from exhaustion and hunger, it would have been laughable.'

They heard her breathing in short, sharp gasps in the dark.

'One poor brave fool who had, until then, concealed his identity as an engineer tried to tell the Khmer Rouge idiots how it should be done. They paraded him before us at a merit festival. He knew nothing about the revolution, they said, and yet he was trying to tell them what to do. He was the living proof of imperialist arrogance. No doubt he died to prove their point. We never saw him again.' She paused again, her voice trembling now, choked with emotion.

'Qualifications, they told us, were *saignabat* – the invisible signal. All that mattered was physical work, *saignakhoeunh* – the visible signal. That was tangible. Therein lay honour.' Elliot realized now it was anger he heard in the scratch of her voice, years of pent-up fury. 'One listens, one obeys, one says nothing. It takes intelligence to create such evil, stupidity to enforce it. You cannot reason with stupidity.'

Elliot glanced at McCue, who appeared not to be listening. He was staring vacantly into the fading light of the fire.

'In nineteenth-century Cambodian history there was a sage called Puth,' Serey went on. 'Puth prophesied that his country would suffer a dreadful upheaval, that traditional values would be turned on their head, houses and streets would be emptied, the illiterate would condemn the educated. *Thmils* – infidels – would take absolute power and persecute the priests.' A tiny shower of sparks burst from the embers of the fire and caught her face briefly in its light, eyes glazed now, lost in painful memory.

'As an educated woman I might once have poured scorn on such prophecies. But Puth also predicted that the people would be saved if they planted the kapok tree. In Cambodian the word for this tree is *kor*, which also means "mute". It was said that only the deaf-mutes would survive this period of chaos. Say nothing, hear nothing, understand nothing.

'I knew the canal we were digging would never carry water. I said nothing, my children said nothing. We just kept digging.'

From somewhere, perhaps a mile away in the direction of the city centre, came the crackle of automatic fire. A short single burst that was smothered by the night, leaving the silence to be broken again only by the screeching of the cicadas. They sat for so long in the quiet after Serey had finished speaking, that Elliot thought she must have drifted off to sleep. McCue had never stirred. The fire was virtually dead. The brief flare of a match momentarily illuminated the room, sending undefined shadows dancing around the bare walls as Elliot lit a cigarette.

McCue inclined his head a little and turned to look at him. His voice was a hoarse, broken whisper. 'Whatya gonna tell her old man?'

'Tell him what I told you.' Serey's voice drifted softly across the room, and Elliot peered blindly in the dark in a vain attempt to catch the outline of her face. 'I don't expect to see him again.'

McCue's head drooped forward and he shook it slowly. 'Guess you win, Elliot.'

But Elliot felt no satisfaction. Only an emptiness. And a desire to sleep.

The sound of voices pierced his restless slumber. Shrill, insistent, argumentative. His eyes flickered open to the hard, painful glare of daylight. He blinked away the grit, but they still stung from the smoke that had filled the room the night before. McCue was sitting back against the wall below the window, the smoke from his cigarette drifting in lazy blue ribbons in the still light.

'What's going on?'

McCue's expressionless glance across the room reflected his indifference. 'Who knows? They're all in the garden.'

Elliot rolled over and climbed stiffly to his feet to pick his way through the debris to the back door. Serey and Ny were on their knees, digging with calloused hands in the soft damp earth of what had once been a carefully tended flower bed. Now it was overgrown with weeds and creepers that snagged on their arms and wrists. The boy, Hau, stood defiantly before them, hands on his hips, brows furrowed, anxious and intense, speaking rapidly in a husky high voice. His thin brown legs poked out like sticks from the green canvas of the shorts McCue had made. McCue's T-shirt hung voluminously from his narrow shoulders, gathered at the waist and tucked into the shorts. He bore little resemblance to the pathetic creature they had found huddled in the back room only twenty-four hours earlier. Children, Elliot thought, had the most extraordinary resilience. And, yet, for all his lack of height, and his meagre twelve years, they were old and knowing eyes that he flicked darkly towards Elliot as he appeared in the doorway. Even more incongruous was the Kalashnikov slung casually across his shoulder. A hand slipped instinctively towards the barrel and held it firm. Ny glanced back over her shoulder, but her mother paid no attention and kept digging.

'What is it?' Elliot asked.

Ny said, 'He want guide you through city tonight, put you on road west. My mamma forbid it.'

'We could do with a bit of help,' Elliot said. 'If the boy knows the way . . .'

'You can find your own way!' Serey's voice was sharp and hostile, but she did not stop digging.

'Now that's what I call gratitude.' Elliot hawked a gob of phlegm up from his throat and spat it into the bushes.

'Why would you need my gratitude?' Serey asked. 'Is my husband's money not enough?'

Elliot glanced at the boy who was watching him intently. The boy averted his eyes towards his sister and there was a brief exchange between them. Then he turned again to his mother, uttered a few short words, and strode past Elliot into the house, the Kalashnikov rattling at his side.

'What did he say?'

Ny opened her mouth to speak, but Serey cut in. 'He said he is doing it anyway and that I cannot stop him.'

Elliot shrugged. 'I guess you can't.'

Serey stopped digging for the first time, and she turned on him a stare leaden with hatred. Steam rose around her from the sodden earth, the rain of yesterday evaporating with the heat of the sun. With the slightest shake of her head she turned back to her digging. Elliot inclined his head to meet Ny's gaze. It wasn't hatred in her eyes. It was sadness. Or something more. Pity perhaps. He looked away. Hate was easier.

A single harsh word from her mother recalled Ny to the task of digging. They had made a hole nearly half a metre deep. Elliot trod through soft earth towards them.

'What are you digging for? Gold?'

'As good as,' Serey said. And he heard the sound of her fingernails scratching on metal. He crouched down to watch as both pairs of hands intensified their digging, scrabbling hard to uncover a rusty metal box about a foot square and six or eight inches deep. Serey muttered something in her native tongue as they lifted it out and dragged it on to the mound of earth they had dug out. Burrowing insects scuttled away from the sudden light. She fumbled with the clasp, but it was rusted solid.

Elliot took out his knife. 'Here, let me.' After several attempts he broke the clasp and prised back the lid. Inside lay a heavy-duty black plastic bag gathered and tied securely at the neck. Serey held her hand out for Elliot's knife. He handed it to her and watched as she slit open the bag to reveal its hidden treasure: gold and silver jewellery; necklaces and bracelets, earrings, brooches; diamonds, rubies, emeralds glinting in the slanting sunlight. Thousands of dollars' worth. Elliot stared in amazement.

Serey kept her eyes lowered. 'We were once very wealthy, Mistah Elliot. When one had no need to worry about food, one spent one's money on the luxuries of life, the beautiful things, the expensive things. One would have needed ten thousand bowls of rice to buy a single diamond. But you can't eat diamonds. Now, perhaps, my diamonds will buy a few bowls of rice.'

From the bottom of the bag she drew out a bundle of notes. US dollars, maybe five thousand in hundred-dollar bills. She tossed them to Elliot. He caught the bundle and looked up, surprised. 'What's this for?'

She looked at him steadily. 'I do not wish to be in my husband's debt. Or yours.'

Elliot felt the cold touch of the golden handshake, the dismissal of the hired help.

Serey delved again into the bag and lifted out a thin, tattered book embossed with the colonial crest of pre-revolutionary Cambodia. 'What is it, Mamma?'

Ny took it from her and flicked it open. A photograph of a pretty young woman, barely recognizable as the woman kneeling beside her, stared out from its faded pages, a curious half-smile recalling happier days in another life. Serey was still looking at Elliot, defiance in her eyes.

'It is my passport,' she said, then turned to Ny. 'And yours and Hau's. It is not worth much now. But it is who we were, and who we will be again.'

Elliot rose slowly and walked back to the house. Serey took the passport from Ny and slipped it back into the bag. As she got unsteadily to her feet Ny said to her, 'Mamma . . .' And she turned to look as Ny picked up the wad of notes from where Elliot had left it lying in the dirt.

CHAPTER THIRTY-SIX

Lisa awoke feeling doubt: about who she was, about who she had always thought herself to be. She had come in search of her father and found herself instead. But a self who was still a stranger, full of contradictions, of responses she did not know herself well enough to predict. She was, at the same time, excited and frightened by this new self. The book of her life had quite suddenly opened up an unexpected chapter, leading her off on an eccentric spiral of delicious uncertainty.

The door opened and she saw that it was Grace, and was suddenly self-conscious, as if the older woman might have read her mind.

But Grace seemed not to notice. Her eyes were blank, a hunted look in the lines around them. Her movements were quick and nervous. Lisa smiled uneasily in an attempt to disperse her sudden sense of foreboding. 'I was just going to get dressed.'

'Get packed. You must leave quickly.' Grace's tone was cold and impersonal. Yet more confusion filled Lisa's mind.

'Why? Where are we going?'

'I am going nowhere. You are going home.'

'Home?'

'I have booked your flight. But first you will need to sort out passport details at your embassy. Move.'

And she hurried out leaving Lisa feeling foolish and deflated. Gone were the revelations of the new Lisa, the unsuspected Lisa who had emerged so recently from the cocoon of her past. Suddenly she was the Lisa she'd always been. Young and naive and frightened. She glanced about her in the bedroom's half-light, sunlight flickering around the edges of the shutters. Everything seemed alien now. All the intimacy between her and Grace dismissed by those few harshly spoken words. *Get packed! You're going home!* The eyes that didn't want to meet hers. Now, another piece of the old Lisa re-emerged. The stubborn Lisa. The petulant child who wanted to stamp her foot and scream, *Won't! Won't do it!* She started to dress hurriedly.

Grace wandered through the cool semi-darkness of the dining room, drumming her fingers along the length of the table. Through the French window, the sun spun soft patterns of light among the green tropical foliage, bright and optimistic, a visual echo of the chattering birdsong, the creak of the cicadas. A normal day, a never-ending cycle. Always the same. And yet, for her, nothing would ever be the same again. It seemed unfair, and unreal, that for her there should be such turmoil and change in the midst of such normalcy. It set her apart, somehow, from the world. She felt disembodied, a ghost haunting the familiar life she had known, but unable to touch it or be touched by it.

Nor could she understand why. Why she should risk everything, even her life, for this girl. Was it guilt? The thought almost brought a smile to her face. Conscience was for those who drew lines of moral distinction. She had never done that, would not know where those lines should be drawn. As Lisa's naivety blinded her to her innocence, so Grace's cynicism had never allowed her a sense of guilt. Of course, deep inside she knew the answer, but she shied away from letting it crystallize in her thoughts. That would be too painful.

She caught herself reflected in the glass of the French windows and saw an old face looking back at her, one she barely recognized. And yet it was an accurate reflection of the way she felt. She shivered, sensing cold sweat on her palms. Tears pricked her eyes and she wanted to weep. The layers of self-protection she had wrapped around herself across the years had somehow been stripped away, leaving her exposed and vulnerable. She heard the crunch of tyres on gravel as her chauffeur brought the car to the front of the house, and turned as she heard a footfall in the doorway behind her. Lisa stood framed against the hall, her face set and flushed with defiance.

'I came to find my father,' she said. 'I am not leaving until I do.' For a moment there was no sound, except for the squawking of birds in the garden. Lisa's defiance faltered in the face of the naked hostility which hid the tears in Grace's eyes.

'Do you really believe he is still alive? After all this time?'

Lisa didn't know what to say. 'You said it yourself last night. He's dead, Lisa! You must go home!'

Lisa shook her head. 'I was wrong – just looking for reassurance. He's not dead. I know it.'

'What do you know?' Grace's voice was jagged with contempt. 'You don't know anything.'

'I – I don't understand.'

'No, you don't!'

'Mr Tuk said—'

'Hah!' Grace's eyes blazed as she moved down the length of the table towards the trembling English girl. 'Tuk used you like he uses everybody. He double-crossed your father when he went into Cambodia, tried to have him killed. And then you stumbled into his nasty little web, the perfect insurance against your father's return, a hostage to vengeance. You thought I was your friend. You were my prisoner. Tuk gave you into my safe keeping to do with as I would until you were no longer required.'

The blood pulsed painfully at Lisa's temples, confusion and disbelief crowding her mind. She wanted to run away from this, didn't want to hear any more. But a vast weight seemed to bear down upon her, robbing her of any ability to move. Grace stood no more than a foot away from her now, her face twisted and ugly, her voice rising in pitch, almost to a scream. Flecks of spittle gathered at the corners of her mouth. 'You thought the General raped you. Well, he paid for the privilege. Paid me. Paid dearly. And there would have been others. Dozens of them. Wealthy Thais willing to splash out for a girl like you.'

'No!' Lisa screamed. She desperately wanted to wake up, prayed for the nightmare to end. If she screamed loud enough—

The slap of Grace's palm across her face nearly knocked her over – the same hand that had so tenderly held her in the dark the night before. But still she could hear herself screaming. And again the hand smacked the side of her head. This time she stumbled and half-fell across the table. A voice was still screaming, only it was no longer hers. It was Grace.

'Get out! Go! Before it's too late!'

A deep sob tore itself from Lisa's chest, tears burning acid tracks down her cheeks. She lay across the table unable to move. Grace's hands took her roughly by the shoulders, pulling her to her feet, as if she were no more than a rag doll. Through the tears Lisa saw the blurred and distorted features of Grace's face only inches from hers. Hot breath hissed in her face. 'Don't you understand? He's going to kill you !'

A girl appeared in the doorway, Lisa's case in her hand. 'The car is ready, La Mère Grace.'

Grace collected herself, brushing the tears away from her eyes. 'Take the case out to the car.' Her voice sounded abnormally controlled. The girl melted away into the hall. Lisa pulled herself free and took a step back. She was no longer weeping, but she shook uncontrollably. She stared at Grace with an intensity close to pain.

'I hate you,' she whispered, and she turned and ran into the hall. Grace heard her footsteps recede and then the slamming of the front door. Slowly she sank into a chair, staring vacantly into nothingness. She felt empty, sucked dry of blood and life. For a long moment her face was calm, without expression, before suddenly crumpling, and she wept as she had not done since she was a child. She did not hear the scurry of feet across the hall and the cry of her name. Only the shaking of her shoulders by urgent hands caused her to look up.

'La Mère Grace, La Mère Grace. They are taking Miss Lisa!'

It took a moment for Grace to assimilate what the girl had said. With an effort she pulled herself out of the chair and ran through the hall, wiping the tears from her eyes. On the steps, heat and light rained down like blows. Her tear-blurred vision created the mirage of Tuk's white Mercedes gliding on air towards the gate. But she heard the crunch of its tyres on the gravel, and saw Lisa's panicked face pressed against the rear window, her mouth opened wide in a silent, terrified scream. And she knew it was no trick of the light.

CHAPTER THIRTY-SEVEN

In the hours before they left, while they waited for darkness to fall, Elliot was aware of the boy watching him. Big saucer eyes that fixed themselves, unblinking, on Elliot's hand as the Englishman absently fingered the tiny silver medallion that hung from his neck. McCue had stripped down his M16 and was cleaning it with an instinctive professionalism. They could hear Serey in the kitchen boiling up a pot of rice. Ny seemed lost in time and space, sitting cross-legged on the floor, staring at the wall beyond Elliot. The boy's eyes flickered up to meet Elliot's, and held his gaze for an inordinate length of time, staring with unselfconscious candour. Finally he turned away towards his sister and whispered something to her. The only indication that she had heard was a slow refocusing of her eyes on Elliot. 'He want know what you wear round neck.'

Elliot felt, between his thumb and forefinger, the contour of the small figure set in its circle of silver, familiar and comforting. McCue glanced up curiously from his gun parts. 'It's a St Christopher,' Elliot said. 'Patron Saint of travellers. My mother gave it to me on my sixteenth birthday.' It came almost as a shock to McCue to think of Elliot as having a mother.

'A charm?' Ny asked.

'I suppose you could call it that.'

'And it work?'

'Well, I've made it this far, so I suppose it must.'

Hau scanned his sister's face passively as she offered him a brief explanation. The boy was silent, then, for a long while, his gaze drawn back again to the tiny figure, like needles to a magnet.

McCue said, 'I think the kid would like it, Elliot.' Elliot shook his head. McCue's chuckle was sour and filled with irony. 'I'd never have figured you for a superstitious bastard.'

'Lots of things you've never figured, Billy.'

McCue's smile never wavered. 'We'll need more than a good-luck charm to get us out of here in one piece. It'll take a fucking miracle. How are you on miracles, Elliot?' Serey came in with a pot of steaming rice and set it on the floor. McCue's gaze settled on the sticky brown grains and his smile faded.

'The last supper,' he said.

Small campfires flickered in the dark, ravaged brown faces huddled around the flames, more for comfort than for warmth. Occasional troop carriers rattled down the broad boulevards. Jumpy sentries nervously fingered the triggers of automatic weapons, small heads in pudding-bowl helmets. Smoke rose all across the city like clouds of luminous mist. During the day, thousands of newly liberated Cambodians had drifted in from the south, in search of food, friends, relatives – the past. And now, an uneasy silence had settled on the city, like dust; fear and hunger and weariness afflicting both the liberators and the liberated.

Hau could still feel the burn of his mother's lips on his cheek, the fingers that trembled on his shoulders as she told him to be careful. He had shrugged free of her embrace, embarrassed by her show of affection in the presence of the tall foreigners. He was no longer a child. He was a soldier, a man. As his sister had stepped forward to kiss him, he had taken a step back, maintaining a distance, and made a little solemn bow. And with a nod to the tall ones, he had turned and led them into the dark suburban night, Kalashnikov clutched tight to his chest.

He led them through a maze of empty streets that were as familiar to him as they were unfamiliar to them. He felt good knowing that they were so completely dependent upon him. He took long, loping strides, moving easily through the humid night air, glancing back from time to time to make sure they were still there. And each time he was struck anew, almost shocked, by Elliot's height. To him he seemed huge; a round-eyed giant with strange, pale skin.

He had only the haziest recollection of the Americans who had once moved freely about the streets of Phnom Penh, and regretted that he had not been old enough to learn to speak their language. What little French he had known was gone for ever. He had felt jealous of his mother and sister, how they could speak to these men. He knew they had saved their lives, and he had been puzzled by his mother's hostility towards them. Surely they were to be admired: tough, strong, seemingly invincible, like the soldiers in the American movies he had seen before his life had been torn up by the roots. He felt both proud and safe in their company, and he enjoyed the respect with which they treated him. They had saved his family from the Khmer Rouge. It was his duty to save them from the Vietnamese.

It took them nearly an hour, skirting the campfires around the fringes of the city centre, to reach the highway that would take them south-west towards the deep-water port of Kompong Som. They lay in wait for more than fifteen minutes watching a convoy of trucks heading out along the highway, before an unnatural silence fell upon the west of the city. The sky had clouded over, virtually obliterating the moon. You could very nearly touch the darkness. They crouched, huddled together, behind the wall of a derelict factory, creeper growing up all around them where it had broken through the cracked pavings. The only sounds the creaking of the cicadas and the whine of mosquitoes.

Hau could feel the heat from the bodies of the two men, could smell their sweat, see it glistening on their faces. He wished he was going with them, that he did not have to go back. After all, what was there to go back to? But he had a sense of duty, too, towards his mother and sister. He was the man. It was up to him to look after them. He felt the hand of the American slip into his and grasp it firmly. 'Thanks, kid.' And for some unaccountable reason Hau felt tears well in his eyes and he was glad it was dark. His sense of safety was slipping away, and he felt less like the man and soldier he wanted to be, and more like the small boy he was.

The taller of the two soldiers, the one his mother had called English – a concept of which Hau had no grasp – pressed something small and hard into his hand. He looked down to see the tiny figure of St Christopher, bowed by the load on its back, and looked up quickly to find the Englishman's eyes hidden in shadow. He clutched it tightly in his hand and felt strangely moved. The big man ruffled his hair and both men moved out from the cover of the wall and off into the night, silent shadows quickly swallowed by the dark.

A voice called out somewhere away to the right, a high-pitched voice, nasal and shrill. An engine roared loudly in the dark, and lights flooded the road beyond the wall. Hau pressed his back against the brick, and heard the clatter of hard soles on tarmac. Almost immediately the night erupted in a blaze of fire and noise. Giants in silhouette flickered across the factory's flaking wall, crouched and running. The whine of mosquitoes was replaced by the whine of bullets pinging off concrete surfaces. To Hau, pressed in sudden terror against the brick, the shadows on the factory wall seemed to grow massively in size, huge dark spirits advancing through the night towards him. He watched, transfixed in horror, as their definition melted at the last, diverging and vanishing. The footsteps ran clattering off to the left and right. The harsh rattle of automatic fire fibrillated in the still night air: five, six, seven bursts that seemed to come from all around, echoing back off the factory wall. Above the roar Hau thought he heard the grunt of a human voice, the thud of a body on tarmac.

Then the shooting stopped, as suddenly as it had begun, the chatter of guns replaced by a chatter of frightened, excited voices, before silence returned. The only sound was the erratic splutter of an idling engine.

Hau felt his heart beating in his throat, heard the roar of blood in his ears. His knuckles burned white as he clutched his Kalashnikov in fear. He took a deep breath and ran silently along the length of the wall, bent double, stopping just short of a breach in the brickwork. His breath came in short trembling bursts, and for a moment he could not move. He relaxed his grip on the AK-47 and realized that he was still clutching the St Christopher, its fine silver chain dangling from between his fingers. Carefully he laid his weapon on the ground and slipped the chain around his neck. The bowed figure seemed to burn against his chest. Creeping forward, then, on his knees, he peered cautiously through the shattered brickwork.

The road lay bathed in the sulphurous light of a jeep's headlamps. Beyond their haloes of brightness, dark figures moved stealthily among the shadows of the darker buildings rising behind. Far away, to his right, Hau saw another figure crouched behind the skeleton of a rusted saloon car that lay at an odd angle, half on the road, half on the pavement, caught in the full glare of the headlamps. The figure was tense and motionless, and Hau realized that the other figures moving beyond the lights were slowly but surely encircling it.

Closer, sprawled awkwardly across the camber of the road, a man lay face-down in the gutter, a pool of blood spreading through the dusty, broken surface. His automatic rifle lay near the faded centre line, casting a long shadow across the ground, reaching out towards his lifeless hand.

With a shock like a fist in the gut, Hau recognized the Englishman. His hand rose instinctively to the medallion that hung around his neck, and he was overwhelmed by guilt. But it was anger that fuelled his sudden, foolish bravery as he snatched the Kalashnikov, stepping out from the cover of the wall and swinging it wildly in the direction of the jeep across the street. Bullets spat from its muzzle in quick succession, hot metal burning his hands, smoke and the acrid stink of cordite flashing up into his face. The front grille of the jeep seemed to dissolve under the sustained burst of fire, bullets ploughing through glass and engine cowling and rubber. Shattered head-lamps extinguished the glare, and dark fell across the street like blindness.

Hau was only vaguely aware of the chatter of McCue's M16, away to his right, and the startled shouts of the Vietnamese. He stumbled through the dark, almost tripping over the prostrate figure of Elliot. *Don't be dead*, he whispered to himself again and again. But Elliot's body seemed lifeless and leaden as he tried to turn it over. *Don't be dead, don't be dead, don't be dead!* A hand pulled him roughly aside and, briefly, he felt McCue's sour, rasping breath on his face. Automatic fire seemed to rattle all around them, punctuated by shrill Vietnamese voices and the sound of running feet. A radio crackled somewhere nearby. But in the darkness there was confusion, and in confusion, safety.

McCue grunted as he strained to lift the dead weight of Elliot on to his shoulder. Hau saw the faintest grim outline of his face, and as the American made for the hole in the wall, Hau scampered across the road to retrieve Elliot's M16. A burst of fire whispered past his face, bullets splintering the brick behind him. Something sharp caught his forehead, just above the right brow, slicing like a razor across the bone. He hardly felt it, but was blinded almost immediately by the blood that ran into his eye. He slung the Kalashnikov across his shoulder and raised the M16, emptying its magazine in wide sweeping arcs of fire across the street. He heard a man scream above the roar of the weapon, before the mechanism jammed on an empty chamber, and he turned and sprinted for the wall, throwing himself through the gap after McCue. Behind him, AK-47s chattered in the dark, but carried no threat now as he ran breathless down the narrow canyons, between towering derelict buildings.

Beyond the far wall that marked the boundary of the former factory, a tiny street led steeply down between old apartment blocks, opening up at the foot into what had once been a small park, now overgrown and threatening to swallow up the streets around it. He stopped to listen. There were no sounds of pursuit. The air was filled with the sweet scent of jasmine blossom, and somewhere far away he heard the distant roar of an engine. A break in the thick cloud overhead opened up on an unexpected glimpse of the moon, and a ghostly light washed the park. McCue was kneeling by a tree, head bowed, gasping for breath that caught in his throat. It was a dry, hacking sound. With a brief backward glance, Hau ran across to join him.

Elliot lay on his back, his chest and arm soaked darkly in blood. His face was chalk pale in the moonlight, and Hau thought he recognized death in its waxen pallor. He placed the tips of his fingers on the Englishman's neck, just below the line of the jaw, and felt the faintest pulse. McCue turned, his face a mask of blood, and for a horrified second Hau wasn't sure whether it was his or Elliot's. Perhaps McCue saw the horror in the young eyes, for he ran the back of his hand across his face to smear the blood away. He looked at it for a moment, then back at the boy, and was surprised to see his face wet with silent tears.

The two women sat huddled in the dark, embracing their unspoken fear. Time was marked only by the sporadic appearances of the moon as it tracked its way across the south-east Asian sky behind thick layers of broken cloud. It was hard to say how long Hau had been gone. Each minute seemed as eternal as the night itself.

At first, Ny heard nothing, but she felt Serey's grip tighten around her arm and tensed. Then sudden fear gripped them both as the front door crashed open and heavy footsteps staggered up the hall. A gross, misshapen shadow loomed in the doorway. For a moment it stood quite still before lurching forward and falling to the floor, unfolding and dividing as it did so, into two. One half hit the floor with a sickening thud. The other remained crouched, heaving and issuing a sound like the bark of torn bellows. A smaller figure appeared in the door behind them. Serey let out a gasp and rushed to pull the boy to her breast. There was no drawing away this time, no standing on masculine dignity. It was a child's sobs that she felt tearing at the young chest.

'What happened?' Ny stood in uncertain isolation in the centre of the room.

'It's my fault,' Hau sobbed. 'All my fault.'

'No.' Serey tightened her grip on him, but he pulled away.

'I took his luck. He gave me his luck and they killed him,' he wailed.

'For fuck's sake, someone get the fire going! I can't see a goddam thing!' McCue was ripping the blood-soaked clothing from Elliot's chest.

The first flames sent their shadows dancing around the walls. Elliot's white skin was touched with blue. The bullet had torn through his chest just below the left shoulder, miraculously missing bone, and coming out cleanly through his armpit. But that had left a mess of torn muscle and flesh. McCue shook his head.

'He's lost too much blood. And a wound like this won't stay clean for long.' He slumped back against the wall and took out a crushed pack of cigarettes with shaking hands.

'What you going do?' Ny asked, her eyes burning with fear and concern.

'Nothing.'

Serey said, 'We must dress the wound.'

'No point, lady! He's a dead man.'

'He will be if you don' do nothing!' Ny's voice rose in pitch.

'For fuck's sake!' McCue threw his cigarettes on the floor. 'He's going to die! Sometimes you just have to accept it! *He* would. *He* knows.' He pulled himself up on to his knees and drew out his pistol. There was something close to hysteria in his voice as he pressed the barrel against Elliot's temple. '*He*'d do it. I mean, you saw him. He didn't give a shit, why should I?' He tensed, his face a mask, as he squeezed on the trigger with a trembling finger.

Hau's confusion and consternation propelled him towards the figure kneeling as if in prayer, but Ny held his arm. 'Your friend had . . .' she searched desperately in her memory for the word '. . . cancer.' It seemed strange on her tongue, innocuous, just a word. Yet the effect on McCue was electrifying. He turned wild eyes on her.

'What kind of shit is that?'

She nodded towards Elliot. 'He tell me. Mistah Slattery come here to die. He had something bad inside him. Growing. A sickness.' She fought to recall Elliot's words, words spoken on

387

a dark night on the Great Lake that might now save his life. 'He going to die anyway, even if no one shoot him.'

The fire in McCue's eyes seemed suddenly extinguished, his finger relaxed on the trigger and he allowed his hand to drop, the pistol trailing loosely at his side. But he remained kneeling, limp and exhausted, like a man whose prayers for release have not been answered, and whose faith in God is shaken.

Hau unclipped the chain at his neck and knelt beside McCue, leaning forward across the prone figure of Elliot to return the St Christopher to its rightful place. He looked up at his mother.

'If I give him back his luck, maybe he won't die.'

CHAPTER THIRTY-EIGHT

Sarit hovered nervously near the arrivals door. Half a dozen cigarette ends lay about his feet, his crumpled white suit grey from the ash of countless others. He dabbed with a grubby yellow handkerchief at the sweat running down his brown face, gathering in the wrinkles and dripping from the ends of his meagre moustache. The evening flight was half an hour late, and his agitation had been increased five minutes earlier by the arrival of two uniformed police officers who stood now smoking and chatting idly by the door

When at length he spotted the face he had been waiting for among the passengers off the London flight, it was with a mixture of relief and trepidation.

'Mistah Blaih. So pleased to see you again.' He smiled effusively and shook the big Scotsman's hand. 'I got car waiting.' And he steered the conspicuously European face quickly out to the taxi rank, and the anonymity of the night.

'Sorry if you've been waiting long, Sarit. The bloody flight was late, then there was all that palaver coming through customs. You got the gear?'

'Oh, yes. Best there is.' Sarit opened the door of the taxi. 'Where to?' He slipped in beside Blair.

'Just take us into the city. We'll drive about for a bit.'

Sarit gave clipped instructions to the driver.

'What about the girl? What did you find out?'

Sarit mopped his face and sat back. 'Difficult, Mistah Blaih, very difficult. Bangkok dangerous place since Tuk running things.'

Blair found his wallet and slipped out a few notes. 'Course it is, Sarit. Better, though, to eat half a loaf in fear than have no bread at all, eh?'

Sarit spread thin lips across nicotine-stained teeth, in what he imagined was a smile. 'Sure, Mistah Blaih, sure.' He took the notes and rubbed them gently between his fingers, as if he thought they might be printed on rice paper and crumble before he could spend them.

'So?'

'They say he tried to have Mistah Elliot killed. But nobody know if he succeed.' Blair felt the skin stretch tightly across his face, but he held his anger somewhere deep inside.

'And his daughter?'

'Don't know who she is, but he got some white girl. La Mère Grace selling her for big bucks. You know, rich European like Thai girl. Rich Thai like white girl.'

The acid of his anger burned now in Blair's gut. 'What did you get me?'

Sarit drew out a cloth-wrapped bundle from under his jacket. 'Colt point four-five, Mistah Blaih. M-nineteen, eleven A-1.'

Blair unwrapped the automatic pistol and weighed it in his hand. It came in at just over a kilo, and had an effective range of about fifty metres. Loading from a seven-round box magazine, it had considerable stopping power. 'Ammo?'

Sarit produced two magazines from each pocket. 'I don't mind telling you, Mistah Blaih, I was pretty damn nervous waiting around airport with this stuff on me.' He paused for an apprehensive moment. Then, 'What you planning, Mistah Blaih?'

'Don't know yet, Sarit.' He snapped a magazine into place and flipped the forward safety catch off, then on again. He nodded towards the driver. 'This guy to be trusted?'

'Sure, Mistah Blaih. He like eat frighten half-loaf, too.'

Blair grinned. 'You're a greedy bastard, Sarit.' He paused. 'I might need you later. Tell him to drop me at the end of Sukhumvit Road.'

Tuk's villa lay in darkness behind its high walls. A single light twinkled through the leaves that fluttered in the hot night breeze. The gates were locked. Blair pressed the buzzer and waited. A female voice crackled across the intercom. 'Yes?'

'Tell Mr Tuk that Sam Blair is here to see him.'

'You wait.'

Blair glanced at his watch. Almost eleven-twenty. The curfew would be in force in a little over forty minutes. He ran a hand quickly over the bulge beneath his jacket, an instinctive act of reassurance. A high-pitched electronic whine preceded a dull clunk, and the gates swung open.

A girl in a yellow dress opened the door to him and he stepped into the large, air-conditioned entrance hall. The hard glare of electric light reflecting off cold tiles momentarily hurt his eyes.

'This way, please.' She led him into Tuk's study, where the light was gentler, lying in soft pools beneath occasional lamps. Tuk rose from behind his desk, looking fresh and cool in a neatly pressed white shirt. But his smile could not disguise his tension. He held out his hand.

'Mr Blair. What brings you to Bangkok?'

Blair made no attempt to take the proffered hand. He waited until the girl had closed the doors behind him. 'I've been hearing stories, Tuk.'

Tuk's hand hung uncertainly in mid-air for some moments before he let it fall to his side. 'One always does.' He sank back into his leather swivel chair.

'About how you tried to have Elliot killed on the Cambodian border.' Blair walked into the centre of the room, keeping his eyes on Tuk.

'I have many enemies, Mr Blair. It is inevitable, a man in my position. People will always try to discredit one.'

'It's not true, then?'

'Mr Elliot crossed the border safely into Cambodia. What has become of him since, I have no idea.'

'And his daughter?'

'His daughter?' Tuk frowned, a look of implausible consternation creasing his brow. Then enlightenment, equally implausible, flickered across his dark eyes. 'Ah, yes, you mentioned her when we spoke.'

'You've seen her, then?'

'No. I told you on the phone.'

'That's strange, Tuk. Because I've been hearing other stories. About a white girl fetching big money. White pussy's a valuable commodity among wealthy Thai businessmen, I understand.'

'Of course. It is the way of the world. We both know this.'

'So you know about it?'

'One hears stories, of course, just as you do. But I have no personal knowledge.'

'Do you mind if I have a drink?'

'Please, help yourself.'

Blair crossed to the drinks table and poured himself a large whisky. 'You know I spent some time in Angola?'

'It is common knowledge. But, I don't . . .'

Blair waved his hand and Tuk stopped short. 'Some people think I'm a nice guy, Tuk. I think I'm a nice guy.' He sipped at his whisky. 'What do you think?'

Tuk felt a tiny trickle of cold sweat run down the back of his neck. 'I think you're a nice guy, Mr Blair.'

'Of course you do. Trouble is, sometimes people who think you're nice think you're soft, too.'

'I don't think you're soft.' Tuk was irritated by having to play this childish role. But fear held him glued to the script.

'Good. I'm glad.' He took another sip of his whisky. 'Good stuff this.'

'Best Scotch.'

'Makes me think of home.' Tuk smiled nervously. 'See, there was this laddie in Angola. He thought I was soft. His first mistake. He was taking money from the other side, feeding them our position. Second mistake. I cut his dick off and stuffed it down his throat.' Blair drained his glass and replaced it carefully on the table. 'Sometimes I'm not such a nice guy.'

Tuk reached suddenly for the top drawer of his desk. Blair was there in two strides, grabbed his arm and slammed the drawer shut on his hand. Tuk screamed and tried to pull away, but Blair held him firm. His voice was almost a whisper. 'See what I mean?'

'You've broken my wrist!' Tuk squealed.

'What a pity. That'll put you out of action for a while.'

Tuk flashed him a venomous look. Blair opened the drawer and lifted out a small pearl-handled revolver. The distant rasp of the buzzer on the gate failed to register, even in his subconscious. 'Very pretty. A real girl's gun.' He slipped it into his pocket, and was about to shut the drawer when his eye caught the familiar gold crest, on dark blue, of a British passport.

'Well, well, well.' He lifted it out. '*Dieu et mon droit.*' He let go of Tuk's arm and walked back around the desk to face him. Tuk doubled forward, clutching his wrist. 'So Lisa never called

394

on you? Odd that you should have her passport, then, isn't it?' Tuk turned frightened eyes in his direction. Blair seemed calm, almost benign, as he drew the Colt .45 out from the belt beneath his jacket and levelled it at Tuk's head. 'I'll give you ten seconds to tell me where she is.'

The door opening took Blair by surprise, and brought Tuk a flicker of hope. Blair took a step back and glanced towards the door, without removing Tuk from his sights. A small, beautiful, Eurasian woman, all in white, stood framed in the doorway. If she was surprised at what she saw, she gave no sign of it. There was a vacant quality about her eyes. 'Grace!' Her name slipped involuntarily from Tuk's lips.

'Don't fucking move, lady!' Blair shouted at her.

Tuk took courage from the interruption. 'Don't be stupid, Blair! If you harm me you'll never find her!' He glanced triumphantly at Grace, and felt his bravado ebb before the cold, dead stare she returned.

'You are looking for Lisa?' Her voice carried the same detachment as her eyes.

Blair glanced warily from one to the other. 'You know where she is?'

'I'll take you.'

'No!' Tuk screamed.

'But we may already be too late. He is having her killed tonight.'

Blair tensed. A shudder ran through him and his eyes glazed as he turned them back on Tuk. 'Goodbye, Tuk,' he said.

CHAPTER THIRTY-NINE

I

A white light filled her head. Somewhere, beyond the clouded edge of consciousness, soft music dripped like rain. Voices drifted across the horizon like shadows, dark and lacking definition. Out of the mist a face emerged, ugly and grinning, eyes burning with hideous desire. She felt hands touching her, warm and damp, like soft breathy kisses, and she rose towards the distant vague outline of the ceiling before tilting forward and revolving slowly through the palest of blue skies. The same grinning face appeared time and time again, ballooning out of the blue. Then a door opened on to darkness, and for the first time she felt the vaguest sensation of her own body, limbs moving through cold air. Somewhere inside lay the seed of consciousness, a tiny eye straining to focus on a reality hidden by thick suffocating folds of obscurity.

The touch of cold stone, beneath bare feet, worked slowly through her, until she was consumed by it. The lights that drifted by overhead appeared like frozen pinnacles. Rough brick grazed her arm and felt warm, a heat that grew until it burned, searing through her icy interior.

Slowly, so slowly that she was hardly aware of it, the inner eye was enlarging its perception, focusing her mind first on a sense of her own nakedness. A hand gripped her arm, propelling her forward, though she still felt as though her feet were gliding over the concrete beneath them. She turned her head through a lengthy arc and saw the brown hand that held her white flesh, and the dark pinpoint needle marks below. Cold water dripped from the ceiling and touched her breast like an icy finger, and with a sudden unbearable perception she heard the splashes of a thousand drips echoing off wet stone, the clatter of leather, and metal studs, on concrete.

Another door opened, this time on light and space. A cavernous echoing vault supported on pillars. A distant pool of light grew closer, drawing her into its centre until, at its vortex, she was compelled to stop. The hand that held her arm relaxed its grip and fell away. She was aware simply of standing now, her nakedness bathed by the cold white light. She heard the scuffle of feet, the clearing of nervous throats Somewhere, behind the growing perception of the inner eye, she heard her own voice screaming. But there was no sound. Her lips did not move.

Time seemed to drift along the edge of consciousness, like a sailboat on the horizon, remote and elusive. There was no way of judging its speed or size or distance, before a gradual clearing of the mist in her eyes dispelled the illusion, and the focus of her horizon drew closer – darkness beyond the ring of light, along whose edge she saw, for the first time, the watching faces. Hands raised glasses to dry lips. Dark eyes consumed her with an inner fear of their own unnatural lust. She stared back blankly at the brown, hungry faces, with only a distant awareness of what it was they wanted of her. A frown crinkled her brow – something familiar in one among the watchers, fat and ugly, a far-off recollection of his mouth, twisted by passion, looming over her, close hot breath against her, the sweet smell of opium. And yet there was something comforting in the familiarity. She tried to smile, but found that she could not.

Suddenly, and yet slowly, fingers grasped her hair and jerked her head around. Dead eyes gazed into hers. A uniformed arm rose with measured intent, a gloved fist at the end of it rising above her, before crashing down and striking her hard across the cheek. She felt no pain, but a wave of weakness ran through her. She felt her legs buckle at the knees, but the hand still grasped her hair, she could not fall. The eyes that stared into hers gleamed now with unspeakable malice. Another blow, this time striking her full in the mouth. Again there was no pain, but as the hand released her and she fell, she saw her own blood, crimson, splash across the white of her legs.

II

Row upon row of dark deserted warehouses drifted by. Blair stared anxiously from the window, searching for light, some sign of human existence. He turned towards the Eurasian woman seated beside him, and wondered at her calm. She was almost serene. It only increased his disquiet.

'You're sure you know where we're going?' He had surrendered himself to her completely, as had all the lovers she had known. But it was not passion that won his surrender. Like a drowning man, he had been forced to grasp the only hand which held out the hope of survival. Lisa's survival.

Grace still held, in her mind's eye, the image of the dead and bloodied Tuk. A frail figure, crumpled in his leather desk chair, his abject terror at the point of death somehow erasing long years of corruption – like a mortal sin forgiven at the confessional. Death had come as a release, for both of them, from the power of his evil. She turned and looked at the red, perspiring face of the Scotsman. 'My driver will find the place.' And for the first time she was curious. 'You were a friend of her father?'

Blair would not accept the past tense. 'I am a friend of her father – unless you know something I don't. I heard Tuk tried to have him killed on the border.'

'And failed. Jacques crossed safely into Cambodia. If anyone can be safe in Cambodia.'

'You knew him, too, then?'

A faint smile crossed her lips. 'Once. In another life, it seems.'

'And Lisa?'

The smile faded. 'I have done her great harm. I came tonight to plead for her life, though I knew I would fail.'

Blair regarded her with bewilderment and distaste. He guessed this was the woman Sarit had named as La Mère Grace, responsible – if Sarit was to be believed – for what amounted to Lisa's sexual enslavement. Why should she care whether the girl lived or died? And yet clearly she did.

'What is this place we're going to? If Tuk wanted her dead, why not simply kill her?'

'Tuk never did anything simply. It is his way of avenging himself on Mr Elliot, for having failed to kill him.' She looked away at the endless dark buildings. 'You have heard of snuff movies?'

Blair felt a chill run through him. 'Yes.'

'In Bangkok there is a live version. If you are rich enough, and sick enough, you can pay to see a girl beaten nearly to death, like a long, lingering foreplay, and then shot dead – like an orgasm.'

Blair found it difficult to speak. 'And this is what he planned for Lisa?'

'I told you. We may already be too late.'

He was trembling now. 'If we are, I'll kill you.'

'If we are, I would not want to live.'

His anger was overlaid by confusion, like oil on water. 'I don't understand.'

She shook her head. 'Neither do I.'

'Madame, we are there.' The chauffeur's voice refocused their attention. The car drew to a stop and the engine idled gently in the darkness. They had drawn up in front of a large brick warehouse, devoid of any sign of light or life. It looked to Blair like all the others they had passed, with nothing to mark it out.

'Are you sure?'

'Follow me.' Grace slipped from the car and her heels echoed back off the cobbles. Blair strode after her, down a narrow lane between rising walls that disappeared into the night sky. At the far end they could see lights twinkling on the black waters of the Chao Phraya. The place smelled damp and rotten.

Halfway along, a figure stepped out from the shadows of a small doorway to block their path. His white shirt caught the reflected light from the water beyond. The butt of a revolver glinted in his belt, but his face was still masked by shadow. There was surprise in his voice.

'La Mère Grace.'

Her voice seemed remarkably calm. 'Is it over?'

'Not yet. Soon.'

'Tuk said we could watch.'

'I don't think so.' He stepped forward so that they saw his face for the first time, a squat, brutish face, a man of about forty. He cast a wary eye over Blair, then grinned dismissively back at Grace. 'From what I hear you're next. Who's the old man?'

Blair listened impatiently to the exchange. 'What's he saying?'

'He's not going to let us in.'

The Thai did not expect such speed from the silver-haired

foreigner. His hand never reached the revolver in his belt, and he barely had time to be surprised when his face smashed hard against the wall. A sharp inhalation drew blood into his throat, and he choked briefly before an arm encircled his head and a swift jerk snapped his spinal cord. His body went limp and Blair slid him gently to the ground.

Grace's shock caught in her throat as she gasped, paralysed by the sight of the figure sprawled at her feet. Blair grabbed her arm, fingers biting into soft flesh. 'Go, lady! Fucking move!' She caught a glimpse of the pistol in his hand as he pushed her ahead of him, through the door and into the vast, damp interior. A tiny lamp, somewhere far overhead among unseen rafters, cast a feeble light in the emptiness of the warehouse. Grace kicked off her shoes and ran across the huge expanse of concrete floor, kicking up tiny clouds of dust, dodging the massive iron hooks that hung on great chains from the darkness above. The patter of her feet, the clatter of his shoes, the rasp of their breath, echoed around them like ghosts mocking them from the shadows, telling them they were too late.

On the far wall, a small lamp glowed beside a large, rectangular hole in the brick. As they reached it, Blair saw that it the opening to a lift shaft. The iron gates were drawn back, but there was no lift, only rusted metal cables reaching up and down into the void above and below. Grace pressed the lower of two buttons set in the wall below the lamp, and the cables went taut, as power coughed life into the pulley, and the whine of the summoned lift ascending surged up the shaft.

They waited in tense, breathless silence as the seconds crawled agonisingly by. Somewhere, far away, Blair imagined he heard the voice of a girl screaming, but he couldn't be sure it was not just one, among many, of the sounds issued by the rising lift. As it drew near ground level, light spilled out from the shaft, casting their shadows long across the dusty concrete.

Blair grabbed Grace's arm and pulled her into the bright box of yellow light. He punched the down button and they began their slow descent.

'Will there be someone at the bottom?'

'I don't know. I don't think so.'

He pushed her across the floor. 'Get up against the wall!' He dropped to the floor, pressing himself into the boards, and levelled his gun at the brick that drifted slowly upwards. It was a full minute of painfully slow downward progress before a black rectangle opened up from the floor and rose before them. Blair tensed. The light from the lift fell out to illuminate a long empty corridor. There was no one there. Blair scrambled to his feet and jumped down before the lift had come to rest.

As Grace followed the sound of a gunshot echoed dully from beyond the door at the end of the corridor. 'Oh, God!' She felt as if the bullet had pierced her own flesh.

With acid burning in his throat, Blair sprinted the length of the corridor. As he kicked open the door, another shot rang out.

A ring of men drew back from the centre of light, startled faces turning towards the door. A man in a brown uniform and black knee-length boots stood under the light, a gun smoking in his hand. Lisa was on her knees, battered and bloody, her face almost unrecognizable. The man had fired two blank shots, the prelude to a live third round, the climax of the performance. His left hand grasped her by the hair, his right pressed the barrel of his gun against her temple. He too had turned a startled face, his concentration broken. Blair raised his pistol and, two-handed, fired three shots in quick succession. The first two bullets struck in the chest, the third in the face. The man in the brown uniform spun away out of the light, like a pirouetting ballet dancer, dead before the smack of his head hitting the concrete reached them. His gun clattered off into darkness and Lisa fell in a lifeless heap.

Grace appeared at Blair's shoulder, a moan of anguish on her lips. She pushed through the ring of stunned faces, dropped to her knees and drew the naked Lisa into her arms with tender hands. Blair advanced in grim silence, pistol still levelled, his eyes flicking back and forth among the men who had been denied their pleasure.

'If she's dead I'll kill every last one of them!'

Grace whispered, 'She's alive!' And she brushed blood away from the girl's face with the back of her hand.

'Then let's get her out of here.' Blair moved, cautiously, into the light. With his free hand he helped Grace pull Lisa to her feet. Lisa groaned, her eyes rolling, as she drifted back to consciousness. Blair saw the great red weals across her chest and back, inflicted by the discarded riding crop that lay at her feet. He wanted to put a bullet between every pair of watching eyes.

'She needs a doctor quickly.' The urgency in Grace's voice blunted his anger and he turned his attention back to the battered girl.

Between them they half-carried, half-dragged her out of the circle of light. As she passed him, Grace's eyes met the General's dark gaze. Her mouth curled in hate as she drew a gob of spittle on to her tongue and spat it into his face. He did not flinch. Blair lifted Lisa into his arms and hurried out of the door and up the corridor towards the lift. Grace lingered for just a moment, before breaking the General's gaze and darting after him.

When the door slammed shut on the basement, the General wiped the spittle from his face and took two steps into darkness to stoop and retrieve the fallen revolver. His face darkened by the fury of humiliation, he pushed the others aside and strode to the door. Light rushed towards him from the lift at the far end of the corridor. Blair, the girl supported on his arm, stood under the light, fumbling with the button to set the lift in motion. The silhouette of the retreating Grace had almost reached him, a white shadow in the dark corridor. The pulley motor surged into life, jerking the cables tense and shaking the frame of the lift. Blair glanced up as the General raised his arm to shoot. Grace was no more than two paces away. The shout of warning died on his lips as the gun flashed in the dark and Grace fell forward, lightly, like a wounded bird. Blair fired blind at the figure at the end of the corridor, but the jerk of the lift sent the bullet whining harmlessly off into space. As the lift rose he crouched to his knees and held out his arm in a futile gesture of help. Grace lifted her head, her face dimming in the fading light.

'Tell her . . .' Her voice, though feeble, still rose above the drone of the motor. 'Tell her I'm sorry.' And she vanished in the darkness below as the lift rose into the shaft.

She heard the steps of many feet before a hand pulled her over and she found herself staring up into hungry eyes intent now on fulfilment. The General's fat lips spread across white teeth. Blair heard the shots before the lift reached the ground floor, each one like a fist in his solar plexus. He closed his eyes. 'Jesus God,' he whispered.

Grace's chauffeur stood by the car as Blair emerged from the shadows. Her eyes widened at the sight of the battered and bloodied girl in his arms. 'Where is La Mère Grace?'

'Dead.' The finality of that one small word struck him as if for the first time. He laid Lisa carefully in the car, and turned back to the Thai girl who stood small and fixed, eyes brimming. His hands grasped her shoulders and he felt her frailty. 'You must get us away from here. Fast.' She nodded mutely. He said, 'What about the curfew?'

She shook her head. 'It is not a problem.'

As the car pulled away across the cobbles, he saw, in the rearview mirror, the girl's tears shining wet on her cheeks, and he was glad that someone, at least, would cry for Grace.

*

A lamp burned in the dark by the bed. The doctor fluttered over her, nervous and sweating, frameless spectacles magnifying myopic eyes.

'Well?' Blair's impatience increased the doctor's agitation. He would be well paid for this illegal night call, but he was still scared.

'She has a broken nose, concussion. Two, maybe three, broken ribs. It is impossible to say what internal injuries there might be. You must get her to a hospital.'

'Not in Bangkok. Can you give her something to kill the pain?'

He opened his bag. 'I can give her some sedatives.'

'I don't want her falling asleep. She needs to walk out of here.'

The doctor pushed his spectacles up on the bridge of his nose and turned wide eyes on the big Scotsman. 'I do not think this would be wise.'

'I'm not asking you to think. I'm asking you to patch her up as best you can.' Blair's voice was tight with restraint, clipped short by the rage he fought to control. The stink of dirty socks and sweat in the airless heat of this tiny bedroom was choking him. He went out to the smell of stale curry and cigarette smoke that permeated Sarit's apartment. Sarit glanced up from the telephone and nodded. After a further exchange he replaced the receiver and turned towards him, the ubiquitous cigarette dangling from his lips.

'Is done, Mistah Blaih. Eight-thirty in morning. First flight to Hong Kong.'

'Hong Kong? Couldn't you do better than that?'

Sarit shrugged and mopped the sweat from his brow with a damp handkerchief. 'Sorry Mistah Blaih. First seats on London flight not before end of week.' He nodded towards a bag lying near the door. 'La Mère Grace girl, she bring Miss Lisa's stuff. You want her get dressed?'

Blair looked at his watch. It was a little after four a.m. 'In a couple of hours, when the doctor's finished.'

'She gonna be alright, Mistah Blaih?'

'I hope so, Sarit. I hope so.'

The towers and turrets of the Grand Palace caught the rose-coloured light of the early morning sun across the river. In the foreground the concrete and steel constructions of the twentieth century jutted skyward, obscuring the view, until they turned away north, leaving the river behind. The traffic was already brisk: taxis, trams, buses, private cars, *samlors* – this great south-east Asian metropolis awaking after the dark hours of curfew.

Blair sat in the back of the taxi behind Sarit, rigid with tension. Beside him Lisa's glazed eyes gazed out from behind dark glasses at the receding city. Her sense of pain was vague, somewhere far away, as if her body and her mind resided in separate places. She had no clear idea of what was happening. The sights that spooled by the window were like flickering images on a screen, remote and unreal. She had an urgent longing to close her swollen eyes and sleep, but the man who sat beside her seemed ever-present, his fingers closed tightly around her arm, urging her to stay awake, to move with him, walk with him, carry the pain.

Blair glanced at her and felt the burden of responsibility. 'I suppose they'll have found the body by now.'

Sarit turned and breathed smoke through his yellow teeth. 'Tuk? His servants will have phone police last night. They look for you for sure.'

'And Grace?'

Sarit chuckled. 'Hah! You no worry about her. She never be seen again, that certain.'

Blair was little comforted. He examined himself in the rearview mirror. At a glance the black hair dye took years off him. But it seemed, too, to emphasize the lines on a face which appeared paler, more drawn. The man who stared back at him made him feel older inside. He felt trapped in his neatly pressed suit, prisoner of an image that was not him. He reached into an inside pocket and took out a British passport in the name of Robert Wilson. The face of the man in the rearview mirror looked back at him from page three. His heart skipped a beat. The glasses! He'd forgotten the glasses. He drew them out from his breast pocket and slipped them on, heavy tortoiseshell-framed spectacles.

Sarit grinned. 'No worries, Mistah Blaih. Even I don't recognize you.' And he turned around, still chuckling, to face the front, smoke rising as he lit another cigarette.

The airport terminal was relatively quiet, and the Scotsman cursed the early hour of the flight. Airport security men, carrying small sub-machine guns, cast inscrutable eyes over the comings and goings. Blair knew the girl would attract attention. Her dark glasses could not disguise her bruised and swollen face, and she could barely walk.

Sarit collected their tickets from the Cathay Pacific reservations desk. He was anxious to pass them on to Blair and be gone. 'Dangerous to be seen together,' he said with a little nervous laugh. 'Goodbye, Mistah Blaih, good luck.' He hurried away, leaving a trail of cigarette smoke in his wake.

The girl at the check-in desk took their luggage and gave them two adjacent seats in non-smoking. She looked doubtfully at Lisa. 'I hope you enjoyed your stay in Bangkok.'

Blair smiled. 'Very much.'

She handed him the boarding cards. 'Gate five. Boarding in ten minutes.'

Lisa was rapidly losing her grip on consciousness. Blair held her firmly round the waist, whispering constant encouragement. They passed through security, where officers insisted on searching her handbag. Blair waited patiently, aware all the time of curious eyes upon them. A stolid middle-aged woman, hair drawn tightly back from her face, scanned each of their passports thoroughly before waving them through immigration without a word. Blair breathed an inner sigh of relief, and looked along the signs for gate five.

'Stop!' The voice came like a blow to the back of his head. Blair turned to find a blue-uniformed security man advancing towards them. 'Passports, please.'

Blair quelled his instinct to react physically – attack or retreat. He forced an even tone.

'We've already been through immigration.'

'Passports!' The security man held out his hand. Blair nodded and took the passports from his inside pocket. The security man took his time, browsing through each of them, checking their faces against the photographs. Finally his gaze rested on Lisa. He reached out and took away her dark glasses. Misted blue eyes squinted at him from the slits that separated the black, bruised swellings above and below. Something like shock registered on his face. 'What happened?'

'She was involved in a motor accident.' Blair watched keenly for a reaction. He could detect none, and added, 'We're going to Hong Kong to see a specialist.'

For several seconds the Thai continued to stare at her, then he thrust Lisa's glasses towards Blair. 'You wait here.' He turned away.

Blair protested, 'But they're boarding our flight.'

The Thai stopped and emphasized with a sharp, chopping movement of his hand, 'Wait!' He crossed the hall and disappeared through a door.

Blair felt sick. He glanced each way along the hall, and saw a second security guard watching from a distance, his hand resting on the black leather of his holster. There was no way forward, no way back. He could do nothing but stand and wait.

A clatter in the doorway jerked his head round to see the

guard returning, pushing a wheelchair ahead of him. 'Is a long way to walk,' he said, with real concern.

It wasn't until the wheelchair had been folded up and taken off the aircraft, and the steward had pulled the door closed, that Blair felt able to relax. The smiling Chinese face of the stewardess loomed over him. 'Is there anything we can do for her?'

'I'll let you know.'

He watched through the window as the plane taxied away from the terminal building to sit, on hold, at the end of the runway for several minutes, before revving its powerful jet engines and sprinting down the tarmac to swoop up into the pale blue sky. As they climbed steeply, swinging north-east towards Hong Kong and safety, he glanced at Lisa and saw that she was unconscious.

PART THREE

CHAPTER FORTY

For three days Elliot hovered between life and death, sometimes consumed by the fire of his fever, sometimes shivering uncontrollably. In flashes of lucidity, between bouts of delirium, he was aware of a young face fluttering over his, a small feminine hand wiping his brow with a cool, damp cloth. He had the impression of being surrounded by countless tiny diamonds of light, a gently curving universe that shone with the fire of a million stars. He floated here, adrift between light and darkness, and dreamt that he heard the slap of water, the dull chug of a small motor, and, once, that he lay in the arms of a naked girl, her soft brown skin burning where it touched his.

The pain in his chest and shoulder pulsed like a heartbeat. At times it appeared to envelop him, smothering all other awareness so that nothing else existed; a relentless, endless pounding of his brain.

When, finally, his fever burned itself out, consciousness came like a waking dream. He lay on wooden boards covered with coarse rush mats, swaddled in blankets and bundles of cloth. He gazed up at the familiar diamonds of light. But even as he focused they seemed to fade. The light was dying around him, and yet the air still glowed. For some moments his sense of disorientation flooded his mind with panic. He attempted to raise himself on one elbow, but fell back with the pain that forked through his chest, while the boards beneath him rocked gently from side to side. The slap of water on wood increased his confusion with the realization that he was on a boat. It came to him then, as he gazed upwards, that he lay beneath a canopy of rush matting arched across him. Tiny chinks of fading light shone through the gaps in the woven pattern. This vessel could be no bigger than a sampan.

He tried again to pull himself up, this time gritting his teeth against the pain, and pressed his face to a slit in the matting to see the sun dipping behind dark, scattered clouds. As it set across a wide expanse of water, its liquid gold seemed to spill out towards him. He fell back on to the mat, breathless and sweating.

A ragged cloth partition at his feet was suddenly drawn aside, and in the dusk he saw the light of concern in Ny's young eyes. 'You hungry, Mistah Elliot?'

'Thirsty.' His voice creaked in his throat, like a rusty gate.

'How you feel?'

'Dried up. Like a raisin.'

She disappeared behind the curtain and returned with a cup of water. 'Mamma boil it. It good.' She helped raise his head, lifting the rim of the cup to dry, cracked lips. His mouth soaked up the water like a sponge. It caught in his throat and he choked, spilling it to cling in droplets to the thick growth on his chin.

'You been very sick, Mistah Elliot.'

'I guess. How long?'

'Three day.'

'Three days!' He felt as though a slice of his life had been excised by a surgeon's scalpel. What had happened in all that time? 'Where are we?'

'South.'

'South where?'

'Kampuchea. On river Mekong. We tied up till it dark.' She gave him more water and he felt it track cold down to his stomach. The effort of raising his head exhausted him, and he let it fall back on the bundle of cloth that served as a pillow, confused, uncertain as to whether this was another delirium.

'How?' he asked. 'How did we get here?'

'Mamma,' Ny said. 'She bring us.' She paused. 'Mistah McCue, he go to shoot you, but I tell him 'bout your friend, 'bout his cancer.'

She leaned over him and dabbed his forehead lightly with a cool cloth. He rolled his head to one side and looked at the bandage on his shoulder. 'Who did this?'

'Me and Mistah McCue. It good. Clean dressing. You been very sick.'

The murmur of voices came from beyond the cloth partition. 'Who's there?'

'Mamma, she cook rice and fish. Hau catch fish. He very smart.'

'And Mr McCue?'

'He there, too. You hungry?'

He nodded.

Nothing had ever tasted so good before. She fed him with chopsticks, morsels that exploded flavour on his tongue. But it was hard work eating – his jaw felt stiff and his throat swollen – and he tired quickly, lying back to drift again into the netherworld that had held him for the past three days.

He dreamed he heard the cough of an engine, the slow chug-chug of a propeller, water whispering past his ears. Then silence, a sensation of floating through space, followed by darkness and a dreamless oblivion. When next he opened his eyes he could see nothing. He heard the splash of water against the sampan, then smelled smoke – the sweet tang of tobacco. The red end of a cigarette glowed in the dark, and by its light he saw McCue's face. He was squatted on the boards beside Elliot, smoking in silence.

'Give me a pull at that.'

Without a word McCue leaned over to hold the cigarette to his lips. He took a deep draw and coughed violently. 'Better?' McCue asked.

'Sure.' The smoke drawn into his lungs made him feel giddy. 'What time is it?'

'Night. Does it matter?'

Elliot felt irritation rising in his chest. 'Yes, it matters. Where are we?'

McCue's voice remained calm and even. 'We crossed the border a couple of hours back.'

Elliot frowned. 'What border?'

'Into Vietnam. Just like coming home, eh?' His voice was edged with irony. 'We set off just after sunset, then about a mile up river we cut the engine and just drifted over in the dark. Easy as pie. You can see the lights of Chau Doc from here. Ever been to Chau Doc? It's a shitheap.' He held the cigarette to Elliot's lips again. Elliot took a light draw and managed this time not to choke.

'How the hell did we get here?'

McCue shrugged, as if it had been nothing. 'She did it. Mamma Serey. She's quite a lady. Just sort of took over. You were as good as dead. Me, I'd given up. Didn't see the point no more. She took the kids and her jewellery into town, bartered for food and a sampan. They came back with a cart. We got you on it, then they hid you and me under all kinds of blankets and shit and wheeled us right past the noses of the Vietnamese, down to the docks. The place was crawling with refugees, soldiers. All kindsa stuff was going on. It was chaos. Shit, no one blinked an eye at an old woman and a couple of kids wheeling a cart. We been on the river ever since. Same on the water, too. All kinda boats going up and down, and the gooks not giving a shit. They don't know what's happening any more than anyone else. We never even been stopped. Not once.' He chuckled. 'Some lady, that Mamma Serey.'

Elliot lay back, staring wide-eyed into the darkness, trying to block in McCue's sketch of his lost three days. But his thoughts were as confused as the scenes McCue had described. He could form no picture of a Phnom Penh alive with refugees and soldiers; just empty streets and desolation. Neither could he picture the river, or the sampan in which he now lay; only the wide, empty waters of the Tonle Sap, and the small open boat in which they had so nearly perished. He felt lost in a void. And, for the first time that he could remember, he realized that he was not responsible for his own life. A huge burden had been lifted. He could embrace death with an easy conscience.

'Why are we in Vietnam?'

McCue breathed a lungful of smoke into the darkness. 'She reckons we can make Long Xuyen in a couple of days. I know a guy there, or did, if he's still alive. Ethnic Chinese. Hated the Viets. I was stationed there for a couple of months. He and I played a lot of cards together, drank a lot of whisky, lost a lot of money. It's not so far from there to Rach Gia, on the coast. I thought maybe he could help.'

Elliot laughed. The easy laugh of one who will never have to face the problem, of one suddenly free to no longer care. 'What are you going to do, Billy? Just waltz into town, say "Hi, remember me?" Five years since the Yanks pulled out. Not many white faces around these days, I'll bet.'

'A few Russians, though.' Elliot heard him grin in the dark. 'That'd be some irony.'

'Know any Russian?'

'*Da svedanya.*' He paused. 'You?'

'*Skajitay pojalsta gdyeh astanavlivayetsya avtobus numer adin.*'

'Shit, I'm impressed. What the fuck does that mean?'

'Excuse me, please, where does the number one bus stop?''

It was the first time Elliot could remember hearing McCue laugh. 'Hey, Elliot, I never knew you had a sense of humour.'

Elliot let his eyes close. The mere act of talking had tired him.

He was not sure if he had slept for any length of time, or merely dozed for a moment, before he next heard McCue's voice. But it came to him as if in a dream and he had to force his eyes open. There was the faintest grey light around them, and McCue was smoking another cigarette. 'What? What did you say?'

'I said quit snoring. I can't get to sleep, and they can hear you in Chau Doc.'

'Give me a cigarette.'

McCue lit him one and Elliot took it in his right hand. There was a foul taste in his mouth again. He said, 'Who's on watch?'

'The boy. I done my stint. It'll be dawn soon, then we'll start the motor and get moving.' He shifted to straighten a cramped knee.

Elliot took several draws on his cigarette. 'I suppose I should thank you.'

'What for?'

'My life.'

'Nothing to do with me. It was the girl. Changed your blankets when they was wet with you sweating, laying cold cloth on your forehead to stop you burning up, cleaning and changing your dressings. You'd think she really cared for you. Can't think why.'

'I dreamed I slept with her.'

'No dream, pal. When you was shivering your life away, she just stripped off, and wrapped herself up in the blankets with you, to stop you freezing to death. I can't believe these people. You treat them like shit, and they return it with kindness.'

Elliot was pricked by irritation. 'I don't need their kindness!'

'Why? Afraid you might feel you owe 'em something? 'Cause you do. Your life.'

'Who needs it?'

'You, presumably. I mean, you was busy thanking me for it just a minute ago.'

'I was being polite,' Elliot said. He felt McCue's eyes on him without having to turn to see them.

'How come you never told me Mikey had cancer?' There was no change of tone, yet the question was laden with accusation.

'He didn't want me to. I only found out by chance. He didn't want anyone's pity.'

'I mean after you'd shot him.' There was an edge there now.

'There didn't seem any point. Would it have made a difference?'

'To me, yes.'

They heard, from the distant bank, the first cawing of tropical birds as the sky lightened.

'You know, I can't figure you, Elliot. It's like you want to be hated.'

'Maybe I deserve to be.' He saw that his cigarette had burned down to the filter. 'Get rid of that for me, would you.' McCue took it and stubbed it out in the bottom of the sampan.

'What are you talking about?'

Elliot turned his head and their eyes made contact. 'You know what I'm talking about, Billy. People like you and me, we do what we do because we know something about ourselves that most people never do.' McCue's eyes flickered away in discomfort. 'We've all been face to face with the other side, the dark side. Of ourselves. You know it, don't you? The place you keep all the nasty things you've done or thought, that little seed of evil that's in us all. Only we let it grow, didn't we? Till it choked all the good in us, all the love. I mean, all that shit about duty and honour. You stop believing in that pretty quick when it's kill or be killed. They know that, the ones who send you out there. They know that war is fuelled by evil, and they reward it with medals and citations. Christ, I mean how else are they going to persuade kids to go on killing each other day after day? And when the dark side takes over, how else are any of us going to excuse it?'

The brief burst of passion in him was snuffed out by fatigue. He lay gasping for breath.

McCue was staring down at his hands. He was silent for a long time. When he spoke it was in a monotone. 'I had a puppy once. In Nam. Inherited it from this kid that got blown away by a frag grenade. I only had the mutt a few days. But I was pretty sore inside. Hurting. Angry. He'd been my buddy, that kid. I never made the same mistake again. That's why I volunteered for the Rats. Make no friends, lose no friends.

'So, anyway, they gave me his puppy. And I would take it and just sort of squeeze it till it yelped, or twist its paw till it would try to bite me. Shit, somebody or something had to suffer for all that pain, and it was going to be that fucking puppy.' He shook his head. 'I grew up on a farm, Elliot. Never hurt an animal in my life. But I was hurting that dog, and suddenly I knew it was in me. I got scared and gave it away, 'cause I knew I was gonna kill it.' He paused to light another cigarette. 'Maybe I should have. Maybe I wouldn't have done all the other things I done.' He glanced self-consciously at Elliot. 'What did you do that was so bad?' It was more a defence than a question.

'Killed a lot of women and children.'

'All that Aden shit? Everybody knows about that. You didn't know they was there. You were just some kind of scapegoat, right?'

Elliot shook his head. 'I knew they were there, alright. They were waving a white flag, as if that somehow wiped the slate clean. I had friends cut to pieces all around me. We were supposed to be protecting these people and they were feeding the enemy every damn move. I was mad. I was so mad I just didn't care any more. I didn't fire the first shot. But I still pulled the trigger. I was the officer, I could have stopped it. I was more guilty.'

He reached out for another cigarette. McCue lit one and handed it to him.

'People used to ask, "What's it like to kill someone? How many people did you kill?" They never asked what it's like to see your best friend blown to bits by a mine, how it feels to be covered in his blood and hear him screaming in agony with his guts hanging out.' The pain in Elliot's shoulder had begun to throb and he felt dizzy and sick. 'You know what I'm talking about. You said it yourself, you never let yourself get close to anybody ever again, never owe anybody anything. And the guilt . . .' he closed his eyes. 'Well, that's something you've just got to live with. The knowledge inside, of who you really are and what you did. Death's too easy. Life's much harder. That's the real punishment.'

He groaned, a long breath rattling in his throat. McCue leaned over him. 'What's wrong?'

He felt sleep, like a mist, slowly rolling over his consciousness. 'Nothing that dying wouldn't cure.'

McCue laughed. 'You ain't gonna die, Elliot. Like you said, that'd be too damned easy.'

It was dark. The mist rose up around him. He heard voices. Whispering. But he couldn't make out what they said. He wanted to call out, but when he opened his mouth no sound came. A body lay in the swamp beside him, blood running rich and dark in the mud. He was scared. He knew they were all around, and when they found him he would be killed. A shadow loomed out of the mist, a dark figure towering over him. It leaned in and he saw its eyes, eyes without pupils or irises, just whites, shot with red veins. At last he found his voice, as terror dissolved control, and he cried out. An arm reached towards him and he grabbed the wrist.

He opened his eyes wide, the cry still on his lips, and saw Ny's pain. He let go her arm and lay breathing heavily. Light burned through the chinks all around them. The air was hot and humid and fetid, and he was covered with a fine film of sweat. 'I'm sorry.'

She rubbed her wrist. 'You have bad dream.'

'Yes. Bad dream.'

'I change your dressing now.'

He watched and winced as she removed the dressing. There was an area of bruising all around, and it was red raw where the dead flesh had been cut away. From the smell and the colour in the centre he knew it was still infected, but it was not as ugly as he'd been expecting. He drew his breath in sharply as she took a small bowl of yellowish liquid and began gently swabbing it clean from the inside out. Even as he wrestled with the urge to yell with pain, he thought how absurd it was that he should feel the need to disguise it. Would she think him any less a man? Should he care? He gasped and tried to speak. A distraction. 'What are you cleaning it with?'

'Piss,' she said.

'Jesus Christ!' He tried to jerk himself away.

PETER MAY

'Please stay still, Mistah Elliot. Mistah McCue, he say it . . .' she searched for the word. 'Sterile.'

'Yeah, he would.' He paused for a moment, then, 'Whose piss?' he asked.

She smiled, a coy little smile, keeping her eyes lowered. 'Mine.'

He lay back and closed his eyes, wondering what further indignities life could heap upon him.

'Mistah McCue drain wound for couple of days. Lot of pus. Smelled real bad.'

'Didn't feel too good, either.'

'Much better now, but infection still there. We make – poultice.' She pronounced the word carefully, proud of her new vocabulary. She lifted his arm with great care and washed out the wound in his armpit where the bullet had come out. He clenched his teeth and breathed stertorously through his nose. 'It hurt bad?'

'Yeah, it hurt bad. Jesus—!'

The cloth partition was drawn aside and Hau crouched down to enter, carrying a bowl from which steam rose like smoke. He looked anxiously at Elliot for a moment, then grinned.

'What the hell's this?'

'Poultice,' Ny said.

'What's in it?'

'Rice. We boil rice and mash it and wrap in cloth. Mistah McCue say very good to draw infection.'

'Seems to me Mr McCue's been saying a lot of things.'

427

'Lot of thing,' Ny repeated seriously. 'Very smart man, Mistah McCue.'

'Yeah, very smart. I'll bet that's hot.'

'Very hot. It hurt, maybe.'

'No doubt Mister McCue told you that.'

'No, Mamma say. She know 'bout poultice, too.' She gently pressed the first steaming bundle into his shoulder, and it hurt like hell.

Later, both wounds freshly dressed, he was able to sit up a little, propped against his backpack, while Ny fed him rice and fish from a bowl. Hau squatted in silence by the partition, watching gravely. Their sampan put-putted through the water, making steady progress. The chinks in the matting gave him a splintered view of the river. It was busy, small boats plying wares up and down between villages in the delta. The wash from a laden ferry boat, sitting very low in the water, rocked their little craft from side to side, the deep throb of its engines receding north.

'How come we haven't been stopped?' he asked.

Ny shrugged. 'Many Cambodian here. Refugee.'

On the far bank he saw the rusting hulks of American patrol boats blown asunder by the Viet Cong, epitaphs for a high-tech superpower defeated by a people in black pyjamas.

Hau's voice broke into his thoughts and he turned to find the boy's eyes on him. He spoke haltingly, with the embarrassed reticence of a child confessing to some dreadful misdemeanour. Elliot looked at Ny. 'What's he saying?'

428

There was the faintest smile on Ny's lips, as if she were secretly amused. 'He apologize for what happen to you.'

'It wasn't his fault.'

'You give him your charm. He believe he take your luck.'

Elliot smiled and shook his head. 'No, no. I gave him my luck. My fault.'

'He give it back to make you well.'

'Tell him to keep it. I'm doing alright without it.'

'No, you no understand. He already give it back. The night you shot.'

His hand reached to his neck and found the familiar St Christopher there, and for some reason he felt tears rise in his eyes. He looked away. 'Tell him, then, that he saved my life. Tell him – tell him I owe him.'

Ny spoke quickly, softly, to her brother. Elliot watched him as, initially, the boy frowned, before grinning broadly. His eyes blurred, and a large tear rolled down his cheek. Elliot grinned back at him. He turned to Ny. 'Tell him big boys don't cry.'

Ny returned a quizzical look. 'Don' they?'

Elliot closed his eyes to shut out the world, but found it was still there, in the dark. And he wondered how it was that vice could succumb so easily to virtue.

It was night when he woke, startled to discover that he had slept at all. Time had passed, with the shutting and opening of his eyes, in a dreamless slumber. He felt the gentle sway of the sampan as it lay in some secret mooring. The air was filled with the sawing of the cicadas. He was still propped, semi-seated, against his backpack. His legs felt stiff and sore. He tried to move them to ease the ache and felt the pain revive in his shoulder.

A match flared in the dark, and he made out McCue's face behind it. The American lit two cigarettes and passed one to Elliot. 'Funny the things you hear in the night,' he said. 'A fish jumping to catch flies, something moving through the rushes, some goddam insect whining away in the dark aiming to suck your blood. In the daylight you might not even notice – there's a rational explanation for everything. But in the dark, well, your imagination gets its turn. Comes up with some damn strange answers.' He paused. 'You alright?'

'Sure.'

'I used to love the dark. Kinda freed you from thinking about things the way they really are. Then you find yourself crawling along some goddam tunnel. It's black like pitch. And whatever your imagination comes up with ain't half as bad as what the gooks got waiting. After that, if you survive, you never trust the dark again – or your imagination.'

Elliot gazed up into the blackness and thought he could see stars through the chinks in the matting. 'What's brought this on?'

'Dunno. Fear, I guess. In the dark you can believe you ain't never gonna see nothing again. In the daylight it's hard to believe you're ever gonna die.' He cleared his throat. 'Funny thing is, I never used to be afraid of dying. Didn't seem to matter much one way or another. But when you got a kid, it's their life, too. You got responsibilities. You only get scared of dying when there's some point to living. And what makes it worse is, you know it was always the ones who was scared that got it first.' He stood on the butt of his cigarette. There was irony in his chuckle. 'One thing that's easier in the dark, though.'

'What's that?'

'Baring your soul. I mean, you can't see my face and I can't see yours. In the daylight I'd be scared I could see you laughing.'

'I'm not laughing at you, Billy.'

'Maybe in the dark you understand a little.'

'A little.'

'Ny told me you got a kid, too. It's hard to think of bastards like us as having kids – counting as someone's daddy.'

Elliot watched the glow at the tip of his cigarette dying away. He shook his head. 'That little girl's got no daddy. He died sixteen years ago. And even if he was still alive she wouldn't want to know him.'

'That's sad, Elliot.'

'No. It's history.'

The curtain was drawn aside, and the faint yellow light of an oil lamp spilled through from the other half of the cabin. Serey's face looked drawn and pale as she crouched in the half-light, but there was a brightness in her dark eyes that Elliot had not seen before. 'Time,' she said.

McCue sighed. 'My watch.' But he made no attempt to leave. He lit another cigarette and chucked the packet to Elliot. 'Not many left.' He took a long draw on it. 'Tell you a funny story.'

Elliot glanced at Serey, but she remained impassive, waiting patiently.

'I spent some time upcountry with my unit in Nam before I was in the Rats. Always used to pull night watch. Used to love it. Me and the dark, you know. So anyway, my bunker was next to this lake, full of lungfish – you know, they got lungs and sound like humans breathing. Well, sometimes, in the dark, they would get stranded in the mud. You couldn't see them, but you could hear them, like horror-movie monsters breathing right in front of you.'

Elliot managed to extract a cigarette and light it.

McCue went on, 'So one night I was just lying there, thinking and listening, and I hear very clearly, right in my ear, this voice saying, "Fuck you." Shit! I knew I was a dead man. I grabbed my rifle and all I could see was this lizard, about eight inches long, just sitting there. I looked at it, and it was looking at me. There was this moment of just nothing, then it blew out its gills and said, "Fuck you," again. Christ, I'm shaking and waking the other guys. "Hey, man, this lizard just told me to go get fucked!" They're grabbing their rifles, too, and the three of us – three grown men – have this stand-off with an eight-inch lizard. Finally the little bastard said "Fuck you" for them, too.'

Elliot laughed till the laughter caught in his throat and he choked, and lapsed into a fit of coughing that pulled and hurt his shoulder. But the pain didn't matter. He had forgotten how good it felt to laugh. He saw McCue still grinning as he pushed past Serey to the outer cabin. Her face showed no understanding.

The sampan rolled as McCue clambered out to sit up back. Elliot's smile faded. Serey turned away. 'Wait,' he said. She hesitated, still holding back the curtain. 'Why are you doing this? You'd have been safe if you'd stayed in Phnom Penh.'

She took a long time to answer. 'After four years under the Khmer Rouge, I'd forgotten I was still a human being. I just remembered, that's all.' And she dropped the curtain and was gone.

CHAPTER FORTY-ONE

Long Xuyen lay in the heart of the delta. Nature had been generous here. It was the richest, most productive area of Vietnam, the rice bowl of south-east Asia. Its comparative wealth had been almost shocking to the conquerors from the north. It had also been the breeding ground for revolt. The Viet Cong and their cadres had worked tirelessly among the peasants, to turn them against the puppet regime of the Americans. There had been little to choose, back then, between the corruption of capitalism and the harsh and unforgiving dogmas of communism. But the communists possessed the more effective weapon. Fear. And they used it to good effect.

Life had changed little for the people since 1975. They worked in the paddies as long and as hard as before – for as little return. There were more rules and regulations. Enterprise and initiative were frowned upon. What little education existed had been replaced by re-education and indoctrination. The new religion was the atheist state but, as the French had failed to establish Catholicism, so the communists could not exorcize the Buddha, or the dozens of other schisms and sects. The history and essence of the East lay too deeply in the hearts of the people.

Here, as elsewhere in the world, racism and bigotry had always existed. But now it had the blessing of the state. As the Asians in Africa and Europe, and the Jews in Europe and America, are the object of jealousy and hatred, so the ethnic Chinese in south-east Asia are envied and despised – for their flair in commerce and trade, their stubborn refusal to discard an ancient heritage many generations removed. Now, under the communist authorities in Vietnam, hatred of the Chinese had been institutionalized. The Chinese community was harassed and persecuted. They were blamed for the country's economic ills, driven from their businesses and their homes. Four years after the war had ended, fear still stalked many streets.

Tran Van Heng was one such ethnic Chinese, driven in late middle age to the very edge of despair. It was from this man that McCue hoped to receive help.

The American squatted just beneath the cover of the rush matting, fear fluttering in his belly like butterflies caught in a net. He had exchanged his ragged black pyjamas for a pair of neatly pressed dark trousers and a white, short-sleeved shirt. He had shaved, and his face felt strangely naked. Serey and Ny had returned with the clothes from a market in town shortly before dark. Now they sat in the cabin behind him, boiling up rice over a small stove. But he wasn't hungry.

They had arrived at Long Xuyen in the late afternoon and

berthed near the harbour among dozens of other sampans upon which hundreds of Vietnamese ate and slept, lived and died in a floating ghetto. Their presence there was unremarkable, and went virtually unnoticed. During the last hours of daylight, McCue had stayed out of sight, sitting with Elliot in the rear half of the cabin, waiting, hoping, for Serey and Ny to return.

Lights from the gently bobbing flotilla were reflected now on the dark waters. The smell of cooking rose like hope above the stink of human waste. The murmur of voices and the tinny scratch of transistor radios drifted gently through the night. From the direction of the harbour, the persistent twang of Vietnamese pop music blared from some waterside café. McCue felt a hand touch his arm. He turned to find Ny crouched beside him.

'When you go?'

'When I finish this cigarette.' It was the third he had smoked since he'd made himself the promise.

'You scared?'

He nodded. 'Sure am.' He glanced beyond the sleeping figure of Hau in the bottom of the boat to where Serey was dishing out bowls of rice. Her face bore a serenity, as if she knew that after everything she had been through nothing could harm her now. 'I wish I was brave like your Mamma.'

Ny smiled. 'You brave, too. You eat later.'

'Sure. Later.' He threw his cigarette into the dark and heard its brief hiss as it hit the water. The last thing he felt, before he clambered across several boats to the wooden landing stage, was the gentle squeeze of her hand on his arm. He carried the touch with him like a lover's last kiss, not knowing when, or if, he might feel it again.

He felt acutely vulnerable. Unarmed and alone, a strange face in a land where his countrymen had suffered a humiliating defeat. Curious eyes fell upon him as he walked through the lit area of the harbour, then flickered away in feigned indifference. Curiosity was not encouraged by the authorities. Cafés and some shops were still open, their yellow lights burning harshly in the dark. He hurried away from the lights of the harbour, seeking the dim anonymity of the backstreets.

It was nearly ten years since he had last been here, and yet little seemed to have changed. The crumbling French colonial homes with their peeling shutters and broken balconies; the jumble of market stalls and cavernous dark shops; the rusted iron gates and dilapidated signs painted with extravagant Chinese characters; all remained much as memory had preserved them. The narrow streets of broken pavings and pitted tarmac, the evil smells that rose from cracks in the sidewalk. All appeared to have ignored the passage of time. He passed the terrace of a café where three men in his unit had been blown apart when a bomb planted by a shoeshine boy had exploded. It was in darkness now, closed for the day. And although its windows had long since been replaced and its terrace patched, the walls still bore the scars of the explosion.

In the main square the Catholic cathedral still stood, a

poignant reminder of another age. In the streets off it, the homeless still slept in doorways and huddled against walls. Sullen-faced boys, and clusters of pasty-faced teenage girls clutching babies, called to him, jostling him as he went by, arms outstretched, begging for alms. A straggling rank of idle trishaw drivers grew suddenly animated, squabbling and fighting among themselves for his business. He shook his head and pushed quickly through, not wishing to attract attention. But suddenly he stopped, reigniting hope of a fare, and the drivers clustered around. Two uniformed and armed policemen stood under a light at the far end of the street. They had seen him, and were looking his way. With no streets off, he could not avoid them without turning back. In his alarm he turned to the nearest of the trishaw drivers. 'You speak English?'

'Yes, yes, speak English,' he said eagerly. 'You Russian?'

He hesitated. 'Yes. Can you take me to Chinatown?'

'Sure. Chinatown. No problem.'

McCue climbed in the back of the trishaw to a cacophony of complaint from the other drivers. His driver just pushed them aside and mounted his cycle. He began pedalling towards the policemen at the end of the street. As the trishaw approached, one of them stepped out with his hand raised. The driver braked and drew up alongside. The policeman looked suspiciously at McCue, then rattled off a series of questions at his driver. Perhaps fearing the loss of his fare, the driver began to argue, waving his arms. There was a lengthy exchange between them before the second policeman, losing patience, stepped up to McCue and spoke to him directly. His eyes were hostile and suspicious.

McCue looked at his watch and shrugged. '*Skajitay pojalsta gdyeh astanavlivayetsya avtobus numer adin,*' he said with as much authority as he could muster. The policeman looked back at him blankly. For a brief, irrational moment, McCue feared he might be directed to the main square, and told that the number one bus left on the hour every hour. He leaned forward to tap his driver on the shoulder and wave him on. '*Da svedanya, da svedanya!*' The driver remounted his bike and pedalled away, leaving the two policemen to watch them go, resigned to their impotence. Even the police were afraid of a higher authority. McCue breathed a sigh of relief.

In spite of the persecution, Long Xuyen's Chinese quarter was still thriving, just coming to life it seemed, as the rest of this provincial town prepared for sleep. The streets were choked with people and traffic – trucks and bicycles – while the alleys spilled over with street markets selling everything from shoelaces to Peking duck. Ancient Confucian and Buddhist temples jostled with down-at-heel cinemas and seedy bars.

'Let me off here,' McCue called to his driver. The man, his wiry body sweating in shorts and singlet, drew his trishaw into the pavement and turned, grinning expectantly. McCue took off his watch and held it out. 'Rolex,' he said. 'Best there is. Okay?'

The driver took the watch and examined it gravely. Then his face opened up in a grin, and he nodded vigorously. 'Okay.'

McCue looked around him, ignoring the stares of the local

Chinese. It all looked and smelled so familiar. Somewhere, further down the street, was the House of a Hundred Girls, the brothel he had frequented during his stay here eight years before. But perhaps, in the new morality, it would no longer be there. He took a left, pushing through the crowds of straw-hatted shoppers patronizing one of the less salubrious street markets. A food stall selling sweet buns was crawling with cockroaches. At the far end of the alley he took a right, turning into a quiet, cobbled street. Here the shops, and the factories that contrived to reproduce the vital parts of foreign-made motorcycles, were closed and shuttered.

Halfway down, a light burned above the door to a private apartment. It was a door McCue had passed through many times. But as he stood before it now, he hesitated. What if Heng no longer lived here? He might have moved away, or been put in prison. He could be dead. McCue wiped the sweat from his palms and knocked on the door.

He waited almost a full minute, and was about to knock again when the door opened a crack, and a sliver of light fell out into the street. Dark eyes in a wrinkled, yellow face peered out at him, wisps of silver hair scraped across an otherwise bald pate. 'Hello, Heng,' McCue grinned. 'Is there a game tonight?' There were several moments of stunned silence before the door opened a little wider, and astonishment shone out from Heng's shrewd old face.

'Billee?' he said.

*

440

A ring of curious faces hovered around the edge of the pale light cast by an oil lamp on the table. They watched in grave silence as McCue ate hungrily, washing down rice and fried chicken with warmed rice wine; two boys and a girl, the children of Heng's younger brother, Lee, Lee's wife Tuyen, and Heng's wife Kim. A wizened, white-haired old crone, Kim's mother, sat somewhere beyond the reach of the light, rocking slowly back and forth, muttering inward imprecations. She no longer existed in their world. From time to time, McCue glanced up to meet Heng's eye and nod as the old Chinaman exercised his rusted English.

'For time after seventy-five, Billee, they let us carry on; shop, private trader, factory. Then last year they start clampdown. Many Chinese and Vietnamese taken from town to work in New Economic Zone.' His chuckle contained no humour. ''Nother name for labour camp. Working in field. I lucky. They take my shop, everything I got, and they make me work in co-operative making wheat noodle.'

'Sounds real lucky, Heng.'

'Lucky for sure, Billee. I too old to work in field. I die there, maybe. Then war with Cambodia, and now they say China 'bout to invade in the north. Things get real bad for *Hoa* then.'

McCue nodded. The *Hoa* was the name the Vietnamese gave to ethnic Chinese living outside China. He knew that if China sent troops into Vietnam's northern provinces, all *Hoa* in Vietnam would be regarded as potential fifth columnists.

'They even start draft for Chinese boys. You know what is draft, Billee?'

'Heng, I wouldn't be here now if it wasn't for the goddam draft.' McCue finished his wine and wiped his mouth with the back of his hand.

'My grandfather used say to us, "China is our home. Vietnam is only our second home." We Chinese don't want to fight Chinese. And we hate communist, we don't want to fight for communist.'

'Shit, the Chinese are communists, too, Heng.'

'Yes, Billee, but they still Chinese. Is different.'

Billy shook his head. 'I don't understand. If the Vietnamese are frightened of a war with China, why would they enlist Chinese in the army?'

'Because they want rid of Chinese in Vietnam, Billee. They want us killed. Putting our boys in army is one way. I spend twenty *taels* of gold in last year keeping my boy out of army. You know – bribe. That more than six thousand dollar. It cost nearly three thousand dollar just to live.' He shrugged. 'Food very expensive on black market. I no can afford carry on much longer. My son in hiding now.'

'Where the hell d'you get the money?'

Heng spread his lips in a wide grin, revealing his three remaining front teeth, like tombstones crumbling in a grave-yard. 'Money all in gold, Billee. They no find my gold.'

'So what are you going to do?'

'Oh, we got to leave Vietnam, if we gonna stay alive.'

'When?'

The old *Hoa* shook his head sadly. 'Is not so easy, Billee. My

442

cousin work on boat at Rach Gia for six month. We all give him money and he buy gasoline and keep it safe for trip. But not so easy now. At first many people leave Vietnam by boat, and government no worry. Now they make it hard. Shoot you if you try leave. We must wait for good weather, then two day only on South China Sea and we get to Malaysia.'

'We're just coming into the better weather now, aren't we?'

'Sure. But it cost much money. Many people need pay for boat. Not easy organize such thing.'

'We got money, Heng. Dollars, gold, some diamonds.'

Heng's brow furrowed doubtfully. 'Dangerous try take foreigner, Billee. Take time, too.'

McCue reached across suddenly and grabbed Heng's bony wrist. It was an act not intended to threaten, but one born of desperation. 'We haven't got time, Heng! We can't tie up in that harbour indefinitely without someone getting curious, sooner or later. They find us, we're dead, man!' His eyes burned fiercely into the old Chinaman's. Then, conscious that he had crossed the line beyond polite Chinese etiquette, he released Heng's wrist. 'I'm sorry.'

The *Hoa* rubbed the bruised flesh on his arm and stared back thoughtfully at McCue. 'You got gun?'

'Sure we got guns. Four automatic rifles, two pistols.' He grinned nervously. 'Awesome, huh?'

'Crossing dangerous,' Heng said. 'Many pirate.'

'Pirates?'

'Thai fishermen. They attack boat people. Steal their money, rape their women, kill many men. Plenty bad story 'bout Thai pirate.'

McCue's optimism rose like the smoke from the oil lamp. 'Then you're going to need us along for protection.'

Heng nodded solemnly. 'Sure Billee.' He paused. 'How much money you got?'

The sampans rose and fell silently in the dark, like the shallow breathing of sleeping bodies. There were no lights anywhere along the harbour. McCue stepped carefully across the boats. From one of them, the muffled voice of a man cursed him for disturbing his sleep. Ny's face appeared in the shadowed margin of the mat roof above their sampan, one half of her face caught pale in the moonlight. McCue crouched down, pushing past her to enter the cabin. He saw pinpoints of light reflected in Serey's eyes, and a movement behind her told him the boy was awake, too.

'What happen?' Ny whispered.

'Is Elliot awake?'

'He is awake.' Serey's voice seemed strained and brittle.

McCue pulled back the curtain and saw the glow from Elliot's cigarette.

'You want food now?' Ny asked, and he felt a stab of guilt. He had eaten and drunk well, and they had made do with rice and dried fish.

'I'm not hungry.'

'Well?' There was impatience in Elliot's tone that annoyed McCue.

'They was going anyway,' he said. 'His family and some others. They've got a boat at Rach Gia and they been saving fuel.'

'When?' It was Serey's voice this time that carried a hint of impatience.

'Not for another month.'

'Jesus Christ!' Elliot hissed. 'We can't hang about here for a month!'

'I talked them into going early.'

'How long?'

'A week – at the most. Someone'll come for us.'

He heard Elliot expelling air through his teeth.

'Even that's pushing it, Billy.'

McCue was angry. 'Fuck sake, Elliot, what d'you want – club-class tickets on the first flight out?'

'That'll do nicely.'

Serey's hand touched McCue's arm. He turned towards her. 'How much?' she asked.

He hesitated. 'A lot. Probably just about everything we ... everything you got.'

CHAPTER FORTY-TWO

The winter sun washed the room with its pale morning light. Outside a cold wind rattled the empty branches of the trees. Lisa sat in front of the mirror on the dressing table, and raised an arm slowly to brush her hair. Despite the heavy strapping, the pain from her broken ribs was still intense. It hurt just to breathe. The worst of the swelling on her face had subsided, bruises faded to the colour of jaundice yellow. The red slash of her lips heightened the chalky white of her skin. She looked ugly and tired. She felt like death.

After four days in the hospital in Hong Kong, and the thirteen-hour flight home, she had been exhausted and slept for eighteen hours, waking to a strange bed and a numbing disorientation. Only when a drawn-looking Blair had come in with a cup of tea did she remember where she was. The strain of his concern showed around his eyes.

'How are you?'

She shrugged. 'Alright.' She pulled herself up to lean against the headboard.

He handed her the cup. 'Do you feel up to a visitor?'

'Who?'

He sensed her alarm and his face clouded with guilt. 'I'm sorry, lass. Perhaps I should have waited. I called your boyfriend to let him know you were safe. He insisted on coming.'

'Here?'

He nodded.

'When?'

He looked at his watch. 'About an hour. If you don't want to see him . . .'

She shook her head. 'It doesn't matter. I'll have to see him sometime.' She made it sound like a dental appointment.

Now, as she stared at the stranger in the mirror, she heard a car draw up in the road outside, a door slam shut. She did not know how to be with him. He belonged to another life, as different and remote as a butterfly's former larval existence. The sound of his feet crunching on the gravel path filled her with dread. But there was a lack of urgency in his step, a secret reluctance, almost as if he too were afraid.

The murmur of voices in the hall, tones and cadences indistinguishable as words, rose and fell like mumbled prayers. But she detected anger in them. Then footsteps receded towards the back of the house and she felt relief at the postponement of their meeting. A drowning man will grasp at anything to delay the moment of death. And yet, surely, death itself could not be worse than the fear of it? She sat for long minutes of patient anxiety, listening for a footfall in the hall. When, eventually, it came, she felt herself stiffen, a chill spreading through her from an icy core. She turned her head as the door opened and he walked into the small front bedroom.

He seemed taller than she remembered, his hair redder, his skin paler. Whatever he had prepared himself for, whatever he had expected, he could not disguise his shock. His lips moved, but no words came. He took a moment to regain his composure.

'How are you?' The banality of his question, the strained politeness in his voice, spared her the burden of having to play a role.

'As you see.'

He stared at her for a long time. 'Why didn't you call?'

She sighed and turned back to the mirror. His reproach was like the memory of a bad dream. 'What do you want, David?'

A gasp of exasperation escaped his lips. 'I've been worried about you.'

'Have you?'

'Yes, I have! If I hadn't called Blair . . .'

'What has he told you?'

'Enough.'

She remembered that he had once wanted to marry her, and tried to imagine what that would be like. A semi-detached existence somewhere in the commuter belt; keeping his house, raising his children, barbecues in the garden with the neighbours on summer evenings. She had no idea, now, what she wanted from life. But it wasn't that. Perhaps it never had been. She shook her head. 'Then you know that I'm not who I was.' She turned to meet his eye but found him staring at a spot on the floor. Perhaps he had already realized that. Perhaps, after what Blair had told him, he was simply going through the motions 'I'm sorry,' she said, 'not to have lived up to your expectations.'

He darted her a look, and she saw real pain behind his eyes, though she could never have been certain it wasn't just the pain of failure.

'But thank you for your concern,' she added cruelly.

Blair heard the front door closing, and shortly after a car started and drove off down the street. The slow, tick of the clock grew thunderous in the silence that followed. He was surprised at the boy leaving so soon, and wondered if he should go through to her. But he did not stir from his armchair. She would need time and space to recover, if such scars as she must carry inside would ever heal. He let his head fall back on the rest and felt a kind of despair. It seemed that everything in Elliot's life was destined to be touched by tragedy.

The room was warm and bright, filled with the reflected light of the sun on the river. He closed his eyes and flirted with sleep, drifting in a netherworld of waking dreams, not quite asleep, not quite awake. A sound came to him from the conscious world and he opened his eyes with a start. Lisa stood by the window, staring out across the river. He had not heard her come in. She turned as he stirred.

'I'm sorry, I didn't mean to disturb you.'

'You didn't. I just – I'm tired, I guess.'

She nodded. 'He's gone.'

'I heard. He didn't stay long.'

'There wasn't much point.'

'What happened? What did you say to him?'

She shrugged. 'I told him it was over, that's all.'

'He didn't strike me as the type to give up so easily.'

She moved away from the window and eased herself into a chair. 'What did you tell him – about what happened in Bangkok?'

'Not much. That you'd fallen foul of some unscrupulous individuals who had tried to harm you. He wasn't very sympathetic, then?'

'David has never sympathized with anything or anyone in his life, except himself. He never really knew or understood me. I took his fancy, an object to be desired and possessed. I think he'd begun to realize, even before I left, that I wasn't really up for sale. And now that the goods are shop-soiled . . .' Her voice trailed away.

'I didn't go into detail.'

'You didn't have to. And, anyway, I don't think he'd have wanted to know.'

'I'm sorry.'

'Don't be. To be honest, I'm relieved. I might have felt in his debt. He was there for me when my mother died and I needed a shoulder to cry on.'

Blair raised a sceptical eyebrow. 'And now you don't?'

'I don't need anyone.' Her voice was defiant – the defiance, Blair thought, of disillusion. She would recoil from warmth, as a puppy which has been beaten shrinks from the approach of even a friendly hand. She had lost her trust, along with her innocence. And mistrust was always a crude defence against further hurt. It precluded the possibility of love.

'You make me think of your father,' he said.

'My father's dead,' she said dully. She looked up to meet his gaze. 'Isn't he?'

His mouth set in a grim line. It was something he had not admitted, even to himself. 'Yes. I suppose he is.' He reached for his pipe and lit it. He did not feel like smoking, but it was something to do. Blue ribbons rose in the still air. The silence lay uneasily between them. Finally he said, 'I never told you what happened. At the end, when we got you out of that place.'

'We?'

'I'd never have found you if it hadn't been for her. You'd be dead.'

She frowned. 'If it hadn't been for who?'

'Grace.'

She looked away quickly and he was unprepared for the venom in her voice. 'I hated her!'

'Maybe you had good reason, I don't know. I don't want to know. But she died saving your life.'

He was unprepared, now, for the pain he saw in the look she turned on him. 'Grace is dead?' She remembered the velvet touch of her fingers, cool lips on her skin.

'They shot her as we escaped from the warehouse. There was nothing I could do.'

A shudder seemed to run through Lisa's body, like the shock waves of an explosion. She closed her eyes and put her fingers to her temple, pressing it as if there were a great pain there. 'But why? I don't understand. Why would she want to save me?'

Blair's mouth was dry. 'She said – she just said to tell you that she was sorry.'

Lisa sat for what seemed like a very long time before she drew in her lower lip and tears came to her eyes. Then she wept, painfully, like a child, and Blair knew that there was hope for her in her pain.

CHAPTER FORTY-THREE

The sound of raised voices from the quayside filtered through Elliot's uneasy slumber. He opened his eyes to find McCue crouched beside him, his M16 raised vertically by his side. His face was a mask of sweat and strain.

'What's going on?' Elliot manoeuvred himself on to one elbow and the sampan rocked. He felt giddy, and found it hard to focus in the fading light. The combined effects of his wound, the fever, the unrelenting heat, and more than a week spent lying on his back, had robbed him of his strength.

McCue raised a finger to his lips and whispered, 'Army. They're checking papers, looking for draft dodgers.'

Elliot swallowed hard. He felt weak and vulnerable, and fear lay like poison in his belly.

'What can we do?'

'Nothing. Just sit tight and hope they don't search the boat.'

Elliot reached behind him to grope for his holster, and drew out his pistol. He said, 'I'd almost begun to think we might just make it.'

They had waited five long days, through the heat and rain,

virtual prisoners in the sampan, for word from Heng. But none had come. Serey and Ny had made several trips into the town, trading in the still thriving black market for food. But the strain of the interminable waiting in cramped and unsanitary conditions was beginning to tell. In the heat, the stink of human waste hung in the air, and thick clouds of flies swarmed around them, infesting their food, getting in their mouths. Through the endless hours, McCue had been like a caged animal, his patience and his nerve gradually disintegrating. He had growled and snapped at everyone, insisting on sitting out back at the open end of the boat as soon as it got dark, in spite of the risk of being seen. Twice, Elliot had dissuaded him from repeating his perilous trip across town to the Chinese quarter in search of Heng. Now, he crouched in rigid concentration, listening intently to the sound of soldiers searching the sampans around them. Elliot guessed that the American would relish an end – any end – to this prison sentence: even death in a firefight with the Vietnamese.

Elliot wondered why he felt fear, before it struck him that it was not for himself, but for Serey and Ny and the boy. After all they had been through, they didn't deserve to die like this. But he knew, also, that he had no power over the events that would unfold, and no strength with which to meet them.

The clatter of boots on wooden boards drew nearer. Their sampan rocked, and McCue had to steady himself with his free hand. A shrill male voice reeled off a series of demands, and Elliot recognized the voice that responded as Ny's – a brave medley of stuttering Vietnamese and Cambodian. He tried to peer through chinks in the matting, but it was already almost dark and he could see only the lights of the harbour across the water. The soldier's voice grew less shrill in response to Ny, adopting instead a tone of confident superiority. Elliot could almost see the leer on his face.

The curtain was drawn quickly aside and Hau scuttled through, clutching an AK-47. His face was sickly pale with fear. In the seconds before the curtain fell again to obscure the view, Elliot saw, beyond the squatting Serey, Ny's bare legs framed in the curve of the canopy, and the soldier's in khaki fatigues tucked into army boots. At first her voice was insistent, argumentative, before finally falling in pitch to adopt a friendlier tone. She talked quickly, with growing confidence, drawing eventually, to Elliot's consternation, a laugh from the soldier. It was an odious laugh, laced with lust. Elliot watched Hau's face, hoping to discern something from the boy's expression, but there was no clue in his studied intensity.

At length, Ny and the soldier left the sampan, stepping out across the other boats. The sound of their voices, and those of other soldiers who had been conducting the search, drifted away into the night. The silence that ensued within their cabin was laden with disquiet. Elliot and McCue exchanged glances, fearing the worst. Hau, head bowed, stared unblinking at his feet. McCue leaned forward to pull back the curtain. Serey sat as before, squatting by the small stove where she cooked their food. Her face had a waxen quality about it, but was otherwise expressionless. She was staring off into the middle distance.

McCue said, 'What happened?'

She didn't turn. Her voice was dull, mechanical. 'She told him that we were refugees and had no papers. He wanted to search. She said that her little brother was very sick and must not be disturbed.' She paused, and McCue saw a nerve quivering at her temple, like a butterfly trapped beneath the skin. 'She pointed out that there is an empty sampan beyond the landing stage, and suggested that if they went and searched it together he might find something more interesting than an old woman and a sick boy.'

McCue let the curtain fall and slumped back into the cabin. Shame prevented him from raising his eyes to meet the boy's. Elliot lay back and screwed his eyes closed. Anger and frustration welled up like vomit inside him. There was nothing to be done.

Gradually, after the soldiers had gone, normality returned to the floating community around them; the sounds of voices, hushed at first, gained in confidence; transistor radios scratched the hot surface of the night; the smell of woodsmoke and cooking rose above the stench of sewage. Oil lamps were lit, their yellow reflections flickering across the gently undulating surface of the river. At one point Elliot thought he heard a girl's voice raised in a cry, coming from somewhere beyond the landing stage. But he could not be certain he had not imagined it.

It was almost an hour before they heard Ny's soft step returning across the boats. McCue drew the curtain aside as she stooped to enter the outer cabin. Her face showed nothing, but he saw, as she squatted silently beside her mother, that her hands were trembling, and there was the hint of bruising around her lower lip. Hau pushed past the American and went out to join them. McCue let the curtain fall, and studied the dirt that drew black lines under his fingernails. Elliot stared at the rush matting overhead for a long time, before he closed his stinging eyes and gave himself up again to the strange dreams that haunted his hours of shallow sleep.

A vast expanse of desert stretched before him, the sand rising and falling in great dunes. The sky was black and starless, and a large yellow crescent moon, lying on its back, rose slowly out of the horizon. He shivered, realizing that he was cold and wet. When he looked up again the horizon was see-sawing up and down and the sand had turned to water, the dunes transformed into great black white-topped waves looming overhead. Above the roar of the water he now heard the baying of a dog, or was it a wolf? Desolate howls in the night. He opened his eyes and heard Ny sobbing on the other side of the curtain. Outside, a heavy downpour dropped rain the size of marbles on to their awning. A fine wet spray showered through the matting. Everything was soaked. McCue still sat by the curtain, his hand cupped around a cigarette.

Elliot forced himself up into a seated position, and pulled the curtain slightly to one side. He could make out Serey's silhouette, squatting still by the stove, cradling her daughter's head in her lap, muttering words of comfort like some religious incantation. He looked at McCue. 'How long's she been like that?'

McCue shrugged. 'Difficult to say. Feels like a lifetime.' He raised his head slowly towards the heavens. 'I guess even the gods are weeping for her.'

'Shhhh! What's that?' Elliot raised his hand, suddenly, straining to hear above the roar of the rain.

McCue listened. 'I don't hear anything.'

'I'm sure I heard . . . There it is again!'

This time McCue heard it, too. A voice calling softly in the dark from beyond the awning. 'Mistah Billee . . . Mistah Billee.' McCue grabbed his automatic and scrambled through the cabin, past Serey and Ny and Hau, towards the back of the sampan. A small, frightened figure crouched there in the dark. McCue recognized Heng's young nephew, Lac. Ny had stopped sobbing now and was sitting upright, clinging to her mother's arm. Hau moved forward, Kalashnikov primed for use. McCue raised a warning hand to stop him.

'What is it, Lac?'

'You come, Mistah Billee. Come now. We leave for Rach Gia tonight.'

CHAPTER FORTY-FOUR

I

The five-ton truck rattled and bumped through the narrow streets of the sleeping port towards the harbour. Beneath its canvas awning huddled more than thirty ethnic Chinese – men, women and children – three Cambodian refugees, an American and an Englishman. The curious stares drawn at first by the two white faces had dulled to indifference during the three-hour drive from Long Xuyen.

Elliot and McCue sat at the back by the pull-down flap, Elliot propped uncomfortably against the side of the truck, his left arm held in a makeshift sling to relieve his shoulder. His face was drained of colour, a grey mask of pain. He felt sick and weak. Heng sat with them, chattering with nervous animation, drawing power and prestige from his association with the round-eyes and their formidable array of weaponry.

Twice, on the main highway, they had been stopped at road-blocks, and fear had crouched with them under the canvas as they listened above the idling of the motor to the voices of their driver and the security police. There had been long exchanges on each occasion, before money changed hands and they were waved on their way.

The lights of the harbour reflecting on still waters opened into view as the truck lurched past the towering shadows of boat sheds and warehouses. Thousands of small craft lay moored here, hundreds of larger fishing boats and trawlers dotted about at anchor in the bay. Here and there navigation lights winked in the dark. McCue peered through a rent in the awning. The docks lay silent and deserted, making the truck's engine seem unnaturally loud. The driver pulled into the shadow of a tall warehouse and cut the motor. Frightened faces, about to adopt the personae of boat people and refugees, spilled out on to the cobbles. McCue half-lifted Elliot to the ground. He turned and caught Heng's arm. 'What about patrols?'

Heng grinned nervously. 'We pay plenty, Billee. They look other way.' He moved off, whispering cryptic instructions in the dark, urging the group to follow him along the quayside.

McCue swung a pack over his shoulder and nodded to Serey and Ny.

'Go.'

Hau lifted the other pack, and his Kalashnikov, and trotted after them.

They hurried past the silent hulks of sleeping trawlers, avoiding the ropes that moored them to great, rusted metal rings set in concrete. The stink of rotten fish and diesel and seaweed rose up from the water. McCue supported Elliot with difficulty, and quickly lagged behind as the ragged group, clutching bags and suitcases crammed with precious belongings, hurried after the old Chinaman. A figure detached itself from the rest and waited until they caught up. It was Ny, her face serious and concerned. She tugged at McCue's pack.

'I take.'

McCue hesitated for only a moment, before swinging the pack from his shoulder and passing it to her. Elliot reached out a hand and caught her arm. He gave it a tiny squeeze and their eyes met for a moment, but he could find no words.

Two hundred metres on, the group had stopped at the top of a flight of narrow stone steps leading down to a small open boat that rose and fell on the gentle harbour swell. As Elliot and McCue and Ny rejoined them, Heng was engaged in a furiously whispered argument with a young man in the boat. McCue climbed down the steps. 'Jesus Christ, Heng! We're gonna try and cross the Gulf in this?'

'No, no. Boat only take us to trawler. It anchored in bay.'

'So what's the hold-up?'

''Nother truck. It late. Should be here since an hour. Lien, he say we got to wait. Trawler captain, his family on truck. He not sail without.'

'How many people on the truck?'

''Bout fifty.'

McCue looked at the boat. 'We'll never get that many people in. Tell him he can come back.'

'No, Billee, he say it too dangerous come back. It be light soon.'

McCue drew his pistol from its holster and pointed it at the young man's head. 'Then tell him I'll blow his fucking head off if he doesn't go now.'

Heng shook his head and gently pulled McCue's arm down. 'No, Billee, you no blow head off. Lien, he my son.'

McCue closed his eyes in despair, then reholstered the pistol. 'So what do you suggest? We hang about here till the cops decide to pick us up?'

Heng turned back to his son and there was further argument before, finally, the young man threw his arms in the air and clattered away to the back of the boat to start the outboard. 'We go now,' Heng said. He waved to the group waiting above.

'What did you say to him?'

'I tell him we go. Chinese son always obey father.'

Sitting perilously low in the water, the little boat ploughed its ponderous way across the bay, straining against the heavier swell. Its wake glowed in the dark. There was an uncanny quiet among its human cargo, no longer afraid, but brooding silently on the lives they were leaving behind, the homes they had known all their lives. They had given up everything – property, possessions, friends – in exchange for danger and uncertainty. It was the price they were prepared to pay for freedom, or at least the chance of it. Had they, perhaps, known the fate of their predecessors on this journey into the unknown, they might not have thought it worth the risk.

The hull of a thirty-metre trawler rose above them out of the swell, and as they drew alongside a rope ladder tumbled down, unseen voices whispering urgently in the dark. One by one the refugees clambered up into the night, silhouettes against the starlit sky, laden with bags and suitcases, until only McCue, Elliot and Lien remained. McCue grunted as he took Elliot's weight over his shoulder and prayed that the rope would hold. The muscles in his arms and legs strained and burned, as he pulled them both slowly up, rung by rung, until helping hands reached over the top rail to relieve him of the weight. The veins on his face stood out, along with the sweat, as he climbed over the rail and crouched there gasping for breath. He glanced around and saw that there were, perhaps, another thirty or forty already on board, eyes shining with bright astonishment at the unexpected appearance of two white faces among them. Ny squatted on the deck cradling Elliot's head in her lap, tipping it forward to receive water from a flask. Then she held it out for McCue, who took a long, grateful draught.

As he drew the back of his hand across his mouth, he saw a small, wiry figure in black pyjamas striding angrily towards them from the wheelhouse. The man was middle-aged and balding, cheeks clapped in below prominent cheekbones. A wispy black moustache grew down from the corners of his mouth, endowing him with a permanent expression of sadness. He grasped Lien's arm, as the young Chinese climbed over the rail, and shouted in his face, spittle gathering on his lips. He waved his hand urgently in the direction of the harbour. Lien seemed unable to respond, glancing helplessly towards his father. Heng stepped in, placed a gentle hand on the man's shoulder and spoke in soft rapid tones. McCue glanced at Serey. 'What's going on?'

Serey shrugged. 'This man is the captain. He think we should have waited for other truck.'

Somebody shouted. Fingers pointed shoreward. Everyone flocked to the rail to see the lights of a truck sweep across the bay. It jerked to a halt on the quayside and its lights went out. Almost at once, headlights sprang up in several sidestreets, engines coughed in the night, and five jeeps roared over the cobbles to surround the truck. Soldiers spilled across the quay to force its occupants down at gunpoint. The wretched figures huddled together in fear and failure.

Aboard the trawler, frightened eyes glanced anxiously at the captain. He stood wild-eyed and helpless, staring out across the water. McCue grabbed Heng and hissed, 'I thought these guys had been paid!'

Heng shrugged, but McCue could see he was scared too. 'Maybe not enough. Maybe they decide, so many, no more.'

McCue looked back towards the harbour. 'If they had been on time, that would have been us.'

Heng nodded. 'We lucky, Billee.'

McCue flicked his head towards the captain. 'What about him?'

'He lose family. Even if he go back now, they put him in jail. Never see them again.'

McCue felt a moment of pity for the slight figure in black pyjamas, as he stared hopelessly towards the shore. 'What'll he do?'

'Who know?'

A sense of panic rose in McCue's breast, a response to the fatalism in Heng's voice. He looked at the faces around him and knew that however desperate their plight, all these people would accept the captain's decision – to go or stay. They had, all of them, come so far and sacrificed so much, and yet he knew not one of them would raise a voice in protest if the captain should decide to return. There was utter silence on the deck, save for the sleepy murmur of a child's voice raised in query. Angry voices drifted across the water from the quay. Still the captain faced the shore, but the fire that had burned in his eyes had gone, replaced by despair.

Suddenly he shouted an instruction to two crewmen who scuttled aft to winch up the anchor, then he turned and pushed through the silent figures to the wheelhouse. Moments later the engines spluttered to life.

McCue stood on the rear deck as they inched past the dark shape of the island that stood in the neck of the bay – the last point of risk. But no coastguard launch swooped from the shadow of the island to cut them off, and their speed increased as they drew out into the choppier waters beyond, towards the open sea and the Gulf of Thailand. A cool breeze whipped his face as the first light grew in the sky to the east. And gradually, as it receded, the coastline detached itself from the sky to form a dark barrier along the horizon. The harbour's twinkling lights grew faint with distance, until one by one they were lost in the dawn. He lit a cigarette, and turned his back for the last time on the shores of south-east Asia.

II

Elliot's eyes flickered open, but he could not see immediately. Where he lay was in shade, but beyond that a wide slash of brightness forced him to screw his eyes closed against its stabbing glare. Slowly he was able to focus on the interior of the wheelhouse cabin, the captain silhouetted at the wheel against the sunlight streaming low through the window. He was lying on the lower of two bunks built into the back wall. The comfort of dry soft sheets against his skin came almost as a shock.

Another silhouette moved through his peripheral vision and crouched at the bedside. Ny smiled and held out a cup of milky liquid. 'You feel better?'

He found, with some surprise, that he did. His whole being no longer ached and, although still weak, the disabling fatigue which had held him trapped so long in his makeshift bed in the bottom of the sampan had gone. A dull ache in his belly told him he was hungry. 'Yes,' he said. 'Much.'

Slowly he pulled himself into a sitting position and swung his legs over the edge of the bunk. She handed him the cup. 'You drink.'

'What is it?' He peered at the liquid.

'Doctor prepare. He say good for you.'

Elliot looked at her in astonishment. 'What doctor?'

'Chinese.' McCue's voice came from close by. Elliot turned to see him leaning idly against the open wheelhouse door, a cigarette dangling from his lips. 'One of the refugees. Got a whole bagful of medicine. Done a pretty good job of patching you up.'

Elliot glanced down at his shoulder and saw that fresh clean dressings had been professionally applied to his wound. He tried moving his arm and, although stiff and still sore, found mobility returning.

Ny said, 'He give you sed . . . seda—'

'Sedative,' McCue said.

'Make you sleep. He say you need plenty sleep, plenty food.'

McCue nodded towards the cup. 'And plenty of that stuff.'

'So what is it?'

McCue shrugged. 'Some kind of saline, glucose solution. Who knows. Doc reckons you lost a lot of body fluid and salt. Got to get it back in there.'

Elliot took a sip and curled his lips in distaste.

'Good?' Ny smiled.

'Shit,' Elliot said.

McCue grinned. 'Be a good boy, now. Take your medicine like a man.'

Elliot held his breath and drained it in a single draught. He glanced up to find the captain looking back at him with narrowed eyes, his face set in studied indifference before he turned away again. 'What's up with him?' Elliot asked.

McCue's expression glazed over and he looked away out the window. 'Nothing much. His family missed the boat, that's all. Wife, two daughters and a son. Army lifted them, and about forty others, on the quayside.'

Elliot looked down into the cup, and its emptiness stared back. 'How long have we been at sea?'

''Bout twelve hours.'

'We made it, then.'

'Guess so.'

Hau appeared in the doorway, carrying a makeshift tray with steaming bowls of rice, chicken and fish. He grinned at Elliot, and trotted across the cabin to place the tray on the bed beside him. Elliot frowned. 'Who's this for?'

Ny said, 'For you.'

'Chicken? Where the hell did we get chicken?'

'Everyone give a little food for you.'

'Why?' Elliot shook his head in consternation.

'Mistah Heng say they look after you, you look after them.'

Elliot glanced at McCue. 'Their faith is touching. I just hope it's not misplaced.'

McCue looked back at him with steady, unblinking eyes. 'So do I. They're good people, these, Elliot.'

Hau held out the bowl of shredded chicken, his face shining with anticipation. Elliot took it from him and tried a piece. Hau flicked a glance at his sister, then peered into Elliot's face. 'Good?' he asked uncertainly.

468

Elliot smiled and ruffled his hair. 'Good,' he said. And the boy's face broke into a wide, disarming smile of sheer pleasure.

When he had eaten all he could, Elliot rose from the bunk and lurched unsteadily to the cabin door. The air was cooler out here in the freshening breeze, the sun tilting low in the western sky. He was astonished at the sight that unfolded here. The sixty or seventy refugees who had made it aboard had turned the deck into a floating camp. Children peeped out from a canvas awning raised over the forward hold, providing shade for most of the escapees. Above him, on the roof of the wheelhouse, several women squatted, cooking over wood and charcoal stoves. The rear quarter of the boat was festooned with sun-dried fish and clothing strung up on poles to dry. He was aware of the eyes that turned towards him, ready smiles springing to trusting faces. It made him feel uncomfortable, like a boy stepping up to receive first prize for an exam in which he had cheated.

McCue lit a cigarette and passed it to him. 'The last one,' he said. Elliot looked at its glowing tip for a moment then passed it back.

'You have it. This seems like as good a time as any to give up. I always meant to, anyway. Might get cancer or something.'

'Yeah,' McCue drawled. 'Pretty dangerous – smoking.' He took a long pull at it.

Elliot watched Ny and Hau pick their way back across the deck to rejoin their mother just inside the awning, and saw Serey looking back at him from the shadows. She had remained sullen and distant since that first night in the camp near Siem Reap – it seemed so long ago now – when he had fired above the heads of her fellow prisoners. She had never trusted him. A spiritual instinct, perhaps, that recognized lost souls. He looked quickly away toward the horizon.

The two men stood for a long time, watching as the sun dipped its gold into the sea. Darkness fell quickly, and Elliot spotted a strange distant glow in the sky, far away to the south-west.

'What the hell's that?'

McCue followed his gaze. 'Heng says Exxon or somebody's got oil and gas rigs about a hundred and ninety Ks off the coast of Malaysia. They'll be floodlit and burning off gas. He was told they could be seen on a clear night more than a hundred Ks away. A kinda signpost in the sky.'

'Where does that put us, then?'

'About halfway, maybe. Should hit the north-east Malaysian coast by tomorrow night.'

'Why don't we just head straight across for Thailand?'

McCue shrugged. 'Turns out the Thais ain't too keen on boat people. Safer heading for Malaysia.'

By midnight the trawler was set dead on course for the Exxon rigs, jets of waste gas burning thirty metres into the night, a distant second sun suspended in darkness. In the wheelhouse, the captain left the wheel to the ship's mate, and curled up on the top bunk. Most of the refugees were huddled together, asleep beneath the forward awning.

Elliot sat out on the deck, leaning back against the

wheelhouse. He heard the cry of a child as it awoke from a disturbing dream, then the comforting murmurs of a sleepy mother woken, too, from a fitful sleep. A group of five men sat up on the bows, smoking, and talking quietly. Their voices carried gently in the wind, just audible above the constant rhythm of the engines and the sound of churning water. The rising moon dusted the deck with silver.

McCue appeared from the rear of the vessel and sat down beside him. Elliot leaned his head back against salt-crusted boards. 'I could do with a cigarette.'

McCue smiled at his hands. 'Thought you'd given up.'

'Never did have much willpower.'

McCue produced a pack from the breast pocket of his jacket and held one out. Elliot looked at it, surprised. 'I thought you'd smoked your last one.'

'I traded some bits and pieces for a couple of packs. Chinese love to trade.'

Elliot took the cigarette and let McCue light it for him. 'Bad for your health,' he said.

McCue shrugged. 'So's dying.' He lit one for himself. 'And we could die tomorrow. So who gives a shit?'

They sat smoking in easy silence for some minutes. McCue asked, 'What's the game plan when we get to Malaysia?'

'I'll call Ang at his hotel in Bangkok. If he hasn't given up on us, he can come and get his family and we can go home.' He glanced at the American. 'What are you going to do when you get home, Billy?'

'Gonna take a bath,' McCue said. He grinned and, as his smile faded, added, 'Then I'm gonna get the hell out of this shit. Take the family to America. *Klongs* ain't no place to bring up a kid.' And as he said it, he realized how long it had been since he had thought of his wife, and his child. He found it hard, somehow, to recall their faces with any clarity, and that brought pangs of guilt and regret. 'Guess I've missed them,' he said. 'What about you?'

'Something I never ask myself,' Elliot said. He flicked the last inch of his cigarette off into the dark. It would be like asking a blind man directions, he thought. 'I'm going to get some sleep.'

He lay for a long time on his bunk listening to the sobbing of the captain above him. It was ironic, he thought, how you could envy another man his pain. The ability to be hurt was a precious gift.

III

The scream of rending metal and splintered wood tore into his dreams. The world jarred and tipped sideways. A grey dawn assailed his waking eyes in the seconds before his shoulder hit the floor, and all consciousness was consumed by a moment of supreme pain. Blood-red light seared his eyes, through lids screwed tight shut. He heard his own breath scrape in his throat, even above the screams and murderous whoops that came from the deck below. The engines had stalled and the boat rolled and yawed in the heavy swell. He opened his eyes and found himself looking into the dead, staring eyes of the ship's mate. Blood oozed thickly from a deep gash in the dead man's temple. Elliot rolled quickly over on to his knees and saw the captain lying dazed and frightened on the cabin floor, where he had fallen from his bunk. The rattle of automatic fire came from the deck, several short bursts. A cacophony of human panic carried on the stiff sea breeze.

A shadow appeared in the doorway. Elliot looked up to see a squat, ugly face contorted by fear and rage. The man was small, thickset. His brown shirt was torn and stained black with blood. A dirty white rag tied around his forehead was speckled with red above murderous eyes. In his hand he carried a long-bladed knife. As he came at Elliot, his voice rose in a blood-curdling howl, the blade flashing over his head. Elliot fell back, fumbling desperately for the pistol in his holster. It snagged on his belt as he tried to draw it out. The shadow of death loomed over him. He could smell the man's sweat. A gun roared in the confined space, blotting out all other sound, and the dead weight of his attacker fell forward, pinning Elliot to the floor.

Elliot was again crippled by pain, unable to move. A hand tugged at the shoulder of his dead assailant and pulled the body aside, and Elliot saw the captain crouching over him, a revolver in his hand. He helped the Englishman to sit up, and Elliot finally freed his pistol.

From the deck, another burst of automatic fire raised further screams. The captain scampered across to the cabin door and peered cautiously out. He ducked back in at once, his face pale with fear. He shook his head. Elliot pulled himself up on the wheel and snatched a quick look from the window. In the grey light of the dawn he saw another, smaller, fishing boat pulled up alongside. A boarding party of more than a dozen men fanned out across the deck, wielding daggers, marlin-spikes, cudgels and hammers. Several bodies lay, prostrate, near the awning over the forward hold. The shadowy figures of rudely awakened refugees ran forward and aft, trying to escape the ferocity of their attackers. Blades rose and fell, glinting in the growing light. From the cover of the awning came another burst of fire. Two men crashed through the forward hold and down into the belly of the boat.

Elliot ducked down and glanced quickly round the cabin, eyes darting into every dark corner, before he spotted his pack, and his M16, stowed beneath his bunk. He slithered across the floor and grabbed the rifle. The captain still crouched by the door, afraid to move.

'Lights!' Elliot hissed. 'How do you switch the fucking lights on?'

The captain looked back at him blankly. Elliot pointed at the ceiling lamp in the cabin. The Chinaman looked at the lamp, brow furrowed in consternation, before it came to him what Elliot wanted. He darted across to the control panel at the wheel, waited for Elliot's nod and flicked a switch.

Lamps on the wheelhouse roof flooded the decks with light, creating an immediate sense of unreality, mock carnage played out on a pantomime stage. Elliot sidestepped from the door, like a player from the wings, and saw startled faces, caught in the unexpected glare, turn towards the wheelhouse. He released half a dozen short bursts of fire, picking his targets. Six men fell. Another burst came from the awning and two more men hit the deck. Of the remaining boarders, one leapt overboard and three vaulted the rail in a desperate attempt to get back to their boat. But the other vessel had already drifted clear, engines gunning, propellers churning, attempting to get away. All three landed in the water, splashing frantically, knowing that death was only seconds away. Elliot picked them off with single rounds.

A strange silence followed, broken only by the wailing of a child. A pulley hanging from the end of a rope swung back and forth against the swell. Elliot scanned the deck for McCue. He shouted, 'Billy!' No response. A movement caught his eye as a crouching figure emerged from the shadow of the awning. It was Hau, wild-eyed and trembling, clutching his Kalashnikov. One by one anxious faces emerged from the darkness behind him.

A hand touched Elliot's shoulder. He turned to find the captain nodding towards the port side of the boat. He followed the Chinaman's eye line, and saw the arm of a torn khaki tunic draped over the winch cable, a bloody hand dangling from its sleeve. He jumped down from the wheelhouse and hobbled across the forward deck, stepping over bodies. As he drew nearer, he saw McCue lying on the far side of the winch wheel, and he broke into a run. A marlinspike stuck out from the American's chest. There were several gaping knife wounds in his neck. Blood had spread into a large thick pool on the scrubbed wooden deck. His eyes were open, staring blindly, the face reflecting, in its moment of dying, a look of surprise. Perhaps he really had believed in his own immortality. He seemed smaller in death than in life.

Elliot stooped to pick up McCue's discarded M16 where it had fallen. The feeder mechanism was jammed. He turned, in a moment of sudden fury, and hurled the useless rifle out over the rail, through the salt spray, a yell of sheer frustration ripping from his throat; a gesture of futile defiance – as if it were possible, somehow, to take revenge on death. He turned back to face the small group of refugees who had gathered round, and saw Ny and Serey and Hau among them. 'We were so nearly there,' he said. But their faces were blurred and he couldn't see that they were weeping for him, too.

The wind and spray whipped their faces as the trawler ploughed bravely on through rising seas. The forward awning flapped and strained at the ropes which held it. The sky was thick and dark with cloud so low you felt you might touch it. They stood in silence as, one by one, they buried their dead; bodies wrapped in sheets slipped over the rail to be swallowed for ever by the black angry waters of the South China Sea. Six refugees, including a child, and one American a long way from home. Tears were lost in the rain that fell now in sudden squalls.

Elliot watched as McCue's slight frame, wrapped in its make-shift shroud, slid into the water. It barely made a splash. He remembered the night at the *klong* house; McCue's surly and suspicious disposition, the pretty, open face of the Thai girl he had married. Sweet and sour. The baby in the back room beneath the mosquito net. A mother without a husband, a son without a father. Elliot had entered their lives and stolen their future. Ironic, he thought, that he should be the one to survive.

He replayed the events of an hour before. Five minutes of madness. Nothing had been gained, except for the loss of innocent lives. Their attackers had not allowed for armed resistance. Clumsy and brutal, they too had paid with their lives. By accident or design they had rammed the trawler in attempting to draw alongside, and holed her just above the waterline. And now, in the rising seas, they were shipping water. If the storm that threatened should break, there was every chance they would sink.

He felt an arm slip through his and looked down to see Ny peering up at him. The deck, he realized suddenly, was deserted. The others had slipped away in silence to take cover under the awning or in the wheelhouse, where the Chinese doctor had set up a makeshift hospital to treat the wounded. From below came the sound of men working in the hold to try to patch the breach in the hull. The trawler dipped sharply, and a huge wave broke across her bows. The spray drenched Elliot and the girl.

'Sometime, Mistah Elliot,' she said seriously, shouting above the wind, 'people need someone. Just to hold. Just to be there.'

Did she mean him, or her? He took her in his arms and held her as the thunder crashed overhead, and a great fork of lightning turned darkness to light.

The storm broke with a terrifying ferocity, clouds three thousand metres deep, forming vertical air movement up to one hundred and fifty kilometres per hour. Great white-topped waves gathered into towering walls of water that broke, repeatedly, over the trawler, threatening to engulf her. The captain fought to keep his craft head-on to the wind. But it was an impossible task. The forward hold filled rapidly with water, despite the efforts of the refugees, and the boat yawed and slewed hopelessly under the furious onslaught of the storm.

The awning was torn away in the first hour, and the wheel-house windows smashed by the force of the waves. It was impossible to stay dry, to cook, to do anything but be sick, and seek whatever shelter or security could be found. Most of the refugees lashed themselves to the deck, or the rails, or crammed into the wheelhouse. Not one of them believed they would survive. Death was inevitable.

For fifteen hours the storm vented its unrelenting anger upon them, retribution for their daring to seek escape in a world where freedom is as rare a commodity as wealth – a gift granted only to a few. Each time they plunged into yet another chasm opening up beneath them, it seemed impossible that they could climb back out. Miraculously, the very force which had drawn them down would throw them up again, a few moments of optimism before another trough of despair. One could not fight such power. Surrender was the only option.

It was the early hours of the following morning before, finally, the storm abated – a gradual process as though the sea had slowly tired of failure, fatigued by its efforts, anger spent. The trawler, which had slipped out of the harbour at Rach Gia forty-eight hours before with such optimism, was battered, bruised and slowly sinking. Listing badly to starboard, the forward hold was almost entirely swamped, and the crippled craft made erratic progress through the still heavy swell. Their maps had been ruined, navigation gear in the wheelhouse irreparably damaged. The sky remained black with cloud, no stars available to guide them. The captain, almost dropping from exhaustion, scanned the horizon constantly for their signpost in the sky – the gas flares of the oil rigs off Terengganu. But he saw nothing, and could only keep the boat head-on to the wind, in the hope that this was the prevailing westerly, and not some distortion of the storm.

By the time daylight crept over them from the east, the captain estimated that they would sink in less than six hours. Elliot lay huddled together with Ny, Serey and Hau where they had lashed themselves to a rail in the lee of the wheelhouse. Further weakened by constant vomiting, he could barely move. Two more men had been lost overboard, a child had died, choking on its own sick, and a woman three months pregnant had miscarried during the night.

Gradually, as the sky cleared and the sun beat down to

steam-dry the deck and its litter of human cargo, hope germinated again from the depths of despair. Stoves were lit, and the smell of cooking carried on the smoke. Clothes and goods were laid out to dry. Families and friends regrouped. But the spectre of death still moved among them, and few words were spoken.

Elliot drew himself into a seated position, leaning back against the wheelhouse. Serey handed him a bowl of rice and fish. He ate with difficulty, fighting back the urge to let his stomach empty itself yet again. His shoulder ached and his head was pounding. Hau held out a water bottle and he took it gratefully, the warm liquid washing away the foul taste of salt in his mouth. He drained the container and sat gasping for several seconds. 'I could do with some more,' he said.

Serey said simply, 'There is none.'

He looked at the three faces in consternation and felt the stirrings of conscience, like the first warning shiver of a coming cold. 'What about you?'

'Your need is greater than ours,' Serey replied.

A shadow fell across them, and the young doctor who had changed his dressing on the first day out, crouched down beside them, his face grey with fatigue. He laid down his precious bag, kept safe somehow during the storm, on the deck. 'We must change your dressing,' he said. The sound of a child crying bitterly for its mother carried on the breeze.

By mid-morning the sun blazed down on the stricken boat. Every scrap of shade was occupied, makeshift tents and awnings contrived from whatever materials were available. The trawler's nose dipped low in the water. The angle of the deck made walking impossible without holding on, scrambling from one fixture to another. Numerous makeshift rafts were in the process of construction; there was no lifeboat. It seemed such a cruel stroke of fate that they should sink now. The sea was dead calm, a deep, inviting, marine blue. But the only invitation it offered was death.

Elliot fought the pain and the heat and the nausea, to try and complete their raft in time. With Hau's help he had stripped all the wooden planking from the back of the wheelhouse, and showed Serey and Ny how to lash them together to create a dozen thicker planks, like logs, nine inches deep and eight feet long. With a machete he cut four thick, pliable stakes long enough to overlap the width of the raft deck. He laid them down seven feet apart, and the others manoeuvred the lashed planking to lie across them. It was a simple matter, then, to lay the other two stakes across the top, directly above the bottom two, and lash the notched ends together to hold the raft firmly in place.

They were visited frequently by other groups building rafts, to see how it should be done, and Elliot demonstrated how to make a paddle rudder and mount it on an A-frame at one end of their rafts. In return they provided food and cigarettes. Large areas of the deck had now been ripped up, and there were a dozen rafts at various stages of construction, the trawl nets providing more than enough rope for the purpose.

Elliot was in the process of lashing the last of their belongings to the deck of their raft when a shout came from the forward part of the boat, followed by a chorus of voices raised in excitement. Elliot looked across as Ny scrambled up the steep slope of the deck to grasp the rail. She gazed out across the sea for a moment, and when she turned back her face was shining. 'Land!' she called. 'There is land!' And she broke into a babble of Cambodian.

Elliot climbed painfully across the deck to see for himself. There, in the shimmering distance, a dark green line of tropical vegetation broke the horizon. He looked up, and for the first time noticed that there were birds circling overhead.

CHAPTER FORTY-FIVE

Half-filled cardboard boxes stood around the living room. Clothes lay draped over chairs. Piled in twos and threes, drawers containing the letters, jewellery, diaries and bric-a-brac that one collects over nearly forty years were stacked in the middle of the floor. Lisa sat cross-legged in front of the fire sifting through her mother's things, deciding what should go to Oxfam and what should be consigned to the cardboard boxes.

The house was haunted by memories, and these were the last tangible reminders; mother-of-pearl hair clasps with strands of her hair still caught between the teeth; a pile of scratched Elvis Presley singles; a box of black and white photographs of her mother as a child during the war years. These were all that remained of an unremarkable and unhappy life. A sad and meaningless legacy, to be wrapped in newspaper and packed away in boxes, as her mother had packed away all memories of her husband in an attic trunk.

Lisa heard the sound of hammering from the front garden. She crossed to the window. A young man from the estate agent was knocking a FOR SALE sign on a pole into soft earth on the garden side of the wall. A light drizzle blurred the glass. She turned from the window and winced a little as the pain in her ribs reminded her of things she would rather forget. She was comforted by the thought that this memory, too, would fade with the pain.

She picked her way across the floor and sat at the table. Before her, spread out on the cloth, were all the cuttings of the court-martial, and her parents' wedding photographs. She had read and reread every word, examined every detail of every picture. She looked again at the press photographs of her father, and traced the line of the scar on his cheek lightly with her fingers, smearing the newsprint.

However hard she tried, she found she could not recall with any clarity the features of the woman who had died for her in Bangkok in the damp basement of a dockland warehouse. Even the face of her mother had receded to the backwaters of her memory. There were, she supposed, always photographs to remind her, but these she could hide away in boxes in the attic. It was her father's face that remained etched on her memory. It was his face she saw when she closed her eyes at night, though she had glimpsed him only once, sheltering beneath a tree at her mother's funeral.

Bangkok was a million miles away. It belonged to another existence, to a person she had been only briefly. Soon London, too, would be just a memory, along with the house. It was possible to put everything away, or behind you. It was possible to be someone else, the sum total of all those people you had been, but different from any one of them. It was possible to start again, to build a new life. If only . . .

Her gaze rested again on the photograph of the young man in dress uniform grinning shyly by her mother's side on the church steps. She wished she could hate him for what he had done to her. She wished she could have met him, if only to dislike him. She wished at least she had got somewhere near the truth. Perhaps then she could have forgotten.

She sat for a long time gazing into the flames of the gas fire, before reaching a decision. She drew the phone towards her and dialled for a taxi.

Blair led her through to the room at the back, and the view over the river. 'I didn't expect to see you again so soon,' he said. It had been less than a week since the doctor had declared her fit enough to return home. He took her coat.

'I didn't mean to disturb you. I needed to talk.' She touched the back of the chair she had sat in for so many hours, talking, listening, learning to trust again, and feeling scar tissue grow over mental wounds. 'May I?'

'Of course.' He waved her into the seat. 'I'd have thought we'd done enough talking to last a lifetime.' He settled back into his armchair and lit his pipe. It was true, he thought. They had talked a great deal. Mostly about her father, feeding her longing for detail – about his life, where he had been, what he had done. But his instinct told him that she had returned now to ask the questions he had hoped she never would. 'What have you been up to?' Perhaps he hoped he could deflect her.

She shrugged. 'I've put the house up for sale, and I've applied for a job. In Edinburgh.'

'Nice city. Doing what?'

'Secretarial. A lawyer's office.'

'Seems a bit of a waste. I thought you were going back to college.'

She toyed with the buckle on her belt, avoiding his eyes. 'I changed my mind. It just seemed like a step back. Anyway, I don't think I was cut out to be a journalist.'

He watched her for a few moments, until the silence forced her to look up. 'Know anyone there? In Edinburgh?' She shook her head. He nodded. 'Running away, then.'

She was stung to defend herself. 'I've got nothing to run away from.'

'Except the past.' He tamped down the tobacco in the bowl of his pipe. 'Only you can never do that. You carry your past with you always. Wherever you run, you'll only find yourself, waiting there for you when you arrive, like an old friend – or enemy – you can't get rid of.'

'You always have all the answers, don't you, Sam?'

'If I'd had all the answers at your age, I wouldn't be where I am now. I suppose you've got to find your own answers.'

She tutted with irritation. 'Maybe when I'm your age I'll be as smug as you.'

He grinned. 'Coffee?'

'No thank you.' She was still annoyed.

'Well, I'm making some anyway. If you change your mind give me a holler.' He eased himself out of his chair.

'I want to know about the massacre in Aden.'

He hesitated for only a moment. 'I already told you about that. A long time ago. Milk, no sugar, isn't it?' He headed for the kitchen.

'You told me a version of it,' she called after him. 'I want to know the truth.'

He stopped and turned, sudden anger in his eyes. 'Do you? Why? So you can hate him? Consign him to the past, like another bad memory? No, no, that would be too easy, Lisa. It's far easier to hate than it is to love. If you're going to feel anything for him it should be pity. And you should carry that pity around with you for the rest of your life, and maybe one day you'll be able to forgive him!'

Tears sprang to her eyes. 'I'm sure he wouldn't have wanted me to pity him.'

'No, he wouldn't. He'd have hated it. And he'd have rather you'd hated him. You're just like him, you know. He always wanted the easy way out, too.' He put his hand to his forehead. 'No, that's not true. I'm being unfair to him. He took it all on himself. All the responsibility, all the guilt. But his way of coping with that was by shutting everything and everyone else out. He just died inside, emotionally.'

He turned and stared out across the river. 'We all died a little.' His laugh was without humour. 'They talk about the innocent victims of war. But sometimes the real victims are the ones who survive.

'Oh, yes, we walked into that village and killed all those people. It was no accident, and I'm not going to try and excuse it. We lost control. A moment of madness. It happens. But, you see, what happened, happened as much to us as it did to them. They died, but we had to live with it, and I think dying was the easier of the two.'

A small boat drifted by, a young couple in winter coats and scarves laughing at some shared intimacy.

Blair turned towards Lisa. 'What I told you before, about what happened – it was our defence at the court martial. It's what we told our wives and our girlfriends and our parents. It's what we wanted the world to believe, what we wanted to believe ourselves. How could you tell anyone, or even admit to yourself, what it was you'd found inside? Something dark and evil that you'd never even suspected was there. Something so rotten you can't ever wash the taste of it from your mouth. Like coming face to face with the devil, only to realize you've seen the face before, looking back at you from the mirror when you shave in the morning.'

The tension in the room was electric. Lisa sat rigid, her look of horror quickly replaced by one of guilt. She felt as if she had desecrated a grave, uncovered a body it had taken years to bury. And the corpse was still alive. She said feebly, 'I'm sorry,' and couldn't bring herself to meet his eye.

As if to deflect his own pain, he said, 'Most of us learned to live with it, one way or another. But it was Jack's name in the headlines, his life that could never be picked up on. When your mother disowned and divorced him there was no way back. Whatever capacity he'd had for love turned to hate, most of it directed towards himself. I said before, it's easier to hate than to love. It's also easier to be hated than to be loved. He lost his humanity. He cared for no one, least of all himself, and that way expected nothing in return. He was a lost soul, Lisa, lost and lonely. So don't ever hate him.'

She stared at the floor, and he stood for a long time without speaking. He felt old and tired. Fat drops of rain began to fall outside.

'I'll make that coffee now,' he said.

CHAPTER FORTY-SIX

A slight breeze stirred the freshly starched tablecloths on the dining terrace of the Batu Beach Hotel. The guests were seating themselves for lunch at their usual tables, overlooking the clear blue waters of the South China Sea. A middle-aged American couple, some Australians, a small party of Japanese, a group of English on a four-centre tour of the Far East.

'Would you look at them!' the American said, his voice rasping with irritation. The Japanese chattered animatedly at their table, cameras still dangling from necks, or laid next to plates.

'What about them, George?' said his wife. She smiled in their direction but got no response.

'You'd think they'd won the goddam war the way they behave.' It annoyed him that they had ignored his overtures of friendship. They were completely wrapped up in their own company. They ate together, went to the beach together, all went in the swimming pool at the same time, and they never stopped taking photographs of one another. It was as if the rest of the world did not exist.

'The war was a long time ago, George,' Yvonne said.

The babble of Japanese voices two tables away rose suddenly in pitch. George glowered in their direction, and saw that something out at sea had caught their attention. Yvonne put a hand on his arm. 'George, look! What's that?'

He craned round and saw, just clearing the headland, a big wooden trawler listing severely to starboard. The vessel was clearly in trouble, shipping water, and limping towards their beach. The forward deck appeared to be crowded with people waving towards the shore.

The waiter arrived at their table with pieces of barbecued marinaded chicken on bamboo skewers, and two bowls of spicy peanut sauce. 'Hey, fella, what the hell's that out there?' George asked him.

The waiter looked up and frowned. 'Boat people,' he said. 'Damn nuisance.'

'Boat people? What, you mean people who've escaped from Vietnam? Refugees?'

'Refugee, yes,' said the waiter. 'Bad news. Very bad news.' And he hurried away.

'Refugees?' Yvonne said. 'Oh, George, how dreadful.'

George stood up and dropped his napkin on the table. 'I'm gonna take a closer look.'

But the Japanese had beaten him to it. They were flocking down the steps to the beach. Several other guests followed.

The trawler ran aground in shallow water two hundred metres offshore, and tipped precariously on its side. Some of the sixty or so refugees who had survived the journey jumped overboard and began swimming for shore. Others, clutching all their worldly possessions, slithered down ropes into the water. Guests, and some staff from the hotel, gathered on the beach to watch. Japanese cameras whirred and clicked. Yvonne caught up with her husband and held his arm. 'These poor, wretched people,' she gasped. 'We must do something for them.'

'It's not up to us, dear. The authorities'll deal with it. Anyway, God knows what kind of diseases they might be carrying.'

'Do you think so?'

The first refugees made it to the beach and stood gasping, looking in wonder at the curious stares of these affluent holidaymakers. An odd silence settled on the sand. Yvonne's grip suddenly tightened around her husband's arm. 'George, there's a white man with them!'

'Where?' He followed her pointing finger and saw a tall, dark-haired European in a white shirt and ragged black pyjama trousers, staggering through the shallows, supported by two Asian women and a small boy. 'Goddam!' he said. 'He could be an American.'

Behind them, a jeep pulled up in the car park overlooking the beach, and two policemen stepped out.

From his comfortable bamboo armchair, in the air-conditioned lounge overlooking the ocean, George could see the white man sitting in the hotel lobby, where he had remained most of the afternoon. He made a curious figure in his ragged pyjama trousers and bare feet. He had a thick growth on his face slashed through by a livid scar on his cheek where the hair refused to grow. His patience, it seemed to George, was infinite.

By inclining his head a little, the American could see down to the beach, where the Asian refugees squatted in family groups in the sand, watched over by an armed Malay policeman. His attention was caught by the arrival of a thirty-foot launch, which had appeared round the headland a few minutes earlier. It passed the wreck of the trawler, and dropped anchor a little closer to shore. A Malaysian flag fluttered on the bows of the launch, and he could just make out the figures of half a dozen armed policemen standing, smoking, on the rear deck.

The excitement of it all had been too much for Yvonne, and she had retired for an afternoon nap. But George's curiosity was aroused. At last he could contain it no longer. He eased himself out of his chair and sauntered through to the lobby. Another policeman stood just outside the main door. George wandered casually through the tropical pot plants. The down-draught from the ceiling fan scattered his cigar smoke. He nodded at the seated figure. 'American?'

Elliot looked up. 'English.'

'Ah.' He tried not to show his disappointment, but his curiosity was not dulled. 'Must have been quite a journey.'

'Yes,' Elliot said. He leaned forward on his knees and examined his hands.

'I mean, uh, you hear about these boat people.' He laughed. 'I guess there's not many Englishmen among them.'

'I don't suppose there are.'

The American stood smiling awkwardly for a few moments, then he thrust his hand out towards Elliot. 'Calvin. George Calvin. San Diego, California.'

Elliot glanced up, hesitated, then gave the outstretched hand a cursory shake. 'Elliot.'

'Pleased to meet you, Mr Elliot. You must have been right glad to make land.'

Elliot nodded.

'If there's anything I can do . . .'

The door of the manager's office opened, and the captain of police appeared in the doorway. 'Would you come this way, please, Mistah Elliot.'

Elliot rose. 'Excuse me.'

'Sure.' George stepped back and watched Elliot shuffle into the office.

Captain Ghazali closed the door, and left Elliot standing in the middle of the room as he crossed to the desk and picked up two passports. He examined them briefly, then dropped them back on the desk and sat down. His eyes were hidden behind dark glasses. 'So,' he said. 'Your passport seems genuine enough. Perhaps you would like to tell me how you came to be travelling on fishing boat PK 709, registered to the Vietnamese port of Rach Gia.'

'I'm very tired, Captain. I've told the story several times already.'

'One more time.' Ghazali smiled. 'For me.'

Elliot sighed. 'I've been on holiday in Thailand.'

'Where?'

'Bangkok, then Pattaya Beach.'

Ghazali grinned. 'Lots of pretty women at Pattaya, they tell me.'

'Yes. Lots.'

'Go on.'

'I was sailing in the Gulf of Thailand.'

'Alone?'

'Yes, alone. I got caught in a storm, lost my rudder and my outboard. I was drifting for several days before these people picked me up.'

'Which explains why there is no exit stamp from Thailand on your passport.' Ghazali removed his sunglasses and sucked the end of one of the legs thoughtfully. 'You must be very grateful to them.'

'I am. I injured my shoulder during the storm. They patched me up.'

Ghazali gazed at him with shrewd eyes. The story was plausible enough. It was Elliot who didn't ring quite true. There was something about him. He didn't look like a holidaymaker out for a sail. The weapons and kit that lay on the seabed a mile offshore might have told him more, had he known of their existence.

'Is that why you are so keen to help this . . .' He glanced at one of the passports. 'This Ang woman and her family? Gratitude?'

'That's right. She told me her husband is in Bangkok. He escaped from Phnom Penh before the Khmer Rouge victory and now has US citizenship.'

'Of course.' Ghazali made no attempt to hide his sarcasm. 'She has no doubt been in constant touch with him.' He shook his head and lifted Elliot's passport. 'I have heard many such stories, Mistah Elliot. One grows weary of hearing the same tune.'

'Why don't you phone Bangkok?'

Ghazali stood up, his patience suddenly worn thin. 'I would not waste my time, or my government's money.' He handed Elliot the passport. 'You will remain here until immigration officials from Tumpat come to clear your entry into Malaysia and stamp your passport. Then you are free to return to Thailand. The border is only twenty miles from here.'

He moved towards the door. Elliot grabbed his arm. 'Wait a minute! What about Mrs Ang?'

Ghazali pulled his arm free and glared at the Englishman. 'Do not touch me again, Mistah Elliot. Mrs Ang and her children will be taken with the other refugees to Bidong.'

'What's Bidong?'

'It is an island some way off the coast. If any country will take them, then it will be arranged by the United Nations High Commissioner for Refugees. They will find many like themselves there. Criminals and drug smugglers. These people have given us very much trouble.'

*

Elliot watched the captain of police climb into his waiting car and drive off. The policeman at the main door touched his arm. 'You wait here for immigration.'

'I know.' He looked down to the beach and saw the first refugees wading out to the waiting launch. Serey was still squatting in the sand clutching her single bag of belongings. Ny was gazing out towards the launch. Hau spotted Elliot and waved.

As he approached them Serey rose to her feet. She knew at once from his face. 'My passport?'

He shook his head. 'They kept it. They say you have to go with the others.'

'And you?' Ny asked.

'They're letting me stay.'

Serey held out her hand. 'I'll say goodbye, then, Mistah Elliot. And thank you.'

He took her hand and shook it. 'For what?'

'Our lives.'

Ny threw her arms round him and pushed her face into his chest. She clung to him for several moments, long enough for him to feel her stifled sobs. Then she turned away and, taking her mother's hand, started wading towards the launch without a backward glance. Hau stood uncertainly for a time, then he too held out his hand. Elliot shook it firmly, and the boy turned away to hurry after his mother and sister, fighting hard not to let the tears show.

Those who still remained on the beach came in turn to shake his hand: the doctor who had dressed his wounds, the

497

captain who had saved his life. They all smiled their gratitude. And he watched them head out to the waiting boat. He had done everything he could. He knew that they did not blame him. He would tell Ang that his family were on Bidong Island. His money and his passport would buy their freedom from there. Yet still he could not turn away. The only reason he could stay and they must go was the colour of his skin, the crest on his passport. But his skin colour had not mattered to any of these people when they had saved his life. He remembered how Ny had washed out his wounds with her own urine, how she had lain with him to give him her body warmth when his fever had left him shivering. He remembered that it was Serey who had got them all safely out of Phnom Penh, that it was Hau who, along with McCue, had dragged him, bleeding, halfway across the city. He had come to rescue them, and it was they who had rescued him.

He turned and walked back across the sand and climbed the steps to the hotel. He found the American, Calvin, sitting in the lounge, smoking a cigar and reading a copy of the *International Herald Tribune*. Calvin turned and smiled as he approached. 'I hear they're letting you stay, Mr Elliot.'

'That's right. I wonder if you'd do me a favour?'

'Sure.' He folded up his paper. 'How can I help you?'

The last of the refugees clambered aboard the launch, helped by the Malay policemen. The anchor was retrieved and the driver started the motor. The relief of only a few hours before

PETER MAY

at safely reaching land had turned now to confusion and uncertainty. A warm breeze blew from the land as the sun dipped low in a sky glowing pink in the west.

The driver gunned the motor, and was about to slip the engine into gear when one of his fellow officers tapped him on the shoulder and pointed towards the shore. A single figure was wading towards the launch. The driver released the throttle and let the engine drop back to an idle. Elliot reached the boat and, with the help of outstretched arms, pulled himself aboard. The officers looked at him uncertainly. Elliot waved a hand dismissively. 'Don't let me hold you back.'

Serey pushed past the others and stared up at him. 'What are you doing?'

Elliot shrugged. 'I guess I'm going with you.'

CHAPTER FORTY-SEVEN

Bidong Island was a lump of rock that rose three hundred metres out of the sea, its steep flanks choked by jungle sweeping down to narrow coral sand beaches fringed with coconut palms. The light was fading as the Malay police launch chugged past the French ship, *Isle de Lumière*, which lay anchored in the bay and served as a floating hospital. As they drew closer they could see that the whole of one side of the hill had been stripped of all vegetation. A tropical island slum of three-storey shanties climbed its slopes. The frames of the wretched dwellings had been constructed from the timbers of the trees felled to make way for them. Walls were made of tin and cardboard and bark, roofs from blue plastic sheeting, or bone-coloured waterproof sacks. The smoke of countless fires drifted up in the dusk, like mist.

As the launch drew in at the jetty, they were met by the stink of human excrement and the smell of woodsmoke. A large crowd of several hundred refugees was gathered on the beach among rotting piles of refuse to watch the new arrivals. At the other end, near the jetty, an incinerator was nearing

PETER MAY

completion, paid for no doubt by meagre sums of money provided to salve the collective Western conscience. Beyond it, on
an outcrop of rocks, figures crouched in silhouette, defecating
into the sea near the wreck of a twenty-metre boat lying in
the shallows.

They were met on the jetty by members of the camp's administration committee, refugees like themselves, overseen by a
group of armed militiamen who stood around smoking. There
was a headcount and an arbitrary division of the newcomers
into groups of six or eight. A cadaverous young Vietnamese in
shorts, a singlet and Ho Chi Minh sandals approached Elliot
carrying a clipboard. 'You with relief agency?' he asked.

Elliot shook his head. 'No. I'm with them.'

'Refugee?' the Vietnamese asked with incredulity.

'That's right. This woman, her daughter and her son are
Cambodian. We're together.'

He looked at them, each in turn, then gave a tiny shrug.
On Bidong Island nothing came as much of a surprise any
more. 'I am Duong Van Minh, interpreter for the camp committee. I have been here five months. There are worse places. I
need your names, then tomorrow you come to administration
centre and register. Tonight I fix you up, temporary accommo-
dation. You follow me, please.'

As darkness fell, he led them through the crowded administrative heart of the camp, just beyond the beach. Here, the
buildings were of a superior quality. Yellow-lit faces peered at
them from windows illuminated by electric bulbs powered

by car batteries. The narrow street opened out into a sort of market square, where all manner of goods were sold from stalls lit by oil lamps and candles: everything from nails and wire and fishing tackle, to curry powder, cigarettes and sewing machines. Craftsmen squatted by campfires peddling their wares or services – watch repairers, woodcutters, artists, acupuncturists. They passed a tailor's shop, a barber's, even a pawnbroker's.

'We have thriving black market,' Minh said. 'Illegal, but necessary. Police look other way. We have restaurant, too, and coffee house. Even library. We are well organized.' They passed a crowd gathered round a noticeboard. 'Most important noticeboard on island,' he said. 'List arriving mail and departing refugee. Find out if you stay or go.'

'Do many go?' Elliot asked.

'Not many.' Minh was philosophical. 'Depend on who you are, if you got money or education, or relative in West. Then maybe some country take you.'

'What about you?'

'Oh, I am alright. I leave soon. I have uncle in United States. And I am trained computer programmer.' He shrugged. 'But I am lucky, Mistah Elliot. Nearly fifty thousand people come to Bidong since first people arrive a year ago. Only ten thousand leave in that time. Even for lucky ones like me, it take time. Some people maybe never leave.' Despite the heat and humidity, Elliot felt a chill run through him.

At an intersection of mean ill-lit alleyways, Minh turned

up the hill, leading them into the packed suburban heart of Bidong, shanties ranked above them like so many coffins stacked around a graveyard. They climbed for more than ten minutes, up through a maze of crudely terraced streets, until Minh finally stopped by a dilapidated three-storey shanty house on a promontory near the top of the hill. From here they had a clear view across the slope, and down to the jetty and bay below. Elliot gasped for breath, his strength rapidly ebbing. Ny and Hau had had to support their mother for most of the second half of the climb.

Minh pointed to a ladder leading up to a wooden terrace above. 'You share middle house till we find something else. You get water at beach in morning. Need to queue, though. Water rationed. Only two litre per person per day. You come to centre for UNHCR (he pronounced it *ungkah*) ration pack every three day. You got money, then is possible to buy more on black market.' He made a little bow. 'Goodnight. See you tomorrow.' And he headed off down the hill.

Elliot looked up at the wooden terrace and smiled wryly. 'This must be home.'

A curtain of bamboo beads hung across the door to the second level of the shanty house. The interior was dark and thick with the smell of sweat. Eyes peered out of the gloom, and they saw that there were already nine other people, men, women and children, squeezed into a room barely three metres by two. There was no sign of resentment at their intrusion. With the patient resignation of the practised refugee, the existing occupants simply shuffled closer together, to create more space. No one spoke. Elliot, Serey, Ny and the boy settled themselves against a wall and stared back at the incurious faces.

The floor was made of wooden slats, and through them, both above and below, they could see the shadows of the other occupants. Smoke drifted up from the lower level, between the slats, making the already thick air almost unbreathable. A child on the level above them had a fit of coughing. Ny and Hau curled up together, like small animals, and were quickly asleep. Elliot leaned back against the wall and closed his eyes. He did not expect to sleep.

A hand on his arm delivered him, abruptly, from a drifting world of jumbled images: vast stretches of sea; McCue's body sliding into the water, a hand waving through the broken foam; a long stretch of deserted beach broken by a solitary figure that he had realized, suddenly, was himself. He opened his eyes but could see nothing in the dark.

'Are you asleep?' It was Serey's voice, very close, barely a whisper.

'No.'

She seemed to hesitate. 'I wanted to apologize.'

'For what?'

'I misjudged you.'

'I don't think so.'

She took his hand and squeezed it gently. He was almost shocked by the warmth of her touch. 'I am grateful, anyway.'

'Don't be. I'm the one who should be grateful.'

'For leading you here?'

'For teaching me something. About myself.' Confessions, he thought, were easier in the dark. He remembered McCue telling him of his fear.

'You had no reason to come here with us.'

'More reason than not to. We all have to live with ourselves.'

He heard her sigh. 'I wish my husband had felt as you do.'

'That was a long time ago. He made a mistake. He regrets it.'

'It was no mistake!' Her voice was sour and rose in anger at the remembered hurt. 'And time changes nothing. He showed that he loved himself more than his family. He betrayed us. My children do not fully understand this. But I do. If he regrets anything, it is his conscience.' She lapsed into an uneasy silence. 'I do not wish ever to see him again.'

'Then why come all this way?'

'I never expected to live,' she said simply. 'I always thought, if there is a chance to survive, then I must take it for my children's sake. Life is an unexpected bonus, but I could never live with betrayal.'

Elliot took a deep, weary breath. 'Your husband is on his way to Malaysia.' He felt her tense at his side.

'It's not possible!'

'I asked an American at the hotel to contact him in Bangkok. He has papers, passports. If I can get us off the island, you could be reunited within forty-eight hours and on your way to a new life in America.'

She withdrew her hand abruptly from his. 'No.'

'You would prefer to stay here?' She did not reply. 'You must go, for your children's sake. There is no future for them on Bidong.'

Still she made no reply, and then he heard a sob catch her throat in the dark. 'If he had stayed, Mistah Elliot, then we might have survived, as a family. Others did. We might all have had a future.'

'You still do.'

'My children, perhaps,' she said. He felt a warm tear splash on his arm, and drew the fragile, trembling body to his side.

Two hours queuing in the stifling heat of the administration centre the next morning, to register and collect their UNHCR rations, did little for the morale of the new arrivals. Anger replaced impatience among the refugees at the contents of the *ungkah* ration pack: nine hundred grams of rice; a tin of condensed milk; three tins of canned meat, fish and vegetables; two packets of noodles; sugar; salt; and two small teabags. There would be no more for three days. 'Official fresh vegetable only available every two month,' Minh told them. 'Can buy on black market, though.'

Elliot drew Minh aside. 'Who supplies the black market?'

'Unofficial,' he said. 'Not legal.'

'But a fact. Where does the stuff come from?'

Minh shrugged. 'Not my business. You speak Fat Bao. He ve-ery rich man. Find him at Vien Du coffee house.'

The Vien Du, or *Venture*, overlooked the sea at one end of the bay. Little more than a wooden shack, it was crammed with crude tables and chairs, a rudimentary bar and a small stage where live vocalists entertained patrons at night. Elliot left Serey, Ny and Hau to queue for water on the beach, and made his way up to the coffee house.

Fat Bao sat at a table by a window which looked out over the sea. A pantomime Chinaman, like an extra from *Aladdin,* a long pigtail hung down his back and a brightly coloured silk robe fell in folds across his belly. A wispy black moustache curled down at the corners of his mouth, accentuating the droop of his fat jowls. Piggy eyes peered shrewdly out from slits in the folds of his face. The coffee house was quiet at this hour, and Elliot drew only a few curious glances as he approached the table. 'Mr Bao?'

Fat Bao looked up from a week-old copy of the *Straits Times* and his lips parted in a broad smile. He waved a hand expansively at the chair opposite. 'Sit down Mistah Elliot. You like coffee?'

Elliot sat. 'Yes.'

Fat Bao snapped his fingers and the barman slipped off his stool to prepare some fresh. 'You wondering how I know you name?'

'From what I hear I doubt if there's much that escapes your attention.'

He grinned. 'Quite right, Mistah Elliot, quite right. Information is power. Power is money. But whole island know already of Englishman who arrive with refugee from Cambodia. I am expecting you. You want escape from Bidong, yes?'

'That's right.'

He leaned confidentially across the table. 'Cost big money, Mistah Elliot, big money. You got big money?'

The coffee arrived. Elliot took a sip. Real coffee, fresh and strong. It tasted good. He shook his head. 'I have no money, Mr Bao. We spent it all getting this far.'

Fat Bao sat back, his jowls wobbling as he spread his hands in apology. 'I am business man, Mistah Elliot. I trade goods from mainland. I buy and sell real estate on island, change currency, lend money. Maybe we can do deal on loan? Very reasonable rate.'

'I don't think so. Do you have a cigarette?'

The Chinaman delved among the folds of his robe and produced an unopened pack of Camels. He pushed it across the table. 'My compliment.' He watched as Elliot unpeeled the wrapper, then he produced an engraved gold lighter and held out the flame.

Elliot took a deep draw. 'It is possible, though, to get off the island?'

'Everything is possible.'

'How come you're still here, then?'

He spread his arms. 'As you see, Mistah Elliot, I have everything I need. Why go?'

Why indeed, Elliot thought, when there was such profit in

human suffering. He said, 'I have a friend on the mainland who will pay whatever it takes to get the four of us off.'

Fat Bao nodded seriously. 'Of course,' he said, as if he had known all along.

'You have contacts on the mainland?'

'Mistah Elliot . . .' His tone reproached the naivety of the question. Then he pulled thoughtfully at the corners of his moustache. 'Four people? Big risk, Mistah Elliot, very dangerous.' A precursor, Elliot thought, to hiking up the price. 'Cost very big money,' Bao said. 'How much you willing to pay?'

Elliot watched his cigarette smoke disperse in the hot breeze from the sea, and flicked his ash from the window. 'You got a pen and paper?'

Fat Bao nodded and leaned over to retrieve a leather-bound writing folder and pen from a bag on the floor. He slid it across the table and Elliot wrote Yuon Ang's name on a fresh sheet. He pushed it back at Bao. 'He should be at the Batu Beach Hotel near Tumpat by tonight. You can negotiate a price with him. How will you get us off?'

Bao gazed thoughtfully at the name for some moments. Eventually, he said, 'Malay fishermen come from mainland with goods for black market. My people have half-dozen small boat. They swim out pushing boat to meet fishermen, 'bout five kilometre offshore. Fill boat with goods then come back. You swim out with boat, but no come back. Go to mainland with fishermen.' He grinned. 'Escape.'

'When?'

'Tomorrow night, maybe. I let you know.'

Elliot scraped back his chair and stood up to drain the last of his coffee. He put the cup back on the table. 'I'll be hearing from you, then.'

'You come tonight, to Vien Du. Pretty girl sing. Big movie star in south Vietnam before communist come. I fix you up good.'

'Some other time,' Elliot said.

The midday sun beat down in the street outside. There was no shade anywhere, and the air was thick with flies. Across the way, on a rocky promontory, stood the remains of a refugee boat converted, by the former moderator of the Presbyterian Church of Vietnam, into a makeshift church and library. From the boat's cabin, the breeze carried the sounds of a refugee class learning English: *'Take me to Times Square.' 'Where is Buckingham Palace?'*

On the long climb back up the hill with the ration packs and water, Elliot told Serey and Ny of his meeting with Fat Bao. They had to stop frequently to rest. Serey squatted, listening in solemn silence, as Ny translated for Hau. The boy greeted the news with the same reserve as his mother. Only Ny seemed cheered at the prospect of seeing her father again. Elliot held her back as they embarked on the last leg of the climb. 'What's wrong with Hau? I thought he'd be pleased to get out of here.'

'We will all be pleased,' she said, 'to leave Bidong. But he is little frightened of going America. Khmer Rouge, you know, they tell us many bad things 'bout the West. They say colour people hated there, treated real bad.'

Elliot wondered if it was possible to suffer any more than they had done at the hands of the Khmer Rouge. But he understood the power of indoctrination. He supposed that the God of his childhood still existed in him somewhere, in spite of the rejected belief of his adult intellect. 'He wants to see his father, surely?'

'Is long time. He remember very little of our father. Scared, maybe, he a stranger now.' She stared down at the dusty ground as they walked.

'And what about you?'

She smiled a little, without lifting her eyes. 'I scared, too, Mistah Elliot. He leave us before. Maybe he do it again.'

'I doubt it.'

She looked up at him. 'I hope not. Mother–daughter love very strong. But girl need father, too.'

He thought of his own daughter who had never known him, and wondered with a stab of guilt if she had suffered for it. Almost as though she had read his thoughts, Ny touched his arm and said, 'Pity 'bout your daughter, Mistah Elliot. I wish I had father like you.'

Minh was waiting for them when they got back to the shanty house. 'I got new house for you,' he said. 'Nearer beach. Move tomorrow.' He and Elliot sat out on the shade of the terrace looking down on the island.

'We'll stay where we are,' Elliot said.

The young Chinese scratched his head. 'I don't understand. Very desirable property near beach. I pull plenty string to get you new house.'

'Why? Because I'm white?'

'You should not be here, Mistah Elliot, with refugee. Make no sense. Plenty sickness here. Hepatitis, typhoid, tuberculosis. Could be on Bidong long time. Not healthy for white man. No resistance. Take house near beach, is better.'

Elliot shook his head. 'We're leaving. Tomorrow night, with a bit of luck.'

Minh nodded, understanding. 'You make deal with Fat Bao.'

'Yes, I make deal, Minh.'

Minh lowered his voice. 'You be very careful, Mistah Elliot. Fat Bao dangerous man. He has no honour. You cannot trust.'

'Thanks for the warning.'

Minh looked at him sadly. 'You don't take serious. I tell you, Mistah Elliot, Fat Bao he cut your throat and take your money. Thirty-five people from camp go missing since I arrive. All involve with Fat Bao and black market. They food for fishes now, I think.'

When Minh had gone, Elliot went inside and searched through the bag of their belongings. Masking what he was doing from the other occupants of the room, he lifted out a bundle of rags and unwrapped his Colt .45 automatic pistol. He checked the recoil action and the contents of the seven-round box magazine, in case of water damage. He did not want to be caught short if things went wrong.

*

The following day came and went under a blistering tropical sun. They went early to queue for water on the beach,
but by the time they were climbing the hill again, with their
eight litres, the fierce heat of the day was reflecting at them
from every surface. As constant as the heat was the babble of
voices, raised sometimes in laughter, sometimes in argument.
All around them people worked and ate and slept and made
love. There was no privacy among the washing lines strung
out across the narrow alleys, but many secrets. This was a
society fraught with mistrust and petty jealousies. Yet there
was, too, a great comradeship. A sense of hunger and hard-
ship shared. It was a microcosm of any slum, anywhere in the
world, where optimism prevails over hopelessness. A ticket
to freedom, resettlement in the West, was the equivalent of
a win on the lottery.

There was no word from Fat Bao, and the day passed slowly,
eating, sleeping, a constant search for escape from the heat
and the flies. Night brought no relief from the heat, and for
Elliot little sleep. His shoulder ached constantly, and he began
to fear that the wound had become reinfected. All day, Serey's
mood had been morose. She had spoken little, and through
the long hours of the night Elliot was aware that she too slept
little, and even then only in restless fits.

In the morning, Elliot went to the tin-roofed medical clinic
in the centre of the camp to have his wound examined. He sat
waiting for nearly three hours, wide-eyed undernourished children and their mothers staring at him with bleak faces. One man,

with a suppurating stump of an arm, arrived after Elliot and sat ashen-faced. The pain expressed by his eyes was past bearing, and yet he sat in silence with a seemingly endless, patient endurance. When it came to Elliot's turn he let the man go first. But there was no room in those eyes for gratitude, only surprise amid the pain. All it cost Elliot was another twenty minutes.

Dr Nguen Xuan Trieu was a middle-aged man with a pale, educated face. He wore wire-rimmed spectacles and examined Elliot's wound with a clinical interest. His English was impeccable. 'A bullet wound,' he said. 'I have not seen many of those since the war ended.' He displayed no curiosity as to how Elliot might have come by it. Nor any sympathy. 'How have you treated it?' he asked.

'It was washed out with urine, and the poison drawn out with poultices.'

'You are lucky to be alive,' he said. 'I have seen men die from a scratch in these conditions. There is a little fungal infection around the new tissue growth.' He dabbed the wound with some white cream and re-dressed it. 'It needs proper attention. Unfortunately I do not have the facilities, or the medicines. Children are dying from malnutrition. There is meningitis and typhoid. I cannot spare antibiotics for bullet wounds.'

When Elliot got back to the shanty house, one of Fat Bao's minions was waiting, a boy who could not have been more than fifteen. He seemed nervous of Elliot, and his eyes flickered over him warily. 'Tonight,' he said. 'Midnight. On beach other side of Religion Hill.'

'Where the hell's Religion Hill?'

'Ask,' said the boy, and he hurried away down the hill, quickly obscured by the washing lines. Elliot glanced up and saw Serey watching him from the terrace.

Religion Hill turned out to be the rocky promontory where the former Presbyterian Moderator had set up his church in the wreck of a refugee boat. The beach beyond it was deserted. The midnight lights of the Vien Du, on the jetty side of the church, cast a faint glow across the white coral sands. Carried on the night breeze, the nasal voice of a girl singing some Vietnamese hit song had replaced the daytime chants of the English class: *'Where is Buckingham Palace?'*

Elliot stepped cautiously on to the beach, disturbing dozens of crabs that scuttled off into the night chasing their long shadows. Two tiny canoes no more than five feet long, crudely fashioned from fallen trees, lay side by side at the water's edge. They were not big enough to hold a man, nor stable enough to remain upright if they could. A flashlight shone in his face, and two figures detached themselves from the shadows of the palms. 'You Elliot?'

'Yes.'

'Where others?'

He couldn't see their faces. 'Turn that thing off.'

There was a moment's hesitation before the light went out. Elliot blinked away the circle of black in front of his eyes. Both men were in their twenties. One had close-cropped hair and a scar on his temple. The other had long greasy hair that flopped over his eyes. The one with long hair glanced nervously, several times, in the direction of the Vien Du. 'Where others?' he insisted.

Elliot signalled towards the trees, and Ny and Hau emerged, followed by Serey still clutching her bag.

'Hurry!' whispered Long Hair. 'Police patrol regular.'

The women and the boy fell in behind Elliot. He said, 'What's the plan?'

'Hold on back of boats and swim. Straight out. Three kilometre. Boat waiting. You see light long way in dark.'

Cropped Head strode down the sand to the boats. 'We help you push off.'

Elliot nodded to Long Hair, indicating that they would follow him. The Vietnamese shrugged and moved ahead.

The water was warm around their ankles as they pushed the boats into the shallows. Elliot remained standing at the water's edge. 'You go,' Long Hair urged. 'Quick.'

'We'll go when you've gone,' Elliot said.

The two Vietnamese exchanged glances. 'Okay,' said Cropped Head. They moved reluctantly away from the boats, towards the beach. Long Hair grinned at Hau and held out his hand.

'Good luck.'

Hau took the hand and was jerked suddenly, almost off his feet. The Vietnamese reeled him in like a fish on a line, clamping a hand over his mouth and pulling the back of the boy's head to his chest. A blade flashed in the dark and pressed into the soft flesh of his neck. A trickle of blood appeared. Elliot stepped quickly back as the other man produced a long, thin-bladed knife from the folds of his tunic. Serey choked back a scream and grasped her daughter's arm.

'What do you want?' Elliot's voice remained steady and calm.

'Open the bag.' Cropped Head's knife was shaking in his hand.

Elliot snatched the bag from Serey.

Long Hair tensed. His eyes were wild. 'I kill the boy!'

Elliot threw the bag up on to the sand. 'Open it yourself.'

Cropped Head moved cautiously past him, keeping a safe distance, then ran up the beach to the bag. 'I don't know what you hope to find,' Elliot said. 'I told Bao we had nothing.'

Long Hair grinned. 'Maybe Fat Bao believe you. Maybe not. We not. You Westerner. Got money there, maybe gold.'

Elliot shook his head. 'And what about the boat waiting out there – if there is a boat?'

'Boat waiting, okay. You disappear. Drowned maybe. Too bad.'

Elliot's hand slipped inside his shirt, and pulled the Colt .45 into a two-handed grip. He knew he had only one shot. The bullet punched a hole through Long Hair's forehead, propelling him backwards on crumpled legs to splash into six inches of foaming brine and turn it briefly pink. Elliot swivelled to face the kneeling Cropped Head, who looked up in stunned surprise from the upended bag and had hardly an instant's blink of disbelief before Elliot shot him full in the face.

Serey and Ny splashed forward to pick Hau out of the water where he had fallen. He clutched his neck, blood oozing through his fingers. Elliot reached them in three strides and pulled his hand away to look at the wound. 'Just a cut. He'll live. We've got to get out of here!'

The singing coming from the direction of the Vien Du had stopped. A flashlight raked across Religion Hill, and there came the sound of raised voices. There was no going back now. And if they missed their rendezvous at sea, they were certain to drown.

Elliot threw Serey's bag into the nearest canoe and they pushed the two boats off into the shallow swell. 'I can't swim,' Serey whispered to him, as they plunged waist-deep through the water.

'Jesus!' Elliot said. 'Now you tell me! Just hang on and kick with your feet. If you keep holding on you won't sink.'

Ny and Hau had surged ahead, hands grasping the rear lip of their canoe, feet kicking up luminescent foam in the dark. When he was certain Serey had a firm grip, Elliot pushed hard away from shore and their canoe slid through the water in pursuit.

They kicked hard at first, seeming to make little progress, until Elliot glanced back and saw that they were already five or six hundred metres from shore. They had cleared the rocky outcrop, and away to their left they could see the lights of the French hospital ship anchored in the bay. Flashlights twinkled on the shore behind them, wielded by shadowy figures running along the water's edge. Aimless shots rang out in the dark.

Soon the sound of water breaking on land faded, and the rocky silhouette of Bidong took shape against a night sky brightly lit by the moon rising from behind the island. Ny and Hau were about ten metres ahead, and drifting further away to the left. From time to time they disappeared completely beyond the rise of the swell. Elliot called to them to stay close. They must not lose each other. He glanced at Serey and saw that she was tiring rapidly, the strain in her arms showing on her face. He was, himself, close to exhaustion.

'Stop!' he shouted. 'Stop!' And he hooked an elbow over the rim of the canoe and hung loose, trying to catch his breath. Ny and Hau worked their canoe back to draw alongside, worried faces peering anxiously in the moonlight.

'What wrong?'

'Nothing. We need a rest, that's all.'

His shoulder had almost seized completely. He looked back, but the swell was so deep now that the island only appeared in glimpses.

'How far now?' Ny asked.

'Don't know. We must be about halfway.' But he felt despair rising in his breast. The second fifteen hundred metres would be much tougher going against the rising swell, and how could they hope to make a rendezvous with one small boat in this vast expanse of sea? They could be swept miles off course by the current. And, yet, if this was, indeed, how goods were brought ashore to feed the black market, then it had been done many times before. Perhaps allowances had been made for wind and current, based on months of experience. 'We'd better go on. Stay close.'

After what Elliot estimated was about fifteen minutes, he ordered another rest. They were all on the point of exhaustion now. It was as much as any of them could do to keep numb fingers hanging on. It would be so much easier, he thought, just to let go, to slip away into the eternity that awaited below. Supporting himself again on the crook of his elbow, he looked around. There was not a glimpse of the island in any direction. Only the sea and, above it, the vast cosmos. Without the moon as a guide, they would not have known which way they were heading. But whatever their bearing, he knew they could not hang on for much longer.

It was Hau who spotted the light. He called out in sudden excitement and pointed away to their left. Elliot strained his eyes and saw nothing. But then, as their boat was lifted again on the swell, he saw it. A bright white light, shining across the water. He lost sight of it almost at once as their tiny craft slid down into another trough, only to spot it again on the next rise. Hope dug reserves of strength from the depths of despair, and they kicked off again in the direction of the light, shouting and calling to the boat.

As they got nearer, their calls were rewarded by the sound of an engine spluttering, then revving hard as the boat turned to head in their direction. Elliot reached across and held the two canoes together, as the wash from the power launch lifted them up, then sucked them in to its side. Light played in fractured patterns across the broken surface of the water, and he saw Yuon's face looking down from the deck. Helping hands lifted Ny and Hau to safety. Elliot turned to offer Serey his hand, but she was gone.

'Serey!' He called again, 'Serey!', in sudden panic, and spun the canoe around, hoping to find her clinging to the far side. She wasn't there.

'What wrong? Where Mamma?' Ny's voice reached him from afar, as if in a dream. He turned this way and that in the water, looking for a glimpse of grey hair breaking the surface.

'Light!' he screamed. 'Give me some fucking light!' A searchlight swung across the water and he swam frantically back in the direction they had come. Nothing. He stopped and tried to tread water, but felt himself going under, and splashed back towards the boat again, gasping for breath. He reached the canoe and clung to it for several moments, head pressed against the bark in despair. Her words rang in his head: *I could never live with betrayal.* And he knew what she had done. He struck out at the water in frustration and anguish. They had come so far.

Two crewmen leaned over to pull him aboard, and he slumped back against the rail. He glanced up and saw the pain in Yuon's eyes. He would never be free of his conscience now. Ny and her brother stood to one side, looking at Elliot with fear and confusion in their faces. They did not yet understand.

'Where Mamma?' Ny asked again in a quiet voice.

'Gone,' Elliot said. 'Gone.'

In little under half an hour they saw the dark shadow of the mainland lying along the horizon, occasional lights winking along the shoreline. They sat in the back of the boat, silent except for Hau, who wept unashamedly in his sister's arms. It had been easy to forget that he was still a child. Only war, and the Khmer Rouge, had made him old before his time. Ny stroked his hair absently, staring off into the middle distance. Yuon sat alone, detached and distraught. A sad and lonely figure.

When they drew, eventually, into the small private jetty, he ushered his family off before him, and Elliot followed wearily at a distance. The launch wheeled off into the night. Yuon turned to Elliot. 'I have a car waiting, Mistah Elliot. We will drive straight to Kuala Lumpur. Will you come with us?'

Elliot shook his head. 'The Thai border can't be more than twenty kilometres away. I'll cross on foot.' He paused. 'I'm sorry.'

Yuon nodded, and Elliot wondered if he would ever really understand.

Ny stepped forward and held out a formal hand. Elliot took it, and they shook hands briefly. 'Goodbye, Mistah Elliot,' she said. In her eyes was the desire to throw her arms around him and hold on for ever, but such a thing no longer seemed possible. He took the St Christopher from around his neck and handed it to Hau.

'I think my luck's all burned out,' he said.

Hau looked at it for a moment, then turned and threw it into the water, and Elliot knew that, somehow, he'd failed the boy.

He watched Yuon, and the children he did not yet know, walk quickly up the beach towards the road, to the car and the future that awaited them. When they had disappeared from view he turned and looked back across the sea. Somewhere, out there, Serey had at last found peace.

CHAPTER FORTY-EIGHT

The *hang yao* passed under a low wooden bridge and Elliot, sitting in the front of the boat, felt its shadow pass over him like the Angel of Death. A shout came from a *klong* house, and he glanced round anxiously, but the man was shouting to a boy who stood waist-deep in the water brushing his teeth. He heard the sound of laughter, breathed in the smell of cooking drifting on the wind. Life went on. Death, even here, seemed remote, a natural end upon which men and women did not dwell unduly. It would come to them soon enough. After weeks in the field life seemed unreal, normality abnormal.

Here too, a white face – a *farang* – on the *klongs* attracted little attention. His presence was unremarkable, a matter of indifference. Another tourist, perhaps. It would take time, he knew, to adjust.

His driver brought the boat to rest at the foot of wooden steps leading up to McCue's house. 'Wait for me,' Elliot said, and climbed the steps with ice in his heart. The rocker still stood on the terrace, but it had an abandoned air, as if it had not been sat in for a long time. The mosquito nets were gone from the windows, and the door stood ajar. The floorboards creaked like snow underfoot as he stepped inside. The emptiness shocked him, like finding somebody naked unexpectedly. A fine film of dust had settled on the floor and the window ledges. The door to the back room, where the baby had lain beneath its protective netting, opened on to more emptiness. Late afternoon sun streamed through the windows, as though trying to shed light on a dark place.

A voice called from the *klong*, and he stepped back out on to the terrace to find a wizened old lady standing on the bottom step. She smiled to show friendship and revealed gums without teeth. 'You look for Lotus?' She held her hand to her eyes, to shield them from the sun, and take a better look at Elliot.

'Yes,' he said. 'Do you know where she is?'

'She no live here any more. Take baby, go back to live in town, work in bars.'

'Do you know where? What bars?'

'She no say. Her man leave her, no come back. Is normal. You friend of her?'

Elliot shook his head. 'I knew her man,' he said. 'He didn't leave her.'

As the *hang yao* sped out from the *klong* into the choppy waters of the Chao Phraya river, Elliot opened his hand and the torn fragments of the cheque that could have bought a better future for Lotus and her child were whipped away on the edge of the wind. To have searched for her in a city of five million people would have been hopeless. Lotus, he knew, was not her real name. It was a name used by countless girls, in numberless bars. And he was not sure he would even have known her again. Just another bar girl with a fatherless child.

At the Oriental Hotel landing stage, he pushed his way through the crowds queuing to cross the river, and picked up a taxi. His fire was all but extinguished, but somewhere, in all his black emptiness, an ember still smouldered. One remaining score to settle. 'Sukhumvit Road,' he told the driver.

All the shutters on Tuk's villa were closed. The gates were padlocked. Elliot gazed through the bars, and was struck by an all too familiar sense of abandonment. The taxi driver leaned through his open window. 'You looking for Tuk Than?'

Elliot turned. 'That's right.'

'He dead,' the driver said cheerfully. And Elliot thought, even revenge is denied me. 'Newspapers full of it when it happen,' the driver went on. 'Some *farang* shoot him. English or American. They don't know. But they say La Mère Grace involve, too.'

Elliot frowned. 'Grace? What happened?'

The driver shrugged. 'Nobody know. They find her body in river. Ma-any bullet. They kill her good. Where you want go now?'

Elliot stood for a moment, then slid wearily into the back seat. 'Home,' he said.

'Where home?'

'A long way from here.'

CHAPTER FORTY-NINE

She stood by the window watching for the taxi. It was five minutes late, but her train did not leave for two hours yet. There was plenty of time. Too much. She wanted to be away. Away from this empty house, stripped of its furniture and its memories. Its cold bare rooms seemed unfamiliar to her now, as a dead body seems strangely unconnected with the spirit that once animated it.

Outside, the February wind slapped sleet against the window and flapped the end of the SOLD sticker on the FOR SALE sign in the garden. A car drew up at the gate. She stooped to pick up her case, all that she would carry from an unhappy past to an uncertain future, and went into the hall. The bell rang as she reached the door, and she opened it to find Blair sheltering on the doorstep, collar turned up against the sleet.

She looked at him with surprise. 'I thought you were the taxi.'

'Can I come in?' She held the door open, and he hurried in out of the cold. He looked at the case still in her hand. 'I just caught you, then.'

'My train's at five.' She put it down again.

He seemed unusually hesitant. 'I didn't realize you were going so soon.'

'I start on Monday.' He nodded, but said nothing. She added, 'I'm afraid I can't offer you anything.'

'That's alright.'

'Not even a seat.'

He stood awkwardly. 'It's not important.'

'Why are you here, Sam?'

He avoided her eyes. 'I didn't know whether to come or not. I'm still not sure it's the right thing.' He glanced at her uncertainly, but she offered him no help. He reached into an inside pocket and held out a folded slip of paper. 'It came yesterday.'

She unfolded the paper. It was an international telegram from Bangkok. It read: STILL IN ONE PIECE STOP HOME TOMORROW STOP J. She frowned and looked searchingly at him. 'J?'

'Jack.' He drew a deep breath. 'It's from your father, Lisa.'

She drank the last of her coffee and wiped the condensation from the window. The traffic in the King's Road was building already towards rush hour. Through the archway opposite, the street lights reflected on wet cobbles. She could not see his window from here, but there were lights along that side of the mews. She felt sick, and as she looked at her watch she noticed that her hand was shaking. An hour and fifteen, still, before her train left. It would take her forty to get to King's Cross, which left her thirty-five to prolong her indecision.

The reasons which had impelled her to travel halfway across the world in search of her father seemed obscure now. She had been someone else then. Devastated by the death of her mother, confused and bewildered by the discovery that her father was still alive. On that day, just before Christmas (was it really only six weeks ago?), that she had summoned the courage to knock on his door, she had feared that he would reject her. Now she was afraid that it was she who could not accept him. For the second time in her life she had accepted his death. Easier, surely, to persist with that acceptance than to acknowledge a stranger as her father. She dropped ten pence on the table, stood up and lifted her suitcase. The tube would be quicker than a taxi.

As she reached the door, a cab pulled up opposite, and a man carrying a leather holdall bag stepped out on to the pavement. Her suitcase slipped from her hand. The scar on his cheek was a livid slash in the suntanned face. He was leaner than she remembered at the funeral. He seemed older, greyer. He paid the cabbie and hurried into the mews, pulling his collar up against the icy February blast.

A fat, middle-aged man tried to squeeze past her where she blocked the doorway. 'Excuse me, miss, are you coming or going?'

Elliot shut the door behind him and scuffed through a pile of mail lying on the carpet, mostly bills and circulars. He opened the cupboard at the foot of the stairs, turned on the heating and set the thermostat, then climbed the stairs and shivered as he switched on the light in the sitting room. The air was chill and the flat smelled damp and unlived in. He threw his bag into an armchair and tossed his coat over it. At the drinks cabinet he poured himself a large whisky. He retrieved the newspapers he had bought at the airport from his coat pocket, and sank into the settee to catch up on the world. He did not immediately notice the light winking on the telephone answering machine, indicating that a message awaited him.

On the foreign pages of *The Times* there was a story about a call from the United Nations for an international conference in Geneva to discuss the 'increasing problem' of the Boat People. He remembered Bidong, the crowds of bleak, malnourished faces that gathered around the noticeboard at the centre of the camp, more out of habit than with any real hope. Vietnam, the story said, would be asked to put a halt to the exodus. But it was as much, Elliot thought, a denial of the rights of these people to make them stay, as it was to force them to leave. The real problem was that no one wanted them.

Another story outlined the UN's refusal to recognize the Heng Samrin regime installed in Phnom Penh by the Vietnamese. The international community, it seemed, preferred to recognize the murderers of the Khmer Rouge as the legitimate government of Cambodia.

Elliot threw the paper aside in disgust and took a stiff pull at his whisky. He wondered why he should feel such anger and realized, with a sense of shock, that it was because he cared.

He stood up and dropped the other newspapers on the coffee table. He didn't need to catch up on the world. Nothing had changed – except in him.

The flashing green light on the answering machine caught his eye. He walked round the settee, rewound the tape and pressed the PLAY button, then slipped back over the settee and lay along its length to listen to the message. His head was pounding still after the long flight. Above the background hiss, he recognized Sam Blair's voice. *'If she hasn't found you before you get this message, Jack, your daughter knows you're alive and she's looking for you.'*

Lisa was passing under the arch when the blast ripped through the windows of Elliot's apartment, sending debris and lethal splinters of glass hurtling out across the mews. The shock-wave hit her in the face like a slap. For several long moments she stood stunned. Her suitcase slipped from her hand and tipped over on the cobbles. Shouts sounded from the street and footsteps ran past her. The mews seemed suddenly full of people. Tiny flames licked around the edges of the shattered windows, dancing in the wind. She saw the dark blue uniform of a policeman. Someone was asking, 'What happened?' Another voice said, 'There's someone in there, I saw a light.'

Lisa picked her way slowly through the debris, as if in a dream, glass crunching beneath her feet. There was a crowd at Elliot's door. The policeman and two other men, one in shirtsleeves, hammered shoulders against wood to break it down. A cloud of dust billowed out into the mews. Lisa's panic

redoubled. She pushed through the gathering crowd to follow
the men inside.

'I wouldn't go in there, love.' A hand caught her arm, but she
wrenched free. It was almost pitch black beyond the door, the
air thick with dust. She choked and covered her face with her
hand and ran up the stairs. The room was wrecked, debris and
dust strewn everywhere, walls scorched black. Flames flickered
around the window frame, sizzling now as sleet drove in on
the wind. Shadows stirred in the gloom.

'Here, under the settee,' one of the men said.

She took a step into the room and saw a hand protruding
from beneath the wreck of an upturned settee. The three men
pulled it aside and crouched over the figure lying beneath it.
Blood had trickled across the face from the left ear, where the
force of the explosion had burst an eardrum.

'Someone call an ambulance!' It was the policeman who
spoke. One of the men broke away from the others to brush
past Lisa and clatter down the stairs.

'Is he dead?' She heard her own voice reach her from somewhere far away.

The policeman looked up. 'The settee must have taken the
full force of the blast. Do you know him?'

Elliot's eyes flickered open as Lisa knelt beside him. He felt
the warmth of her hand clasping his. As the dust settled he
saw her face clearly for the first time.

'He's my father,' she said.